The Marrying of Chani Kaufman

The Marrying of Chani Kaufman

Eve Harris

W F HOWES LTD

This large print edition published in 2013 by
W F Howes Ltd
Unit 4, Rearsby Business Park, Gaddesby Lane,
Rearsby, Leicester LE7 4YH

1 3 5 7 9 10 8 6 4 2

First published in the United Kingdom in 2013
by Sandstone Press Ltd

Editor: Moira Forsyth

A CIP catalogue record for this book is available
from the British Library

ISBN 978 1 47124 671 5

Typeset by Palimpsest Book Production Limited,
Falkirk, Stirlingshire
:d and bound by
:) Ltd, Croydon, CR0 4YY

For Jules and Rosie

'Therefore shall each man forsake his mother and father, and cling to his wife, and they shall become one flesh.'

(Genesis 2:23, 24)

CHAPTER 1

CHANI. BARUCH.

November 2008 – London

The bride stood like a pillar of salt, rigid under layers of itchy petticoats. Sweat dripped down the hollow of her back and collected in pools under her arms staining the ivory silk. She edged closer to The Bedeken Room door, one ear pressed up against it.

She heard the men singing. Their shouts of 'lai-lai-lai!' rolled down the dusty synagogue corridor. They were coming for her. This was it. This was her day. The day her real life started. She was nineteen and had never held a boy's hand. The only man to touch her had been her father and his physical affection had dwindled since her body had curved and ripened.

'Sit down, Chani-leh, show a little modesty. Come, the Kallah does not stand by the door. Sit, sit!'

Her mother's face had turned grey. The wrinkles gleamed as the make-up slid towards her collar. The plucked brows gave her a look of permanent surprise. Her mouth was compressed into a frosty pink line. Mrs Kaufman sagged under the weight of her mousy wig. Beneath, her hair was grey and wispy. An old woman at forty-five: tired. Chani was her fifth daughter, the fifth to stand in a Bedeken Room, the fifth to wear the dress. Nor would she be the last. Like Babushka dolls, three younger daughters had emerged after her.

Chani remained at her post. 'Shouldn't they be here by now?'

'They'll be here soon enough. You should be davening for all your single friends. Not everyone's as lucky as you are today, Baruch HaShem.'

'But when will they be here? It feels like we've been waiting forever.' Chani let out a long, bored sigh.

'When they're ready. Enough now, Chani-leh.'

From mother to daughter, from sister to sister, the dress had been a faithful friend, shrinking and growing with each bride's need. The silver embroidery and countless pearls concealed a thousand scars and jagged seams that chafed the skin. Every alteration marked another bride's journey, delineating her hopes and desires. The yellowed underarms that had been dry-cleaned so many times, spoke of her fears. The cold prickle of anxiety, the flash of white sheets and the enormous waiting bed loomed in each bride's mind. How will it be? How will it be? The question pulsed inside Chani's head.

She stumbled across the carpet. Parting like the Red Sea, her mother and sisters shifted their ample backsides to make room on the divan for her small, neat bottom. Her bride's white prayer book was gently pushed into her hands. The women whispered and mumbled as the prayers rose and fell in time with the rhythm of their breathing, the beat of their hearts. The Hebrew poured out in gentle, female gasps. Chani imagined the words floating up, up, up – winged letters melting into the ceiling.

The hot air throbbed with the mingling of perfume, masking the stink of body odour and stale breath. Their parched mouths were sticky with drying lipstick, their rumbling stomachs hidden under layers of clothing. Some wore two-piece suits consisting of long skirts with matching jackets buttoned up to the hilt. Others paired the compulsory long skirt with a white high-necked shirt underneath a plain navy blazer. The colours were purposely dull, enlivened only by a small brooch, or perhaps cream piping around the pocket. A self-imposed uniform, lending a dowager air to even the youngest in the room.

Like Mrs Kaufman, the married women wore their best wigs – heavy, shiny locks that hid their hair from the opposite sex, the false hair inevitably more luxurious in texture and hue. Young single women announced their state by going bareheaded, although even the most glorious mane was tamed and tied back or cut into a tidy bob.

The rounded backs and shoulders of those who had been brides before her swayed back and forth, their knees cracking as they bowed low. They prayed and sighed for Chani, for the marriage to be good and true, for HaShem to look kindly upon her and her husband. Chani's eyes burnt with tears at their loyalty and kindness.

But where was the Rebbetzin? After the lessons had ended, she had promised to be at the wedding. Chani blinked and scanned the room once more before allowing disappointment to set in. She comforted herself with the prospect that the Rebbetzin was already inside the shul watching from the women's gallery. Chani vowed to look up before she entered the chuppah.

Instead, she had her prospective mother-in-law for company. Chani caught her eye and immediately regretted not being immersed in prayer. Mrs Levy sat resplendent in a dark turquoise silk suit. A matching pillbox hat finished off the ensemble, giving her the air of a glittering, bourgeois kingfisher. She sidled over and breathed noxiously in Chani's ear.

'Lovely dress, Chani – although a little old-fashioned for my liking. Still, very pretty all the same. It suits you, my dear.'

Her mother-in-law's hat had tilted, giving her a jaunty air. Chani suppressed a smirk. Mrs Levy's extravagant copper wig had been coaxed and teased into poker-straight curtains beneath, framing her wily smile. A leopard grinning before it pounces. Chani knew better than to trust it. She stood her ground.

4

'Thank you, Mrs Levy, it's a family heirloom. My grandmother got married in this dress. I feel honoured to wear it.' She smiled pertly and turned towards the divan, leaving Mrs Levy staring in her wake. Having got this far, she would not let the woman rile her now. In time, they would have to learn to tolerate each other. The loathing was mutual, but it was Chani who had carried the prize and this day was hers.

The dress creaked as she sat down. It flowed over her knees and sank in sheeny billows around her feet. The only bits of Chani left free to breathe were her face and hands. The dress crept over her collar-bones and clutched at her throat. The silk pulled tight, giving her an elegant long neck. Over her small, high breasts, flowers and birds bloomed in arcs of silver, traced and retraced in a spidery web over her torso. Her spine was forced upright; the stays were laced so tightly, her ribs screamed for release. A double row of pearl buttons climbed up her back like a ladder. Below her waist, the dress swelled over her hips. Silver leaves unfurled on branches, as the embroidery inched towards the hem.

Her feet jigged in satin ballet shoes and her toes wriggled in the sweat of her stockings. Thick cuffs of seed pearls, a thousand lidless eyes stitched through their very pupils, imprisoned her wrists. She was a truly chaste bride, her clavicle, wrists and ankles expertly hidden from the male gaze. The dress clung to her girlish curves though, hinting at the unexplored flesh beneath.

The dress was her passport, her means of escape from the sticky door handles and eternal chaos of her parents' home in Hendon. She had never had her own room or an abundance of new clothes. Everything was always second hand. Like the dress. Even the love she received was of the hand-me-down kind.

He couldn't remember her face. A slight problem. Baruch had come to identify his bride, to ensure he was marrying the right girl. Not to be cheated like Jacob had been, when Laban had swapped Leah for Rachel on the wedding day itself. Help me, HaShem. What was she like? Until this very moment, her face had blazed in his memory but now his mind had gone blank. Three wide black fedoras obscured his view as the Rabbi, the cantor and his father-in-law bustled towards the Bedeken Room door. He had met her three times and proposed on the fourth – but now what on earth did his bride look like? Hazy with hunger his brain rebelled, presenting him with a doughy smudge for her features. Heat held him in a vice-like grip; smothered in layers of clothing, he swayed on his feet. His uncle and father caught him. They propped him up like a drunk being escorted out of a bar. They hoisted him along, one step closer, then another. He was sweating so much his glasses steamed up. He had no chance now; the door was swinging open.

★　★　★

6

Chani remembered when her parents had time, when her mother had waited at the nursery gates for her. They would walk home together and talk all the way, her mother gripping her hand tightly, listening carefully as she gabbled. She had a faded memory of her mother playing hopscotch with her in the back garden, picking up her skirts and leaping deftly from stone to stone. But then the other babies had followed in quick succession. Her parents staggered through a mire of formula and stinking nappies. On the way home from school Chani carried the shopping, while her mother pushed the buggy and waited for the trailing toddlers to catch up. Eventually when she reached secondary school, her older sisters walked her home.

Her father was a respected rabbi of a small shtiebel in Hendon with a modest following. He was a gentle, slight, quiet man, absorbed in his spiritual world, more there in spirit than in body. His beard was long and feathery like grey candy-floss. He wore the customary black suit, with braces underneath the jacket to keep his trousers up. Her mother always bought him trousers that were slightly too large, perhaps imagining he would grow into them. Yet her father had seemed to shrink as her mother expanded.

Chani adored him. He had been a warm, loving father, full of light and laughter. She remembered the swoop of his thin arms as he swung her through the air. But as his family had grown, his delight in her had been replaced with an absent-mindedness that felt like rejection. He wandered through the house as if dazed by an eternal state of fatherhood.

It wasn't just the other daughters. The community had stolen him from her. In the neglected semi that was her home, the doorbell rang incessantly. A stream of unhappy wives, confused fathers and eager scholars trooped through the hall, needy for her father's advice. He squirreled them away to his study where his door remained shut for hours. As a child Chani would play outside it, just to hear the rumble of his voice. Her patience would be rewarded by a pat on the head upon his exit. She could recognise his trouser legs anywhere. When she shut her eyes she would see the shape of his hunched shoulders, his black velvet skullcap sliding from his bald spot as he had disappeared downstairs.

Her mother had become a machine whose parts were grinding and worn. Once, she had been a slender and supple young woman, joyful and quick in her movements. Over the years, Chani had watched her mother's stomach inflate and deflate like a bullfrog's throat. She had never known her mother not to be nursing a child. Now, when she looked in her mother's eyes, she saw that the light had gone out. Her mother had become a stranger, an exhausted mountain of dilapidated flesh, endlessly suckling, soothing, patting or feeding.

Her father had sown his seed time and time

again in his wife's worn out womb. Chani would shudder imagining each painful birth, baby after baby being urged into the world. She swore that when it was her turn, things would be different. Her children would never be needy for attention. Although her knowledge of contraception was a little vague she had vowed that somehow she would stop at four.

But she had had to be patient, to wait in line until suitable spouses had been found for her older sisters. The vivacious girls, who had thumped up and down the stairs, fought over the phone, alternately cuddled and teased her, had vanished. The family photos arrived from Brooklyn and Jerusalem. Her sisters were fading like ghosts as their own broods increased.

On the phone their voices were flat and hoarse. There was no time to talk, no time to ask all the questions to which she needed answers. Her turn had arrived.

Chani wore no jewels, forbidden as they are in the Torah. A Kallah, a Jewish bride must stand under the wedding canopy, hands ringless, ear lobes unadorned to signal the impending union as a commitment based on spirituality and not material acquisition. Chani looked down at her hands as they glowed against the spine of her prayer book. The nails had been smoothed and painted a clear pink, but they were ugly and too short. She had bitten them down to the quick. Her hands looked childish, the fingers stubby. She missed the blaze of her ring – the fierce diamond, a bauble of obscene size which had looked even bigger against her moist little fist. She had loved flashing it about and had taken to pointing with her left hand and gesturing with it whenever she could.

She opened the book, but the ancient letters skittered and would not be still. Where were the men? Why hadn't they knocked? Surely the singing was getting louder? She couldn't wait any more. But she had to. After all, she had been waiting all her life. She wanted a mirror to check her make-up. Gingerly, she prodded the grip that bit into her scalp, securing her floor length veil. The veil drifted over her shoulders and cascaded down her back. Was it sitting straight? She turned to ask when the door jumped in its frame. The knock forced her mother to her feet. Mrs Kaufman rocked towards the door, shoes squeaking, bunions throbbing.

Her mother grasped the doorknob and turned it. She stepped back, eyes downcast as the door swung open. The two parties, male without and female within, stared at each other. For a moment there was silence, stillness, as if everyone was listening to a single chord that chimed in the dust-mote laden air.

Baruch almost fell into The Bedeken Room. He righted himself, wiped his glasses on his tallis and stuck them back on his sweaty nose. Somebody gave his backside a firm shove, and he was propelled deeper into the room and its heady, alien, female aroma.

And there she was. His eyes met hers and he flamed the colour of chraine. Baruch bent to examine the face in front of him. Her large eyes were mischievous brown, almond-shaped and artfully emphasised with kohl. The lashes were long and sleek. Her nose was long but straight, her skin the colour of milk. The face was sharp and alert. It was not a doll's mask but alive and expressive. Her hair was a twist of slippery jet, pinned into place with pearls. Within moments of the ceremony's completion a wig would hide its liquorice sheen. She was very pleasing. He had chosen well, but surely a good Yiddisher girl would not stare back so? A half-smile played over her mouth and he remembered why he had chosen her.

His hands shook as he pulled the veil over her face. 'Amen!' boomed the men behind him. She was the right girl – but who was she really? He felt dizzy with terror at what he was about to do.

Chani had been on date after date after date. All arranged, each prospective suitor having been carefully considered by her parents and the match-maker. She had suffered hours of cold coffee and awkward conversation. The men that she favoured did not favour her and those that wanted her, she had found dull or unappealing. After each meeting,

11

the boy's mother would call to give the verdict regardless. Her mother made polite noises into the receiver. Then she would hang up, her face a wall of patient disappointment. It was hard enough being rejected, but it was galling to be rejected by a boy you didn't even want. One by one, her peers were getting engaged. She was desperate not to be the last. She did not want just to settle, but it became clear she had little choice.

What was the point in an unmarried Jewish girl? She did not want to be like Miss Halpern, the bible teacher at school, her long, pale face souring with each passing year, her uncovered head bent over tattered exercise books, ignoring the sniggers of the young girls she taught; girls who were on the verge of womanhood, alive with the vitality of hope and promise. So Chani gritted her teeth and persevered.

After a while she had come to resent them all, even the ones that wanted her. She could not bring herself to say yes to the pasty scholar, the squat teacher or the melancholy widower. All highly observant, all seeking a good Yiddisher girl to stir the cholent and light their Shabbes candles. An instant wife – just add water. None of them wanted to know about her.

At night, under her big white knickers, her hands explored her own naked form, enjoying its smells and contrasting textures. She pressed and caressed and felt a momentary electric thrum. But her body remained a mystery to her.

12

Invisible barriers surrounded her. As a small girl, she had wanted to hitch up her frumpy skirt and hurtle down the street for the bus, her legs pumping like pistons. Instead, she had learned to walk and not run, her arms clamped stiffly to her sides. She had longed for freedom of movement but had been taught to restrict her gait.

At school aged fifteen, her garrulousness had got her into trouble. In response, she filled old exercise books with angry scribbling. She was considered audacious but gifted. Her grades soared. Everything interested her – the little she could get her hands on. There was no television or internet at home or school. 'A television is an open sewer in the living-room,' her father growled. After school at Brent Cross shopping centre, she stalked the front of Dixons, mesmerised by the flickering screens and lurid colours of a world which she desperately wanted to plunge into.

Thick, black marker pens violated Shakespeare's texts. Brand new copies of *Julius Caesar* had been desecrated, ugly inky patches hiding the 'inappropriate language' beneath. In art, her favourite subject, Gauguin's nudes had been skilfully doctored. Da Vinci's drawings looked like a patchwork quilt. Buttocks, breasts and genitalia had been covered over with white labels.

Once, she was caught picking off a sticker and was sent to the Headmistress. Nobody knew exactly how old Mrs Sisselbaum was. It was generally assumed she had been born ancient and shrunken, for she was a very short woman. Her wig was styled in an ash blonde Thatcher-like wave. Her hair looked as if it had congealed on her head. The Headmistress had gazed up at Chani without blinking, her eyes magnified by enormous glasses. Mrs Sisselbaum reminded Chani of an albino rabbit. The rabbit had informed Chani that such curiosity was unnatural in a Jewish girl. 'Do it again and you will find yourself looking for a new school, a school for shameless girls like you.' Chani had fled the office, rebellion pounding in her heart. If HaShem had made the naked human form, why was it banned from sight?

She was living under a bell jar. But finally, despite the objections and the obstacles, a match had been struck. Finally she had said yes. She barely knew him from their few awkward meetings, where she had bitten her tongue and spoken in stilted sentences. A nervous, gangly yeshiva boy, albeit one who seemed genuinely kind and attentive. She hoped that the bell jar might finally be lifted. Or at least she would have someone to share it with.

The midnight blue canopy closed over her head; its golden fringes shivered as the wedding party huddled beneath. Cream roses and waxy lilies covered each pole, charging the air with scent. Chani stopped momentarily at Baruch's side.

It felt strange to be standing so close. This was the closest they had ever been. Still they were not touching. Not yet. A breath remained between

14

them. Chani was intensely aware of Baruch's physical presence. She sensed how hot and tense he was under his black suit and prayer shawl. The brim of his hat hid his face. He twitched and tapped his brogue. But he did not look at her. Not directly anyway. She knew he was slyly watching. Bubbles of hysteria welled up inside her. A squeak erupted from the corner of her mouth. The Rabbi shot her a warning look, his eyebrows bristling disapproval.

Round, round, round. Chani circled Baruch, counting to seven in her head as she broke down the barriers between them with each step. She remembered how they had both flinched when their fingers had accidentally brushed in the hotel foyer. The sugar had scattered across the table. Frozen, neither had made a move to clean it up. Both were shomer nageah – observant of the laws of restraint.

Tonight, prohibition would be lifted.

Baruch's foot crashed down on the wine glass. It shattered and the shul exploded into life and sound. 'Mazeltov!' roared the congregation. The men scooped him up and he was thrown about in their frenzied dance. Someone trod on his foot. 'Zimmen-tov und mazel-tov! Mazel-tov und zimmen-tov!' they yelled and stamped. The women clapped from the gallery. Beards flapping, shoulders bashing, the men whooped and swirled around the chuppah. Faster and faster they spun.

15

Chani was a white blur at the edge of his vision. He tried to catch her expression, but he was whirled away. Sweets pelted them from above as children threw them for luck. One caught him on the back of the head.

He was twenty. His life felt narrow: the pressure to succeed, to be a rabbi, to please his father. His quick analytical mind was to be harnessed to The Talmud. The English degree he longed to study remained a blasphemous secret buried in his heart. He listened to Coldplay on his iPod, his father believing that the wisdom of Rabbi Shlomo was filling his ears. Beneath his mattress lay the novels he was banned from reading – Dickens, Chandler, Orwell – but they were no longer enough. He felt controlled – there was no release, no relief.

One night, he took the Tube home after a lesson. A woman sat opposite him. She was huge. Her shirt was unbuttoned revealing two orbs of sunburnt flesh. Averting his eyes, he glanced at the advert above her head. But the advert showed a nubile girl in a bikini. He did not know where to look. He muttered a prayer but his eyes had strayed back to the rosy mounds in front of him. The flesh was alarmingly real in its imperfections. He could see a faint creping at the base of her throat. The breasts held a primordial power over him. He was drowning in the dark chasm between them. The train rattled over the tracks. The breasts shook. He grew hard.

The woman stared. He clamped his prayer book over his erection. The doors opened and he scrambled out.

At night, he pressed his need into the mattress. He hoped his mother wouldn't notice the wasted seed when she did the laundry. He had tried to restrain himself by wearing gloves and two pairs of underpants, but now his dreams were a forbidden landscape of enormous breasts, rising like dunes in the desert. He was lonely and craved something, someone.

Married. Ten minutes alone together in The Bedeken Room. Suddenly Chani missed the crush of female bodies and swishing of skirts. Unusually, she didn't know what to do or say. She tried to imagine what the Rebbetzin would advise in this situation, but her gentle words would not come to mind. She had glanced up at the women's gallery. Where was she?

Chani could not look Baruch in the eye. Her friends had giggled over the theory that this brief respite granted to newlyweds immediately after the ceremony, was actually for the couple to do it. She stiffened in fear. She wondered if Baruch was thinking the same.

A cake stand had been set up. Tier upon tier of flaky delicacies glistened on doilies. Below were two bottles of mineral water and two crystal goblets. Neither Chani nor Baruch had eaten or drunk since the day before. They stared at the cakes. Instinctively, they reached for the same almond slice.

'No, go on . . . you have it. Please,' croaked Baruch.

Chani mumbled thank you, whispered a blessing and nibbled the cake. She could have scoffed the lot. Munching in silence, they avoided eye contact.

'Feels strange doesn't it, being married?'

'Mmm.' Her mouth was still full.

'Is it like you imagined?'

She shook her head vigorously. 'I am not sure what I imagined,' she said. 'It feels very, um, quick.'

'Yes, it does. I guess it's the same for everybody.'

'Probably.'

'Well, they'll be coming any minute now, perhaps we should . . .' His words tailed off into silence.

Baruch sensed he should kiss her but he had no idea how. Anyway, he hadn't brushed his teeth all day so decided against trying. Chani felt a large, bony hand close round hers. She wished her hand wasn't so sweaty. Side by side, holding hands, they chewed and swallowed one more pastry each, until the door opened and they quickly let go.

The week before the wedding, Baruch had sat in Rabbi Zilberman's office. The room was a dusty grey box. There were two doors, both locked, but there were no windows. Papers covered the desk. Books filled the shelves and lay scattered on the floor. There was barely room for two plastic chairs.

The filing cabinets closed in on him. A huge photo of a beloved sage hung on the wall. The old man stared at him, cataracts glowing blue-white, his hands frozen claws hanging from gaping sleeves. Had he suffered wedding night nerves?

Under the photo sat Rabbi Zilberman, a study in monochrome. His beard was streaky charcoal, his black suit speckled with dandruff. His sad, grey eyes examined Baruch. Rabbi Zilberman officiated at the synagogue that Baruch's family attended in Golders Green. Baruch was more familiar with the rabbi's rounded back, bent in supplication at the front of the shul. The rabbi's son, Avromi, had attended Baruch's school in Hendon and was one of his few and closest friends; but Baruch's relationship with Rabbi Zilberman had always been one of deference and formality. Whenever he had visited Avromi, Rabbi Zilberman would acknowledge Baruch with a curt nod and a stern, patriarchal smile, the corners of his mouth flexing upwards momentarily, his expression remaining sombre. After enquiring politely after Baruch's parents the rabbi would move swiftly on, a whirling column of dark wool and white shirt, leaving the two boys silent and awkward in his wake. That had been the extent of his familiarity with the thin, grey-bearded man sitting opposite him until these strange, compulsory tutorials had begun.

The rabbi started. 'You are responsible for all your wife's needs,' he said. 'You must feed her,

19

clothe her, provide a roof over her head and pay for all her material necessities. But you must also give her pleasure in your relations with her.'

Baruch shifted in his seat. Pleasure. It sounded so simple. He had gone as far as to do some private research on the subject at Swiss Cottage Library, far away from the shtetl of Hendon. He had even swapped his yarmulke for a baseball cap for further anonymity. Too shy to ask, he had roamed the stacks lost like Moses in the desert, until he had found the right section. There, he sat immersed in sex advice manuals, a world so taboo to him that his heart raced with guilt. But he could not stop. Fascinated, he read on and stared at diagrams that made his ears burn red with shame. Clitoris, stimulate, arouse, labia, climax – the female body made no sense at all.

At school, he had glanced at the grubby men's magazines passed from desk to desk. The pictures had made his head swim – the women so brazen, their mouths glistening and open, their flesh sleek and pneumatic. He could not equate them to Chani. He had never even seen her elbows. Yet he was duty-bound to give her pleasure.

'An orgasm, Rabbi?' he offered. Realising his mistake he flushed, the rash of acne on his left cheek suddenly backlit.

Rabbi Zilberman raised an eyebrow. 'Yes, I believe that's what they call it nowadays.' But he did not probe further.

'How will I know if I have pleased my wife?' He

had to ask. This was his chance. His mouth had gone dry, but the words had slipped out.

'You will know with time, with practice. She may even tell you, but do not waste time chattering about frivolous things. Action is important, not words. A child is a wonderful mitzvah. And, to have relations with her whilst she is pregnant is a double-mitzvah!'

Pregnant. Baruch had almost forgotten that these mysterious relations could lead to such a thing. He wasn't ready to be a father yet.

The Rabbi seemed to expand and fill the room. 'And Baruch, just as we do not eat like animals, we do not have relations like them either. HaShem created us with physical desires and marriage liberates us to enjoy those desires in the right way. Not like beasts in the field.' Rabbi Zilberman was eyeballing him.

Like beasts in the field? But how was this anatomically possible? He remembered the pictures – but surely the behind was the wrong place? Baruch was very relieved that HaShem had solved this problem for him.

The Rabbi was not done yet. 'And when your wife is niddah, you do not go near her. Don't even touch her until her bleeding has finished and she has purified herself in the mikveh. Then you may rejoice in each other again just like on your wedding night. But all this your wife will know. Consider the time when you cannot have relations as a time to get to know each other again like brother and sister, to solve any disputes and to deepen your friendship.' The rabbi spoke calmly with no embarrassment. Baruch stared at the rabbi's ear. It all sounded very wise and sensible and it was not news to him. He had studied the family purity laws in the Gemarah, a text so dry and remote that any possible eroticism had been bleached out. He had learnt basic biology at school but the mechanical realities still baffled him.

How could she bleed from down there each month? The thought was making him nauseous.

Two days before the wedding. Chani washed, combed, brushed and scrubbed herself raw. Sitting in the little cabin, she waited for the light to go on above the door. The bathroom was a delight. Immaculately clean, its surfaces gleamed, unlike the one at home. The walls were painted pastel pink. Matching pink towels lay neatly folded on a heated rail. There had even been a brand new toothbrush and a fresh tube of kosher toothpaste, a mini pack of earbuds, a nail file and a pair of nail scissors and tweezers. All laid out just for her.

That morning Chani had performed her last internal check just as Rebbetzin Zilberman, the Rabbi's wife, had instructed. The soft bedikah cloth had remained brilliant white. Not a drop of blood. She was ready for the mikveh, the ritual bath.

The Rebbetzin had accompanied her and was

waiting in reception. Chani examined the framed notice on the wall:

Before beginning cleaning preparations remove:
a) jewellery
b) false teeth, dental plates (for temporary caps ask your Rabbi)
c) false eyelashes
d) bandages, plasters
e) make up
f) nail polish
Then cut and file nails of hands and feet. Brush teeth, floss, rinse mouth and use the toilet (if necessary).
Then bathe and shower before immersion. Check and remove any dried blood or pus, dried milk from nipples, remnants of dough, nits or lice, splinters or scabs, ink or paint.

Chani was pretty sure she did not have any lice or dried milk on her. Wrapped in a fluffy towel, her hair streamed as she sat on the edge of the bath. Under her breath she recited the prayer prior to tevilah – immersion.

May my husband's eyes look only towards me and my eyes look only towards him . . . may my husband consider himself more blessed because of me than of any other blessing in the world . . .

She imagined that behind the doors of the other cubicles, there were young brides waiting like her.

It was impossible to know. It was one woman at a time in the mikveh.

Bing! The light went on. Chani leapt to her feet, checked that the towel was secure and opened the door. Outside, the mikveh pool shimmered invitingly. Its deep blue waters rippled, reflections glinting on the white ceiling and against the white tiled walls. It was larger than she had imagined. The pool was about ten feet long and seven feet deep. It filled the bare room.

'Hellooo dalink, open your towel and let me check you.'

Chani jumped. Behind her stood The Mikveh Lady. She was a wizened nut of a woman. Her hair was wrapped in a faded blue headscarf. She wore wooden clogs and navy tights. Her smile was warm and honest but her eyes were as sharp as needles.

Chani opened her towel. The Mikveh Lady gazed intently at every part of her body.

'Vat a sweet leetl brite you are,' cooed The Mikveh Lady. Chani felt ridiculous. All her life she had hidden her nakedness from prying eyes and now here she was, her body being scrutinised by a total stranger.

The Mikveh Lady asked her to turn so as to check for any strand of hair that might have been shed and clung to her back.

'Nails, dalink?'

Chani presented her hands for inspection. The Mikveh Lady held them and examined each ragged crescent. Then she flipped them over and peered at her palms.

'Feet?' Chani held each foot up.

'And have you combed your hair down there?' asked The Mikveh Lady.

Chani was not sure what on earth could be hiding in the hair down there, so she nodded dutifully.

'Ok zen, my dalink, in you go. Sock yourself vell, my dear. Immerse yourself fully.'

Three steps, then two strokes and she was in the middle of the pool. The water was warm. She sank down and it closed, womb-like, over her head. Her heart thudded in her ears. Rising to the surface, she could see two dark, watery shapes standing by the edge of the mikveh. She burst through and gulped a lungful of air. When she opened her eyes, she saw Rebbetzin Zilberman smiling down at her. Next to her stood The Mikveh Lady, smiling the same ecstatic smile.

Chani clamped her hands over her meagre breasts. She had not expected the Rebbetzin to come in and watch. A small bubble shot out from behind her. She prayed that the Rebbetzin had not noticed.

The Rebbetzin spoke softly.

'Chani, you need to immerse yourself three times and then recite the blessing. Don't touch the walls to push yourself under because your palms will not be fully purified. Spread your fingers and toes as wide as you can. Let the water wash every crevice. Ready?'

Chani nodded and sank deep into the mikveh. She knew that when a woman prays underwater, her prayer flies to HaShem immediately. She hung suspended in time and space, her limbs spread-eagled, the water entering every fold. She opened her eyes. The water did not sting. It was pure and natural.

Please HaShem don't let it hurt on my wedding night. Please HaShem make it easy and quick.

She dipped twice more. Finally she rose to the surface and recited the blessing. Reborn. She was ready to be married.

CHAPTER 2

THE REBBETZIN

November 2008 – London

Another day. Another immersion. Another new bride.

The Rebbetzin and Chani walked to the end of the alley alongside the railway arches. Above them, the sky was a tumultuous blanket of grey and a chill wind whipped their long skirts into tangled knots. At the end of an unremarkable suburban street was a small industrial zone housing a mechanics' workshop and a car park. Right at the end, stood the low, flat mikveh building. Concealed, unobtrusive, no sign announced its presence but the women of the community knew where it was and valued its private location.

'So maybe you could give Baruch a little gift on your wedding night, a token to mark the start of your new life together?'

'Like what?'

'A small box of chocolates or some new cufflinks? Or a new leather siddur with his name embossed onto it?'

'Why would I need to give him anything when he's getting me? Aren't I enough?'

'I'm sure you're plenty, Chani – I'm only making a suggestion.'

The Rebbetzin was smiling but she had seen the fear in the girl's eyes. It was easy to spot. She had taught many girls how to count the nights and the days, how to prepare themselves for the mikveh. Even the ones who were terrified of water, who could not swim – eventually they too had succumbed. And it had been fine. More than fine. The brides would emerge dreamy-eyed and smiling softly, the water pouring off their pale, smooth skin, their thighs pressing together modestly below the dark triangle of hair.

But Chani was different. She lacked the bovine passivity typical of many of the other girls. She was needy for answers but the Rebbetzin was not sure it was her place to supply them. She thought about Mrs Kaufman, Chani's mother. She hadn't been surprised when the woman had called to say she couldn't make it today. Mrs Kaufman had breathlessly explained that the youngest daughter had fallen down the stairs and needed to go to hospital – please could The Rebbetzin accompany Chani to the mikveh without her? Chani had arrived subdued, the disappointment reflected in her eyes.

And who would answer Chani's questions now? The Rebbetzin decided to speak. It was her duty. 'Chani, it will hurt a bit the first time, but let it happen. Try to relax, breathe deep and slow. With time, your relations will get better. It's a whole new world for both of you. But a man's needs often outweigh the woman's. When you are niddah, you can rest. Still a woman can take great pleasure in her husband too, explore each other . . .'

The Rebbetzin had said too much and felt embarrassed. Chani was staring at her. She couldn't read the girl's expression. In the gloom of the railway arch, Chani's eyes gleamed. A train tore through the air above them. The Rebbetzin thanked HaShem for the welcome distraction.

They continued in silence, each deep in her thoughts. The Rebbetzin thought about Baruch. A talented yeshiva bocher and quite a catch. A little neurotic, it had to be said, but which boy isn't? He was friendly with Avromi, her eldest. They had gone to the same school, the same class in fact. Baruch came from a fine wealthy family. His parents were regular members at her husband's shul. It was also a healthy family on the whole. A little diabetes on the paternal side, but who doesn't have a little diabetes these days? On the other hand, Chani's family was of a poorer yet worthy lineage; full of tzadikkim and therefore more traditional in its leaning. But too many daughters alas. Poor Mrs Kaufman, what a headache it must be to find them all husbands. How she must have longed for a son.

The Rebbetzin had been a little surprised at the shidduch. Not only were there differences in

29

familial background, Chani was not the malleable sort of daughter-in-law Mrs Levy had in mind. To begin with, Chani had not attended sem although in the Rebbetzin's opinion that was not an insurmountable issue. It had rankled with Mrs Levy, however. Chani was also spirited and had had a certain reputation at school, but then it was easy for any lively, curious girl to be branded in that way by the community. So why did Baruch choose her?

She was bemused that his parents had finally agreed to the match. The Rebbetzin knew that Mrs Levy had been dead against it. Had they been persuaded by Mrs Gelbmann? The woman was a shrewd matchmaker and rarely made a mistake. Perhaps she knew of a suitable girl for Avromi. A good, haimisher girl from the right sort of family. Yes, that was exactly what was needed. Or was it too late for that already? Was he beyond that sort of girl now? Her mood grew darker as she thought of her confused, lost son.

They passed the garage and as usual the mechanics were gawping at them. Two frum women in their dowdy clothes, their long, dark skirts hobbling them. Chani's wet hair had left a stain across the back of her jacket. How did they look to the outside world? To men who were used to seeing female flesh from every angle? The Rebbetzin pulled her cardigan tightly around her, crossed her arms and walked swiftly on. She held her head high, not looking to the left or right. Let them stare. There was nothing to see.

They stopped at the end of the residential road. The Rebbetzin gently embraced Chani. 'Call me before Shabbes if there's anything you need,' she said.

'But I'll see you on Sunday, won't I?'

The Rebbetzin pulled back holding Chani at arm's length. She examined the small, bedraggled creature in front of her.

'Of course, I'll be there. Now stop worrying and try to enjoy these last couple of days at home with your family. I'm here if you need me, Chani.'

And then they had gone their separate ways. The Rebbetzin walked slowly up Golders Green High Street. She felt like a fraud, having not been to the mikveh for months. She had her reasons. The attendant had stared at her stomach but the Rebbetzin had worn her loosest, darkest clothes. They flapped around her, turning her into a giant crow. Let her think what she likes.

The roar of traffic engulfed her. A Hasid dressed in sombre black like a spectre from the Polish past, gabbled Yiddish into his mobile and dodged between two red buses, his woollen stockings winking as he hurried along. A bus driver slammed on his brakes and thumped his horn. The Hasid ignored him, hopped onto the kerb and began to weave his way expertly along the crowded pavement, still talking furiously as his ear locks swayed in rhythm with his pecking gait. In his right hand, he clutched a plastic bag bulging with pastries or pickled herring. He looked downwards, avoiding female eye contact, hurrying, hurrying, because there is never enough time in the day to do all that HaShem commands.

The world of the goyim passed him by regardless. Some stared a little, but most of the non-Jews were used to the be-hatted, be-wigged members of the Charedi community living in their midst. The Rebbetzin watched him disappear into a Judaica shop. Two Japanese women stopped to talk in the doorway of a Chinese restaurant. Behind them, headless, plump Peking ducks sat on their skewers, gleaming in all their non-kosher glory under the hot lamps. An elderly African man, bundled into a navy wool coat, pushed a wicker shopping basket past a Big Issue seller who stood numb with boredom and despair, against the sleek, dark glass of a pizzeria. She entered the Jewish home stretch.

Past the little kosher cafes. Past Carmelli's the baker's. Inside, people were pushing and shoving, handing money over the counter in exchange for plastic bags bulging with sweet, warm bread or poppy seed bagels. The door opened releasing a doughy fug. Cinammon rogellach, syrupy baklavas, doughnuts oozing jam, marzipan rolls, crisp florentines, giant macaroons each with its own cherry nipple. The trays were emptying fast. In a few hours, the stampede would disappear leaving till receipts and greasy napkins to clog the gutter. It was Friday and that meant only one thing.

Shabbes. It was due in six hours and the Rebbetzin had done nothing in preparation. And Shabbes waits for no man or woman. On the seventh day HaShem ceased from all work and blessed the seventh day and declared it holy – a day of rest. Shabbes. It would arrive at precisely 4:12 pm. At 4:13 pm, she would no longer be able to flick a switch. Even this was considered work. She had ten people to feed, five of them guests. She hadn't even made the chollahs. There were a few honey-coloured plaited loaves left. Should she buy two?

The goyim dawdled by, unaware of the mounting pressure their fellow Jewish citizens were under. The women were already in the kitchens preparing for the evening feast. A gaggle of schoolgirls dawdled past, chattering, laughing, avoiding the inevitable list of chores that would be mounting up at home upon their return. She walked on and crossed the street. She nodded to fleeting acquaintances. The rush of Shabbes filled the air. Past Yarok the grocer's, where the fruit shone in obscene shapes, the brilliant colours tempting a long queue of customers. The carrots were giant fingers, heaped in a barrel. She needed potatoes and onions for the cholent but she did not stop.

Kosher Kingdom beckoned. The supermarket window was full of neon offers. She had neither any Kiddush wine left for the blessing nor any kneidele for the chicken soup. Instead the Rebbetzin turned into her small road. She padded down the quiet street. The privet hedge hid her from view, but she felt the eyes watching her receding back. The net curtains twitched. There goes the Rebbetzin Zilberman the mouths muttered. Let them mutter. The bins overflowed, the front gardens were a jungle or ugly bare squares of practical concrete. Elms shorn of their foliage spread amputated limbs skywards provided the only relief from the greyness of the pavements and the repetition of humble semis. The houses sagged against each other. No one really cared about appearances here. Who had the time or the energy when there were so many more important things to do?

Her front door banged shut. The house seemed to wrap itself around her, hold her in its dark corridors and soothe her with its familiar smell. It was hers for now; her husband was in his office at shul and Michal and Moishe had not returned from school. She had no idea where Avromi might be. She quashed the familiar flicker of anxiety. She would worry about him later.

Peace. Silence. The house sighed as she kicked off her shoes and stalked through the hall in her stockinged feet. Each step left a faint, sweaty print on the dusty wooden floor.

After the darkness of the hall, the sunlight in the kitchen blinded her. She squinted against the glare. The fridges hummed their usual tunes. The meat freezer clicked and gurgled. Meat to the left. Milk

34

to the right. The meat fridge gleamed silver, the milk fridge blazed white. In their separate cupboards the pots and plates lined up like opposing troops ready to be mobilised. The meat plates had gold scalloped edges whilst their enemies in the milk camp, bivouacked in pale green. In separate cutlery drawers, the foot soldiers slept uneasily. The dairy spoons were stacked one on top of the other secure in their own tray. In the darkness next door the meat knives glinted knowing their turn would come.

She opened the meat fridge. The huge chicken leered at her; its gaping hole a mocking mouth.

Roast me! *Eat me!* screeched the mouth.

'Roast yourself,' muttered The Rebbetzin and slammed the fridge door.

Her wig itched. Where was her knitting needle? She needed to poke about and give her hot, tight scalp a good scratch. She thumped upstairs, her feet registering the threadbare carpet through the gossamer of her stockings, her hand sliding up the chipped banister.

The bedroom was a mess. It smelt of morning breath and apathy. One sock here, one sock there – her husband had been too tired to dump them in the laundry basket. Yesterday's skirt lay in a crumpled circle on the floor. The curtains were still drawn. In places, the heavy material had come off its hooks and sagged unevenly. Fingers of daylight stretched across the ceiling. She yanked back the curtains and shoved open a window.

Better. She could breathe.

The wardrobe yawned open. Her husband's suits swung gently on their hangers. She gave them a push making them dance like merry Hasidim at a wedding. All black, all the same cut. Her husband had thrown out his navy pinstripe, his charcoal grey and summer linen years ago.

The Rebbetzin sighed. There was no change on her side of the wardrobe. As usual the same long, drab skirts lined up in a thrilling variation of navy, black or dove-grey. Her shoes sat in obedient pairs underneath; they were all the same soft black Italian loafers; save for one white pair for the summer. The Rebbetzin sighed for all the shoes she used to wear. Vicious winkle-pickers with their brilliant silver buckles, red patent stilettos that had crippled her, brash yellow trainers with neon green laces, squidgy flip-flops and wobbly cork platforms.

The dressing table was squashed up against the bay window. Her wigs rested on their stands; each a hard white faceless balloon. She sat at the mirror. It reflected their bed, a huge mahogany wonder that divided into two single beds for when she was niddah. The bed parted silently rolling on greased wheels. The heavy mattress hid a zip that could not be felt when done up. It had been a wedding present from her parents. She had been over-whelmed at their generosity as a bed such as this one must have cost a few thousand. Their under-standing had also moved her for theirs did not separate.

The bed had remained in half for weeks and the pine chest of drawers deliberately placed in between was covered in a thin layer of dust.

Several weeks ago. Tiny kicks. All day long. The Rebbetzin was forty-four and she knew this child would be her last. Her pregnancy had been a gift. After Moishe she had thought it impossible. His body had ripped its way through her and she had believed the damage had done its worst. For a time, being barren had seemed a relief until the old longing had returned sharper than before and had remained unanswered for many long years. Yet here she was, her stomach rising once more like dough in a tin. The old stretch marks tautening like rubber bands. The joy swelled her heart, softening the lines on her face, her smile a beacon. She had pushed the old fear away, the tearing and clawing at her insides, the splitting open of her body. It had been like dying.

She would bring this last one into the world even if it killed her.

Something was wrong. The bed was wet. The Rebbetzin sat up. A spasm. The pain came again as a dull ache.

'Chaim? Chaim!'

'Whatisit?' grumbled Rabbi Zilberman.

'Something's wrong – the baby – I can feel wet –'

The Rabbi snapped on the light and kicked back

the covers. A crimson stain had spread from between his wife's legs. They were lying in it.

He leapt from the bed and stared down at his pyjamas. The liquid had soaked through the thin material gluing it to his flesh. He trembled. Her blood was niddah and therefore so was she. Surely in an emergency all laws would be suspended? He was torn. One law forbade him from touching her and another law ruled that everything must be done in order to save another's life. He didn't know what to do. This had never happened before. This was women's business.

'Wha – what should we do?' he stammered.

Her baby was leaking out of her and Chaim was asking her what to do. Such a husband she had. She heaved herself onto all fours, her hands scrabbling at the sheets. Where was it? Her fingers tangled with gloop.

'Ring for an ambulance!' she snapped. No. No. Please HaShem. But she knew the baby was lost.

Rabbi Zilberman couldn't move. Which law must he obey? He felt faint sickened by all that blood. He had to help her but his limbs had rebelled. He remained where he was.

'Chaim, *do* something!'

'I'll – I'll call Hatzollah,' he mumbled.

He stumbled across the room to the phone on the bedside table not daring to look at the bed. He gripped the receiver. But he couldn't remember the number for the Charedi ambulance service. The Rebbetzin groaned.

'I can't remember the number!'

His wife turned to stare at him. She lurched across the bed, snatched the phone out of his hands and dialled 999 instead. Pain rippled through her. Her thighs were warm and wet. The nightdress sagged between them, its material so dark, it looked black.

'Hello – hello – yes, I need an ambulance. Yes, for me. For my baby. No, not labour – now, please. 36 The Drive, Golders Green. My name – yes – Rebbetzin – I mean, Mrs Zilberman – thank you, yes – I will – thank you.'

She sank back and waited. There was nothing else to do. Her husband remained standing, frozen by indecision.

Chaim felt a fool. How selfish he had been worrying about the laws. Saving another's life should always come first. On instinct he had leapt away from her blood but it had been more than that. He had been repulsed by it. Her belly had been so smooth, perfect in its gentle swelling. The life that was so carefully concealed had spilled out of her, creating such chaos. The illusion of containment had been shattered and the wet messy truth of her womb had been too much to bear. Beneath the disgust, he was afraid. More than the loss of his child, the blood seemed to carry with it an ominous meaning that he was unable to grasp.

He felt sick with self-loathing at his cowardly response. Why hadn't he just dialled 999? It had been a terrible mistake, a loss of self-control and now he had to try and mend things. He tried to form an apology in his head, but it was no good. The words seemed pathetic.

He shuffled closer to the bed.

'Rivka –'

He could only say her name. Instead he reached out a clammy hand to pat her shoulder. She stared up at him, her mouth a rigid line of distaste.

She swatted his hand away.

'Rivka – I don't know what came over – the sages say –'

'I don't care what they say! This is not the time –' she grimaced with pain. 'Bring me a towel – bring me two . . . and go into my drawers and bring me a clean nightie.'

The Rebbetzin Zilberman slumped further into the bed. He obeyed the order relieved just to be useful. He emerged from the bathroom with a heap of towels in his arms. Bracing himself to deal with the carnage, he stripped the duvet off his wife. So much blood. Who would have thought that such a little baby could cause so much blood? He wanted to close his eyes at the sight but forced himself to continue. She parted her legs and he pushed a rolled up towel between them. Then he heaved her upright. Her nightdress was rucked up around her hips. She lifted her arms and he pulled it over her head. Then he slipped the clean one over her shoulders, helping her push her arms through its sleeves.

He was grateful that he could perform these small actions for her although he still felt deeply uneasy. But it was not enough. It would never be enough.

'What else can I do?'

'Nothing. Just get dressed yourself – they'll be here any minute,' she muttered.

'Ok then.'

His voice quavered. Rabbi Zilberman felt impotent in the face of the painful female mystery unravelling before him. A few minutes ago, she had been pregnant and all had been well. It was hard to comprehend how their joy could dissolve so suddenly. The child must have been truly holy, for HaShem to have called it back before it had even taken its first breath. His child might have been a great tzaddik or rebbe. Still he had wanted to see his child, to see its tiny face screw up and hear it bawl for the first time. To hold his son. For he was sure it had been a son.

The memory of an old loss returned as keen and sharp as the shoyket's knife and the ghost of another child hung in the air between them, a small, spectral wisp.

She watched him as he dressed. There was nothing more to say. He had failed her, his wife, his beloved companion and best friend of all these years. Perhaps she had been too old to bear another child but Isaac was born unto Sarah when she was ninety. HaShem had made it possible.

When he turned to look at her, her eyes were

shut. The lids were violet against her pallid skin. They flickered with movement but her face had the quality of a mask. It was only then that he noticed her hair was uncovered. To disturb her now seemed ridiculous but her immodesty bothered him. Other men would see her hair now. He was being absurd. What did it matter – surely HaShem would –

The doorbell rang and he raced to answer it.

The paramedics spoke in low, kind voices and lifted each limb carefully, as if she were a china doll. And indeed she had broken, broken open, the life was still flowing out of her. Her heartbeat had slowed, reverberating in time with the pain. The voices seemed to swim near and far.

They touched her. The Rebbetzin had always tried to avoid any man's touch but her husband's. But these strangers, these goyim had carried her and spoken to her with a compassion that she had desperately needed. And here she was, her flesh exposed. She no longer cared. These men knew what to do. They carried out their actions with a smooth confidence, showing no fear or hesitancy and she was glad of it. It was a relief that someone else had taken control.

Her husband had scurried about, clearing the way for the stretcher, busying himself with opening the door to the men, shooing the children back to their rooms. Dressed in their pyjamas, they had crowded the doorway.

'Dad – Dad – what's wrong with Mum?' Moishe demanded. But Michal, his older sister, had realised what had happened. She gripped his wrist and pulled him out of the way. He shrugged her off easily.

'Get off, Michal! I want to know what's wrong –'

'I'll tell you later – let's just let these guys do their job.' Her voice shook a little but Moishe relented, retreating to watch from his doorway.

Avromi stepped forward to help the men.

'Stay out of the way and don't interfere,' snarled his father.

The Rebbetzin heard the hurt in Avromi's muttered reply – her husband had still not forgiven their son his fall from grace.

She was grateful for the sheet they had laid over her, covering the cruel evidence. She did not want her children to see the stain spreading from between her legs, soaking the wadded towel.

The stretcher lurched down the stairs, the men negotiating each step. Rabbi Zilberman followed their progress, giving instructions as he watched his wife bump along downhill. 'Careful, lower her a bit, left a bit – slowly round this corner please –' It made him feel a little less useless. The men tolerated his twittering patiently, understanding his need to be involved – but finally the senior paramedic, a large and thickset Irishman intervened: 'Rabbi, don't worry yourself – we've done

43

this a few times before, we'll see her down the stairs all right now –'

So Rabbi Zilberman held his tongue. They carried her out of their bedroom, feet first – like a corpse. He did not like it, but what could he say to these goyim? Still they were good men, and had their place in this world and the next.

He felt stupid, a real nebbuch. He could not even help lift the stretcher, now there were other more capable men to do that. He wanted to walk alongside the stretcher so he could look into her eyes, but there was no space in the narrow hall. Besides when he had gazed down at her on the landing, she turned her head away.

The ambulance waited against the kerb. Its siren was silent but the lights flashed, bouncing and flickering against the dark windows of the little houses. And sure enough, the curtains twitched and the lights came on. Faces filled the windows. Mrs Meyer and her husband stumbled out, wrinkly with sleep. His skullcap was lop-sided, his dressing gown cord dragged through the puddles. Mrs Meyer wore huge, monkey faced slippers with beady eyes, a present from her grandchildren. Her stripy socks had concertinaed around her ankles but her hair was wrapped in a snood.

More neighbours appeared peering at the stretcher. 'The Rebbetzin . . . the Rebbetzin . . .' they muttered.

And there she lay, her hair dangling over the edges of the stretcher.

A small crowd had gathered and the paramedics found themselves surrounded by an audience. They were used to rubbernecks as long as they did not get too close. The men worked quickly and efficiently ignoring the onlookers but this crowd was different. It whispered, it spoke, it wailed and worse; it gave advice:

'Pray for the Rebbetzin Rivka Zilberman! HaShem will save her!'

'I am a doctor and I am telling you, she needs oxygen –'

'My son Simcha – he is a doctor – I'll call him –'

'Her hair – what about her hair? For shame that a married woman should appear like this!'

It was this last comment that spurred the Rabbi into action. He knew he should have done something before they brought her out. If a woman's glory was her hair then the Rebbetzin had been crowned with greater glory than most. Her hair was long, lustrous and had remained conker brown marred only by a grey streak here and there. From the day of their wedding, she had covered it as the Torah dictated. He had run his fingers through it so many times in the privacy of their bedroom, that even now his hands retained the memory of its smooth, glossy weight. Long snaky locks brushed the tarmac.

'Cover her up!' he cried. He moved next to the

burly Irishman and shook his shoulder. The senior paramedic had been kneeling next to the Rebbetzin as the stretcher was being lifted into the back of the ambulance. He turned to gaze at the Rabbi over his shoulder. The Rabbi's hair formed a wispy halo as the streetlights shone down on him. His eyes were pools of terror.

'Sir, Rabbi – she is covered – we put a blanket on her to keep warm – please just let us get on with our job.'

'No – you don't understand – her hair, you see – just pull the sheet over all of her –'

'Sir – she isn't a corpse.' The senior paramedic was losing his patience.

'Yes – yes – I know that – but her hair, it's uncovered –' Rabbi Zilberman was gabbling.

The crowd swayed in agreement. Suddenly Mrs Gottlieb barged her way to the front, her magnificent bosom constrained by her camel hair dressing gown. She flourished a long, loose piece of material like a victory banner and waved it under Rabbi Zilberman's nose.

'See, here we are – no need to make a fuss,' she announced importantly. She knelt at the Rebbetzin's side shielding her. With a flick of her wrists the hair was caught up and neatly bound. The scarf was twisted and knotted tightly. Every stray curl was hidden. The Rebbetzin's eyes flashed open and stared up at Mrs Gottlieb. Mrs Gottlieb was struck by the emptiness in those eyes – 'as if no one was there' she would repeat

46

to her enthralled guests at her coffee morning, later that day.

The crowd breathed a sigh of relief. Yes, yes, much better.

The men heaved the stretcher into the back of the ambulance. The Rabbi clambered in after them. The doors clanged shut and with a roar, the ambulance jolted into life. The sirens screamed and it screeched away from the kerb.

The show was over. The residents slowly dispersed. Tomorrow there would be plenty to talk about.

CHAPTER 3

BARUCH

November 2008 – London

Baruch rose early and donned his phylacteries. Although he intended to recite Shacharit, morning prayers, in synagogue with everyone else, this particular morning he had woken feeling the need for individual prayer. In shul, he enjoyed the sense of unity and fellowship brought by communal prayer. It was pleasant to start his day immersed in ritual, surrounded by familiar, friendly faces. However, the mutter of male voices was also a distraction, and he was not always able to muster the intensity achieved when praying alone.

To make matters worse, in the week leading up to the wedding, his father had insisted on accompanying him to shul each morning rather than davening at his office, as was his custom. Mr Levy's presence always seemed to suck the air out of the room, not least because of the musky aftershave that made Baruch's head swim.

Baruch loved the silence of the early morning and the cold glow of the light. His family were still asleep. The only sounds were the flutter of wings and chime of birdsong coming from the tree outside his window. He felt safe and alive, every thought sanctified, his mind empty of everything but HaShem. The leather boxes were bound securely to his forearm and forehead, the dark straps laced so tightly that the pale flesh of his inner arm tingled.

After, he carefully unwound the tefillin, kissed them and put them back in their black velvet bag, pulling the drawstring tight. The bag was stored in his desk drawer with his tallis folded neatly on top.

His room was narrow but cosy, a simple cell containing his few possessions. Soon he would leave this room behind forever. It had become a temporary respite between one yeshiva and the next. His old school uniform still hung in the wardrobe and his dusty, dog-eared files and exercise books remained stacked on the shelves. Gazing at these familiar objects comforted him, warding off the sense of fear that had been nagging away at him for weeks.

Fear of the unknown. First, marriage and then, eventually, a new life with Chani in Jerusalem, pursuing his rabbinical studies at a top yeshiva chosen by his father.

The small, plain side-room lent an intimacy to proceedings. Men stood behind benches made of a light wood that creaked with the supplicants' movements. The walls were white and the carpet a deep, soft blue. The black and white stripes of the married men's prayer shawls provided pattern and the golden Hebrew lettering above the ark was its only decoration.

Baruch tried to ignore his father's gravelly singing voice, but serenity evaded him. He wondered briefly at his father's need to stand so close. The room was small but it was not full. He realised that this was probably the last time in a long time he would daven Shacharit with his father. In a few days' time he would daven as a married man, wrapped in his own prayer shawl that had been chosen and bought for him by Chani.

How different he seemed from his father. Out of the corner of his eye, he observed his father, catching him as he rocked forward on his heels. He had always thought his father to be taller, but over the years he had shrunk and hardened to the compact, muscular mass occupying the space on his right. He towered over him now and the difference pleased him. To Baruch, his father represented the cold, hard outside world, a world of smooth talking wheeler-dealers that laughed and shmoozed each other over the phone. Even now, the flash of his father's mobile glowed eerily through his tallis, a flickering neon heart.

He was glad he would not be entering his father's world. His father had made sure of it. Baruch was not businessman material. There was only room for one mache in the family and his father had retained his heavyweight title. His brothers Yisroel and Ilan would swim in their father's stream, snapping at his heels, small dog-sharks defending family territory and increasing profit by collecting rent from tenants packed like rats in a hole. His two younger sisters, Bassy and Malka, would eventually marry into equally wealthy, powerful families.

Baruch could never understand how his father could daven with a clean conscience when he made his money from other people's discomfort. His father wasn't a bad man. He gave generously to charity, albeit in large, public gestures. The new Torah scroll at shul had been commissioned and paid for ensuring his father was always mentioned in the rabbis' prayers. And the decaying roof of the girls' school his sisters attended had been replaced at his father's cost. A small plaque on the wall on the top floor clarified any doubt as to who had made the improvement possible.

His father's eyes were shut tight, a fissure of wrinkled flesh scarring the right side of his face. His dark beard was trimmed neatly. His cufflinks glinted, their shine replicating the glossy leather of his shoes. On his head sat a fedora, black as night, containing not a hint of lint. Every morning Mr Levy would lovingly brush his hat before setting it at a jaunty angle, hiding his black velvet skullcap beneath. His father's hair was thick and curly, like his own, and showed no sign of thinning.

Beneath the tallis, his powerful body was neatly hidden, folded under a crisp white shirt, cloaked by a fine, bespoke suit. But when his father placed a hand on Baruch's shoulder and squeezed, his boxer's grip remained tight as a steel clamp.

His father had been a Whitechapel boy and a local champion. The cabbies had loved him for his mean left hook. But at the age of eighteen, someone bigger and faster had left him reeling, and unable to rise to the count of ten. When the world had returned, he had found that he couldn't see out of his right eye, the enlarged, warped pupil eclipsing his hazel iris, giving him a dark Belladonna stare. The blow had torn his retina and shattered the orbital bone below. That was the end of his days in the ring. Another punch and he may never have been able to read his siddur again. Besides, boxing was not a seemly pastime for a nice Yiddisher boy.

Mr Levy had been hungry for success. As the son of a lowly Hungarian refugee, his need to prove himself was powerful. Baruch's grandfather had been a fishmonger selling pickled herring to the Jewish wives of the locality, women who spoke only Yiddish. Mr Levy, though, had wanted acceptance not from his own kind, but from the white lads, the rough and tumble non-Jews who had tripped him up and trampled his skullcap in the dirt. He was sick of the stink of fish, the wet slither of briny entrails, and when his boxing days came to an abrupt end, he knew he had to find another way to make his fortune. No matter how hard he washed his hands and scrubbed his nails, rubbing lemon juice into the raw cuts, the stench of ripe cod lingered.

His sons had never had to plunge their hands into vats of slimy herring. He had made sure of that. Mr Levy was a provider. His house was large and luxurious, the carpets plush, the windows triple-glazed. Baruch had grown up warm, comfortable and loved. For all his materialism, Mr Levy was a doting father. Baruch appreciated his father's efforts and had never lacked for anything. Nor had he ever wanted for anything. Apart from the freedom to choose his own path.

CHAPTER 4

CHANI

November 2008 – London

On her way back from the mikveh, Chani sat at the front of the bus, leaning forward as if to urge the bus up the hill. At the back sat several boisterous observant Jewish schoolboys, shovelling crisps and chocolate into their mouths as they mocked and bragged, revelling in the freedom of an early Friday home time. They swiped at one another's skullcaps, their ties loosened, their shirts untucked. They wore the uniform of Baruch's old school and she wondered whether he had ever sat at the back of the bus and behaved so inappropriately. It was hard to imagine. Several rows behind her, sat two young Polish women, slim and glamorous in their immaculate jeans and make-up, talking quietly.

Through the huge windscreen, she watched the world below hurry towards Shabbes and felt a pang of guilt. She should be helping her aunt and sisters prepare the evening meal. This was to be her last Shabbes at home. But it didn't feel like her home any more. She felt displaced – she had neither left nor fully arrived. And now that she had finally reached the point of impending marriage, a state she had thought she would never reach, she felt oddly flat.

Chani was making the same, monotonous journey she had made almost every day of her adolescent life. But this time her mother should have been with her, staring down at the shoppers below, making idle observations about the faces familiar to them. Aunt Frimsche had offered to accompany her to the mikveh instead but Chani had refused. If her mother could not come with her then she would rather go alone. Besides, the Rebbetzin would be there waiting for her.

The huge window shone, warmed by the late autumn sunshine. Chani could see herself reflected in the glass. She felt she looked smaller and paler than usual. A crease furrowed her brow. The chrome of the seat backs gleamed in endless succession behind her. Usually she revelled in such lofty solitude, enjoying the scrape and thump as the bus pushed past the trees. She would stare into the thick, dark green canopies and imagine the trees swaying at night undisturbed, when the traffic had stopped and the streets were silent.

But today she felt neglected. The trees passed by unnoticed. She deserved more than this; a girl marries only once unless she is unfortunate. As the Kallah, she should have come before her silly little sister. Chayaleh, whose hair she had always

55

brushed, whose coat she had always buttoned, whose hand she had always held on the way to school, had now fallen down the stairs and been taken to casualty. Chani wondered whether *her* older sisters must have resented her in the same way but even so, she was certain that her needs had not taken precedence over their first visits to the mikveh. If in the days before the wedding, the Kallah is to be treated like a queen, then why was her mother absent? Another person could have taken her sister to hospital. Chani swallowed hard and stared ahead, gritting her teeth. She would not cry today.

The glow that had enveloped her as she stepped out of the mikveh had dulled. As the bus rumbled on, Chani tried to re-kindle the preciousness of those initial moments after her immersion. She had felt protected, coated in an invisible shield of virtue. The water itself had felt ordinary but she had been imbued with a deep sense of peace, as if her every action and thought had been sealed with HaShem's approval. The abrasive rub of a towel had seemed sacrilegious. Afterwards, in her cabin, she had remained naked for as long as she had deemed politely possible, allowing the air to dry her. The Rebbetzin had waited patiently outside. Chani had examined herself carefully in the mirror but could detect no outward change. Her expression was perhaps a touch deeper, more soulful she had decided, but her body remained slight and lissom. It had not bloomed into womanly voluptuousness. The droplets had traced wet paths over her skin, between her small breasts, over her flat stomach, and had mingled in her dark nest below. She had licked her arm to taste the water. It had no taste. It had been just water after all, even if it was pure rainwater. But it had meant everything.

There was nothing left to be learnt now, no more private tutorials with the Rebbetzin, whispering together behind closed doors to prevent the Rebbetzin's children hearing of matters so intimate and feminine. The mysterious knowledge of Jewish womanhood and wifely duty had been passed on and stored faithfully in Chani's heart. In a month, she would return to the mikveh alone. There may not even be another visit for a while. Chani froze. She was not ready to have a child. But if HaShem willed it, so it would be. There was nothing she could do. The inevitability of her life and role as a woman sank in. Suddenly, Chani felt burdened with her future responsibility, with the weight of being a wife and mother. This new world was hurtling towards her. She had wanted this next stage of relative freedom and adulthood to start so desperately, but now life seemed all too serious. She felt unworthy in her half-baked state. But Baruch would not want a skittish wife; she must pull herself together.

Her stop was coming up but Chani remained seated. She had time. She would just spend an hour there. Ahead loomed the other temple at which she worshipped: Brent Cross Shopping Centre. Its grey towers rose above the concrete loops and gaudy billboards of the North Circular. Chani felt that she was owed some form of compensation even if she supplied it herself. It was her bride's due.

Her heart beat a little faster. In her pocket was her purse and inside that, safely tucked away, was her only credit card. She hadn't spent this month's paltry salary earned as an art assistant at her old school. The endless days of mixing paints, cleaning trays and guiding ineptly held brushes were over. She had saved for a day like this and intended to squander her money on whatever she desired. The anticipation of such reckless spending sent a shiver of pleasure down her spine.

Pleasure. The Rebbetzin had used that word. Chani's greatest pleasure was shopping but the Rebbetzin had alluded to a darker, more mysterious pleasure that had sounded almost as exciting, unlikely though this seemed to Chani at that precise moment, as the bus steamed towards her Mecca of mercantile delights.

Until that conversation, Chani had associated her wedding night with intense and terrifying pain. She knew she would bleed. The purpose of the Sheva Brachot – the seven nights of feasting and entertaining that followed the wedding night – was to keep the newlyweds apart to prevent them from having relations again until the bleeding had stopped, for even the blood

58

shed during the loss of virginity rendered the bride niddah. Unavailable. And if there was blood, naturally there would be pain, Chani had reasoned. She winced at the thought of how narrow she was down there, in her holy of holies. So if she was to bleed, then something must have to penetrate that small, dark space. That something must belong to Baruch. It apparently had the potential of giving pleasure according to the Rebbetzin. Well, thought Chani, the Rebbetzin must know about such things; she is a wife after all, and has been one for at least twenty years. So the Rebbetzin must have had plenty of practice at doing – well, whatever it was that gave pleasure.

If only she had not stopped short. If only the Rebbetzin had continued her small speech about these obscure events that she would soon experience first hand. What had she meant exactly by the phrase 'explore each other'? Had the Rebbetzin explored Rabbi Zilberman? The thought of the Rabbi's woolly beard grazing his wife's soft flesh was rather unpalatable. And disrespectful. Chani promptly banished this unholy vision. Instead a distant memory resurfaced. Chani had tried to bury it in a dusty, forgotten corner of her mind but of late, it had come back to haunt her.

Five years before, she had gone on the Year 9 Cornwall Walking Tour. A crocodile of one hundred girls marching in neat pairs, their long, flapping skirts drenched with dew, their voices hoarse from singing psalms, had wound its way along the clifftops of North Cornwall. It was a drizzly yet humid afternoon full of midges that ate them incessantly, however frantically the girls beat the air in front of them. The path was narrow but the brilliant green grass spread for metres on either side of them. The girls were sensible, steering well clear of the cliff edge, carefully following Mrs Dean, their P.E. teacher's lead. She was a small, dark figure in the distance, the only non-Jew amongst them and because of this and the practical nature of her subject, she was the only woman allowed to wear trousers. Her trousers were a source of fascination for the frum girls she taught and they would often be caught staring at her legs when they should have been listening to her instructions. If it wasn't her trousers, then it was her dyed blonde hair worn in a tight, swishy pony-tail that cast a spell over them. Being a goya, she did not have to cover it even though she was married. Its artificial brilliance was a shocking but enthralling sight.

Next to Mrs Dean strode the Deputy Head, Mrs Bernard. She was an unusually tall, broad woman and although she was at the front of the line, her bosoms were even further ahead. Wherever she went, they went first. The Deputy Head wore a wide straw sunhat held on by a piece of elastic that cut into her many chins. She was not Charedi but was dressed accordingly in a long skirt and long sleeves. It was rumoured though, that she too wore trousers out of school.

Chani walked next to Shulamis, her best friend. They were singing so loudly, that they did not realise the line had stopped. Their cagoules had given them tunnel vision and muffled distant sounds. They barged into the pair in front. What was happening? Why the delay?

'Stop, stop!' yelled Mrs Bernard. The Deputy Head was jumping up and down, waving her arms about as her chest bobbed in a disconcerting manner.

It was too late to turn back one hundred girls. For there, on the murky grey sand below lay mounds of pasty flesh, human bodies as naked as Adam and Eve had been in Gan Eden before the apple incident. They had stumbled onto a nudist beach.

'Back, girls, turn back!' howled the Deputy Head. Dutifully the line turned. But coming towards them along the coastal path from the opposite direction were two figures. The figures grew closer and it was plain to see that they were naked too. There was nothing the teachers could do to prevent their girls from witnessing such abomination. Yet being good, frum girls, they politely turned their backs or averted their eyes. It was not for them to see such things. Not yet anyway. There was only one girl who remained transfixed.

The walkers were a middle-aged couple. They

carried walking sticks and wore floppy sun-hats with corks hanging from the brim. On their feet they wore leather sandals. But it was the items on display between the hats and the sandals that had Chani riveted. The woman's pendulous, blue-veined breasts swayed like white party balloons, gently nudging each other in rhythm with her waddling gait. Her navel was hidden by folds of flesh that collapsed around her hips like saddlebags. A murky tangle of hair spread outwards across her upper thighs. The woman beamed at Chani.

However it was her male companion's body that caused greater dismay. Patches of bristly grey hair grew over his sunburnt torso. He was rake thin, his sternum dipping inwards to reveal a small rounded abdomen similar to a starving child's. Beneath this belly, a forest of dark curls grew and amongst their luxuriant foliage dangled even stranger pouches of violet flesh. And between these pouches a pink snout seemed to quiver. The snout had an eye, which stared at Chani. It gave her a sudden wink.

'Good morning, ladies,' said the owner of the snout. His grin flashed from under his hat.

No one answered him. There were a few snorts and titters, as the couple passed along the column. But the girls stood motionless, staring anywhere but at the greeter.

'Chani Kaufman – *turn around!*'

The Deputy Head had spotted her. Chani jumped and turned the other away.

'I will be speaking to you later and –' Mrs Bernard paused to refill her lungs.

'*To your mother!*' for a few seconds the Deputy Head held back for dramatic effect. '*And* to Mrs Sisselbaum.'

There was a collective intake of breath. Chani gazed at the ground in pretend humiliation; she wasn't sorry. Finally HaShem had granted her a front row seat at a spontaneous revelation of all that had been concealed from her. However it had not been a pleasant sight. In fact, the man's parts had disgusted her. How ridiculous they had appeared, bouncing about in mid-air. Surely these hidden wonders had been HaShem's idea of a joke. They were not mysterious or beautiful. They seemed useless and ugly. She remembered the adulterated art books and her visit to Mrs Sisselbaum's office. What a waste of all those white labels, Chani thought.

What Chani had not known, was that later that evening Mrs Bernard found herself in a quandary. She was caught. She had made an example of Chani by forcing her to sit separately at dinner. But quarantine was not enough. She would have to speak to the girl. There was one small problem though; she had threatened to tell Mrs Sisselbaum of Chani's brazen behaviour.

Yet if the Head found out that the whole of Year 9 had been led onto a nudist beach, heads would roll and hers would be the first on the block. Mrs Bernard had been reading the map, but she had not realised the beach marked on it had a special purpose. Had she known, she would have made every effort to find a detour, however lengthy. It was her duty to protect her girls in every way, including screening the scenery where necessary.

The other staff could be trusted to keep shtum. The girls were unlikely to tell the Head, but they might tell their mothers and that could lead to complaints. It was more likely that they would conveniently avoid regaling their families with this particular episode since the tour was a resounding success. The girls were delighting in their freedom and in each other's companionship. A strong bond was growing between them. What happened on the Cornwall Walking Tour would hopefully remain on it.

Mrs Bernard called Chani to her side. It was hard to dislike the girl. Chani had character and the Deputy Head liked girls with spirit far better than the meek do-gooders that the school aspired to produce. Chani broke the mould and it made a refreshing change. Mrs Bernard was not a religious woman. It concerned her that all forms of self-expression were bled out of these girls as they grew older. Chani she was sure would suffer, for it was always worse for the brighter, feistier ones, always harder for them to do what was expected, to have their individuality bleached out of them until they became the softly spoken, modest, virtuous girls deemed ready for marriage. However, she would have to come down hard on her because Chani should have obeyed her instructions immediately; Chani knew only too well when to turn away. She had been deliberately disobedient.

As for informing her mother – poor Mrs Kaufman was barely coping as it was. It would be cruel to burden her with the petty crimes of her offspring. She envisaged Chani's mother, huge and sorrowful, her face a sad moon, her swollen ankles bulging over her scuffed shoes. She could not do it. The woman had enough tzurris already. Yes, a little rachamim, a little mercy was needed. Mrs Bernard smiled at her own graciousness.

Chani arrived looking suitably penitent. She stood with her hands clasped in front of her, head bowed. She peered up at The Deputy Head through her fringe. The Deputy Head mustered her guns.

'Yes, Mrs Bernard.'

'Chani Kaufman, your behaviour today was inappropriate at the very least.'

'Yes, Mrs Bernard,' Chani whispered.

'What's that?' snapped the Deputy Head.

'I'm very sorry, Mrs Bernard,' said Chani, a little louder.

'I should jolly well think so! A Queen Esther girl does not behave like you did today! How dare you disobey instructions. When I say turn around, you jolly well do it at once.'

The Deputy Head's bosoms were quivering. Her face was puce.

'But, but – I didn't hear you –' stuttered Chani. She was actually feeling a little worried now. Everyone had turned to stare and the scraping of plates had abated. The hush was eerie.

'Didn't hear me? Didn't *hear me*? I don't believe you.'

Chani's head drooped lower. Tears prickled her eyelids. She would cry a little. It usually helped. She raised her head, just as the first tear began to trickle down her cheek. She gulped and squeezed another one out. Her eyes shone with liquid apology.

'Plea-please, Mrs B-b-bernard – I didn't mean to –'

The floodgates opened. Chani wept and shook. Mucus poured out of her nose and her mouth opened in a hideous wail. She looked and sounded awful. And she was getting louder by the second. Mrs Bernard had to put a stop to this. Hysteria was a highly contagious disease amongst young girls.

'There – there – Chani, stop, enough now. Ok, ok, I believe you are sorry. Here, have a tissue, go and wash your face.'

Mrs Bernard handed Chani her last wrinkly but clean tissue. Chani accepted it gratefully and blew her nose like a trumpet. From behind the tissue, she gasped, 'Will – will – w – you tell my mother and Mrs Sisselbaum?'

The Deputy Head paused. An empty threat was detrimental to her authority.

'We shall see, Chani. Let's see how you behave for the rest of the tour and we shall take stock at the end of it.'

Chani swallowed and nodded manically. Then she gazed up at The Deputy Head through red-rimmed eyes. 'Thank you, Mrs Bernard,' she whispered.

'You may go now and join your friends. But remember, I will be watching you.'

Mrs Bernard watched Chani slink back to her cohorts. They surrounded her like a rugby scrum, embracing her and nagging for details – 'what-did-she-say, what-did-she-say?' But Chani took her seat in silence, settling herself as if she were a grand dame of the theatre. They could wait a little; she had plenty to say.

The Deputy Head turned away to hide her smile. She knew Chani's game and admired her style. And later that night, when all the girls were tucked up in bed, she sat with her fellow staff and laughed so hard at the day's events that tears ran down their faces and bladders were in danger of being released.

The bus edged into its bay. Chani's thoughts returned to the present and to Baruch.

She tried to imagine her husband-to-be naked. He would have a snout. This was an unavoidable fact but hopefully it would be more appealing than the walker's appendage. It must be this instrument that would enter her. It was hard to imagine that flaccid tentacle being capable of invasion. The necessary hydraulics were beyond even Chani's vivid imagination.

And please HaShem, make him not so hairy. She couldn't abide the thought of a hirsute body rubbing up against her own sleek skin. Chani tried to remember how hairy Baruch's wrists had been, but it was hard to tell for like her own, they had always been covered. Yet, his knuckles were smooth and that was a comfort.

The bus stopped. Chani forgot her fears as the doors flung open. Her earthly paradise beckoned and she hurried to meet it.

The crowds swirled around her like brilliant tropical fish. She watched them as if through a thick pane of aquarium glass, their voices loud and distorted, and their clothes bright and strange. Chani sat on a bench and stared in fascination. An Indian family ambled past, the children lagging behind their parents, eyes wide, gazing at Chani as she stared back at them. Their mother fluttered in a burgundy sari, sequins glittering as she walked. A vermillion dot graced her forehead. Chani admired her straight back and the delicate, gold bangles illuminated against her flesh. Brent Cross was a porthole through which she peered at the wider world. She longed to know what it was like to be a part of all that was forbidden to her.

How did other people live? Did they feel and think like her? What was it like to roam freely in the world and not have to think about your every action and its spiritual consequence? On her father's side, she had distant cousins in America who led secular lives. Her mind boggled at all the questions she would them ask if the opportunity arose.

What did the non-kosher world taste like, for example? Every morning she walked past a cafe on her way to school. A salty, smoky tang wafted from its doorway. Shulamis had told her that the smell was that of bacon. How had she known? Shulamis had shrugged and said another girl had told her. What did bacon taste like? In America, you could buy bacon flavoured kosher crisps – a puzzling concept, as how did the kosher producers know what bacon tasted like? Was a goy involved in the taste testing?

Then there was Christmas. She had admired the decorations and the trees. Definitely better than the giant Chanukiah outside Golders Green station. She knew Christmas was the goyim's biggest high holiday and it had something to do with the birth of Yoshki, the man they called Jesus. Did they dance wildly like the men did on Simchat Torah? Did they daven? Were they overwhelmed with sheer joy? Her father was known to shake with happiness on Simchat Torah.

Obviously the whisky helped. And what exactly did they eat? She had heard of kosher turkeys that were available for the more liberal Jews. A kosher turkey to celebrate the birth of Yoshki. An interesting concept. Her father referred to Christmas as Bank Holiday. Apparently Yoshki had been a devout Yid. What had happened along the way, Chani wondered.

Whenever she walked past the large crucifix outside the local church, she would glance swiftly up at the painfully thin body and the tousled hanging head. He was so emaciated that she could see his ribs. His pierced feet and hands made her shudder but she had to look. Only for a second or two if no one was watching her of course. Her great-grandmother would have spat three times outside the church to ward off the evil eye. But Yoshki was almost naked and this was another reason to catch a glimpse. A frum boy in a loincloth. Why was he always suffering?

It was the young women that interested her most though; what they wore and how they presented themselves to the world, in ways that she could not. She envied their freedom of choice, of colour and texture, of self-expression and individuality. What would it be like to wear trousers or bare your arms in the summer? What about the feel of a ridge of material between your legs, but nothing catching around your ankles? And the ease of movement, never being too hot, never having to experience tights sticking to the backs of your legs in the summer heat?

She knew it was rude to stare, so she tried her best to observe them surreptitiously. If she caught someone's eye, she would look away, glancing at the blank screen of her mobile. She was waiting for Baruch to call. He had said he would speak to her before Shabbes came in. It would be their last chat before the wedding. Until now they had spoken once a week without fail. He would call her every Sunday night at eight o'clock. So far, he had not let her down.

Chani clutched her shopping and pounded down the steps to the exit. He still hadn't rung. Her heart flooded with disappointment. A queue of people hustled to get onto the bus and she staked her place in the line. She hopped on board as the doors hissed shut behind her. The bus swerved away from the kerb and Chani was thrown against the driver's window. 'Sorry, love! Hold on tight now!'

She couldn't find her pass. Fumbling through her bag, her fingers scrabbled in the gritty dust in its seams, blindly recognising a hairbrush, her keys, the splayed edges of her prayer book, ragged tissues and a defunct biro, when her phone buzzed in her pocket.

Flustered, she waved a ten pound note at the driver. 'I'm sorry – can't find my pass – do you have change?'

'Nope, love. No change.' The driver shook his head ruefully. 'Go on, I'll let you on just this once!'

'Thanks!' she gasped as she boarded the bus. Her mobile had stopped. It had been Baruch. She couldn't speak to him on the bus. Everybody would hear. Chani realised she had little choice. If she didn't call him back now, they wouldn't speak until they were married. Squeezing past knees, buttocks and a stroller, she stumbled up the stairs. There was a seat at the back. Swaying down the aisle, she flopped onto the banquette and dialled his number.

'Hello, Chani?' He sounded relieved.

'Hi, Baruch – sorry I missed your call, I was getting on the bus back from Brent Cross – I couldn't find my pass but the driver let me on for free –' she gabbled. Why did I tell him all that? Now he'll think I'm a real nebbuch.

'Hey, what a mensch – good for you – I'm always losing my pass – How come you're at Brent Cross anyway? I thought you'd be home with your family. I'm tripping over mine –'

'Same thing at my house . . . and well, I'm heading there. Um, it's a long story. I just needed a bit of time –'

'To yourself?'

'Yes. Exactly.'

'I know how that feels. It's a madhouse at mine – I managed to get away to call you. I'm in Hendon Park by the swings. I rode here on my bike.' His voice quietened. 'It's nice to speak to you right now, Chani –'

Chani squirmed in her seat. She had been doodling on the window with her forefinger but broke off to concentrate on Baruch's words. None came. Was she supposed to reply now? Her reticence had created an uneasy lull. Instead she waited for Baruch to continue, but he remained silent. She sensed the flagging of his expectations and felt foolish. If only it were Shulamis on the other end of the line. She would know what to say to her.

She had to say something. 'I bought some nice things, you know.'

'What did you buy?'

Chani fingered the lacy pink plunge bra in the Marks and Spencer bag. It had matching knickers, sheer at the back and frilly at the front. She couldn't tell him. Why had she mentioned shopping? Her face was burning.

'Oh, this and that –'

She had planned to wear this and that on their wedding night. And she remembered Mrs Freidelberg's face looming over her in the queue, so close that she could see the powder caught in the old woman's creases – 'ahhh, little Chani the Kallah, so what are you doing here without your dear mother?' Mrs Freidelberg had almost choked when she had seen what Chani had been clutching. But Chani had brazened it out. 'Oh, just buying a little something for my wedding night, Mrs Freidelberg. Do you think my hossen would like me in these?' She had dangled the bra and knickers in front of Mrs Freidelberg's nose. Mrs Freidelberg had leapt back as if scorched – her mouth had flapped open and shut like a guppy's. 'A little loud, the colour, no?' Verdict uttered, she squinted at Chani, her jowls wobbling in disapproval. 'Not at all,' replied Chani 'Pink is very fashionable. My mother tells me it brings out my brown eyes.' Mrs Freidelberg tilted her head in defeat, and gripped the handles of her basket tightly. 'If you say so, my dear . . .' Inside her basket were some firm support tights and a bra that resembled a harness.

Mrs Freidelberg had bumbled off leaving Chani triumphant. Shabbes was coming and it would be too late for Mrs Freidelberg to kvetch to her mother. She would be well and truly married by then, and hopefully the lingerie would have served its purpose.

'Sounds intriguing . . . anything for me?'

She couldn't possibly tell him. 'Yes, um, well . . .' Chani petered out.

He waited in vain for her to go on. He wanted to say he was looking forward to Sunday but he wasn't certain he really was. He wanted to know what she was feeling. He wanted to know whether she was as nervous about Sunday as he was. His hands grew clammy at the thought of it. Baruch sensed that the conversation was ebbing away.

They would be married in two days and they still couldn't manage a phone call.

As usual, a void yawned between them. Baruch was only a mile away from Chani's bus, but he felt light years separated them. The convention of polite small talk was choking him but it was apparent to him that Chani was not ready yet to leave unfamiliar turf, although they had already spoken on several occasions. And why should she be? After all, they still barely knew one another. He felt trapped. This call could almost be a recording.

Baruch wanted more. He kicked the back tyre of his bike and wondered if he should change tack. A light breeze was stirring the brilliant sea of autumn leaves and they swirled in gusty eddies around his feet, catching against his trousers. He wished Chani was standing here next to him. There was a deep need in him to see her, to read her expressions and move beyond stilted talk. He wanted to know her in every sense, but the more he tried, the further away she seemed.

'How are you feeling?' she asked suddenly.

'I'm fine, I guess –' Baruch was momentarily taken aback by her question. He could hear the rumble of the bus. Perhaps he had misheard her? He waited for her to speak again, to be sure.

'What are you thinking about – I mean, are you thinking about Sunday?'

This was a first. Her words were crisp and clear. Baruch paused, gathering his thoughts, preparing an honest, if somewhat abridged, censored and acceptable answer.

'I guess I'm a little nervous – obviously Sunday means things will change forever for both of us and I think if HaShem allows it, the change will hopefully be for the better. In fact, I can't stop thinking about Sunday . . . how about you?'

'Um, the same . . . yes, it's a little scary, isn't it?'

Come on Chani, say more. Baruch willed her to go on. 'Yes it is. May I ask what scares you the most? Is it not knowing me very well?'

The-wedding-night-the-wedding-night-the – wedding-night. The words revolved in her mind like a washing machine stuck on spin cycle. The engine of the bus seemed to throb to their rhythm.

But of course she couldn't say them. 'B'srat HaShem, all will be well. I will daven for both of us tonight so that HaShem may bless us and keep us, and ensure that our hasanah goes to plan –' she trailed off, the fraudulence of these bland sentiments preventing her from continuing.

'Amen,' said Baruch. Well, what else was he supposed to say? He had tried. His heart sank. Was she so frum that the barriers would never come down between them?

'Baruch, yes, I'm scared, actually I'm terrified – I can't sleep and I can't eat –' gabbled Chani.

She had revealed too much. The poise she had tried to cultivate lay in tatters. This was not how it was done. But there was a sense of relief in her, a welcome unburdening.

'I'm the same – exactly the same – so don't worry – it's both of us – I haven't sleep well for weeks actually – well, since I met you –'

Chani smiled. The doubts still perturbed her, but his confession, although exuberant, had charmed her. 'I have to go now, gotta get off here – I will see you in shul on Sunday, Baruch and . . . it was nice talking to you. I feel better now.'

'So do I, Chani. Good Shabbes and get some sleep. See you on Sunday then . . . well, I guess . . . that's it for now!' His voice squeaked a little.

'Good Shabbes to you too. Yes, see you Sunday.'

Chani leapt off the bus as the doors squealed behind her. She scurried around the edge of Hendon Park, along Queens Road, praying she wouldn't bump into him. Her road could be reached down a small, damp alleyway. Pulling up her hood, she plunged into the safety of damp, overhanging yew, skilfully skirting the dog mess. It was time for afternoon prayers. She would be home in a few minutes.

If Baruch had turned around he may have seen a small, drab figure disappear down the shortcut on the opposite side of the street. However, even if he had seen her, he probably would not have recognised her as the girl that was to be his wife.

She would have been an indistinct feminine blur. His glasses brought the world closer to him, but it was never close enough.

He did not turn around. He remained deep in thought, hands in his pockets as he leant against his bike. The bike was propped up against an old chestnut tree. At his feet lay yellowing spiky husks, their empty shells still waxy inside, as the last conkers lay brilliant amongst the rotting leaves.

CHAPTER 5

THE REBBETZIN

October and November 2008 – London

In the first few days afterwards, waking was the only time the Rebbetzin felt alive. In those hazy moments she believed her belly still to be full. But then she would blink awake to the emptiness inside her. When the bitter reality set in, the dreams began. She was pushing a pram down Brent Street, her baby cooing at her from within. But when she looked down at him, all she could see was blood, dark and viscous, filling the pram to the brim.

The Rebbetzin moved in a daze, her body carrying out its usual functions but food had no taste and sleep gave no relief. Her hands busied themselves with her daily chores but she could not pray. The words stuck in her throat. She tried to read her siddur but it gave her no comfort.

Her husband was a constant reminder of her loss. She ignored him when he called her name. He had used to kneel before her to ease off her shoes, rubbing each hot, sore little foot until the life wriggled back into her toes. Now the thought of his touch repulsed her. The bleeding had stopped but she avoided the mikveh. By remaining niddah she kept him at bay. She had wanted him to disappear so that she could grieve alone in peace but the evidence of his existence invaded her domain and disturbed her silent lament. His hat still hung on the banister, his dirty underpants still surfaced in the mound of washing.

Tears came and they would not stop. They poured down her face when she least expected it, making a visit to the shops impossible. She sent Michal instead. They blinded her suddenly when she tried to read a recipe. She constantly licked them away. Her chin became raw from her hand brushing against it. Her cheeks stung with salt.

When the tears dried, the anger began. Her rage grew into a white heat. It lit her from within, turning her soft gaze into a hard stare whenever she saw an expectant mother, her stomach bulging with life. The women sensed her envy and would stroke their bumps protectively and turn away from her. Such jealousy attracted the evil eye and the Rebbetzin knew why these women crossed the street when they saw her. She was ashamed of her bitterness but she could not control it. The community's tongues were wagging; she had been too old to carry a child. Let them talk. She had nothing to say.

Her husband was an easy target when the screaming started. The Rebbetzin had never raised her voice against anyone; she had trained herself to speak gently even under pressure. Suddenly her throat belched accusations, harsh words and reproaches. Her husband bore them all, his head bowed as if it were his due. And it was. If it got too much, he left the house.

In the kitchen, she clattered the pots and pans, banged down the food on the table and stirred the soup with unusual venom so that it spilled over the sides and congealed in olive splodges. In front of the children, they tried to maintain an edifice of normality, their voices falsely cheerful, but their eyes no longer met. The children were adult enough to sense the unease lurking between them; it surged like an electric current fuelled by their mother's unspoken anger. Meal times had the surreal quality of a farce but no one was laughing. Even sixteen-year-old Moishe behaved himself, relenting from his adolescent sullenness. Between her husband and Avromi a grudging, unspoken truce had been established.

Her pain poisoned her cooking, burning the chollah and souring the cheesecake. Her gefilte fish, usually sweet and delicate to the palate, left an acidic aftertaste. Her tzimmes that had given guests so much pleasure now gave them indigestion. But nobody dared complain. The family chewed and swallowed with difficulty. Moishe would sometimes ask to be excused only to spit out the gristly lumps of goulash hidden in the pouches of his cheeks.

Over the space of a few weeks the initial fury

receded into a seething contempt and finally a cool indifference. She returned to her teaching, but the irony of teaching girls like Chani to use the mikveh every month as part of her wifely duty made her feel deeply uneasy.

The Rebbetzin stared at herself in the mirror. It all seemed such an effort. She felt she was drifting at the bottom of the ocean. The bedroom walls seemed to close in on her. Shabbes was due in four hours. She couldn't think clearly in the presence of their separated bed. The Rebbetzin decided to take a walk in the park and return in time to prepare.

Rabbi Zilberman missed his wife. He ached for her and his yearning formed a knot in his stomach. His chest felt constricted and his heart seemed to beat faster. It was a kind of pain he had not felt before.

When she bent to unload the dishwasher, he gazed at her soft, round rump. Her skirt clung to her hips and he longed to grasp them and press himself up against her, his hands roaming over her belly and across her breasts. But he restrained himself, seeking distraction by sorting out the cutlery, checking each tine for rust or stubborn food particles. He would polish them vigorously with a tea towel and throw each utensil into the meat drawer so that they crashed against each other – which was more than he did with his wife these days.

They had not touched for so long. How much longer, HaShem? A man must wait. He was tired of waiting. It was his own fault – he should have talked about things when she had approached him. But once again he hadn't been able to face it.

It was another Friday afternoon. He sat in his dusty, grey office and thought about the young hossen who had just left. He heard his footsteps clump down the stairs to the street below. Last week, he had spoken to Baruch Levy and the week before to another young man. Marriage was a never-ending business. The young men wore the same dark suits and white shirts, and the same anxious, fearful expression. They sat on the edge of the plastic chair and listened intently to his words. He was a broken record, intoning the same advice each week.

Rabbi Zilberman wanted to lunge across his desk and grab each young hossen by the lapels, look him in the eye, and say: 'Love her, listen to her! When she needs you, run to her. Give to her with your whole heart for in time, if you're lucky, she will be more than a helpmate. She will be your best friend. Forget about talking too much to her! Talk to each other all day and all night if you need to. You must give even when you don't feel like giving. For *this* is what it means to truly love another.'

But he restrained himself. Instead he spoke of duty and moderation. And felt like a fraud.

He would pray. He opened his siddur but the

psalms offered no comfort. The words seemed distant and cold. He would talk to HaShem. Rabbi Zilberman cleared his throat. 'HaShem? Are you listening?' He looked up at the ceiling and saw the cracks. He felt foolish. Perhaps this was not the way to address the Master of the Universe. He tried again. 'Ribbonoh Shel Olem, help me reach my wife, Rivka Zilberman. She's a good woman, a good wife – but I've let her down in so many ways . . .' His voice tailed off. What if someone overheard him in the corridor outside? They would think he was a meshugganeh for sure. And then the whole world would know his business.

There seemed to be no immediate answer from HaShem. He would talk to his wife. He would admit he had been wrong about many things. He would call her and tell her he loved her. No, he had told her already this morning. Nu? So he would tell her again. She would be preparing for Shabbes now. Perhaps now was not the time. If not now, then when?

Rabbi Zilberman dialled home. He imagined his wife wiping her hands on her apron, reaching for the receiver. It rang and rang. Perhaps she had gone out. He waited a little longer, hypnotised by the empty mechanical bleeps. They seemed to intensify his loneliness.

'Hello?'

'Rivka? How are you? It's me, Chaim.'

'Yes. I know it's you, Chaim.'

84

'I – I was just wondering how you were getting on, if there is anything I can do to help?'

'No, Chaim – it's all under control, thanks.'

Undeterred, Rabbi Zilberman ploughed on. 'Well, how are you feeling? Are you tired?'

'No, I'm fine. I need to go. I need to pick up some things before Shabbes comes in – I haven't got time –'

'I miss you.'

There was silence. He heard her breathing.

'I know you do.'

'Do you miss me?'

He had to ask. He saw her standing in the hall, twisting the phone cord between her floury fingers, her headscarf slipping back. There would be a smudge of flour on her forehead, from where she had rubbed the sweat away.

Another silence followed by a long sigh.

'I love you, Rivka.'

Another sigh.

'I know you do. I have to go now – or I won't be ready for Shabbes.'

He sensed she had relented a little; he would grab his chance. 'I'm sorry. We do need to talk. About . . .' He couldn't say it. He couldn't hear her breathing and then she spoke.

'It's late. I have to go already.'

He had lost her again. Desperate he plunged on. 'Rivka, you can't keep grieving like this. HaShem doesn't want you to grieve like this. It's not right. We're not right. We need to talk, we need to change things – please – I'm here for you.'

'I know – I know. But I need more time.'

'How much longer Rivkaleh?'

'I don't know. Just a little longer that's all.'

'Ok, a little longer then. What can I do? I'll see you at home after shul.'

'Ok then, bye.'

'Bye. Rivka –'

'Yes?'

'Good Shabbes, my darling.'

'Good Shabbes to you too, Chaim.'

The phone clicked and returned to its usual hum. He held the receiver in his hand until the line went dead.

The loss of their baby had hurt him too. His grief had been less intense – she had carried their child for four months. He thought of a time before Avromi had been born. His poor Rivka, she was punishing them both. The anger flashed through him – he did not deserve to be treated like this. He had hurt her, but enough was enough. They had three children, plenty to be grateful for. HaShem had been good to them. There were some couples who could not conceive. She should count her blessings and stop with this nonsense. A little longer, that was all he could bear, for to love is to give even when the giving feels like a burden.

The Rebbetzin replaced the receiver and stood for a moment in the cool, shadowy quiet of the hallway.

He was trying – she would give him that – but he didn't really understand. It was more than just the miscarriage. A wave of guilt washed over her; her own callousness irked her.

No, this was her time. First she would pack a box of leftovers for the bag lady who lived in the doorway of a greengrocer's that had closed down. She entered her silent kitchen and marched up to the milk fridge. She pulled out a little potato salad, some smoked herring, a large spoonful of egg mayonnaise and a dollop of shredded beetroot. She pressed the lid down firmly and placed the box in a shopping bag. Rummaging in the bread tin, she located two crusty poppy-seed rolls and from her larder, she took a carton of apple juice.

The Rebbetzin strode past her neighbours' houses, her tall, bony figure wrapped in an old raincoat. Inside, the good wives of Golders Green would be chopping and stirring, their hands moving with a blind certainty as they prepared for yet another Shabbes.

The high street was calmer now. A few remaining shoppers hurried to and fro. Even the traffic had slowed.

The Bag Lady was squatting in the narrow doorway of the shop. The glass windows sheltered her from the wind and rain, but at night she froze. A stained duvet covered her bandaged feet. Her head was wrapped in a filthy headscarf covering her bald, bruised scalp. All her worldly possessions surrounded her and most of these were plastic bags, stuffed into larger plastic bags, some of which had been torn into strips and knotted into brightly coloured ribbons which she wore as a garland around her neck like the flowers draped around a Hindu deity. They fluttered in the breeze. A supermarket trolley filled with stinking rags was parked behind her and she sagged against its metal frame. Her hands lay in an arthritic heap in her lap.

Who was she and whose wife or mother had she been? Whose daughter or whose sister? The Rebbetzin had never ceased wondering. And how could her family abandon her to live out her final days like this – to suffer the cold and the violence of wicked strangers? Or had she abandoned them? Her head was as empty as her plastic bags and in her rare moments of lucidity, she claimed to have been evicted by the council but could not remember from where. Society left her to rot in a doorway, her old bones rendered immobile from sitting on a stone floor. Such neglect made the Rebbetzin ache with bitterness.

It would not happen in her community. The old and the sick were cared for. Her own ageing mother lived in a plush nursing home nearby. Their bones were warmed by central heating and their hearts were warmed by filial love or duty. The visitors arrived like clockwork, bearing gifts of home made blintzes and honey cake. At every Shabbes, Yom Tov or family occasion, these beloved fossils were wheeled out and settled in their favourite chairs at the family table. When they lifted their quavering voices to ask for more cholent or to tell a tale that had been told a thousand times before, they were listened to with respect and their every whim indulged.

She approached with caution. When angered, the Bag Lady had a foul mouth. The Bag Lady squinted at her from her one good eye. The other was sealed with pus. The Rebbetzin knelt before her, holding her breath – the Bag Lady was more than a little ripe.

How can we continue to grow fat and happy and leave such a miskenah to rot on our doorstep? The Rebbetzin had seen the women push their strollers past The Bag Lady as if she were invisible, quickening their step as if she weren't there. These were women who gave tzedakah each week and considered their generosity a mitzvah. She thought of their daughters, the schoolgirls that shrieked and sprinted past her when she cawed at them, believing her to be an old witch and her stare to be malevolent.

It seemed to the Rebbetzin that her community concerned itself only with its own. Those who were not Jewish, or not Jewish in the right way, were of little consequence. Although to be fair, she did not see anyone from outside the community trying to help the poor woman.

The Bag Lady worked her shrivelled mouth in anticipation. She watched as the Rebbetzin opened the box and placed it into her hands. The hands shook but the box did not spill. The Rebbetzin pulled out a plastic spoon from her pocket.

'Thank you, dearie. 'Tis very kind of you. God bless you.'

'God bless you. Eat up now. I will bring you some more soon.'

'Ahhh, there aren't many like yourself, I can tell you. May sweet Jesus love you and keep you.'

Indeed. She stuck the straw in the apple carton and settled it on the pavement within the Bag Lady's reach. 'On Monday,' she vowed, 'I will ring Social Services and get her some help.'

The Rebbetzin continued on her way. She was now out of her community's heartland. The food shops dwindled in number. A strip curtain fluttered in the breeze and from within came the relentless gabble of sports commentary. She glimpsed a huddle of bent backs and the flash of a TV screen. A discount bookstore, a Polish food-shop, an internet cafe and finally a beauty salon offering 'clean, safe, speedy tanning in new upright booths'. Once upon a time, she had used a sun-bed. She remembered lying in a neon coffin wearing nothing but a tiny pair of black goggles, her body silhouetted against the brilliant white rods beneath the warm glass.

A fine drizzle had begun. The Rebbetzin passed Golders Green tube station. A herd of squealing teenagers had gathered outside. They smoked, flirted or punched numbers into their mobiles. Girls flicked their hair or coyly pulled their sleeves over their hands, stretching their jumpers, their long, coltish legs on display beneath pleated school skirts. They were taller than the boys.

She had been one of them once. She had not always been called Rivka. At eighteen she had been accepted to read History at Manchester University. But Rebecca Reuben had never attended a single lecture. She had swerved from her chosen path during her gap-year in Jerusalem. A year of desert heat, dust, ancient stone and the rustling of eucalyptus trees.

She had met Chaim that year. And God.

CHAPTER 6

CHANI

November 2008 – London

The bathroom was warm and damp. The mirror was clouded over save for the mosaic of old fingerprints. Hair clogged the plughole and wet towels lay in a jumble at her feet. She rubbed at the mirror, clearing a window. Leaning against the chilly edge of the sink, Chani stood on tiptoe and gazed at her reflection in the dim and misty light.

The pink bra and knickers seemed to float against her pale skin. Their colour seemed lurid, artificially brilliant in the gloom of the dingy bathroom. Satin cups forced her breasts inwards and upwards, faint blue veins visible above the soft material. The straps were taut and skimpy, tiny gold buckles perched on each shoulder. Below her cleavage dangled a diamante charm. She twisted to make it catch the light and caught sight of her buttocks wrapped like cling-film in a slither of chiffon. This is what a harlot wears, she thought. This was not the impression she wished to create, but still the image fascinated her with its vulgar unfamiliarity. It was the antith-esis of the starched white corset and stockings her mother had bought her at Lieber's. The suspender belt had felt vaguely surgical, the straps thick and clumsy and the elastic had irritated her skin. Then there were the pants in white satin, plain and navel-high.

She wondered what Baruch would think of her looking like this. Would he find her alluring? The billposters along Queens Road showed pneumatic female pop-stars writhing in similar attire, their eyes inky with mascara as wicked and beguiling as a succubus. She didn't want to appear whorish though; God forbid he should think her cheap. Her purpose was to claim some ownership over her wedding night, to mark it as a threshold crossed willingly into womanhood. The pink bra and knickers were her personal celebration. She was delighted by the curves they had created. Yes she would wear them.

Her reverie was interrupted by a fierce hammering on the door. Chani grabbed a towel and wrapped it around her shoulders.

'Chani! What are you doing in there? Shabbes is nearly here. Your friends have arrived down-stairs. You're late!' yelled her older sister, Rochele.

'Coming! Just combing my hair. Be down in a sec.'

'Don't forget to say your broches after you've finished in there.'

'Yeeeeesssss, Rochele . . .'

'All right then, see you downstairs!'

A child wailed below and her sister hurried away. Chani scrabbled out of the bra and knickers, and changed into her smartest Shabbes clothes, a navy velvet skirt and jacket. She brushed her teeth, washed her hands and whispered a brocha. Finally, she thrust the lingerie back into its plastic bag and exited the bathroom. She hid it in the secret zipped compartment of her bride's suit-case. All set for Sunday night. She switched on the Shabbes night-light, closed the door and hurried downstairs.

In the living room, an old armchair had been decorated to resemble a queen's throne. An ivory silk sheet covered the worn corduroy and silver tinsel had been draped around the arms and back. Two plump red velvet cushions with gold tassels nestled in each corner.

Chani was led to the chair by Shulamis and Esti, another close friend from school, the three of them surrounded by a cluster of friends and female relatives. The girls whooped, whistled and clapped. The house shook as they stamped their feet and pounded the carpet. Clumsy with joy they welcomed the Bride with song and dance. The men were praying mincha at shul. The women had already prayed together at home and now out of male earshot, they could sing as loudly and tunelessly as they liked.

'Mazel tov Chani!' they shrieked. The older

94

women ululated, their throats trilling their happiness. Blessings rang out from different corners of the room as the Fahr-Shpiel began.

Chani basked in the attention as her friends gambolled about, entertaining her with ridiculous sketches and jokes. Rochele thumped away at the piano; notes clashed as her fingers forced the dusty keys. Her son, a chubby three year old, was squatting under the piano stool. An elaborate tea party had been set up on a trestle table at the back. Apple cake, cinnamon rogellach, miniature cream puffs topped with syrupy apricot halves, a solid looking cheese cake topped with shiny, scarlet strawberries, tuna and egg filled bagels and an enormous black forest gateau waited to be eaten. Shuli, Chani's oldest sister was pouring the tea. Devorah, Mrs Kaufman's third daughter was arriving early Sunday morning from New York, whilst Sophie was too far on in pregnancy to fly.

'A speech! A speech! The Kallah has to speak.' cried Aunt Frimsche, her mouth full, a crumb quivering on her upper lip.

'Oh, leave her alone, Aunt Frimsche. Let the Kallah relax and enjoy herself.' This was from Rochele, ever protective. Chani didn't want her to leave after the wedding. She hadn't seen her in two years, since she had married and settled in New York. She was shocked at the change in her. Her sister had grown stout, her cheeks bulged and a double chin trembled as she spoke. Her arms stretched over her belly to reach the keyboard. It was impossible to tell whether her stomach was swollen with child or just cake and Chani dared not ask.

'I think – I can manage a speech –' Chani strained to be heard over the clamour. The noise died down the moment she spoke. 'As you know, I'm quite fond of speaking . . .'

'Noooo? Really?' Someone quipped at the back.

'Thank you, Naomi – if I may continue . . . well, it's been quite a journey as you know, it took a while to find the right hossen – but er, here I am and thanks to HaShem and my parents – I'll be a good wife in two days –'

'Amen! But good? Good?! Since when have you been "good"?' This was from Shulamis.

'All right, all right, Shulamis – I will *try* to be good!'

Her school friends nudged each other and sniggered. Chani gave them a mock baleful stare.

'Baruch HaShem! You'll be his helpmate, his right hand . . . may you bring forth healthy and happy children . . . B'srat HaShem,' muttered Aunt Frimsche, swaying gently in her chair.

Ignoring Aunt Frimsche's pious input, Chani plunged on. 'So I want to say thank you to all of you for being here, and celebrating this big moment with me. I can't say I'm not nervous, but I really hope that all my lovely friends that are still waiting and searching, Shulamis, Esti and Sophie –'

'And me! Don't forget me!' hissed Shoshanah, prodding Chani's shoulder. Chani turned round.

'Oh yes, oops – and Shoshi – very sorry, Shoshi, didn't see you there – all find the right man soon and get married! I will daven for you on Sunday and then I will dance at all your weddings!'

'Amen!'

'Hear, hear!'

The women raised their teacups and the room grew quiet save for the clinking of china. A lull descended. The unmarried girls became pensive, avoiding eye contact, absorbed by their private fears. Naomi and Maya, both recently engaged, whispered about their choices of wedding venue and exchanged admiring glances at each other's rings. The older married women shuffled over to the table and examined the carnage. They picked at the leftovers, their fingers sticky with syrup and sugar strands. The sandwiches were beginning to curl at the edges and the black forest gateau was butchered. They stood in small cliques, speaking quietly, ruminating over the week's events, exchanging juicy morsels of gossip.

And soon those that were not family bid Chani farewell and took their leave. Chani was left alone again, save for Aunt Frimsche and two older sisters. Of her school friends, only Shulamis remained. These four busied themselves with tidying up and would not let Chani intervene. She was ordered to sit on her throne and relax, which was easier said than done.

With nothing to distract her, the panic that lurked at the back of her mind overwhelmed her again. She eyed the four women in the room. None of them was approachable. Shulamis was ignorant of her fears and her comprehension of the carnal act itself was even more muddled than her own. She had tried broaching the subject on one occasion in Orli's café over hot chocolate, but Shulamis had become wildly agitated, reeling off crazed assumptions in a loud stage whisper. The woman at the next table had given them a disapproving glare and Chani had had to kick Shulamis hard under the table.

Aunt Frimsche was a definite non-starter. Chani wondered whether Frimsche had even consummated her own marriage to Uncle Ephraim, for theirs had been a fruitless union. Frimsche was a bony, desiccated, old stick; she preferred the ethereal realm of prayer to the physical world. Her aunt was a kind, anxious and quaint soul; Chani found it hard to envisage her as a curious bride, let alone naked and writhing in blessed passion with Uncle Ephraim.

As for Rochele, it had been a while since they had had a truly intimate conversation. Seeing her sister again had been a strange and awkward experience. There had been much to adjust to, including her sister's unfamiliar nasal American twang.

She was not close to Shuli, so that was a no-go too. When Chani was fourteen, Shuli had been married and went to live in Stamford Hill. Now, although she was only twenty-six, in her musty tweed suit, her oldest sister resembled a dowager. She insisted on wearing a woollen beret over her wig, just in case someone mistook her for being unmarried. How anyone could possibly be so deluded was beyond Chani. She was wrapped up like a parcel in all her layers and preferred to speak Yiddish to her children, having married a man who had gone to yeshiva in Antwerp. It was always a struggle to decipher her cousins' English. Their diction was garbled, the words buzzing like wasps trapped inside a bottle, and Chani was often left perplexed as to what they were actually saying.

She would go and visit her mother in the kitchen and bring her a slice of cake. Chani shovelled a dishevelled lump onto a paper plate and carried it to the kitchen. The door was ajar and a strip of neon light glared through the crack. Her feet clipped over the sticky linoleum. The heat engulfed her as she entered. Her mother stood over an enormous soup tureen, patiently stirring, her wrist moving in a slow, circular dance. Her face was covered in a light sheen of perspiration. Behind her, Chayale clung to her skirts, rubbing her face against her mother's bottom. The bandage remained, although now it had been knocked askew and had acquired a few jammy fingerprints.

A toddler, Chani's youngest sister, Yona, sat in

her high chair idly eating Play-doh; gazing at Chani in silent wonder. Out in the yard under the plastic roof, Chani watched Yael dragging washing out of the machine and sorting it into soggy piles. She was fifteen, tall and willowy and wore her long hair in a smooth dark plait. Chani observed a subtle poise and refinement in her mien that had previously been absent. Now that Chani was getting married, Yael knew her time was coming and hence her self-awareness had grown. She spoke quietly and had grown more shy and introspective. Chani felt momentarily wistful at the prospect of her younger sister becoming a woman; the Yael that had gambolled at her side had gone forever.

'Mum. *Mum!*' called Chani and waited for her mother to focus blearily on her.

'Hello, Chani-leh – how was the Fahr-Shpiel? Did you have fun, my darling?'

'It was great, Mum – they made such an effort, so sweet of them – Shoshi and Sarahleh wrote all the sketches and they had rehearsed them at Shoshi's house last week. Here, I brought you a slice of cake.'

'Leave it on the side-board, I'll have it in a minute – mustn't let the soup boil or it will lose its flavour . . . and the chickens haven't even been stuffed yet, I'm running so late . . .'

'Mum, stop, just for a minute and eat a bit, just a pitsel for me – I haven't seen you all day.' Chani refrained from mentioning her mother's absence at the mikveh. She knew her mother felt guilty. Instead, she watched as her mother muttered a blessing and gobbled the cake, the sweetness infusing her weary features with pleasure. She wondered if her mother could allay her fears.

'Mum . . . um, I was wondering – do you remember your wedding night?'

Her mother paused, her jaw frozen like a cow chewing the cud, momentarily startled. She swallowed noisily and stared at Chani, as if seeing her for the first time. 'Chayaleh, go on and lay the table for mummy like a good girl,' said Mrs Kaufman.' Find me eighteen matching forks and knives from the meat drawer please.'

Chayaleh stomped off to do her mother's bidding, sticking her tongue out at Chani as she passed. Chani ruffled her hair.

'Ow! You're hurting my stitches!' squealed Chayaleh.

'Oooh . . . I'm so sorry your Highness . . . I beg your forgiveness –' Chani teased. Chayaleh lifted one shoulder and dropped it, then skipped out of the kitchen.

'You're frightened, my darling, aren't you?' said Mrs Kaufman. She reached over and placed her warm flabby palm over Chani's white knuckles.

'No, not exactly – well, yes, mum.'

'Well . . . I guess every Kallah has to do what she's got to do. All your sisters seemed to manage perfectly well . . .' pondered Mrs Kaufman.

'Mum! That's *not* helping!' She could brook her frustration no longer.

'I know, darling, but it's been so long since I was a bride . . . I'm trying to remember what I felt like . . . your father was very good to me that night . . . I think the important thing to remember is that there can only be one first time for every woman. And to get on with it – let your husband do his duty. Don't stop him. And you must do yours . . . the less fuss, the better . . . and may Ha Kodesh Ha Borech Hoo bless you with a child – He has already blessed you with a hossen, hasn't He? A boy from a good Hasiddisher family, the right sort – and he's a yeshiva bocher. I am sure it will all be fine.'

'Amen. But did it hurt?'

'Did it hurt? Hmmm . . . eight children later – Chani, I can't honestly remember! If it did, it's a fleeting pain . . . it won't last and it will get better with time and practice my darling, you'll see.'

'That's exactly what the Rebbetzin said –' sighed Chani.

'The Rebbetzin?' Mrs Kaufman's eyebrows disappeared under her fringe. 'You talked to the Rebbetzin about your wedding night? Oh Chani, how could you? A little decorum, a little self-respect perhaps? Where's your modesty?'

'I don't see what the problem is. We talked about everything else – in fact, she brought it up on the way back from the mikveh –'

'The Rebbetzin Zilberman talked to you about

your marital duties on the street? IN PUBLIC? Huh! I've always had my doubts about that woman, far too modern –' sniffed Mrs Kaufman. She thrust the crumpled paper plate into the bin and wiped her mouth on her apron.

'Mum – you weren't there, were you?' The accusation slid out. Chani winced as her mother's face sagged. Her mother released a ragged sigh.

'I know, I know – I've let you down again – I'm sorry, but what was I to do? You know Chani, when you have children, there will be days when you make mistakes, when one child takes precedence over another – and there's nothing you can do – I'm sorry – if I could've been there –' Words tumbled out of her mother, the regret and anger mingling together, her voice a croak.

Her mother faltered, her massive body shuddered like a blimp buffeted by strong winds. Chani crept over and wrapped her arms around her mother as far as they would go; inhaling her peculiar aroma, redolent of sweaty wig, fried onions and face cream. She felt her mother's tears seep under her collar and sensed the tension retained in her hulking shoulders. Chani stroked her mother's back, and the shoulders shook in relief.

Baruch pedalled up the hill, his coat billowing behind him, as he made his way home to wash and dress for shul before Shabbes arrived. His eyes watered from the traffic fumes. He wanted to wipe his nose but he dared not let go of the handlebars. Reaching the summit he freewheeled down Brent Street, standing on the pedals, bracing his weight against the bike's sturdy frame. He loved the rush. If he was lucky, he would make the traffic lights and careen across the North Circular into Golders Green without having to brake.

His head was full of Chani, a jumble of images, words and sounds. The catch of her breath. The pale blur of her heart-shaped face. His wife. The fear suddenly resurfaced, threatening to cloud his mood. He knew he wanted Chani but did she want him? Nothing was for sure. What if she didn't? His longing had grown stronger every day since he had first met her and now his need gnawed at him endlessly. He thought of the wedding night and began to pedal for dear life. What if she rebuffed him? What if he couldn't control himself? The wet dreams persisted. He had little hope of curbing his excitement with her if he couldn't manage it on his own.

Her small white hands, the nails that were ragged crescents, her smooth pale skin, her dark eyes bright and quick with a keen intelligence she had tried to suppress. Perhaps she would be a bold adventuress leading him to the Promised Land. The bike swerved beneath him. A crazy notion but he had seen the alertness in her face and liked it.

Baruch wanted to know all her thoughts. He wanted to share his with her, but he feared he would bore her. His thoughts were myriad and overwhelming; he didn't want to drown her. His mind was full of the future, their future – how would it be and how would he support her?

But he was getting to know her. She had been different this time. Until now the phone had made them both feel awkward, forcing them to fall back into a monotonous pattern of stiff, polite formality. This last conversation had felt more real and very soon she would be a tangible presence.

Baruch thought about living in Jerusalem with Chani. The move was imminent. In six months they would be leaving London. How would they cope in a new and unfamiliar environment? Neither of them spoke Hebrew. He would toil over religious texts for hours leaving Chani alone at home in a strange land. The idea filled him with dread. He didn't want her to be lonely. He would spend all his time with her if he could. But he had little choice. His parents had agreed to buy them a small flat in Nachla'ot and to fund his studies on the proviso that he continued them. He had savings of his own but no real transferable skills. Chani would have to find a small, part-time job somehow to support them. Perhaps they could give English lessons? But neither of them had any qualifications.

He cycled faster trying to outstrip his thoughts. The cold air stung but the speed matched the tumult of emotion coursing through his veins. Her voice reverberated through his head and he heard the halting rhythm of her speech above the roar and grind of juggernauts, buses and cars. Each turn of the pedal pushed the nagging doubts to the back his mind. He felt like he was flying, encased in his own bubble, protected by the intensity of his feelings for a girl he barely knew.

CHAPTER 7

THE REBBETZIN

May 1982 – Jerusalem

Rebecca stood in the queue waiting her turn to go through security, a little frightened by the press of humanity behind and in front of her. Men dressed in black and white, wearing black fedoras or fur-trimmed hats swarmed through the barriers, pushing and shoving in their haste to say their evening prayers at the Wall. The tension was palpable as the pious grew increasingly irritable. The stink of sweat, stale clothes and greasy beards wafted through the air. She held her breath, not comprehending how they could tolerate wearing heavy wool suits in the heat. The women were bundled up too. Some wore sweaters over long-sleeved shirts that were fully buttoned. She couldn't help staring at their thick dark tights. The younger women wore long trailing cotton skirts that almost concealed their feet. They hung back from the men leaving a discreet gap.

She was relieved she had worn her longest skirt and a long-sleeved T-shirt. Shifra stood next to her similarly attired except that her top was baggier. They had met when Rebecca started to learn weekly at the campus Beit Midrash, where frum women volunteered to teach secular women the basics of Torah and Judaism. Chaim had persuaded her to attend just once. Shifra was her assigned mentor and Rebecca enjoyed her easy company and so the spiritual knowledge she passed on had not felt like a trial. They were the same age and quickly became friends outside class. Rebecca suddenly felt conspicuously aware of the thin cotton welded to her skin. She wished she had brought a shawl but it was too late to go back.

The female soldier barked an order and the line surged forward, making Rebecca stumble.

'You ok?'

'Yes, yes I'm fine,' she muttered, feeling foolish.

'We'll be through in a minute. This bit is always annoying.'

'Sure.'

But she wasn't sure at all. She felt uneasy, a hypocrite for being there. She had visited the Wall before on holiday with her family but never just before Shabbes. The precinct had always seemed half empty, peaceful in its vastness. The fervour that now filled the air had been missing. Rebecca was beginning to regret agreeing to come. But she had promised Chaim she would go. Just this once. She knew he was here somewhere too. Maybe he was through already.

The line lurched again and they found themselves in a small hall. Inside, there was a conveyor belt and scanner. She had nothing on her since it was Shabbes and it was forbidden to carry. Bored soldiers directed her through the metal detector. They appeared nonchalant, rifles swinging at their hips, jaws working overtime, pounding gum. They joked and flirted amongst themselves, shouting over the heads of the faithful.

The immensity of the precinct made her feel small and vulnerable. At the far end of the square stood the Wall. It reared up, massive and foreboding, its face cast in shadow. At its base supplicants had begun to mass, ant-like, insignificant compared to its bulk.

Tourists, soldiers, students and schoolchildren gathered in small excitable groups. The evening sky darkened to indigo. An Israeli flag fluttered proudly, fabric whipping against flagpole in the stiff evening breeze. There were trestle tables covered in white tablecloths offering an array of soft drinks and cake. Cameras flashed, teenagers hugged and grinned and tour leaders called out names. Young Hasiddim mingled with the secular inviting them to Shabbes dinners. Beggars rattled tins crying out 'Tze-da-kah!' Rebecca spotted a tall, slender bride in a billowing gown and glittering bodice. The girl was laughing, her face suffused with joy.

At the barrier of the women's section of the Wall, a woman handed out cloaks to female tourists who were inappropriately dressed. She glanced at Rebecca and smiled and nodded. They made their way through the narrow gaps between the plastic chairs where elderly women sat hunched up, peering at their prayer books. Some smiled and whispered a greeting. She found herself gently smiling back.

Only a few feet remained between them and the Wall. All around her, women swayed and bowed and the air buzzed with whispered devotion. It was quiet, serene, the fractious disorder of the queue now forgotten. Singing from the men's section floated on the breeze, dying away until another wave of sound flooded the enclosure. She was sure Chaim was there.

They squirmed through the last row of congregants until there was nowhere else to go. She gazed up and up at the massive slabs. Plants had grown through the cracks, the dusty green of their leaves a contrast to the expanse of Jerusalem stone. Its colossal height and thickness gave an impression of perpetuity.

It had stood here for almost two thousand years. Instinctively she ran her hands over its wrinkled surface. The stone was still warm from the sun and its crevices were crammed with hundreds of tiny folded notes. Rebecca wished she had brought a secret plea of her own but she had not known what to ask for. She had had a vague idea but was too scared to put it into words in case the note really worked. She was not sure she was ready for the outcome.

She looked around her. To her left a woman lent

motionless against the Wall, her face buried in the crook of her arm, absorbed in invocation. To her right another woman sobbed. She hadn't expected to witness such an open display of emotion in this sacred place. Shifra handed her a small leather prayer book, the diminutive print impossible to discern. It made no difference, as she couldn't read Hebrew anyway.

Shifra had started to pray. She did not know how to pray. She felt lost. She tried praying in English, saying the words in her head but it felt false. The only prayer she knew was the Shemah. She had no idea if it was the appropriate time to recite the prayer but she had to say something. She leant against the wall and covered her face with her open prayer book emulating the women around her. Under her breath she recited the Shemah, her delivery hesitant and rusty.

'Shemah y'Israel Adonai Elohaynu Adonai Echad.'

Hear O Israel The Lord is Our God The Lord Is One.

She didn't think she believed in God, but nor could she fully deny His existence, frightened that when she needed His help He would not offer it. Instead she wandered in a spiritual no-man's land, too cynical to believe fully, yet too fearful to cut herself off completely. Her parents were Polish refugees from the Holocaust. They did not believe.

But here at this strange, ancient site, she felt something different. It was as if the Wall was a symbol of – and a connection to – a people. Her people. She hadn't thought of them like that before. The Wall was all that remained of their holy place and she understood then that it was not enough just to survive. One had to return.

Darkness had fallen and the heat of the day had faded quickly. Rebecca shivered. They hurried through the twisting, narrow streets of Meah Shea'rim until they reached the main street. The traffic had stopped but the place hummed with human energy. Under the street lights, children scurried. Old Hasidim wearing round fur-covered hats paced slowly, murmuring in Yiddish, hands clasped behind their rounded backs.

The street was bleached of colour, causing the shadows to seem blacker and denser than usual. The men's faces, hands and brilliant white shirts hovered in the darkness. Even the dirt and litter that featured so prominently in the daytime were camouflaged at night. Here and there a bottle gleamed or a chocolate bar wrapper had been wedged between railings, small tokens of modern life. The smell of cooking drifted from every open window and doorway. Salty noodle soup, fried onion, the sweetness of freshly baked chollah, rosemary, golden potatoes and roast chicken. The pots had been covered, the ovens had cooled and the women were waiting for their husbands to return from synagogue. In the windows, candles guttered but remained alight.

On every exterior, peeling white placards were glued, filled with angry Yiddish. The stark block script seemed to suggest an ominous presence that watched and judged and demanded obedience. She could not read the words but she could sense the flickering glances as she entered the ghetto. She was being watched too.

Shifra quickened her pace and entered a dilapidated apartment block. The mirror in the entrance hall was cracked and smudged. A bin bag had burst open and rubbish was strewn at the base of the stairs. A cat shot out past them. There was no light and the stairs twisted upwards into blackness. Suddenly apprehensive, Rebecca put a hand on Shifra's arm to slow her down.

'Wait, I feel a bit weird coming here – I mean are you sure this is ok, for me to be here?'

'Of course it is, Becca. Don't be silly, I want you to be here. I've told my parents all about you and they're expecting you. Come on, my sisters really want to meet you.'

Her anxiety diminished but still she hesitated. 'Shifra, I don't know any of the blessings – nothing – your parents are going to think I'm –'

'They aren't like that, I promise you. They don't judge people like that. Remember, they were like you once. Don't be scared. Don't be put off by these streets and people – they don't know you! You're here and you're with me.'

'What about my clothes? Are they ok?'

'More than ok. I'll lend you a sweater if you like.'

'Yes, please do. I'm freezing.'

'I will. Now let's get up these stairs.'

They climbed in darkness, the marble making their steps and voices echo. The building smelt musty. Cooking odours hung stale in the air. The trapped heat of the day assailed them as they reached the fifth floor stairwell. A strip of yellow light from beneath the closed door illuminated the doormat and handrail. The door was not locked. Shifra pushed it wide and they entered.

A large oval table shimmered with light. A pair of ornate silver candlesticks stood at its centre. The cutlery glistened against white cloth. Shifra's father poured wine into a goblet and raised it to recite the blessing. He had nodded gravely at Rebecca when she had arrived but had not spoken. She sat at the other end of the table amongst the women and waited to sip from the cup. She watched as it was passed down from husband to wife and from oldest to youngest. As it reached her, she took a sip. The wine was cloyingly sweet and she had to fight the urge not to grimace.

She passed the cup to Shifra. Again she sensed she was being watched. She looked up and briefly met the rabbi's eyes. He regarded her carefully, his gaze steady. She sensed he was measuring her worth. Behind the beard, she realised, he was younger than he looked.

The room was close, crammed with people, although calmness pervaded. The younger children wandered freely. Nobody minded. A toddler chewed Lego on the floor while two others hid under the table whispering and giggling.

She had been warmly welcomed and her plate had been filled but she could not eat. Her appetite had evaporated in the heat and the food was too stodgy for her liking; the chicken drumsticks had congealed in their own oily juices and the cabbage salad was soggy and overly sweet. The children stared. She had not known the blessing for washing her hands and had repeated the words after Shifra in a jolting fashion. The water had soaked the stitching around her wrists. Her ignorance embarrassed her and she felt on edge, anxious not to cause offence or humiliate herself. She was determined just to get through the evening, to go home to all that was normal and reassuring. But these people had cast their own spell over her. She stared in turn, mesmerised by the gentle voices and unfamiliar rituals.

At home Shabbes was a miserable affair. They would plod through the blessings over the candles, wine and bread in a desultory fashion, her father usually muddling them up in his halting Hebrew. Her mother's cooking was abysmal. The soup was always tepid and over-salted, the potatoes burnt and shrivelled. The atmosphere was invariably melancholy. She had felt lonely. An only child with her ageing parents, her father lost in his memories, consumed by the need to talk and talk. Just beyond the brightness of the flickering Shabbes candles lurked unspeakable horrors. In the corners of the room, shadows would shift, re-enacting atrocities that had terrorised her dreams. There had been nothing to hold on to, no hope or joy to counteract the gloom. After supper, her father would slump in front of the television and she would be left to scrape and stack the dirty plates.

'So you have come to Jerusalem for your gap year?'

The Rabbi's voice interrupted her reverie. She was surprised to be addressed so directly by him. The table grew silent. The children chewed and stared again.

'Yes. I'm on a one year programme for foreign students at the university.'

'And where are you staying?'

'At the dorms. On Mount Scopus.'

'How is it? Great view, I imagine, of the Old City.'

She pulled a face thinking of the cockroaches in the kitchen. 'It's ok – cramped – I share a room but I'm lucky, I get on well with my room-mate. She's Scottish.'

'Glad to hear it. And what's the plan for afterwards?'

'Oh, a history degree at Manchester. Then maybe law. Or journalism, which I'd prefer – law's so dry. But my parents want me to be a lawyer.' She was rambling now.

The rabbi nodded his appreciation. 'Ahh the parents – always getting in the way! So how are you finding living in Jerusalem?'

'It's strange. It's taken some getting used to. Actually, I think I'm still getting used to it. The new part is nothing like I expected, but I love exploring the Old City. There's something about it I can't explain. It pulls you in.' She hoped that answer would suffice and the attention would shift away from her.

The rabbi smiled, his teeth white and even against the hairiness of his beard. 'I know. It was a shock for me too after Golders. But now I couldn't live anywhere else. The city gets under your skin, seeps into you . . .' He broke off to attend to his small son who had clambered into his lap. The moment had gone.

The rabbi started to sing grace, his voice fluctuating with each cadence. The family responded in an easy, natural manner, flicking through tattered pages of the prayer books. The rabbi sang louder and thumped the table, carried away with his own enthusiasm. The children smirked. She did not know where to look so she stared at the page, any page, desperate not to look out of place.

He stopped abruptly and began to speak in English, his words clear and unfaltering.

'And so on Shabbes we remember who we are. We stop our work and we rest. We have time to think. Time to light candles and say the blessings. But is it enough? Or is it too much? We sit here in our own land. In freedom. It's not always peaceful but here we are. We have returned after thousands of years of exile. But some of us are still in exile, cut off from their spiritual identity forgetting the customs and prayers that have kept our people going. It is easy to forget. It is easier not to pray, not to think about their every action and its consequence. It is easy to eat traif and move away from everything that makes us who we are. After all, six million died in the gas chambers so what's the point any more? Where was HaShem in Auschwitz? In Buchenwald? In Treblinka?'

The rabbi's eyes seemed to bore into her. What had Shifra told him? Who was he to tell her how to live her life, even if she had asked herself the same question time and time again?

He continued, his voice quieter.

'I have no answers. Nobody can explain HaShem's actions or lack of action, some may say. But we have a choice. To keep our identity by continuing in the name of tradition. To keep our heritage even though so many of us died for it. Or to continue Hitler's work by forgetting who we are and turning our backs. It's so much easier to live a modern life, eat what you like, marry whom you like, watch telly on Shabbes. But every time a Jew walks away it's another victory for those who wished and still wish us dead.'

She dared not look up. She was furious with Shifra. She should never have come. She had been an idiot. The sermon had been for her benefit; she was the only traif-eater at that table.

Yet there was something here for her in Jerusalem, something that stirred the blood and ignited her senses however much she doubted God's existence. The city throbbed with a thousand different voices, a thousand different yearning souls: Muslims, Jews, Christians. Its walls vibrated with God's names. It beguiled and teased her, revealing a new face here, but then twisting away, revelling in the confusion it caused. Light and darkness. Knowledge and ignorance. These religious Jews in their black garb repulsed and fascinated her. What were they so sure of? What secrets had been revealed to them? She envied their peace and sense of place. They belonged. She had caught a mere glimpse and had been left unsatisfied.

The walk back was awkward. Rebecca sulked in silence, walking fast so that Shifra had to work to keep up. Shifra had glanced nervously at her but had not spoken. They glided between houses, hearing the singing floating out from open windows. The night had grown still, the darkness unbroken by moonlight.

'I'm not angry with you. But I am angry.'

Shifra paused, gauging her reply. 'Well, you have every right to be. I guess I told him too much about you. I really, truly didn't expect him to say all that – I shouldn't have told him about your parents.'

Rebecca stopped abruptly and faced Shifra. 'I don't mind him knowing about my family and my background. That's not it. I prefer that they know – then it explains my lack of tradition, knowledge, whatever you can call it. I'm not ashamed of my parents. What I did not appreciate about tonight, Shifra, was your father's little lecture about how I should be leading my life. He may as well have stuck me in a pot and boiled me! It's not like I haven't heard it all before anyway.'

Shifra looked down and then away. 'I know – I know – he gets like that sometimes. He's a rabbi – that's his job. They're all like that – they feel they have to, you know. I'm sorry.'

'Look, at the end of the day, he made me think again. Maybe that's why I'm so angry. I am curious. I wouldn't be here otherwise. We wouldn't have met if I hadn't wanted to know a bit more about the religious side of things, learn about what being Jewish is all about, right?'

'True, but I feel bad about putting you in that situation. It wasn't handled very well. I wanted you to feel relaxed, good about being at my house for Shabbes. I just wanted you to feel at home, but that all went a bit wrong. I'm going to have a word with him.'

Her friend looked glum and Rebecca felt sorry for her. She had meant well. It had not gone as expected but they had tried. She slipped her arm through Shifra's.

'Hey, cheer up. Leave your father alone; he can't

help it. Come on Shifra, leave it now, it's Shabbes. Nothing's broken. I'll still come to Beit Midrash and you can continue to bathe me in your holy glow!'

Shifra laughed. 'I'm glad you weren't completely put off then.'

'Seriously, I think I want to know more. Slowly, nothing major, just the basics – no brainwashing or anything.'

'What brainwashing? As if *I* would ever do such a thing. I'm not my father.'

'Ok. Relax!'

'Me, relax?'

'Yes, you! Relax about all those religious dates you're going on for a start.'

'I wish I could.'

They walked on, chattering about everything and nothing until they reached the poles marking the end of the religious area. Beyond its borders cars rumbled and modernisation churned. They would meet again on Tuesday evening at the university for her lesson. Released from the quiet restraint of the religious neighbourhood, Rebecca plunged into the melee of secular Jerusalem. Teenagers staggered past her clutching bottles of beer, the girls garish in tight Lycra and smeared make-up. The chaos swallowed her as she wound her way towards a taxi rank. All she wanted now was to see Chaim.

She waited for him in their usual place, just outside the basketball court. Behind her were the concrete hulks of the dorm buildings. She sat huddled against the wire netting, hugging her knees to her chest to keep warm. In the valley below, the Old City was spread out like a glittering tapestry. The faint sound of the traffic drifted on the night breeze, mingling with the eerie wail of the muezzin. The city seemed so near yet remained as elusive as ever. From her vantage point, it felt as if it belonged to her but however hard she tried, she could never grasp its mysteries or unravel its ancient secrets. Her love of the Old City had intensified with every walk through it she had shared with Chaim during the past six months they had spent together. She could not get enough of its twisting lanes and sudden open spaces baked under brilliant blue sky. Even now, in the darkness, having left it only hours ago, she longed to plunge back into its heart again. Where was Chaim? Perhaps when he arrived they could catch a cab down and have a wander.

Then she remembered Chaim had stopped taking cabs or buses on Shabbat. She respected his decision but it was frustrating at times. Rebecca missed the bars and buzz of the weekend. Now they waited until Shabbat had gone out. Sometimes the wait felt eternal. Yet she would rather be with him than anywhere else.

She glanced at her watch. It was nearly midnight. He was walking back from French Hill where he had dined with friends. She knew he had walked the long route back to avoid walking through the Arab village at night. A crunching of gravel alerted her to someone's presence. The red glow of a lit cigarette bobbed in the darkness.

'Hello.'

'Hey. How are you? How was supper?'

He lowered himself next to her and hugged her tight, rubbing her back against the cold.

'Interesting. A bit unnerving actually.'

'How come?' He passed her his cigarette and she took a long drag.

'It's nothing like home. There's an intensity, a serenity that was . . .'

'Special?'

'Kind of. But the rabbi, Shifra's dad, spoiled it by going on about how secular Jews like me are spoiling the religious return to Israel by not keeping kosher or marrying out. He said we were basically doing Hitler's job for him.'

She could feel Chaim grinning next to her. His amusement irritated her.

'It's not funny, Chaim! He really got to me! He made me feel guilty and it's not his place to do that.'

'No, it isn't, but look at the reaction he got out of you. If you didn't care, you wouldn't be feeling so strongly. He isn't necessarily right. Some of them believe we caused the Holocaust by assimilation or turning away from a Torah life.'

'That's ridiculous! How can anyone believe that?

I'm sorry but that's just crazy. So many really religious Jews died in the gas chambers alongside all the sinners. How can that possibly be true?' The indignation rose inside her. Surely Shifra did not believe that theory?

Chaim shrugged. 'I agree. It's totally irrational. But that's one of the things I like about people who have strong faith – they just believe implicitly and their belief system creates answers for them.'

'Like sheep,' snorted Rebecca.

'Yes perhaps, but to them our lives are pure chaos. No rules, no direction. We just do as we please and to hell with the consequences.'

Rebecca turned to stare at him. She could only catch the dim outline of his profile. He struck a match and the yellow glare momentarily framed his creased eyes and turned his cupped hands scarlet. He had not given up smoking on Shabbat yet. Something of the old Chaim still remained and she was thankful for it. He was changing and if she wanted to keep up, she would have to adjust to those changes. There had been no pressure from him. He was exploring his own path and he wanted to share it with her. Now that she had found him, she did not want to lose him. She was trying to understand and to feel what he felt. And at times, like the fleeting spark of a blazing match, she thought she felt it too. In the Old City, in the light, in the shadows. In the warmth of his body next to hers at night.

'Come on. Let's go home. It's cold.' He stood up and held his hand out to her, pulling her to her feet. Numb with cold, their legs moved stiffly and then they began to jog, feeling the blood circulate, their feet slapping against the gravel path.

CHAPTER 8

CHANI

November 2008 – London

After all the guests who were not family had finally returned to their respective homes, Chani lay in bed thinking. She stared at the ceiling as the darkness evolved into a multitude of shifting colours and incoherent patterns. Her cousin Malka snored gently on a camp bed next to her.

Chani envied her ability to slip off into the realm of the subconscious with such ease. She was tense and wakeful. Her mind throbbed with anxiety. Around her the house ticked and creaked, the majority of its occupants unaware of the cooling of its timbers, the glugging of its pipes, yet each sound seemed to be amplified for Chani's benefit. She thought of her mother and wondered if she had ever wished to live a different existence. Was she disappointed with her lot? The knowledge that her mother was unhappy filled Chani with habitual despondence. This comprehension was not sudden or new to her. All her life Chani had sensed her mother's growing misery. She used to smile more, she even used to laugh. A blurry image of her mother sitting and grinning in a giant, revolving tea-cup at a local fun fair tugged at the edges of her memory. Had she sat in the teacup with her mother or was it one of her younger sisters? It didn't matter, the fact remained, her mother had been happy then.

In the early days, when Shabbes came, her mother presided over the table, a true Shabbes queen resplendent in her glossiest sheitel, smiling gently, indulging her youngest daughters by allowing them to sit in her lap or run riot amongst her guests. Her mother joined in with the lively conversation, playfully arguing with her father. Chani remembered receiving her mother's blessing, the soft kiss on her brow, the sticky residue of her mother's lipstick. Every Friday, her father still sang the psalm Eshet Chayal – *A Woman of Worth* to her mother across the dinner table and Chani remembered how her mother had glowed with pleasure as his quavery voice sang her praises. Nowadays, her smile was wan and she often crept upstairs to fall asleep with her youngest child before grace after meals.

Her mother's sadness seemed to follow her like a cloud, drifting gently over her daughters, but it had irked Chani more than the others. When she questioned her older sisters about her mother's lack of vivacity, they just shrugged and replied, 'That's the way she is now, that's just Mum.' This did not assuage Chani's anxiety. What had her mother been like at her age? Chani had pored over family albums for clues, and found evidence that she had once been different: her mother dressed up for Purim as a tube of toothpaste, her father as a toothbrush – the pair of them, grinning sheepishly at each other. What had their marriage been like before children? There were only a few photos, and most of them were of her parents' wedding. Her mother as a nervous, slim bride wearing the dress, posing stiffly, looked pensive. Her father looked small and puny. In later family photos, Mrs Kaufman's girth had widened but her pillow face remained unreadable. She sat in the midst of her small tribe. Her expression did not change. She had merely increased.

It seemed to Chani that her mother lived under her cloud alone. Shulamis' mother was eternally cheerful. Mrs Feldman had five children and remained slim as a pickle. She moved with alacrity and was a loquacious, welcoming woman. Mrs Feldman never failed to ask after Chani's mother.

Chani sensed the pity that lurked beneath her polite enquiries. Instantly, she would become ashamed of her mother, of her unwieldy bulk and sorrowful air, the shame soon submerged under a wave of guilt at her disloyalty. She wanted to be proud of her, yet simultaneously she longed for a modern mother who wore elegant clothes. She wanted a mother who smelt of perfume not cooking oil. She wanted an energetic mother who took her shopping and most of all, she wanted one who listened and responded.

One afternoon, she arrived home to find her mother in some sort of trance. Her father was at shul, her younger sisters on their way home from school. Mrs Kaufman was sitting on the edge of the shabby sofa in the living-room, her head in her hands, rocking back and forth, muttering to herself, 'I cannot cope, I cannot cope –' Chani was terrified. Her mother seemed to have lost all control. Chani remained frozen in the doorway, her mother unaware of her presence. She called out shakily to her: 'Mum? Mum, are you all right?'

But Mrs Kaufman continued to sway, as if she were davening intensely. Chani edged closer until she was kneeling at her side. Gently she pulled her mother's hands away and peered into her face. Her mother's cheeks were slick with tears and her mouth hung open in a grotesque grimace. Her words became a hoarse whisper until eventually they stopped altogether. Between her knees, her swollen abdomen trembled, larger than ever, distended with new life for the eighth time.

'Mum – mum – what's wrong – what's happened?' Chani demanded. 'Is the baby ok?'

Her mother's breathing had become harsh. A string of saliva stretched from her bottom lip, pooling in her lap. Suddenly, a long, low howl of despair rose up in her throat. Chani gripped her mother's hands and shook her hard. Her mother stopped rocking and blinked groggily at Chani.

'It's a girl,' rasped Mrs Kaufman.

'What is, Mum? What are you talking about?'

'The baby – it's another girl.' Mrs Kaufman's hands rubbed her stomach. 'I promised your father I wouldn't ask the nurse, but I couldn't resist. Stupid me – better not to have known until the birth –'

'Oh Mum . . . I'm so sorry –'

'Your father will be so disappointed. We've been praying for a son all these years but all we get is daughter after daughter! We still haven't fulfilled the mitzvah to produce one of each – and this will be our last chance, I'm sure of it – I'm too old!' wailed Mrs Kaufman.

'Mum – the baby is still a gift from HaShem – you shouldn't resent her for being a girl –'

'Eight girls!' shrieked Mrs Kaufman, her hands clutching at her skirt. 'Another daughter to find a hossen for, another hasanah to pay for – we can't cope! Your father is in enough debt as it is. Your sisters' weddings broke him . . . what are we going to do? And you're still single. HaShem must be punishing us for something –'

Her mother's voice had risen an octave. Chani hugged her as tight as she could. Surely it was her father's fault. Couldn't he have restrained himself? There must be a way to prevent a baby coming. Chani felt a rush of anger towards him and then towards her mother, for clearly she hadn't been wholly innocent either. There were women who refused to go to the mikveh in order to avoid rela-tions with their husbands, but her parents were good people, simply living their lives according to

HaShem's bidding. Her mother would never shirk her ritual duty. Nor refuse her father.

Chani knew her parents loved each other; of this she was certain. She witnessed their deep affection in the gentle, respectful way they spoke to one another, although they seldom touched in their children's presence. Her father had never raised his voice to her mother and however exasperating she could be, he stood by her stoically, never complaining or criticising.

Chani knew one thing for certain. She didn't want her marriage to become a replica of her parents', nor did she want to emulate her mother's example. Not every mother had eight children. However the majority of the women in her kehilla fulfilled their spiritual quota by producing at least one girl and one boy. Most went beyond the call of duty and had four or six children. Ten was an exaggeration but was not unheard of. The pressure to ensure the continuation of the Nation was ever present.

Not everyone heeded its call. Her friend Esti was one of three and her mother was relatively young and fresh. Esti's mother was still of a child-bearing age. Perhaps she had simply chosen not to have another child. And as for the Rebbetzin Zilberman, well, if a rabbi's wife could stop at three then . . . Chani paused mid-thought. She had heard the rumours and hadn't wanted to dwell on them out of respect for the Rebbetzin. Nor did she want to think of her suffering. Still, there must be methods of preventing conception. This was a matter she must raise with Baruch, if she could muster the courage before it was too late.

Her mind swirled. What sort of husband would Baruch be? Would he listen to her? Would he love her? Perhaps he loved her a little already. No, this was impossible – she didn't love him, so why should he love her? Not yet anyway. Would they fall in love? What did that mean? She had heard that phrase time and time again but couldn't imagine doing it herself. It made love sound like a treacherous vat of boiling liquid. It smacked of losing control, something she would once have welcomed.

In her world, people did not fall in love. They were chaperoned into marriage. They met, they married and then they had children. And somewhere along the line; they got to know each other. They became a team, husband and wife, bringing more babies into the world, as HaShem willed it. And if they were fortunate, HaShem smiled upon them and gradually they learned to love each other. Slowly but surely, two strangers became a neat, snug unit carrying out mitzvahs in His Name. Falling in love was for the goyim.

But what was Baruch really like? She had seen only what she assumed was his polite façade, and that was all she had allowed him to see of her. He was her suitor, old fashioned, humble and cour- teous, falling over his colossal feet to open doors for her. It took tremendous willpower on Chani's behalf not to laugh. He was sensitive and attentive to a fault, but what if his behaviour had been a mask? He could be a monster in reality. It was hard to imagine Baruch being anything other than mild and agreeable. Please HaShem don't make him boring!

She harked back to their last conversation and felt a momentary thrill. The excitement was quashed almost immediately as her mind scuttled back to more probing issues. Would he treat her well? What if he beat her? The notion startled her. She would be alone with a stranger, a stranger who was physically stronger than her. She knew it could happen. It had happened. But to whom exactly? She had heard vague mutterings but all had been hushed up, smoothed over by the rabbis. The victim remained silent, the abuse an ulcer buried deep in the kehilla's bowels. The fact remained that Baruch could do what he liked to her once they were behind closed doors. Chani thrashed about in bed, her thoughts spinning wildly. A vision of Baruch screaming, mouth a gaping, angry hole, knuckles gleaming in a fist. She flipped her pillow over to rest on its cool side. Baruch seemed an unlikely tyrant. But how could she be sure?

She hoped she would not disappoint him as his wife. She knew what was expected of her, but her own expectations of love and marriage remained intangible. It was hard to imagine what his were. Chani tried to picture Baruch but his face kept eluding her. Acne – three red spots erupting along his jaw. And small green eyes behind thick panes of glass. There must be more to him. He wasn't that unattractive, was he? She strained her memory, desperate for details. His hair – yes, it was thick and curly. No sign of hair loss yet, Baruch HaShem. Her father's tonsure was not appealing. Yes but why had he chosen her? There were lots of girls desperate to get married. Why her?

It was no good. Sleep evaded her and her mind seethed with questions. She scrambled out of bed, pulled on her dressing gown and crept downstairs to the kitchen. She needed chocolate.

In the darkness of her bedroom, Mrs Kaufman listened to her daughter's tread. She could not sleep. Tormented by guilt, she had spent the past few hours berating herself for being neglectful to Chani whilst her husband muttered about the Baal Shem Tov. Rabbi Kaufman, ever virtuous, was never plagued by insomnia.

Mrs Kaufman tossed and turned, the bed groaned in protest and Rabbi Kaufman was deposited to the edge of the mattress. The duvet rode high over his wife's heaving flanks. Rabbi Kaufman woke to find himself uncovered, his feet numb with cold. He snuggled against his wife's broad back for warmth and resumed his discourse with the ancient sage.

'Chani-leh? Chani, is that you?' Mrs Kaufman whispered.

But no reply came. The footsteps continued unabated, fading with distance.

'I should have gone to the mikveh with her but I am so tired,' she moaned softly to herself, to the darkness, to HaShem if He was listening. I should get up she thought. I should go and check on her. But I can't move. Mrs Kaufman allowed a tear of defeat to trickle into her pillow. She sighed a long, exasperated sigh and prayed for relief. But no relief came. Her snood prickled her sore scalp and her husband's bony knees needled her back.

'Yankel, are you awake?'

'Ugh?' burbled Rabbi Kaufman. Was the Baal Shem Tov standing before him in his bedroom?

'Yankel, wake up! I need to talk!' No, it was definitely not the Besht speaking, Rabbi Kaufman sadly conceded. It was his wife. Indeed the great rebbe was receding, leaving a faint glow against the flickering blackness of Rabbi Kaufman's sealed eyelids.

'What about, Leah-leh? It's time to sleep.'

'Yankel?'

'Yes, Leah-leh?'

'I can't sleep.'

'Try, my dear, try . . . say a brocha.'

'Nothing will help. I've been a bad mother.'

'Oy, Leah-leh, are you starting this again?'

'It's true, I am a bad mother. And it's too late to repair all the mistakes I've made.'

'Nonsense, Leah-leh! You are a wonderful mother to our children and a wonderful wife to me . . .'

'It's not true, you're just saying that . . .'

135

hiccupped Mrs Kaufman, the tears soaking her pillow.

'Leah-leh, enough now! Please try to sleep. There, there, my dearest . . . it will all be better in the morning . . .'

Rabbi Kaufman patted his wife's hand, and rubbed his beard against her polyester nightgown. He held her tightly until sleep claimed him once again and relaxed his grip. The Baal Shem Tov did not return.

Mrs Kaufman continued to snivel. She thought about Chani and how once again, another daughter was leaving her. She replayed their conversation in the kitchen for the umpteenth time.

'I should have told her the truth. It never stops hurting. It never gets any easier this life . . . only harder . . .' she mouthed into the darkness.

CHAPTER 9

THE REBBETZIN

October 1981 – Jerusalem

They had first met in the university canteen. Rebecca had woken late and ravenous – having slept her way through breakfast – and morning lectures. She drifted in, lethargic from hunger and lack of caffeine. She stood in the queue asleep on her feet, shuffling forwards with her tray. The soup tureen steamed, its contents broiling to a salty, flavourless slime. The meat lasagne looked more promising and she helped herself to a large slice, paid and made her way towards an empty table overlooking the courtyard, a bare and dusty bowl bathed in winter sunlight.

Her food had turned into a congealed, greasy mass by the time she sat down, but at least it was filling. She attacked it with vigour, hacking at the pasta with her useless plastic cutlery. Halfway through her meal a shadow fell across the table.

'May I sit here?'

The voice was faintly nasal and the clipped accent sounded like its owner might hail from the Southern hemisphere. At the same time it was soothing and familiar against the backdrop of chaotic Hebrew she had yet to master. She glanced up to see a tall, slim young man, his pale skin stained with a mass of tea-coloured freckles. Beneath a shock of dark auburn, unruly hair, his face was thin and slanted and his sharp chin bristled with stubble. There was something alert and watchful about him. He reminded her of a fox.

'Yes, of course,' she said. He had startled her. She was sure she had tomato sauce smeared around her mouth. The young man sat opposite her and began to wolf down his food without further comment. Rice, chicken, carrots and peas disappeared at an alarming rate. He ate without pause, his fork sifting through his plate and approaching his mouth fully loaded. She tried not to stare.

'Sorry. I'm a fast eater. Barely touches the sides.'

She reddened. 'Oh, I hadn't meant to stare! Sorry – no, don't let me put you off – I'm done anyway.' She rose hurriedly and picked up her tray.

'But you haven't finished.'

'I wasn't that hungry anyway,' she lied. His eyes rested steadily on her face. Flustered, she shook her head, gave him a sheepish smile and moved away.

'At least let me buy you coffee,' he called after her, halting her in her tracks. Her smile broadened into a real one.

'Ok, then. Mine's black with two sugars please.'

'Feel free to take a seat,' he grinned and ambled off towards the queue.

She eyed him as he stood lopsidedly in line. She knew he was pretending not to notice. She liked the stoop of his thin shoulders, the tanned triangle at the base of his neck, the scruffy trainers and faded jeans. He seemed to be appealingly at ease in his own skin.

Chaim was twenty-three years old and South African. He had emigrated to Israel four years before, having lost his place at Johannesburg University after failing his exams. Too much partying and too little study. He had come to Israel at his parents' insistence. They had felt it would straighten him out and in many ways they had been right. He had completed the army and hated it, but the experience had toughened him. He had learned to toe the line, to be disciplined and work as part of a team, traits he had previously shunned. However, he was a pacifist, deeply uncomfortable in that environment and was relieved when his tour of duty was over.

He had come to Jerusalem because his grand-mother lived in a sprawling apartment in the Rechavia suburb and at first he had lived with her until he felt he needed his own space. He continued to visit her every other day even after he had rented a room at the university dorms. He was in his second year of a Philosophy and Politics degree and had no idea what to do afterwards. Open a philosophy shop perhaps. For his keep he gave private English lessons or proof read essays written in English by Israeli students.

He spent his spare time exploring the Old City, wandering freely through all four of its quarters, learning its strange rhythms, delving into its hidden beauty spots. He roamed the Arab and Christian streets where tourists and Israelis feared to tread. He sat in crumbling coffee shops and drank bitter coffee sweetened with cloves. The vendors had come to know him and greeted him as a friend, challenging him to backgammon contests that he would inevitably lose, only to return the next day and lose again.

He said he felt safer there than in Johannesburg or anywhere else in South Africa. In the midst of the Old City, in the narrow, blood-stained streets that had been fought over for centuries, in the darkness of a musty café, where the tables were sticky with Coca-Cola and the air buzzed with radio static and the harsh rattle of Arabic, he felt at peace. To him, it was the eye of the storm.

He spoke of these things to Rebecca and she begged him to take her with him.

Beneath the docile, charming exterior was a slightly lost soul. He was searching for something and for someone with whom to share his search. Chaim came from a liberal Jewish family. He kept almost none of the traditions, but the Old

City and the intensity of the beliefs it harboured, raised questions. The holy sites at which the pilgrims of all three faiths came to worship aroused a sharp interest. He wanted to know what drove their conviction and in what ways it helped them to survive life's adversities. Moreover, he wondered whether there was something in it for him, whether believing and doing in the name of something greater led to one becoming a better person.

He was certain there was something more to life. He wanted more than the material world could deliver and he spoke of this yearning frequently to her. He wanted to live a life of meaning – whatever that meant. At first it perturbed Rebecca. She did not want to get involved with a daydreamer and he seemed to be leaning in that direction. But then again, he spoke of ideas and theories that were new and inspiring. He engaged her mind and her imagination, a rare ability in a man in her eyes.

It was easy with Chaim because he was at ease in himself, gentle and unassuming. He liked women and they responded in kind. He was courteous and flirtatious in a playful, harmless way. They found him a sensitive listener. In fact, he preferred female company and at first she had thought that perhaps she was simply one of many.

Fortunately, the appreciation was mutual. He found ways to intercept her paths around campus, to bump into her accidentally at a cash-point or to find her sipping coffee at the canteen. Afternoons spent together spread into evenings and then nights. He was not her first, but her few previous dalliances that had seemed so potent at the time, now paled into insignificance.

As for him, he had found someone with whom he could truly communicate. He spoke to her about everything, his desires, his dreams, even his fears. She drank it all in and in turn related her own inner world to him. All that she had held most intimate, she now willingly shared. He was nothing like her previous boyfriends. He was her friend, her lover, her companion. It felt like plunging into a warm sea and discovering she could swim.

Rebecca did not know exactly why, but her lessons with Shifra brought her a sense of peace even though she often argued her way through them. Afterwards, walking back to her room, she would mull over what she had learned, ordering it in her head, readying herself to discuss the lesson with Chaim. She loved these intimate, spiritual debates she could now share with him. It had brought them closer. She was still not sure she believed, but she was beguiled by the intricacies of each passage and how it related to religious life. She had become more aware of the changes in season and how each had its own festivals and ritual. Time moved with greater purpose, its rhythms punctuated by prayers, each bustling week ending in the slowness and quiet of Shabbat.

She became a frequent guest at Shifra's for Friday night dinner and made her peace with Shifra's father. She had circled him warily at first, bracing herself for further criticism but he refrained as if having sensed her hurt. Instead he went out of his way to welcome her, to talk and joke with her. She was almost disappointed, having longed to interrogate him on his ideas. Now he spoke openly and warmly to her, encouraging her to ask questions. Shifra shone with quiet pride.

Slowly she felt at home there. The blessings and the rituals became familiar and now she could say them on her own. And when she did, she felt a sense of rightness, that she was doing things as they should be done. The children still stared but if she smiled, they smiled. She began to feel accepted.

The changes happened slowly. At first they were barely perceptible, but as her learning deepened they started to seem appropriate. She continued to struggle with the notion of belief. Did she believe now? Something was stirring in her heart but she was still uncertain. When she raised her doubts to Chaim, he had told her that his own faith was still fragile. It came and went but he found in carrying out the mitzvot, in saying the blessings, it intensified. By doing, even if his belief meandered, he could restore the connection for which he was searching. After all, it was human to err and doubt was part of the journey. She tried harder, and he was right. When she carried out even the smallest, most basic mitzvah, such as giving to charity, she felt as if she were becoming a better person for it.

She stopped mixing milk and meat and joined Chaim in eating in kosher cafes only. The television and radio were silenced over Shabbat. She pushed her jeans to the back of her cupboard and began to wear skirts and dresses, seeking colourful garments that were soft, flowing and feminine. She started to prefer herself without make-up, her face bare and clean. What had once seemed unattractive now seemed natural and right. Chaim had told her she did not need it anyway.

In turn, Chaim began to cover his head, sometimes with a white knitted kippah, and favoured light coloured clothes that were loose and comfortable, beneath which he wore a prayer shawl against his skin, the tiny plaited strings dangling over his baggy jeans. His hair grew into a thick, curly nest which soon became one with his beard, giving him a wild, biblical appearance which Rebecca secretly liked, although she complained about how scratchy he was to kiss.

Their relationship deepened. They had so much to talk about, but words were chosen with greater care. Sometimes they had no need to talk at all. Rebecca had never been with anyone with whom she could sit in silence. Previously she had always felt the need to fill any lull in conversation, hating the inane chatter that would pour from her lips. Now they exchanged long, slow glances that lingered and became smiles. And it was enough.

Until one night he pushed her away.

Outside, a cold desert wind whipped litter and dead leaves into a frenzy. Even though her room-mate was absent, they spoke in whispers. They grew warm and sleepy. She rested her head on his chest and he cradled her against him, their breathing falling into the same easy rhythm. She reached for him.

To her dismay, his fingers gripped her wrist under the covers and gently removed her hand. She froze. He had never refused her before.

She raised herself up onto her elbows and gazed down at him.

'Don't you want to?'

He turned his head away, taking his time in answering. Then he sat up and pulled on an old T-shirt. She watched in silence, a knot forming in her stomach.

'I want to, Becca. Nothing's changed about the way I feel for you. What has changed is the way I view us, our relationship. We shouldn't be doing this. We're not married.'

She had been expecting as much. Nevertheless, she felt as if he had struck her. God mattered more to him now than her. He could resist her. She was losing him, in the one place they had always shared so intensely, so intimately. Frightened, she sat up in a huddle against the bedframe.

'What does that mean for us then?'

He faced her and reached for his cigarettes. The sudden blaze of yellow illuminated his face, but his eyes were closed against the glare, revealing nothing. The darkness swallowed them again.

'It means that we should get married. I love you. I respect you and therefore this is wrong. We should not even be touching unless we're married.' His words fell heavily, his voice sounding flat and dogmatic. She shivered, panic clutching at her heart. This was not the Chaim she had known.

'But I'm not ready to get married. I'm eighteen years old, for crying out loud, Chaim! And you're only twenty-three.'

'I know. But I'm ready. I know I am. I spoke to the rabbi about us and he said that if we love each other, we should get married and be done with it. There's a place for sex in Judaism and that's within a loving, close marriage. Not like this, Becca. This just cheapens everything. Listen, the rabbi told me that when two people get married, it's like bringing together two halves of the same soul that was once split and placed into two unborn children. Then they grow up and go their separate ways, living separate lives, unaware of each other's existence, until they meet and marry if they're lucky enough to find each other again. Like I found you.'

146

Rebecca exhaled slowly. She could not believe what she was hearing. She felt completely unprepared to deal with his sudden desire for celibacy. He was hurtling away from her. She could not keep up.

'Why do you suddenly feel this way now? It never bothered you before, our unmarried state.' She hated the note of sarcasm creeping into her voice. She sounded petulant, childish. Chaim appeared so definite, so adult in his convictions. Perhaps she was not the right one for him. She pictured him standing next to a small docile woman, her hair wrapped in a head-scarf, the material pulled low on her brow, her features meek and mild. Bland. That woman was not her.

Chaim was staring at her. The darkness had thinned and glowed petrol blue against the denser pools of shadow. He was thinking of a response, choosing his words carefully. Silently she urged him to hurry up, her heart pounding.

'I don't know. The more I study, the more I feel I'm reaching some sort of truth about how we're meant to live. I want to be the best person I can possibly be. And that means doing the right thing by you. I want us to start again.'

He was beginning to sound like Shifra. Her Chaim, the old Chaim – always so cynical, self-deprecating and humourous – was disappearing.

'You're changing. I don't like it. It's all happening too fast. I can't keep up. I've done enough, Chaim. I've gone as far as I can down the path you're on but I'm not sure I can follow you any further. I've ditched the trousers, given up the traif, started keeping Shabbes for you . . .'

'For me? What about for you? Doesn't any of this mean anything to you, Becca? I thought it did. I thought it made you feel good. Better.' He was beseeching her now. Hurt filled his eyes. She wished she had been less blunt. But that was it: she had done it for him.

'It does. But I wouldn't have done any of it if you hadn't started to turn frum on me.'

A flash of teeth in the darkness. He was grinning now at the strangeness of the term.

'I'll never be like one of those penguins. Come on Becca, you know me, I'm not like them.'

'Chaim, I know what you're like and it doesn't matter what your personal style of being frum is – you're there and I'm not. So maybe we should call it a day.'

He grew very still. She could not tell whether he was angry or just hurt. She had wanted to jolt him out of his reverie, to make him see that he had gone too far. Now she was beginning to feel like the boy who cried wolf. She waited.

'I don't believe you. I don't believe you want us to end. If you need more time, Becca, I'll wait. There's no rush.' His voice was a croak, as if she had winded him. She could still reach him, but the effort made her feel cheap and spiteful. She was testing him, knowing deep down she did not want to let him go.

148

'You can believe what you like. I think you need a different sort of girl to be your wife. The proper frum sort, someone who has been frum from birth, who can help you and guide you . . .'

His hand shot out and grasped her forearm. He was gripping so hard it hurt. She pulled away.

'Becca, stop it! I'm sorry – did I hurt you?'

She shook her head, rubbing her arm to release the tingle.

'I want you. I love you. I don't want some silly, boring girl like Shifra – no offence to Shifra. I want us to go on this journey together. I don't want to be with anyone else.' A pilot light of relief flickered once more. He had not abandoned her. Still it was not enough. She could not let it rest.

'But you won't sleep with me any more? How can you give that up?'

He sighed. 'Because I know we can be even better if we follow the right path.'

Rebecca sagged. She felt hollow with exhaustion. 'Ok, Chaim – I need to think this over. I need to take it all in.'

'I'll give you all the time you need.' He moved to embrace her but she evaded him. 'What is it?'

'You don't want us to sleep together. You want to be shomer nageah.'

He looked bewildered, caught out like a child that had promised to behave. 'We can still touch – just not . . .'

'Fuck?'

He laughed uneasily. She had never used that

word before to describe what passed between them in the heat of the night. Now it seemed a sullied thing.

'Don't cheapen it, Becca.'

'I'm not. You're the one telling me it's wrong, it's dirty, dishonest.' She felt the anger rising like sap. He had better be sure what he was asking for.

'You know I don't mean it like that. Becca, please.' He reached out for her hand and this time she let him.

'Ok, so what do we do?'

'We carry on.'

'Just like before but without the sex?'

'No. We can't even sleep together any more, Becca. I want to – it's going to be really hard resisting you – but I have to do this. I've made a choice.'

'You can always change your mind.' She moved into his arms.

'I'm going to try not to. And you need to help me.'

'How?' She knew how but she needed to hear it from him.

'By not provoking me. By not seducing me.'

'Ha! Now I sound like Lilith!' She squirmed against him, enjoying her power.

'I mean it, Becca.' He shook her lightly then he kissed her hair, burying his face in it, breathing in the smell of her scalp, the grease of her roots.

Then he sat up, softly letting her go. He reached for his jeans and began to pull them on. She watched in silence.

'Where are you going?'

'Back to my room. It's easier that way.'

'You can sleep here. In my bed. I'll sleep in Kate's.'

'No, Becca. You know that won't work. We'll miss each other too much. Get tempted.'

'We'll miss each other more in separate rooms.'

'Well, maybe that's a good thing. We can learn to savour things in the long run. It will be even more special if we hold back until then.'

He really was serious. Now he was pulling on his old hooded sweatshirt, kneeling to retrieve his trainers from under the bed, searching for his right sock.

'Like I said, I need to think about it.' She said it to regain some sense of herself. But she had already decided.

'Ok, you do that. I'm not going anywhere.' He shuffled over on the bed and hugged her tight, burying his face in her neck. 'I'm going to miss you so much,' he mumbled, his stubble scratching her skin. For once she did not pull away.

Her heart felt as if it was about to burst. She let him hug her and then he pulled away to unlock the door.

Chaim stood framed in the yellow light of the corridor. She remained a huddle in the bed, knees, ankles and feet long dead from lack of movement. She could not believe he was really going.

'I'll see you tomorrow. Meet me for coffee in

the Humanities Cafe at second break. I have a lecture at three.'

'Ok.'

'See you. Sleep well.'

'You too. Laila tov.'

'Laila tov.'

He closed the door behind him leaving her sitting in the dark.

CHAPTER 10

BARUCH. AVROMI

May 2008 – London

Baruch glanced at his watch. He had crept through the women's section, keeping as close to the wall as possible. His legs seemed to move in huge, jerky steps of their own accord. His size 14 feet resembled flippers in his brogues. He concentrated on planting them carefully. Closer and closer he sidled towards the mechitzah. On the other side of the screen lay refuge: the men's section.

The women ignored him, but Baruch knew better. He was being watched and assessed. Their eyes monitored his progress through their territory, storing information like security cameras. Their soft perfumed shapes were only a disguise. All female creatures were actually secret agents on a mission to marry or marry off. This knowledge unsteadied him and he wobbled mid-step, one foot in the air. He glanced about him to check no one had noticed. And that's when he saw her.

She had been standing next to the ice sculpture, on the edge of a gaggle of girls.

Chani had been engrossed by the prospect of bitter chocolate ganache topped with maraschino cherries. The cherries nestled in the dip of the swan's clear frozen back. She had already had two helpings but was bored and needed something to do before the dancing started. She gripped the silver ladle in her hand and dipped it into the steaming vat. The ladle was pleasingly smooth and heavy in her palm, and caused thick, shiny undulations as she stirred.

The chatter ebbed and flowed around her. It was the usual idle nonsense picked over by young single women, waiting their turn.

Usually it started like this: 'How are you?'

'I'm fine Baruch HaShem.'

'No – how *are* you?'

'I'm FINE, Baruch HaShem. And you?'

'Baruch HaShem, fine.'

Then they got down to business: –

'. . . and he's going to Or Yeshiva in Yerushaliyim – they're renting a flat in Mea She'arim –'

'When's the wedding?'

'Next Tuesday at the Watford Hilton.'

'Well, I heard his younger brother's looking, he's so cute –'

'Dovid? I've known his family for years, they'd only accept a Bobover –'

'Guess that rules me out then. Plenty of Bobover

girls in New York – where does Benji's Kallah come from?'

'Brooklyn.'

'Typical. Those American girls get all the luck.'

'Well, I've heard her parents had hoped for a shidduch with a son of an old family friend but it fell through. They were engaged and he broke it off.'

'Why? Wasn't she good enough for him?'

'Sounds like she wasn't. And then Benji rescued her.'

'Nebbuch!'

Although the act of spreading gossip was considered a serious transgression, here it provided urgent relief. It was therapy for the girls who were still waiting. To each, the unbearable reality of the shelf seemed to draw nearer every day. They gleaned some comfort from not being alone in their unmarried state. It was always the same. The same talk, the same food eaten by the same girls. One by one they would disappear, joining the ranks of the newly anointed, the young married women. They stood patiently shifting their weight from hip to hip, their feet aching in elegant shoes that were neither too high nor too low. Their eyes rested on each other but their minds fluttered uneasily. They wore clothes that made them appear older, sensible, almost matronly. Stiff skirts hid their knees in velvet or wool but the stockings they wore were of the thinnest denier, enough to conceal their flesh but give the impression it was bare. Jackets were tightly buttoned although the room was tropical.

Some of the girls were barrel-like already; sugar dulled each disappointment. There was always a ready supply, the dessert table groaning with sticky pastries and crystallised fruit. Their hands reached blindly for their next fix. It did not matter what went in, as long as their jaws continued to grind. Others remained whippet thin; they ate with their eyes, gazing wistfully at the bride in her finery.

Every wedding they attended rubbed salt into the wound and every bride with whom they danced saw the yearning in their eyes and breathed a sigh of relief that her turn had come. Spinsterhood was a living hell and was to be avoided at all cost.

He saw her thin shoulder blades, shifting and flexing beneath her black cashmere sweater, its elbows a little worn and faded. Had he been close enough Baruch would have noticed that the sweater had become slightly bobbled. But it was what the sweater concealed that interested Baruch – her slender back, the outline of her spine visible under the wool, melting into the narrow waist that twisted as she lent forward to grapple with the cherries. Her hair was a smooth, black coil. A restless energy in her slight frame made her movements quick and neat.

He wanted to see her face. Turn, turn. He couldn't wait. He was trespassing.

Her friend had noticed him staring. She spun round and gave Chani a nudge. The cherries tumbled off the spoon, staining the white cloth.

'Shulamis! Look what you've made me do, you idiot!' yelped Chani, giggling. Her white shirt cuff had been splashed with juice.

'Someone's watching you!' hissed Shulamis.

'Who? I'm not turning round, so you have to look – but don't make it obvious – try and be a bit subtle.'

'Ok, ok – keep your hair on – you never know, he might be looking at me for once –'

'He might be but it's unlikely.' Chani rammed her elbow into Shulamis' well-insulated rib. Shulamis' face fell causing Chani to regret her jibe. She put an affectionate arm around her friend. Beneath the boisterous exterior, Chani knew that Shulamis lacked confidence and was sensitive about her weight. She had not had as many shidduchim as Chani and was becoming increasingly anxious about her single status. She loved Shulamis and hated to see her hurt. She was a dear, loyal friend. They were partners-in-crime: equally playful, slight misfits, lacking the poise and quiet dignity of their peers. They found the sober maturity of their friends stultifying. Yet at times it was necessary to assume the cloak of adulthood if they didn't want to be left behind.

'I'm sorry. You're right, he could be staring at either of us.'

Shulamis shrugged. 'You're forgiven! Actually, I don't care – let him stare.'

Curiosity gripped Chani even though experience had taught her that a young man's attention was a fickle thing. She had been stared at before. Enquiries had been made, the phone lines had buzzed and then nothing had happened. The young man heard she was a little too lively and moved on. It would probably be the same this time, but a flicker of hope refused to be doused. Chani composed herself, straightened her back, lifted her head, and shifted away from Shulamis. A veneer of modesty was called for.

Baruch knew the girls had been whispering about him. This was what girls did. He had two sisters and they spent most of their time in a huddle in the kitchen. Nothing went unnoticed in their world, the glance that lingered a little too long or the blush that flared at an importune moment. He was young, he was single and therefore an object of subtle female inspection wherever he went. He hated it: the constant evaluation of his eligibility, his family and his prospects. But this was the ghetto he lived in and there was no escape. The only exit was through marriage. It was time.

He was no Adonis and knew it. His face was long and thin but his shy smile was warm and wide. His hair was soft and thick but his head was cone-shaped, as if the forceps had squeezed too

158

hard at birth. His glasses gave him an owlish air through which he peered myopically at the world. Chani was probably not as attractive as he perceived her to be. He needed a second opinion. He would ask Avromi.

The mechitzah was taller than him. The screen was covered in rampant ivy. A rose nestled here and there amongst the shiny, dark leaves. There was something primeval about such lush growth. Baruch pushed against the end screen and slipped through. The leaves felt scratchy – they weren't real. Nor did they provide full coverage. Gaps appeared framing flashes of black and white as the men shuffled to and fro on the other side.

He was through. The colours disappeared and the jostling began. The sour smell returned. The men steamed in their wool suits and furry black hats. A stink of fish balls filled the air. Avromi was listening intently to Rabbi Weisenhoff. Baruch's heart sank.

Rabbi Weisenhoff spoke in a hoarse whisper but when imparting spiritual wisdom his voice became barely audible. His forefinger would stab the air, its nail yellow and thickly ridged. His eyes widened with the intensity of his words, stretching the pouches beneath and making his eyebrows rise like wisps of cloud. The Rabbi was old and alone. His wife had died many years ago. He had lived long, too long and now only his love of learning sustained him. His emaciated body required little nourishment; food irritated his gullet making him cough and splutter so he refrained from eating in public. He preferred to talk.

On any other day, Baruch would have greeted the rabbi and joined the discussion. He was very fond of the kind, gentle man. Rabbi Weisenhoff was a great teacher, passionate but patient and Baruch loved listening to him. But time was of the essence. The girl might move away and he may never know who she was or whether she was as pretty as he had thought. He moved a few paces behind the rabbi and tried to catch Avromi's eye. It was no good. Avromi was having his face tickled by Rabbi Weisenhoff's beard. He was staring at the ground, nodding along to the rabbi's mono-logue. The rabbi was leaning on Avromi for support.

Baruch slipped away to a quieter spot by the wall. The air hummed with male voices, the words inarticulate but the noise swelling around him. They seemed to be saying 'zuh-zuh-zeh, zuh-zuh-zeh' or 'wus-wus, wus-wus'; the mingling of Yiddish and English creating a hybrid tongue: Yidlish.

Avromi's mobile bleated in his top pocket. He ignored it, not wishing to insult the rabbi by answering. The Rabbi stopped.

'Somebody is calling you, Avromileh, you should answer.'

'Thank you, rabbi – I'm sorry, please excuse me.'

'Please.' The Rabbi proffered, his palm open.

Avromi acquiesced although he didn't like leaving the old man on his own. He led the rabbi to a chair and settled him in it, ignoring his faint protests when the ringing stopped. Moving away, he flipped open his phone and redialled.

'Bruch?'

'Quick, come over to the wall, next to the bread rolls – I need to show you something.'

'Okey dokey. Coming over.'

Baruch waited for his friend to push through the army of dark shoulders and suited backs. Avromi was handsome and Baruch felt a momentary stab of envy. Suddenly he was relieved that the mechitzah existed; he felt sure the girl would prefer Avromi. Baruch was ashamed for having these thoughts. Avromi was his closest friend, his brother in all but a shared name and he should not resent his looks. Avromi was tall and broad-shouldered, with clear olive skin and dark and lustrous eyes.

As usual, Baruch felt deeply inadequate. He hated being ugly; or so he considered himself. When he walked down the street with Avromi, he was well aware of how girls stole glances at his friend but ignored him. Avromi never seemed to notice the discrepancy in their appearances or the girls' interest. Or if he did, he never alluded to it. He usually liked to talk about girls with Baruch. Avromi had confidence and more importantly, a dusting of worldliness. He was a university student and met girls regularly in his tutorials, albeit goyishe ones. Of late, however, he had seemed distracted and at times, a little distant. Baruch assumed that the heavy university workload was taking its toll.

'Bruch!' Avromi grabbed Baruch in a bear hug. 'What's up? Where's the fire?'

'It's this girl,' gasped Baruch.

'A girl, eh? Who's this marvellous creature then? Do I know her? Have you two been on a shidduch then? You didn't tell me, you crafty bugger –'

'I don't know her. I don't even know her name. Maybe you know who she is since you know nearly everyone. She's over there.' Baruch pointed to the mechitzah.

'Oh. I see. So what do we do? Pole vault over?'

Baruch grinned uneasily. 'No-no – I was hoping that we could find a hole and take a peek when no-one's looking – she was just over there, at that point.' He pointed to the spot at the mechitzah where he imagined Chani to be standing.

'Baruch, this place is booby-trapped with rabbis – how on earth do you expect us to look? If we get caught, my dad will roast us alive!'

Baruch's face fell. He gazed down at his enormous feet.

'All right – stop with the broken-heart act – show me this girl, let's just be quick about it! Now's our chance, they're all toasting the groom!'

The men had turned. Somebody was rambling

into a microphone. Baruch and Avromi scuttled towards the mechitzah.

'She's probably moved away – she was standing just there with her friend, talking. They saw me staring –'

'What's her friend like? Would I like her?'

'Um, fat.' Baruch felt awful for saying it; who was he to talk?

'Great. Couldn't you have picked a girl with a lovely friend for me? You only think about yourself, don't you?' teased Avromi.

'Well, maybe she's got a great personality.'

'Stop with the sales pitch and show me your princess. Hurry up already.'

They were speaking in whispers. Behind them the men broke into a loud chorus of 'L'chaim! L'chaim!'

Baruch grabbed his chance and peeped through a hole. They were still there. Baruch HaShem. She looked even better framed by a ring of plastic leaves. She was facing his way and he liked what he saw, her small sharp face, the soft, pink mouth and the straight fringe that accentuated her eyes.

Avromi gave him a poke. 'Budge over and let me look – which one is she?'

'The girl in the black V-neck jumper – she's facing this way, she's got dark hair, tied back – she's small and thin –'

'Oh yes, yes – think I've got her. Very nice, Baruch. She's pretty.'

'Really? Do you think so? Be honest, Vrom – I need to know – can't always trust these stupid specs, y'know. Tell me what you really see and think. You know girls better than me.'

'I don't but in my humble opinion, I would say she's a very nice looking young lady. Nice hair, too. Not frizzy like all the other girls. Lovely smile too . . . nice legs. Shame about her friend, definitely likes her lokshen pudding.'

'Right, thank you – very much. That's enough – let me look – quick, they'll finish soon.'

'My pleasure, Bruch. Go ahead – I'll keep a look-out.'

Avromi vacated the viewing spot. Baruch took another look. She did have nice legs. She had nice everything. Satisfied, he turned to Avromi.

'But who is she?'

'Haven't got the foggiest. She looks like a Kaufman, judging by her colouring – they all have that black, straight hair and pale skin. But there are loads of 'em – I think there are eight daughters in that family. So we have to find out which one she is . . .'

'*Eight* daughters?'

'Shhh!'

Eight daughters. Baruch knew that if they identified the wrong daughter, all would be lost. He had to find out her name and be certain about it.

Avromi scanned the room.

'I've got it! We'll ask Shmuel. His older brother Eli married one of the older Kaufman sisters – don't ask me which one –'

And before he could stop him, Avromi had melted into the crowd. He returned with another young man in tow. Avromi was tugging the young man's sleeve and the young man was grinning sheepishly.

'Hello, I'm Shmuel,' said the young man.

'Hello, nice to meet you,' said Baruch.

'Avromi says you've seen one of the Kaufman girls – or at least you think she's a Kaufman.'

Baruch gestured to the gap behind him. Shmuel checked the room and assumed the position. Baruch and Avromi shielded him.

'Ok, she's the one in the black V-neck.'

'Got her. Yup – she's a Kaufman . . . I know there are still four living at home and she must be the oldest. There's a Rochel, and then I think a Sophie . . .' Shmuel was counting on his fingers.

'She must be Chani. Devorah, my sister-in-law, has mentioned her to me before actually. I think, she wanted to suggest – a – a –' Baruch was staring at him. Sensing the delicacy of the situation, Shmuel moved on. 'Yes well, erm, that's Chani Kaufman.'

'Chani. You sure?'

'Pretty much so.'

'Chani Kaufman.' He tasted her name.

'Anything else I can do for you two gentlemen?' said Shmuel.

Baruch surfaced. 'No – that's great. Thank you so much, Shmuel. You've been a real help – if you ever need the same favour, I'll do my best although I don't know any girls . . . or their names.'

Shmuel grinned. 'Any time. Good luck with Chani anyway.'

'Thanks. I'll need it.' Baruch looked grim. Mentally he had leapt ahead, anticipating all the obstacles that lay strewn like boulders across his path. Avromi punched him playfully on the shoulder.

'Getoveryourself, Bruch! Cheer up, it may never happen. May you both live to one hundred and twenty and have hundreds of grandchildren.'

Baruch wasn't sure about the hundreds of grand-children. At least he knew her name. So now he could begin.

Avromi's mobile trilled in his jacket pocket. He glanced quickly at the screen.

''Scuse me, guys, I have to take this,' he said, carving a furrow through the black suits as he slipped out through the service doors, leaving Shmuel and Baruch staring curiously after him.

He entered the hell of the kitchens and caught the eye of the young Hasid who was peering into a steaming cauldron in the name of super-vising kashrut. The Hasid – dressed all in black – looked out of place amongst the spotless white aprons and gleaming chrome, but he continued to poke his nose into fridges and pots and did not watch Avromi as he made for the fire escape stairs.

Outside on the metal platform, two waiters were

smoking, slouched against the brick wall. They eyed Avromi who gave them a friendly nod as he clattered down to the first level.

'Hi, you still there?'

'Yup, still here, still waiting . . . where are you?' Her voice was a little waspish. He said he would call her at four but had been sidetracked by Baruch's girl-spotting adventure.

'I'm at a wedding – you know you can't call me here.'

'Well, I thought you said you'd call at four. It's now five.' He could not ignore the hurt in her tone. It was his fault.

'I know, I know, I'm sorry, I got held up. Anyway, how are you? What are you up to?'

'I'm good, thanks. Watching telly, tidying my room, in the hope my sweet prince will visit.'

Avromi let out a low laugh. 'I'll come over tonight but it will be late. I'll slip out during the dancing and catch the train into Euston. But I doubt I'll be there before ten. The dancing will go on til the early hours so my parents won't suspect a thing. Is that ok?'

She sighed. 'I suppose so. I'll just languish on my silk sheets and eat figs in my underwear.'

Avromi blushed and chuckled again, enjoying her flirtatiousness. He was still uncertain how to handle it. All his usual confidence seemed to dissipate whenever Shola was in the vicinity. She made him feel shy and self-conscious and excited all at once. No other girl had had that effect on him.

He barely noticed the young frum maidens from his own community. His eyes passed over them, their dowdy modesty and quiet manners rendering them invisible. Chani had seemed an insipid imitation of womanhood in comparison.

'Well, I am looking forward to seeing your underwear – I mean with you in it – and feeding you figs.'

Shola giggled. 'Ok then, my prince, see you later.'

'Bye.'

He was never sure how to end the conversation. He wanted to use a term of endearment but sweetheart or darling just sounded forced. They were not sweethearts in the purest sense of the word. Avromi sighed, tucked his phone away and trudged back upstairs.

Now was not the time to think about it. He tried to block out the memory of her voice as he pushed back through the kitchen doors. The roar of machinery and the barked orders of the head chef did little to dispel his thoughts of Shola. Through the glass porthole, he glimpsed a heaving sea of black wool. He thought of her silky skin, her laughing eyes and brilliant, pussycat smile. What would she make of this wedding? Of all the men dressed alike? Of the beards? And rabbis attached to them? The separation of the sexes? He dreaded to think.

It did not matter. She would never witness one like it for herself. She was part of his other life, his university self – a delicious, forbidden secret that filled him with delight and horror in equal measures, but one he could not give up. Not now, not yet.

He plunged into the crowd, his heart thudding with the daring thrill of it all, when he spotted Rabbi Weisenhoff sitting alone where he had left him, looking old and forlorn. Guilt crashed over him, causing his ears to burn and his palms to sweat. How could he carry on like this? He felt the habitual disgust creep over him. He felt cheap. Sullied. How could he continue to converse with a rabbi as wonderful and wise as Rabbi Weisenhoff when he had trespassed so sinfully? He did not deserve to shake the rabbi's hand. And he had willfully lied to Baruch, pleading a lack of know-ledge when it came to girls. A shudder of shame rippled through him and he shook himself to be rid of it.

Then there was Shola herself. Had he been a true mensch, he would never have got involved, he would not have succumbed. He could not blame her; she was free to do what she liked.

Avromi forced all thoughts of Shola out of his mind and made his way over to the hunched, tired rabbi. He bent over him and spoke loudly into his hairy, waxy ear and helped the rabbi to his feet, steadying him as the old man threatened to stumble. Together they wound their way towards the side exit, leading to the lifts. He would hail a cab for the rabbi and once he had seen him safely inside, he would turn back to his friends and act as if nothing had happened.

He also knew that the guilt would evaporate the minute he stepped out at Euston, only to resurface at gale force when he was alone, making his way home, slipping in to his parents' house like a ganif in the middle of the night.

CHAPTER 11

BARUCH

May 2008 – London

If he wanted to meet the girl he had glimpsed at the wedding, Baruch knew that he would have to talk to his mother, a thing he dreaded. His mother had her own ideas about whom he should meet and marry and her ideas did not correlate with his. He had baulked on previous occasions when she mentioned meeting the shadchan, the local matchmaker, Mrs Gelbmann. His older brothers had been introduced to their wives through her. He knew what horrors awaited him in the woman's stuffy front parlour, behind the swathes of tightly drawn net curtain. He would be interrogated, weighed up, his details logged and filed away in an ancient giant ring binder, his very being reduced to a couple of pages.

There was no other way. Even when he had seen a girl he liked, he would have to go through the shadchan to meet her. Mrs Gelbmann knew everyone and only she could ring the girl and suggest the match. If he was serious about meeting Chani Kaufman then he would have to pursue his interest in the way convention demanded. He was engulfed by a vision of a gloating Mrs Gelbmann clutching her ring binder, her harpy's leer stretching her cracked lips as she crooked a chapped finger at him.

But first he would have to convince his mother that Chani Kaufman was worth meeting. She was not on his mother's list of suitable candidates, carefully selected from the upper echelons of the wealthy and prominent in the community. Doubtless she had never even heard of the Kaufmans.

His mother was on the phone in the lounge. She was lying on the sofa, her feet crossed at the ankles, a cushion supporting her neck. Her heels lay on the floor, their cruel spikes abandoned. The phone rested on her abdomen, rising and falling with her breathing. She twisted its cord between her manicured fingers, her long nails a coral pink.

His mother smiled wearily at him but continued her conversation.

'I know, Shoshi, there's nothing we can do, we have to sit and wait.'

His mother fell silent. He could hear the urgent click and ripple of words coming faintly from the receiver. Baruch took a seat next to his mother's feet. She waggled them at him and raised her eyebrows. He waited, watching her face.

'It will all be ok. Listen, it's normal for the first baby to be late. Do you remember my niece Sora-Malka? She was two weeks late and suddenly her contractions started over dinner, and her husband delivered the baby in ten minutes flat on the kitchen floor before the ambulance could even get to them! Baruch HaShem, everything was fine. The paramedics only had to deal with the afterbirth.'

'Mum . . . Mum . . .' he whispered, pulling gently at her forearm.

'Shoshi-leh, I have to go now. Baruch's here. He needs to talk to me . . . Yes, I will . . . im yirtzeh HaShem all will be well. Bye, Shoshi, bye, bye . . . yes, I will . . . ok . . . bye.'

His mother grunted as she sat up, replaced the receiver and let out a long sigh. Automatically her hands rose to tidy and check her wig. His mother wore a coppery concoction that fell in loose waves to her shoulders. The hair was thick and shiny and looked effortlessly natural. It suited his mother and he knew that it had cost his father dear.

'That woman never stops talking! Such a yenta! She sends you her regards by the way. Nu, Baruch? So what can I do for you? How was yeshiva today? Did you daven for Mrs Goldmeyer? She's critically ill now. I heard from her neighbour that they doubt she'll pull through this time. Poor woman.'

It was now or never. 'Mum, I need to talk to you about a girl.'

His mother's fingers froze. Her eyes widened, sooty fronds of mascara catching. 'A girl? I thought you weren't ready yet for girls. *Now* my day's getting interesting . . . what girl? Is she one of us?

173

Someone I know? She better be. Do I know the family? Nu? Tell me!' His mother prodded him playfully.

Baruch began hesitantly. 'Er, you probably won't have her heard of her, I mean, I don't know the family . . .'

'Spit it out, Baruch! What's her name?'

'Chani Kaufman.' There. He had said it.

'Kaufman . . . Kaufman . . . hmmm . . . I know a Mrs Haufman . . . nope, can't say I've heard of that name . . . are they a Golders family?'

'Mum, I don't know. I just know her name. I saw her at the Vishnefski wedding –'

'You saw her? I thought a good Yiddisher boy like my son didn't look at girls . . .' teased Mrs Levy.

'Well, I was late and I had to sneak through the women's section to get to the mechitzah. It was kind of mortifying – all these women pretending not to see me but they were watching me all the while . . .'

His mother snorted with laughter. 'They couldn't exactly miss you, could they? So you were creeping through the women's bit like a ganif and then what? Keep going!'

'I'm trying Mum, but you keep interrupting me.'

'Ok, ok I'll be quiet already.' His mum made a zipping motion and clamped her mouth shut. Her eyes bulged with expectation.

'Well, I was trying not to look, honest, Mum, I really was but I couldn't help it because there she was. Just standing with her back to me with her friend –'

'You saw only the back of her?'

'*Mum*! Let me finish. I saw only the back of her and well, she looked really nice –'

'I bet her toches did!'

'*Mum*!' Baruch shot her an exasperated look.

'Ok, ok – I'm sorry. Forgive me.' His mother gazed down meekly in mock repentance.

'So, I noticed her. There was something about her – her hair – I don't know –'

'What's her hair like?'

'Shiny and black . . . long, I think. She had it up as far as I remember in one of those, one of those . . . you know how Malka likes to wear her hair?'

'In a pony tail?'

'Yes – anyway,' Baruch hurried on fearful of more interference, 'I just liked how she looked, how she stood. She was slim and sort of delicate. I didn't have time to hang around and wait for her to turn round so when I got to the other side, I found Avromi and another guy called Shmuel and we found a hole in the mechitzah and when all the other men weren't looking we took a peek –'

'My son was peeking through the mechitzah! Baruch! Well, at least she's skinny and not a shloomp.' Mock angry, his mother was finding it hard to hide her amusement.

'Mum! Come on, there was no other way, I had to find out who she was and see her face –'

'Of course. And what was it like, her face? And by the way, was this girl aware that boys were watching her?'

'Uh, well, her friend caught me staring as I was passing through and I think she told her –'

'And she continued to stand there and let you look? Very nice, Baruch . . .'

'It wasn't like that, Mum. It happened really quickly. Anyway, I was where I shouldn't have been. It wasn't her fault.'

'Her face?' insisted his mother.

'She's very pretty as far as I could tell. Avromi thought so too, and the other guy –'

'Nu? Details? Details, Baruch. What colour were her eyes? Nose – how big?'

'Mum, you're impossible . . . I think she has dark eyes, probably brown. She's pale and well really pretty . . . small-looking. I *don't know*. I just really liked her. And Shmuel knew who she was because his brother married one of her older sisters.'

'Pale, you say? Sounds like she's Ashkenazi. Baruch HaShem – I don't want a Sefardi daughter-in-law – they're trouble. Who's this Shmuel?'

'Some guy who was there. He was really nice. A mensch. But I don't know him personally – Avromi knows him.'

He watched his mother as she ruminated over the scanty facts, waiting for her verdict. He sensed it would not be favourable.

'Baruch, I don't know the family and you know

how I feel about families . . . they have to be the right sort. I'm not happy about the fact I've never heard of this girl.'

'I knew it! The first girl I show any real interest in and there's a problem.'

'Baruch, you know the rules. Your father and I have to approve of the match. What about the Rosen girl we wanted you to meet? Or Libby Zuckerman? Both of them lovely, haimisher girls – intelligent, pretty, frum, skinny like pickles the pair of them. What more could you want?'

'I want to choose my own girl. I don't like the Rosens, they're arrogant and as for Libby, I'm not her type – I know I'm not.'

'Not her type? Look at you, tall, good-looking, a yeshiva bocher, a mensch. You're my son, what's not to like? You've practically grown up with Libby – we've known that family for years. Mrs Zuckerman said she'd be thrilled if you two made a match.'

Disappointed, Baruch stared down at the table. He had known his mother wouldn't approve.

'Give Chani a chance, Mum – that's unfair. I like her and I want to meet her. Please help me out here,' he muttered.

Mrs Levy relented. 'Ok, Baruch. I want you to be happy. It's my duty to help you find a wife you like. First I'll tell your father and get his ok on it. Then I'll go to Mrs Gelbmann and ask her if she knows Chani Kaufman. She may be on her list.'

'Thanks Mum. I really mean it,' Baruch reached across the table and squeezed his mother's hand.

Mrs Levy smiled ruefully. 'On one condition.'

'Yes? What?'

'That if she's not the right sort from an acceptable family, you'll move on and agree to meet a more suitable girl?'

'Ok. But please give this one a chance.' Baruch coaxed.

'One chance. Once your Dad agrees, I'll call Mrs Gelbmann and arrange to see her as soon as possible.' His mother stood up and moved towards the phone.

'Thanks, Mum.' He hugged his mother and kissed her cheek.

He was filled with trepidation and in his heart, he sensed trouble lay ahead.

CHAPTER 12

AVROMI

September 2007 – London

They had met in Avromi's law tutorial group on the first day of university. She had sat next to him, closer than he would have liked but there was little space around the table. Avromi had purposely chosen to sit next to another male student, but the spaces around the table had begun to fill up and to his dismay, half the tutorial group consisted of young women. He had not expected there to be so many female law students. In fact, he had not expected there to be so many girls at university altogether.

There were girls simply everywhere – of every shape, size and colour. He was assailed by the plethora of female flesh on display and at times he found the abundance of legs, arms, thighs and breasts that seemed to taunt him with their insouciant presence, more than he could bear. He would look away in an attempt to mind his own business but there, dancing down the corridor ahead of him, was a neat, round toches wrapped in tight denim.

Avromi now understood why his father had been so reluctant to allow him to attend. Had his mother not insisted that her son took a degree and experienced university after he had excelled at his A-levels, he would not be here. She had wanted him to have something to fall back on should a rabbi's salary not prove adequate. His father had grudgingly agreed on the grounds that Avromi would proceed to yeshiva immediately after he had finished his law degree. It was strange to think that his parents had once been students themselves. They had even met at university.

When she bent forward to write, he noticed the softness of her skin just under the jawbone, and could see a pulse throbbing lightly beneath the translucent honeyed surface. Her dark hair was cut into a chic bob, the shiny curls falling around her sharp cheekbones, softening her features. She was of mixed race, slender, yet something undeniably tough lurked beneath her femininity. The girl wore a battered leather biker jacket and beneath the table he glimpsed a short, tight skirt, revealing long legs encased in black tights. He averted his gaze and focused on heading up his file-paper.

Every time she moved in her seat, she gave off a sharp, fruity tang. Avromi pulled his chair away an inch in order to lessen her proximity. The girl looked sideways at him, flashing him a warm, open smile.

'Sorry, am I squashing you?' she whispered.

'No, not at all, it's just a bit of a squeeze in here.'

'Isn't it? Hi, my name is Shola, by the way.'

'Mine's Avromi.'

'Avromi? That's a bit unusual, where's that from?'

'Oh, it's Yiddish, it's just a shortened version of Abraham. Where does Shola come from?'

'Shola is Nigerian, my dad's Nigerian and my mum is English.'

'Right. Nice name.'

'Yiddish, you said? Does that mean you're . . .'

'Jewish?'

'Yes. There are some Orthodox Jews around where I live in Stoke Newington and they speak Yiddish. So that explains the suit and little black cap you wear.'

'Yes, I'm one of them – well, not *exactly* like them, they're ultra-frum, I mean ultra-religious. I live in Golders Green and we're a bit different. Different communities, same religion, sort of thing.' He felt he was rambling but Shola was staring at him, her mouth slightly open.

'Wow – I've never actually spoken to one of your people before. You seem very, well, secluded.'

'Yes. Sadly that is the case. But come to think of it, I have never properly met, one of your type before either.'

Her eyes creased in amusement and she let out a snort.

'My type? And what exactly is that?' she teased,

head cocked to one side. She chewed her pen as she waited.

To his chagrin, he felt his face burn. Shola raised a perfect eyebrow enquiringly.

'I meant, you know, you're, you're . . .' He raised his hands in a helpless gesture.

'Black? Or female? Which is it?'

'Both actually,' he mumbled.

'Well, it's a first for both of us then. Nice to meet you, Avromi,' she said, holding out her hand.

Avromi eyed the small, brown palm extended towards him. His blush spread to his ears. He tried to smile.

'Shola, I'm really sorry, but I'd love to shake your hand, but I am forbidden to touch girls.'

Shola's mouth fell open in disbelief. She pulled her hand in like a shot.

'You mean, you can't even shake my hand, because I'm a girl?'

Avromi nodded sadly.

'Wow. That's pretty hardcore. Is that rule for the whole of your life or just for now?'

'Until I get married.'

'Blimey,' said Shola. 'That can't be easy.'

'It's not,' sighed Avromi. 'I mean, I can hug my sister and my mum . . .'

'Uh huh,' Shola chewed her pen thoughtfully, gazing at him.

At that moment, their tutor walked in and greeted the group. Avromi thanked HaShem for his appearance. He felt shaken, at odds with himself. He had never felt this way before but then he had never met an outsider who questioned him so directly. He liked her frank approach, although it was somewhat unnerving. Even more unsettling, though, was her undeniable prettiness.

CHAPTER 13

THE REBBETZIN

August 1982 – Jerusalem

'Come and see the shul. It's just a few minutes walk from here.' He pulled her hand, but she held back, resisting. She wanted to go home. The groceries from the shuk that they had just spent a long time choosing, were weighing her down. It was hot and she longed for the cool dimness of her room.

Although they no longer shared the same bed, Chaim and Rebecca continued to see each other every day. Their relationship intensified despite the lack of physical intimacy. He began to pray daily at a local synagogue. He would reappear, often hours later, an ecstatic smile across his face, eyes shining, his voice hoarse. Rebecca preferred to pray at the Wall. She had taken to visiting it without Shifra, at different times of the day, savouring the changes in light and atmosphere. At prayer times, even though she was jostled by the pious, she enjoyed the thrum of activity. At other times, the precinct was almost empty and a quiet peace descended. At midday, sunlight scoured the old stones and the only shade to be found lay between the cracks in its surface. Compared to Chaim's shul – which she had not yet had the courage to visit – the realm of worship and prayer seemed real and rooted in time and place.

'Chaim, stop nagging. I'll come and see it when I'm ready.'

'You keep saying that. Please. Just this once. We can drop in on our way to the bus stop – no need for a detour. Just for five minutes.'

'Ok, just this once,' she sighed.

He flashed a grateful grin and began leading the way through the maze of winding streets, his sandals slapping the pavement as he picked up pace. Soon they were at the edge of a busy main road full of grey, dilapidated buildings. Chaim stopped outside a padlocked metal door. It was narrow and sloped towards the pavement on one side. There were no windows. It was the entrance to a bomb shelter.

'Here?'

'Yup.' He patted the door affectionately.

'You have to be kidding me. A shul in an old bomb shelter?'

'Kind of makes sense, doesn't it? Worshipping HaShem where people run for protection from missiles – turns the negative into a positive.'

'But what if there's an attack? Where will people in this area go?'

'It will still be used as a shelter. It can pack in a lot of people, believe me. And it's deep.'

'Isn't it really claustrophobic praying down there all together?'

He smiled at her and shook his head. 'Becca, it's amazing. It just adds to the atmosphere. Please come tonight. Please.'

Suddenly she was curious. She had never been in a bomb shelter before.

They returned before sunset. A few men in knitted white kippot and loose white shirts were gathered in front of the metal door that was now open, a brick pinning it back. She caught a glimpse of a long flight of concrete stairs descending into darkness. A single, naked light bulb lit the first ten or twelve steps. There was nothing to announce this was a shul, no notice board, no sign. She could have been entering a cellar bar or a nightclub, except the clientele looked curiously benign and gentle in their baggy clothes and dangling tallis strings. They greeted Chaim with warm smiles; one even embraced him. Their voices were soft, their cadences lilting and foreign. At their feet lay various musical instruments. One wore a guitar slung across his back.

Chaim introduced her and they smiled and nodded but did not shake her hand. The one who had hugged Chaim stepped forward and introduced himself as Yossi. He was short, tow-headed and bespectacled. His eyes shone with kindness and merriment. He reminded Rebecca of a hobbit.

'My sister's coming with some of her friends and

I'll introduce you to them,' Yossi said, beaming at her. 'Don't worry, you won't feel lonely here.'

'Thank you, that's very thoughtful of you.'

'No problem. Enjoy. Sorry I have to leave you, but we need to set up. I'll catch you later, Chaim.'

He turned to go in, carrying a bongo drum under each arm. Slowly the others peeled off after him, one by one. Rebecca watched them disappear down the mouth of the shelter. Chaim was waiting quietly at her side. She turned and raised an eyebrow at him.

'Bongos?'

Chaim grinned mysteriously. 'You'll see. Let's go in. Yossi's sister will find you.'

The door to the women's section was easy enough to locate. Inside, the flight of stairs was well-lit, neon strip lighting bouncing off the thick, smooth concrete walls. She could see cracks and indentations in their surfaces. Mosquitoes and moths moved in a frenzied, whirring dance against the lights. She took the plunge, feeling her way against the narrow walls for balance. The stairs were steep and her feet made a faint crunching sound as she descended.

The room was long and low, separated by a partition of movable screens covered in white fabric, through which she could hear the rumble of male laughter. She tried in vain to single out Chaim's voice, but the voices had blended into an incoherent tide of sound.

The women's section was quieter, although it was largely empty. There was little embellishment or beauty. Décor was plain and functional reflecting the brutal interior of the concrete shell. The olive green carpet was stained and patchy. There was a whiff of mould and damp patches bulged ominously where the plastered walls met the ceiling.

White plastic seats were arranged in neat rows, stopping halfway to the front leaving a large vacant space before the ark. In keeping with the place, it was a simple alcove covered by a navy velvet curtain embroidered with golden Hebrew lettering. A few women hovered at the edges of the room, chatting and smiling. Some were young and single, bare headed like her. Others wore berets or head-scarves, their trailing ends twisted into a neat plait. Not a wig to be seen, although she was sure a few would turn up.

Gradually the room filled and the temperature rose. Women trooped down the stairs singly or in small clusters, warmly greeting one another. Children skidded and shrieked, running between the men's and women's sections. The noise level rose. Rebecca's face felt sticky and her forehead greasy. Under the weight of her hair, her nape was moist. She shifted uncomfortably in her seat; her thighs were sticking to the plastic through the thin cotton of her dress. The walls seemed to sweat, their surfaces covered in a light sheen. She wondered how much longer she could endure.

A light touch fell on her shoulder and she twisted

round to find a sturdy young woman peering at her. Her hair was pulled back but a frizz of blonde curls formed a halo, framing her features. Hazel eyes gazed out of a chubby face.

'Are you Becca?' The accent was softly American.

'Yes, you must be Yossi's sister.'

She grinned. 'I certainly am – for my sins. My name's Tovah. Come and sit with us. I hear it's your first time here, right?'

'Yes. Is it going to get much hotter in here?'

'It sure is – but by then you won't even notice the heat. It's part of the total experience here. That's what you get if you hold a crowded service in a bomb shelter. The air-con broke and we're still raising money to fix it. What's a little sweat between friends, I say.'

'True,' she replied, wistfully thinking of the cool Jerusalem evening above ground. She could have been walking through the breezy streets with Shifra by now.

Tovah led her to join three young women who were leaning against the wall nearest to the ark. This was the hottest part of the shelter, but a large fan had been left on and she edged as near to it as possible without wishing to appear rude. The girls looked her age. Two wore brightly coloured bandanas as headscarves, giving them the air of Russian peasant women at a market. Their legs were bare and brown sandaled feet peeped out from beneath their long gypsy skirts. Married already. She was surprised at how young they were.

'This is Becca. Becca this is Marty, Rahel and Suri.'

One by one the girls smiled, inclined their heads and widened their small circle to include her. Before they had time to exchange pleasantries, a burly squat man with a bird's nest beard approached a small raised platform.

The rabbi spread his hands wide and a hush fell.

'Friends, it's wonderful to see so many of you here tonight. Anyone who is new here, please make sure they are not alone; regulars, please make the newcomers feel especially welcome. It's going to be a fantastic service. I can just feel it. Those of you that have kindly brought instruments . . .' The shimmer of a tambourine interrupted the rabbi, who chuckled and held a hand up for restraint.

'It seems some of you can't even wait for me to finish. As I was saying, feel free to join in at any time. I trust you know the melodies and even if you don't, I'm sure you'll pick them up.'

The cantor's deep, mellow voice swelled across the room. Suddenly, swaying female forms obscured her view of the front of the shul. A violin played somewhere to her right. The men answered in response, following the cantor's lead. A drum began to pound, and then another drum answered it. And another. And another. The shelter shook to their beat. Soon the air grew thick with melody and an irresistible energy.

The psalm was sung in Hebrew. She had no idea

of the words or their meaning but it didn't matter. Her feet began to tap in time. To her surprise, the sound around her amplified and she realised that the women were singing softly too. Some of the women clutched their prayer books to their chests and sang with their eyes shut tight, their faces held up to the light.

Tovah nudged her and pointed to the correct page number in her prayer book. An English translation was printed on the opposite page. She began to read through it but soon lost her place as the women began to jig and sway on either side of her. She was jostled from side to side. Tovah grinned apologetically. 'Don't worry about the words, or following the siddur, you can hum if you like. It doesn't matter.' Heeding the advice, she hooked her thumb in the book and let her feet find their way through the psalm.

Then the melody changed and with a surge of excitement, she recognised it as one sung at the Wall on Friday evenings. The refrain was familiar. She sang the words shyly under her breath, not wishing to be caught out. She loved this song. It was beautiful, mystical and textured in its meaning, even sensual.

'Come my Beloved to greet the bride –
The Sabbath presence, let us welcome!'

The Sabbath was likened to a young bride, and although the identity of the mysterious 'Beloved' to whom the poet had referred was a mystery, the idea moved her, of a groom waiting under the

191

canopy as his splendidly clothed bride advanced towards him.

In the sweaty, cramped, underground shul, she felt the music lift her. Her feet pounded and stamped in time. Her clothes stuck to her back but she could not stop. She danced and swayed and sang. The songs changed and the rhythms swirled, the men grew louder and more boisterous and soon the women were singing without restraint.

Tovah grabbed her hand and dragged her to the back of the room. Giggling, Rebecca followed.

'Where are we going?' she shouted into Tovah's ear.

'To watch the men. You can stand at the back of their section and see them. Come on.'

They rounded the mechitzah to find the men dancing in a long, snaking line which proceeded to coil in on itself, looping crazily as the rabbi led them in a frenzied conga. They shook tambourines above their heads, and pounded drums hanging from their necks. Chaim danced at the far end of the room, head thrown back, eyes shut, his mouth wide as he chanted, completely absorbed in the moment. Next to him, a little girl sat on her father's shoulders as he jogged around the room. The child was laughing as she clutched his neck, her little feet bouncing in mid-air.

As the night wore on, the shelter continued to rock with spiritual energy, suffusing the congregants with joy until exhausted and dizzy with happiness, they stumbled out into the fresh night air to make their way home.

Rebecca and Chaim walked along the narrow moonlit street in companiable silence. It was past midnight.

'So what do you think?' he asked, glancing slyly at her grinning face.

'I loved it. I've had a great evening.' She stopped and turned to him, reaching out her hand. 'Thank you.'

In the shadows, she saw his teeth gleam.

'So it was worth it then?'

'Definitely. Chaim,' she said, 'I think I'm ready. Let's get married.'

They walked a few paces further in silence, allowing her admission to sink in. A feeling of joy bloomed in her heart.

Late in the afternoon, when the shadows had lengthened and faded into a promise of darkening coolness, Rivka hurried back from the mikveh. She pattered through the narrow lanes, where the heat of the day still emanated from the thick stone walls of the houses, her sandals shielding her feet from the baked pavement. Under her headscarf her damp hair dripped, the droplets trickling between her shoulder blades where they brought a welcome respite.

Beneath her thin cotton dress, her skin glowed, every pore cleansed and sanctified. She had doused herself in lotions, dabbed perfume behind each knee, each ear and in the crook of each elbow. Her legs were slippery smooth. She had scraped a razor over her armpits until they were raw but nothing mattered in her quest for perfection. They had not touched for fourteen days, her period having lasted longer than usual. She thought of lying naked, skin-to-skin with her husband again, and her stomach tightened with desire. She thought of the laughter and soft talk that always came afterwards and she sighed with impatience. They had been married for five months now but her excitement that followed each visit to the mikveh had not diminished. She loved the whole ritual; the ebb and flow of their relations marked by her courses had taken on a deeper, more natural meaning for her. No longer just a nuisance, her bleeding signalled a possibility to create new life with her husband or simply to delight in his body after a time of physical drought.

Above her, swallows wheeled effortlessly against a diminishing turquoise sky. She could hear children playing within the small, red-roofed houses – a ball thudded and a mother scolded. Perhaps HaShem would answer their prayers this time and she would finally fall pregnant. She picked up her skirt and vaulted the stairs to their apartment, two at a time.

Inside, all was cool and dim. She turned on the lights. The blinds rattled in the evening breeze and moths hurled themselves against the kitchen window. In the dusty, neglected garden below, the scarlet hibiscus closed for the night and date palms shivered and swayed. A yowling catfight had begun in the bushes.

Rivka loved these moments, as the longing for intimacy mingled with the sweetness of lingering anticipation. She still had dinner to prepare. She stirred, sliced, pounded, mixed and fried, every ingredient bringing him closer, every action filled with love. On these nights, her dishes were created with extra delicacy, the spices sharper and more poignant, the textures more satisfying in their contrasts, as if every morsel had been infused with her desire.

The table was laid, the plates blank spaces awaiting fulfillment. Rivka hummed as she polished the wine glasses and stirred the pots. Then she turned the gas down low, leaving the soup and sauces to simmer. She examined her reflection in the mirror, noting her flushed cheeks and wide, shiny eyes. Finally, she unpinned the brooch she had worn since the start of her period as a warning to Chaim, to avoid touching her. She placed it on the table, between their plates.

His key turned in the lock and she raced to open the door. He took one look at her happy face and wrapped his arms around her, squeezing so tight she could barely breathe. He walked her backwards until she bumped against the table, knocking over the wine glasses. He began to kiss her neck, his hands sliding over her buttocks. She laughed and pushed him away until he was at arm's length, so that she could look him in the eye.

'What took you so long?'

'I couldn't get away from Rabbi Yochanan, man, can he talk and talk? But hey, I'm here now.'

She buried her head against his chest, hiding her grin. Then she pulled away and shoved him gently into a chair, just in time to rescue the soup.

CHAPTER 14

BARUCH. CHANI.

May 2008 – London

Mrs Levy surveyed her reflection in the rear view mirror. She applied another coat of lipstick, tugged a mascara wand through her sticky lashes and patted her wig into place. She changed her flats for heels, grabbed her handbag and exited the car only to plunge her elegant court into an oily puddle. Yet again she had parked miles from the kerb.

'Feh!' she exclaimed in disgust. The water had seeped into her shoe and soaked through her stocking leaving a grimy tidemark below her ankle.

She was running late. There was no time to re-park so she slid across the passenger seat and stepped out onto the road. Not too bad. It was a quiet road and hopefully no one would hit her Saab.

Mrs Levy opened the small wooden gate and clicked up the front path, disliking the wet rub of her foot inside her shoe. Just as she was about to press the bell the door swung open. Mrs Gelbmann stood in the doorway smiling graciously.

The two women examined each other. Too much

lipstick as always, thought Mrs Gelbmann. Such a plain woman, thought Mrs Levy for the umpteenth time. And yet she wields so much power. Why doesn't she update her sheitel at least? Mrs Gelbmann was dressed as always in black, reminding Mrs Levy of a giant cockroach.

They did not embrace or even shake hands although they had known each other for years. Instead they exchanged courteous nods and continued smiling benignly at each other.

'Hello, Mrs Gelbmann. How are you?'

'Baruch HaShem, Mrs Levy. And you?'

'Baruch HaShem, everything's fine, Mrs Gelbmann.'

'How are Yisroel and Tali getting on? I hear she is expecting again.'

'Baruch HaShem, just fine – thank you, Mrs Gelbmann. And yes, another one's on the way.'

'That's good to hear. Wonderful news. Baruch HaShem.'

Mrs Gelbmann looked down and noticed that one of Mrs Levy's shoes was wet. Her eyes locked on the soiled nylon.

'Oh it's nothing! I'm such a klutz, stepped into a puddle on my way out of the car!' Mrs Levy gabbled.

Mrs Gelbmann continued to smile but inclined her head apologetically and holding her hand out, beckoned her bedraggled guest in. Mrs Levy touched the mezuzah, kissed her fingers and stepped over the threshold.

'Come in, it's warm inside, you'll soon dry out. Can I take your coat?'

'Yes, please.' She shrugged off her floor-length mink and clacked into the living-room.

The room had not changed since the last time she had visited. That was two years ago when she had come to find a bride for Ilan, her second eldest son. The electric coals still glowed steadily in their iron grate. Above the mantelpiece the ormolu clock continued to remind the unmarried clients that with each gentle tick, time was passing and with it, their youthful charm. On either side of the clock stood framed photographs depicting legions of Gelbmann offspring providing evidence of the fruits of successful matchmaking. Mr Gelbmann himself was frozen in black and white for eternity. A fine husband, beloved but dead.

Four small, shrivelled satsumas nestled at the bottom of a huge, maroon Venetian glass bowl. Mrs Levy eyed them warily. They too had probably been here last time.

Mrs Gelbmann gently closed the door and settled herself into the chintzy armchair opposite her visitor. She held herself ramrod straight and folded her hands in her lap. Instinctively Mrs Levy sat bolt upright, clutching at her handbag propped up on her knees.

'And what can I do for you today, Mrs Levy?'

She had thrown down the gauntlet. The tournament had begun. Refreshments would not be offered until business had been made clear. Mrs

Gelbmann did not favour time-wasters and since Mrs Levy was dying for a cup of tea, she decided to do away with subtleties.

'A small matter, Mrs Gelbmann. One in which you may be able to assist me.'

'Baruch, I presume?'

'Yee-es. This concerns Baruch.'

'I have some lovely girls in mind for him. They all come from excellent, Hasiddisher families with the best credentials –'

'Actually Mrs Gelbmann, he has seen someone and I wondered whether you knew her or knew of her family.'

'Seen someone?' Mrs Gelbmann peered down her aquiline nose at Mrs Levy. Her right eyebrow rose in an elegant, practised arch. Mrs Levy fluttered before her, a songbird caught in its gilded cage.

'Yes, it's rather embarrassing, but he was late to the dancing at the Vishnefski wedding and he had to slip through the women's section and well, there she was . . .' She was not going to mention the fact that her son had peeked through the mechitzah.

Mrs Gelbmann tilted her head slightly. Mrs Levy plunged on.

'He liked the look of her. Apparently her name is Chani Kaufman. Do you know the family?'

'I most certainly do, Mrs Levy. A good family, very frum. They live in Hendon. They are simple, decent people. She comes of good stock.'

'But simple, you said?'

'Her father is the rabbi of that tiny shul on Bell Lane. He survives on his stipend and has managed to raise and educate eight daughters on it.'

'Is the family financially solvent?'

'Well Mrs Levy, how shall I put it? The Kaufmans are not, well —' Mrs Gelbmann gave a little laugh, 'as financially solvent as you and your husband.'

She knew it. Baruch had gone for a penniless beauty.

Mrs Gelbmann regarded the crestfallen Mrs Levy. The room fell quiet as each woman considered her next move. Mrs Gelbmann sensed Baruch's attraction was strong; strong enough for Mrs Levy to remain seated. Perhaps a match could be struck after all. Softly but steadily she would reel Mrs Levy in. The Levys had paid handsomely in the past, demanding that their sons met only the most popular and respectable young maidens the community had to offer. Although Chani occupied a lower rung, it would be foolish to look a gift-horse in the mouth.

'Tea, Mrs Levy?'

'Oh yes please, Mrs Gelbmann. Two sugars. No milk though, I ate a salt beef sandwich for lunch.'

'No problem. If you'll just excuse me —'

'Oh yes, yes.'

It was not that Mrs Levy was a supercilious snob nor was Mrs Gelbmann a mercenary. Each had their part to play and marriage was a serious business. For a successful match to be struck both families must come with equal goods to the table. Should one basket be fuller than the other, an imbalance would occur and a myriad of awkward situations would result, beginning with the payment for the wedding itself. The bride's family would usually provide, with the groom's side oiling the financial wheels where necessary. But should one side struggle so much as to feel beholden to the other then the wealthier party would influence all future decisions, whether their impoverished relatives liked it or not. It was unusual for a match of such obvious differences to proceed.

Mrs Levy did not relish the idea of lording it over another family. She desired joyful and warm relations with her extended family through marriage. Inequality bred underlying resentment not unity. It was never a good start. Besides, what would the neighbours say?

But at the heart of it lay her son's happiness. Baruch always so reliable, so biddable and compliant had made a rare request. She could not dash his hopes. He had never disappointed them. True he had his idiosyncrasies, his love of art and literature (she had found the novels secreted away under his mattress and had left them there), his gaucheness and over-sensitivity, but he was hers and Mrs Levy adored him.

As for Mrs Gelbmann, matchmaking was her livelihood. Although widowed, her profession gave her financial independence, a rarity for a single woman. Nor was she forgotten and set aside as a woman past her prime, alone in her empty nest. Mrs Gelbmann was a vital component of the community, working hard to ensure its continuity. Naturally it was prudent to treat her well.

Of course she was an opportunist. Matchmaking was a challenging and exhausting profession. Unaware of their own mediocrity, young people demanded perfection in a spouse.

In practice, the boy and girl did not set eyes on each other until the date itself. Hence rejection on the basis of physical disparity was a frequent excuse for failure. Too short! Too fat! Where's his hair? Then there were the potential pitfalls in differing levels of observance. Too frum! Not frum enough! The complaints rumbled on and on making Mrs Gelbmann's head ache.

But in this case Baruch had already seen the girl and was anxious to see her again. Half her work had been done for her. All that remained was for Chani to return the compliment. The attraction must be mutual. Yet Chani had rejected suggested matches and in turn had been rejected several times. The girl might be getting desperate. Even if Baruch did not live up to Chani's expectations, there was a good chance that she would agree to marry him regardless. He was a fine catch, better than all her previous suitors. The girl would be a fool to turn him down.

Mrs Gelbmann prepared for battle. She released the brake and wheeled in the tea trolley.

⋆   ⋆   ⋆

The shivering of porcelain interrupted Mrs Levy's brooding. She sat up straight again and watched as Mrs Gelbmann parked the gleaming trolley in front of her. A plate of almond thins nestled beside a fat strudel dusted with icing-sugar. Near the teapot a honey-cake glistened, anointed with golden syrup.

Mrs Levy licked her lips. Her eyes followed the deft movements of Mrs Gelbmann's hands.

'Cake or some biscuits, Mrs Levy? Or both?' offered Mrs Gelbmann. Her smile was genial, neutral, but she knew Mrs Levy was trapped.

'Oh Mrs Gelbmann, I really shouldn't! I'm on a diet,' protested Mrs Levy.

'A diet? What for, you're as slim as a pickle! You haven't put on an ounce. A pitsel of honey-cake won't hurt. Or a sliver of strudel? I baked it this morning,' purred Mrs Gelbmann. In truth she thought Mrs Levy was looking rather plump like a juicy sultana. But flattery got you everywhere. As for the strudel, both women were well aware it had been bought at Carmelli's that morning. Little white lies – the currency of diplomacy.

'Ahh, if you insist, a slice of strudel please, Mrs Gelbmann,' replied Mrs Levy. Resistance was futile. The smell of cinnamon had flooded her mouth with desire.

When both women had finished spearing forkfuls of stodgy sweetness into their mouths, business resumed.

'So,' began Mrs Gelbmann, her voice glutinous, 'tell me a little about Baruch.'

What mother can resist the opportunity to boast about her beloved son? Mrs Gelbmann sat back and waited for Baruch's accolades to be expounded. She helped herself to another slice of honey cake, sensing the list would be lengthy.

Mrs Levy seemed to inflate with pride. She took a deep breath and began. 'My Baruch is a special boy, a very clever boy. He's different from the others . . . he's more sensitive. He's deeper and more spiritual. And *very* academic, Mrs Gelbmann! Top of the class in every subject at school. The Head gave him a glowing reference for the Yeshiva in Gateshead and he did brilliantly there as well . . . so my husband and I, well, we hope . . . well, we would like him to become, im yirtzeh HaShem, a rabbi . . .'

She had stuttered to a halt. Mrs Gelbmann's beady eyes had been fixed on her throughout. She felt uncomfortable, foolish for imparting the last piece of information. The Levys were not in the habit of producing rabbinical scholars, let alone rabbis.

'A rabbi? A most unusual choice for one of your sons, Mrs Levy, if you don't mind me saying. Until now they have all been so, so . . . how shall I put it?' Mrs Gelbmann fumbled for the right word. Materialistic was not it.

'Entrepreneurial?' suggested Mrs Levy, her heart beating a little faster.

'Yee-eess, that's right. They are all highly successful businessmen. Born with an excellent head for financial success.' Shysters, every one of them, with the father being the worst! The apple does not fall far from the tree.

But this third son was apparently different, a future rabbi perhaps.

'Tell me more about your future plans for Baruch if you will, Mrs Levy. How old is he now exactly?'

Her complicated, brilliant but insecure son had become a commodity ready to be bartered. Somehow it had been easier with her other sons. They were cast from a different, less brittle metal.

'He's just turned twenty. At the moment he's living at home having finished his studies at Gateshead. He's been accepted at Or Yerushaliyim and we're hoping he'll start learning there by Pesach.' Eat that thought, Mrs Gelbmann. Or Yerushaliyim was *the* yeshiva; only the elite gained entry. And her Baruch was one of them!

'Baruch HaShem! Or Yerushaliyim . . . how wonderful for you, Mrs Levy. He must be a true yeshiva bocher. You must be very proud,' trilled Mrs Gelbmann. There was always a catch though. Otherwise news of this Levy wunderkind would have already reached her ears.

'Oh we are, Mrs Gelbmann, we are. Mr Levy was thrilled when he received Baruch's acceptance letter,' enthused Mrs Levy.

'And what does Baruch look like? How tall is he? Have you got a picture?'

Tall she could do. 'He's about six foot two. That's pretty tall, isn't it?'

'Most certainly. Especially for a Jewish boy. Is he dark like Mr Levy or fair like you?'

'He takes after me. I've got a fairly recent photo here, taken about a year ago at his cousin Brochele's wedding.' Mrs Levy dug in her handbag and retrieved a dog-eared photo from the confines of her purse. She hesitated wishing she could avoid exposing her poor son to the shadchan's calculating eye. She knew Baruch was ordinary looking.

Mrs Gelbmann scrutinised the picture. Clearly more than a year old. The boy in it was no older than sixteen at the most, his features blurry and indistinct. She noted the protruding chin and heavy spectacles – nothing unusual there, they all looked like that. His skin appeared to be blotchy in places. Or was that simply patchy facial hair? He bore no resemblance to his smoother, darker brothers who had clearly surpassed him in the looks department.

She paused before she gave her verdict. 'Very nice, Mrs Levy. A lovely Yiddisher boy. He looks well. Has he had any illnesses or health problems?'

'A little asthma but he only gets it when the pollution is high in the summer, Mrs Gelbmann. You know our family's medical history from when we met last time. No change there, my father-in-law's diabetes is a little worse but he has it under control – he' s started using one of those injection pens. He's very proud and likes to be independent so it suits us all just fine. And my parents are still alive and well, Baruch HaShem.' No need to mention Baruch's persistent athlete's foot or his garlic allergy.

'Baruch HaShem. Good, good. I suspect you are wondering about Chani?'

Chani. The name was common enough. Would the girl be too?

'Yee-ess, that's why I'm here, Mrs Gelbmann. What's she like, this Chani? Tell me all you know – of course, only what you feel you can safely reveal, Mrs Gelbmann.'

Now it was Mrs Levy's turn to watch the other woman's face. But the shadchan concealed any flicker of emotion or judgment. Her features had become a mask of impartiality as she met Mrs Levy's request with a steady gaze. And when she spoke only her lips moved, her articulation precise. She took her time, revelling in her sway over Mrs Levy.

'Ahh, Chani. A fine young Yiddisher girl. She's nineteen. A bright, pleasant, cheerful girl. Practical, helpful and willing in her manner. Excellent manners. She's about five foot three in height. Has a pretty smile. Slim. She has dark, straight hair worn tied back. Pretty, one would say.'

They were all pretty, even the downright ugly ones, thought Mrs Levy. But Baruch had noticed her so she must be attractive. Until now he had made no mention of being interested in the opposite sex and when she had asked if he was ready to go on a shidduch, he had shuddered in disgust. Mrs Levy had been worried; had even entertained the terrible thought that her son might – God forbid – be . . . be . . . With relief she cast that unspeakable fear aside. There was no place for those of that persuasion in her world. Her Baruch was simply choosy. He'd been taking his time, that was all. Good for him.

But had he been choosy enough?

'The father is a rabbi as I have already said. His family were originally from Vilna and can trace their ancestry back to the time of the great Rabbi. On Mrs Kaufman's side, there are many illustrious rabbonim, including Rabbi Shmuel Ben Tsvi. Her family hail from Kiev.'

Mrs Levy sipped at her cold tea. So the girl was from a family full of rabbis. But the hard fact remained: she was dirt poor.

'So which school did Chani go to and how did she do there? And which sem did she attend?'

The shadchan wriggled in her armchair. This was dangerous territory.

'Well, Chani went to Queen Esther. She's an excellent student just like Baruch, she got straight A's in all her GCSEs and went on to collect two more at A Level, if I remember correctly. At the moment, she's teaching – well, assisting – in art lessons at Queen Esther.'

Mrs Levy smelt a rat. The shadchan had not answered all her questions. She persisted.

'Baruch needs a clever girl to match him, but hopefully not too clever – those brainy types can be troublesome . . . but Mrs Gelbmann, you haven't mentioned her sem experience . . .'

'Chani didn't go to sem. May I offer you another slice of strudel, Mrs Levy?'

Anything, anything to distract her client. Mrs Gelbmann had a sudden vision of herself tap-dancing on the coffee table, twirling a cane and raising a bowler hat.

'What? What sort of good Yiddisher girl with those kind of grades doesn't go to sem?' Mrs Levy yelped in glee. There was light at the end of the tunnel, Baruch HaShem.

Mrs Gelbmann came back to earth with a bump.

'Mrs Levy, Chani wanted to teach, she stayed on for Sixth Form at Queen Esther at Mrs Sisselbaum's request.'

'Mrs Sisselbaum asked her to stay on? What for? She usually pushes them to go on to Gateshead. That's her job, isn't it? Come on, Mrs Gelbmann, let's drop this pretence. Tell me the truth. If this girl is going to meet my Baruch, I need a very good reason for her not going.'

'Well, Mrs Sisselbaum felt she was better off staying on, that she was more suited to – to – well, Chani is the lively type . . .' Mrs Gelbmann stumbled on.

'The lively type?' Mrs Levy narrowed her eyes. The shadchan wavered before her.

'Mrs Levy, Chani is a lovely girl, I mean, lively

as in friendly and warm – a little different perhaps . . .'

'Mrs Gelbmann, you and I both know what different really means.'

The shadchan began to explain but Mrs Levy held up a hand.

'No, Mrs Gelbmann, please don't say any more. She isn't right for my Baruch. Poor, I can just about accept.' Both women knew this to be a fabrication. Mrs Levy hesitated and then regained her momentum. 'But her not going to sem is another matter altogether. If Baruch is to become a rabbi, he needs the right sort of girl, an educated, good, quiet, supportive girl. Not some oddball who stayed on at Queen Esther to teach, sorry, to assist in Art! You and I know perfectly well, that the girls that don't get accepted are trouble. I don't want a difficult daughter-in-law. Baruch is too sensitive to cope with a headstrong girl. I've heard enough, she isn't right for him. So let's move on and find someone who is.'

Oh the bird had flown! Defeated, Mrs Gelbmann began to clear away the tea things.

'Very well, Mrs Levy,' she sighed as she stacked the saucers. 'I will look out for a more suitable shidduch for Baruch. It's a shame though, Chani's truly a lovely girl . . .'

'That she may be! But she is someone else's lovely – not my Baruch's,' snapped Mrs Levy. Enough already. She wanted to go home.

'As you wish, Mrs Levy, I will make enquiries . . .' murmured Mrs Gelbmann.

'Thank you, Mrs Gelbmann, I appreciate it.' She stood up and brushed the crumbs off her skirt.

'We will find Baruch the right girl, im yirtzeh HaShem.'

'Im yirtzeh HaShem.'

Mrs Gelbmann walked her guest to the door.

'Good Shabbes, Mrs Gelbmann.'

'A good Shabbes to you too, Mrs Levy. I'll be in touch.'

'Thank you, once again, Mrs Gelbmann.'

'Thank you for coming, Mrs Levy.'

Mrs Gelbmann closed her front door. She stood behind it listening to the receding clack-clack as Mrs Levy walked away, and with a sigh she returned to her cosy living room to polish off the rest of the strudel.

CHAPTER 15

AVROMI

April 2008 – London

'I can't, Shola, it's just – I can't,' sighed Avromi.

'But everyone will be there, our whole tutor group and we'll miss you.' She stood opposite him on the pavement outside the law faculty, balancing her file and books on her hip. The wind blew her hair across her face but she remained where she was, blocking his path home.

'Shola, you know I don't go to these things. My parents expect me to be home in the evenings. You know how my dad feels about me going to uni as it is – he'd have my guts for garters.'

She gazed beseechingly at him, her deep brown eyes wide and innocent. Her ankles were bent outwards in her baker boy boots, her long, elegant legs braced against the leather. She reminded him of Bambi. 'Just one drink. For me.'

He caved in with a sigh. 'All right, Shola, just for you. But I'm only staying for half an hour and that's it.'

As soon as he had agreed, he regretted it, but

Shola gave him such a sweet, sunny smile that he felt something flip over in his stomach. As he made his way home, Avromi ran through a gamut of excuses for not staying in and studying after supper. He could always tell his parents he was meeting Baruch in Golders Green for coffee.

The student union bar was half full, but a puddle of beer had already leaked across the small dance floor. The place stank of stale booze and lost student nights. Posters announced gigs that had already been and gone. The light was a murky yellow, interspersed with silvery rainbow fragments as a lone glitter-ball spun sadly on its axis.

Avromi wore his usual black and white attire replete with discreet black velvet skullcap, but had hung up his jacket in the cloakroom and rolled up his shirtsleeves to the elbow in an attempt to look less conspicuous. During the first weeks of university he had learned to tuck the strings of his prayer shawl into his trousers, in order to avoid the barrage of questions they provoked.

There was no sign of Shola.

The barman lent over and yelled in his ear. He had a pierced eyebrow and one side of his head was shaved to reveal a tribal tattoo. Avromi stared in fascination. The Torah forbade the imprinting of marks on the body.

'What you 'avin', mate?'

He considered his choices. The wine and beer on offer would not be kosher. There was whisky though. His father enjoyed a dram at the end of a long Shabbes meal and although he hated the drink, if he mixed it with Coke – also kosher – he might manage to swallow half a glass. It might just be enough. He knew full well that he would find the evening unbearable were he to attempt it stone cold sober. So far so good. He would not be transgressing.

'A Jack Daniels and Coke please. With lots of ice.'

'Single shot or double? It's happy hour, two for the price of one, mate.'

'All right then, make it a double.' He paid and took a cautious sip, pulling a face at the medicinal taste.

'Avromi!'

Shola had materialized and was grinning at him in delight.

'I'm so glad you're here!' She moved as if to hug him, but remembered and remained where she was. They stared at each other, smiling awkwardly. Avromi did not know the correct protocol. Obviously he could not kiss her and he had no present for her either.

'Well, it is your birthday and you look quite gorgeous!' Shola giggled nervously. He felt himself blushing and to hide it, he gave her a flourishing bow that brought him face to face with her bare knees. Her feet were clad in her trusty biker boots but the rest of her was new territory for Avromi. She was wearing a dusky pink dancer's dress. It emphasized her slender waist; the chiffon material of the skirt flared out over her hips, stopping at mid thigh. Two gossamer straps held up the dress; its simplicity and fluidity enhanced Shola's delicate frame, making her seem innocent and almost fragile. Her skin glowed like ochre. He gazed at the dip in her clavicle and watched it rise and fall with her voice. Then he remembered his manners.

'Can I get you a drink?'

'That would be lovely. What are you having?' She peered at the glass he was clutching.

'Double whisky and Coke.'

'Ooh, same again please!'

The rest of the tutor group began to appear, forming a boisterous huddle around Shola. Some had gifts and others embraced her. She was lost in a whirl of social activity but Avromi could not take his eyes off her. He leant against the bar, nursing his drink, wishing she would talk to him.

'All right, Avromi! How ya doin'? Can I get you a drink?'

Mike had sidled up to him and was now barking into his ear. Avromi had to lean sideways in order to catch what he was saying – Mike was very short.

'No, Mike, honestly, I'm fine – I've got a drink.'

Mike sniffed at Avromi's glass and returned with another whisky and Coke. What was it with these non-Jews and their need to ply you with alcohol? The room began to feel very warm. Faces crowded round and he was soon embroiled in loud conversation. He could not hear half of what was being said, but for the first time in the evening he felt at ease. A dopey grin spread across his face as he joined in the general banter and bonhomie. To his surprise, he began to enjoy himself.

The bar became more and more crowded. Avromi reached for his second drink, which no longer tasted of anything but was refreshingly cold. A light sheen began to appear on his forehead and his shirt felt hot and stifling. He undid the top two buttons. Well, there was no one from the kehilla to see him.

Avromi leant against a wall and watched the bodies writhe on the dance floor. The room span faster, the air foetid and the floor, slick with spilt liquor, vibrated beneath his feet to the throb of the bass. Girls, their limbs bare, hair flying, revolved past him in a succession of shuddering breasts, shimmying buttocks and juddering thighs. He stared openly and swigged another drink. Suddenly, the wall slid away from behind him and he was left slumped on the floor.

Hands hauled him up and he was bundled onto the dance floor, despite his protests, lurching and swaying with the rest of them.

'Avromi! Are you ok?'

He opened his eyes only to be blinded by the glitter-ball's refractions. He was lying down. On a bench, so it seemed. A face was blocking out the dizzying light, its shadow framed by familiar shaggy spirals. She was kneeling beside him, offering him a glass of water.

He hauled himself upright and tried to speak, but his lips would not work. The room tilted viciously. He lay back down.

He woke to the sting of cold night air. His class-mates were propelling him towards a black cab. Shola was arguing with the driver.

'He won't puke, I promise!' Her voice was insistent and anxious.

'The last time I had a piss-head in here, it took me two weeks to get rid of the stink of vomit. So the answer's no.'

'Please . . . I'll pay double. I just need to get him home.'

The cabbie sighed. 'All right, love, double it is but if he's sick, you'll be paying for the cleaning bill too.'

The taxi throbbed. He sprawled across the back seat and clung to the leather edge of the seat as the cab swung around. Opposite him, Shola watched nervously. She leant forward and reached for his hand, but Avromi had fallen asleep again and was oblivious to the impropriety.

When the cab stopped, he came to again. An

urgent need to vomit forced him upright. He fumbled with the handle while Shola paid the driver. Shola guided him as he stumbled towards the door of her flat.

'Where's your loo?' he groaned.

'Up this flight and first on your left.'

Kneeling over the toilet bowl and gripping its rim, he voided a dark torrent. Afterwards, rising unsteadily, he felt utterly revolted but surprisingly better.

Shola knocked timidly on the door. 'Are you ok, Avromi?'

'Yes, I'm fine. Be down in a minute,' he mumbled.

'Ok, I'll make some tea.'

'Thank you.'

He knelt at the sink and splashed his face with water. He dared not look in the mirror. Instead he patted the top of his head for his skullcap. It was no longer there. He sighed. It was his own blasted fault. This was his punishment for adopting the habits and customs of unbelievers. He would have to find a way of explaining himself to his parents. He should have been home hours ago.

Cautiously, he opened the door and began his way downstairs.

They sat next to each other at the small pine table in the kitchen. Shola had wrapped a grey woollen cardigan over her dress. She was leaning on the table, warming her hands on her mug of tea. Her flat-mates were out and the place was quiet and dark. Avromi held his head in his hands. He still felt very wobbly. All he really wanted to do was to sleep. His mug of tea lay untouched.

'What am I going to tell my parents? My dad will never let this go. This will just prove him right, that I shouldn't have gone to uni in the first place.'

'Can't you make up an excuse?'

'Like what?'

'Like you were at a friend's house and you didn't realize the time, and you missed the last bus home, so you decided to stay the night.'

'Well, that would be lying wouldn't it?'

'Well, yes, but then there's lying and there's lying. You aren't hurting anyone with this lie. In fact, you'd be protecting your parents from the truth, which would only upset and worry them. This way no one suffers. Think of it as a white lie. And you should text them now, so they stop worrying about where you are.'

Avromi blew on his tea and swallowed thoughtfully. Shola was right; he would be transgressing but it was more palatable than the truth. He would just have to daven extra hard for forgiveness. He hated the thought of lying to his parents. But he had already lied to them about where he was going tonight. One more lie would not make much difference now.

'I suppose I could tell them I stayed at Baruch's. Or maybe another friend who lives in Edgware – that's a bit further away and would make the missed-the-last-tube or bus home excuse more plausible.'

'There you go then! It's not so bad after all. Make sure you warn that friend in case they check up.'

'They wouldn't bother. Far too busy.' He sighed into his mug. 'It's not just the lying part, Shola, I am just so embarrassed.' He grimaced, avoiding her eye.

'About what exactly?'

'Getting so drunk, making a fool of myself in front of everyone. In front of you.' He peered up at her sheepishly.

She laughed. 'Don't be silly! There's a first time for everyone to get legless. It happens to all of us. In fact, I think the others might see it as you being a bit more normal, fitting in with us sinners.'

'Really?'

'Like you've won your drinking spurs. However crass that might sound.'

He considered her verdict. 'Right. I owe you one.'

'What for?'

'For looking after me.'

'You're my friend. After all, I invited you to my birthday drinks.'

'It's your birthday and I've totally spoilt it. What a plonker I've been!'

'It's not my birthday any more so stop beating yourself up, Avromi. You're here, aren't you?'

'What do you mean?'

'With me. Now.'

She reached for his hand and gave it a squeeze. He did not let go. Avromi leant forward slowly and kissed her. She tasted of hot, sweet tea. Shola wrapped her leg around his, pulling him closer. His hands cupped her waist then slid towards her hips, driven by an instinct he had been trying to suppress ever since he had first met her.

CHAPTER 16

BARUCH

May 2008 – London

When Baruch came home, his parents were already waiting for him in the lounge. They sat side by side on the cream leather sofa, two consuls supreme in their power. The curtains had been drawn and the standing lamp bathed the pair in golden light.

'Come in Baruch and sit down,' grunted his father. He was hunched over in his shirtsleeves, his braces dividing the white expanse of shirt across broad back.

He entered the arena and took his seat in the armchair opposite. A glass coffee table lay between them.

'Baruch, your mother has seen Mrs Gelbmann today and after discussing matters with me, we've come to the conclusion that Chani isn't for you.'

Baruch stared at his father and then at his mother. Mrs Levy avoided his gaze. She reached for her husband's hand instead.

'But – why? What's wrong with her?' The words spluttered out.

His father glanced at his mother. She was still inspecting the carpet. He nudged her.

'Baruch,' she began hesitantly,' I know how much you wanted to meet her. But darling, she isn't for you. I had a long chat with Mrs Gelbmann and it turns out that for some reason Chani didn't go to sem. You can't marry a girl who hasn't been properly educated in Yiddishkeit. We don't know if she just didn't get accepted or whether it was for some other weird reason but I do know that the ones who don't get accepted are the problematic types. Darling, you're going to be a rabbi, and you need the right sort of wife. Someone who'll be your equal, who'll understand you and your needs, who'll be your helpmate, your –'

Mrs Levy stopped short. She couldn't bear seeing the despair in her son's eyes. He was tight-lipped with frustration.

Mr Levy took over. 'Baruch, we want you to be happy and in the long run, marrying the wrong sort of girl is only going to end in disaster for all of us. For her and her family and our family. There are many wonderful girls out there and I promise you, one of them is for you. But she isn't Chani. Forget her, move on. The best way to move on is to start dating more suitable girls. And I hear Mrs Gelbmann has some lovely young ladies for you to meet.'

He couldn't stand it any longer. In that moment, he loathed them all, Mrs Gelbmann included. They were all against him. Baruch had been staring at the copies of *Good Housekeeping* stacked on the coffee table. They hadn't been touched for ages, their corners still perfectly aligned. For some reason, their presence infuriated him even further: empty promises of perfect lives in perfect homes where choice and variety abounded were so distant from the claustrophobia of his daily reality.

The silence grew. Mr Levy stared down at his spotless brogues, checking for scuff marks whilst Mrs Levy gazed at her son.

Finally he spoke, so low and quietly that his parents had to crane forward to hear him.

'It's not fair. Nothing's fair in my life. I can't even meet the girl I like. Everything's always decided for me. I never complain, I just do as I'm told . . . and now, when I ask for one thing, one small thing – it's denied me.'

Mr Levy shifted uncomfortably. He didn't like displays of emotion; he was an undemonstrative man who believed that this sort of behaviour was best left to women. He wished his son would stop this kvetching.

'Baruch, calm yourself and remember your manners –' he said.

'I am calm!' Baruch sprang from his chair, his long body unfolding in a single fluid movement. He towered over his parents, waving his long arms as if he were bringing a plane in to land.

'Sit down, Baruch! This is not a way to behave.' barked Mr Levy.

'Sit down? What for? I'm always behaving, always

remembering my manners. And now I can't meet Chani because she hasn't been to sem! Loads of girls don't go – it's not such a big deal.' He was squawking now. He knew he sounded ridiculous but he didn't care. The words leapt from his throat, burning his larynx with their force.

Mrs Levy clutched her husband's arm. She tried to speak, but all that came out was a squeak. 'Please, Baruch, I know you are upset but try to understand – we want your best, we don't want to hurt you –'

'My best? What would that be? To be a rabbi and marry some girl I don't even like? I don't even know if I want to be a rabbi.'

His father's head snapped back as if it had been jerked by a string.

'Don't want? *Don't want?* What is this don't want? All your life I have provided for you, clothed you, fed you, LOVED YOU! And this is the thanks I get? Tssss . . . such a grateful son I have.'

His mother broke in. 'Darling, I understand you're frustrated now – and disappointed. But sometimes we have to do the things we don't like in life –'

'Like marry someone that you like and I don't?'

'Baruch! That's enough!' bellowed Mr Levy. The magazines scattered as his father shoved the table out of the way. With a grunt, he was up on his feet, facing Baruch, poised to fight. He pointed a thick forefinger at his son.

'Sit. Down.'

Baruch was beyond obeying orders but danced a step backwards just in case and lowered his tone.

'No thanks, Dad. I'm fine where I am for the moment. Listen, I love and respect you both – but sometimes, I just feel – that I never get asked about what I really want –'

'What do you want?' His mother spoke gently. Mr Levy sank back into the sofa, sensing a lull in the storm.

Baruch hung his head, hands loose at his sides. 'I don't really know,' he said sadly. 'But what I do know is if you won't let me meet Chani, I won't meet anyone else.'

Mr and Mrs Levy were lost. Their darling son was malfunctioning and they had no idea what to do. So they blamed each other.

'I'd have let him meet the girl, if it hadn't been for your nagging.'

'My nagging? Dovid – we agreed. She isn't right – so why are you blaming me now? Typical – it's always like this, something goes wrong and I get the blame – why can't you support me for once in our decisions?'

'I always support you but maybe we were too impulsive – maybe we should have let them meet. What does it matter – sem no sem, money, no money?' Mr Levy airily waved away both impediments. He slumped bored and irritated in his chair.

'Now you tell me! Now after he's not talking to us any more –'

'How long can a boy be broiges for?'

'Who knows? Who cares?' snapped Mrs Levy. A migraine threatened; a magenta cloud of pain hovered over her left eye. She willed it away.

'I think we should let him meet her,' muttered Mr Levy, almost to himself. He took refuge behind a copy of the newspaper. His wife was staring at him; any harder and the newsprint would start smouldering. He cleared his throat, shook his wristwatch and stood up, avoiding her gaze.

'Time to daven –'

'A bit early for you, isn't it, darling?' enquired Mrs Levy.

He grunted and moved towards the door.

'Dovid?'

'Yes dear?' He tugged at the brim of his hat and plucked a prayer book from the shelf.

'We haven't finished talking.'

'I can't keep HaShem waiting.' He pulled at the door handle.

Mrs Levy, moving with a lithe and speedy grace, intercepted his progress and with a firm shove of her buttocks, ensured the door remained closed. Arms crossed, she glared at her husband.

'I think HaShem will understand your delay. Why break a habit of a lifetime? Now where were we? You were saying that we should have let them meet.'

'Oy, Berenice, will you give over? Just for a moment. He'll be out of his room before you know it.' Mr Levy yearned for the rumble of other men's voices, for the privacy of his prayer shawl, but his wife had turned into Medusa and he knew better than to meet her gaze.

Mrs Levy glowered from beneath her ginger wig. 'Dovid, do you want our son to marry beneath him?'

'All I am saying is . . .'

'I'm waiting.' His wife kicked off her heels and leant back against the door, wriggling her toes deeper into the carpet.

'It's really not so bad. She's probably a lovely girl and anyway – how do we know she'll want our great noodle of a son?'

'Of course she'll want him! Who wouldn't want him?' sizzled Mrs Levy.

Mr Levy held his hat in his hands and lovingly stroked its brim. 'Well, if I remember correctly, you weren't exactly overawed by me on our first shidduch . . .'

'True, but I was won over eventually . . .'

'By my gentlemanly charm?' He squinted up at his wife. A smile flickered across her lips. She pretended to swallow a yawn. He waggled his bushy eyebrows at her. Mrs Levy giggled.

'Or by the size of my wallet?'

'Stop it, Dovid. Be serious.'

'I'm trying, but you're even more trying. Give the boy a chance. It'll probably all fall through – the more resistance you put up, the more attractive this girl seems to him. I say we contact Mrs Gelbmann and get her to speak to the girl's mother and see what happens. Probably nothing will happen. And then we can move on.'

'And if they like each other?'

'So they like each other.'

'Dovid, if they decide to get married and the rabbonim agree – we can't stop them. Think about it.'

'I've thought about it. There'll never be a girl good enough for him in your eyes. You're a very picky woman.'

'And so I should be.'

'And so you should be. But remember how it was with Ilan? You rejected all Mrs Gelbmann's suggestions, and that was not such a wise thing to do. People were starting to talk.'

'So?'

'So, sooner or later, no girl would have agreed to meet him. Baruch HaShem he met Dafna just in time. We don't live in a world of endless opportunity. It's a small community.'

'But this is the first possible shidduch. He doesn't have to go on it.'

'It's the first one he's wanted to go on.'

'Right.'

'He's as picky as his mother.'

'And look what I ended up with.'

Mr Levy stuck out his bottom lip in mock offence. 'You're not the only one suffering. Now would you please let me go daven?'

With a sigh, Mrs Levy shifted away from the door.

Mr Levy squashed his hat back on and slipped out.

He plodded down the hall, overcome by sudden exhaustion.

'Ok, I agree. Let them meet,' called Mrs Levy from inside the lounge.

Mr Levy grinned. He would daven for them all.

The kitchen door had been pushed to and Chani hovered outside, eavesdropping, a habit in which she excelled. The adult conversations from which she was barred often revealed nuggets of inform-ation that she would mull over in her quieter hours. The best ones occurred when her mother enter-tained a female guest from the kehilla. After being shooed out she would clomp down the hall only to scuttle back on nimble feet to lean against the door.

In that position she had learned a lot – about the rejections, the disappointments and the quiet rebellions that occurred so subtly they almost went by unnoticed. How they were absorbed, dealt with, quashed. Which esteemed son had dropped from favour; whose daughter complained of her bitter marriage; which rabbi had provoked uproar for his outspokenness.

The lives of those around her seemed to be coated in a smooth, soothing layer of conformity. Nobody appeared to transgress. Instead, they did as their neighbours did and hoped their behaviour was judged approvingly by their peers and most of all, by HaShem. Now and then though, the stillness of the pool was disturbed by the writhing of something dark and undesirable just below the surface.

Today's conversation was about her. She was draped listlessly across the living room sofa when the phone burst into life. Chani scrambled to her feet in hope that it was for her, but the kitchen door remained closed. So she lurked in the shadows as usual. Her mother greeted the caller with enthusiasm. As soon as her mother had finished the formalities, Chani tingled with anticipation. It was clear from her mother's hopeful tone that the caller was Mrs Gelbmann.

A shidduch. It had to be. Mrs Gelbmann would not call for any other reason. Chani strained to catch every word.

'Yes Mrs Gelbmann, she is still available.'

Her mother listened. Chani's heart beat like a drum.

'Go ahead . . . mmm . . . mmm . . . no, I have not heard of them. They live where?'

'That house on the corner? They must be very well-to-do.' Her mother gave one of her loud sniffs. 'And what does this boy do? And what are his parents' plans for him for the future?' There was a pause. 'Ok . . . sounds promising. Tall you say. Not too tall, I hope! Nobody wants a giant in the family! How old did you say? A little young perhaps, but if he's ready he's ready, B'srat

HaShem. Now tell me, how did he –' Her mother broke off. Chani itched to race upstairs and quietly pick up the extension in her parents' room, but she was glued to the spot, desperate not to miss a vital snippet.

'He saw her *where?*' Her mother's exclamation startled Chani so much that she nearly fell through the door.

'Mrs Gelbmann, let me tell you something, boys that look at girls like that are not for my daughter.'

Chani flinched in realisation. It was the boy at the wedding. Shulamis had been right! If only she had turned round and looked. There was no time for regret; her mother was speaking again.

'Very well, Mrs Gelbmann, I hear you. Of course young men look but not so directly, nu? Mmm . . . really? Now that does make a difference. Or Yerushaliyim did you say?'

Or Yerushaliyim. Her heart sank. For most girls, ensnaring a top yeshiva student was considered a coup. Instead, Chani saw the yawning gap in knowledge and experience that would inevitably stretch between them. Why would a yeshiva bocher want a girl like her? She would feel lost. Or bored. Or both. And so would he.

'Yes, but Mrs Gelbmann, we both know that Chani hasn't been to sem. Is he aware of that fact? And more to the point, his parents? Oh. Really?' Her mother was listening intently again. 'Good. Yes. Very good. Ok, ok, I'll talk to her and I will let you know. Thank you, Mrs Gelbmann. Yes and you, yes im yirtzeh HaShem. Goodbye for now.' Her mother hung up.

Chani shot into the living room, her slippers skidding on the lino.

'Chani-leh, I know you were listening!' scolded Mrs Kaufman.

Chani knew better than to pretend otherwise. She threw herself into plumping up the cushions. Her mother shuffled up behind her.

'Well at least you're blushing! Since when has listening in on other people's private conversations been the right thing to do, young lady?'

Chani rolled her eyes at the bookshelf. She spun to face her mother. 'Mum, please, not now! Just tell me! Who is he?'

Mrs Kaufman dropped onto the sofa and patted the space next to her. Obediently, Chani sat down.

'His name is Baruch Levy. He comes from a wealthy family, it seems, although I haven't heard of them. Clearly they don't go to your father's shtiebel.' Another sniff. 'He's a yeshiva bocher with a place at Or Yerushaliyim, but tell me what sort of yeshiva bocher arrives late to a wedding and starts looking at all the women?' queried Mrs Kaufman. She turned to face Chani, her mouth twisted in distaste. 'And I dread to think what you were doing that made him notice you!'

'Mum! All boys look, even frum boys. Surely Dad looked at you? A little glimpse here and there perhaps? I wasn't doing *anything*. I promise. I was behaving myself. I wasn't even aware anyone was looking.' She stopped herself before mentioning that Shulamis had seen him staring.

Suddenly she burned to meet him. She swept aside their differences. He was young, Shulamis had said. And tall. And he had bothered to pursue her this far. If she did not move quickly, he may lose interest and turn his attentions elsewhere.

'Mum – it doesn't matter – I want to meet him.'

Mrs Kaufman, not wishing to appear too keen, was in favour of letting a little time elapse before returning the shadchan's call.

'Very well, I'll talk to your father and I'll call her after Shabbes,' she sighed. 'But let's not get our hopes up. You know how it is, Chani-leh with these shidduchim. So many girls waiting in line. Too many choices for these silly boys, nu? Not a true mensch amongst them! Ok, so you're a little talkative but who wouldn't want you?' She stroked Chani's hair.

'I know, Mum. Can't you call her back tonight?'

Her mother tutted. 'Chani, a little pride, a little decorum.'

'Oh Mum! What does it matter? He'll probably reject me in the long run anyway. Better to get it over and done with now. Or he may just . . . just . . .'

Mrs Kaufman gave her daughter a wan smile. Chani was radiating ripples of panic and her stomach lurched in recognition of her daughter's fears. What if no one wanted her? It had been easier with the others. Perhaps HaShem had His reasons for the delay. She wished He would hurry up though. Soon Chani would lose hope as the shidduchim offered became less and less palatable. She would slip and flounder her way into spinster-hood, jaded by endless disappointment. Mrs Kaufman could not bear to think of Chani growing old alone. As if cursed. The taint would spread, infecting her younger daughters. Not until Chani was wed could another search begin.

CHAPTER 17

THE REBBETZIN

November 2008 – London

The Rebbetzin walked at a smart pace, her feet beating time against the slickened pavements. She passed the mysterious Christian centre on the corner after the station. Today there were no Africans crowding its doors, dressed in their Sunday best, the women looking regal in patterned head wraps and matching dresses. The building was large, square and grey, and had once belonged to the BBC. It looked nothing like a religious building and still smacked of a public institution with its glass barred swing doors and notice boards. She had often wondered what it would be like to attend a service there. She would have liked to hear the singing. The centre behind her, her mind wandered back to the past. They had been so happy once.

The changes began shortly after they had left Israel when the children were still young, and had continued ever since. Most of them the Rebbetzin had accommodated willingly. She had little choice – Golders Green was not Nachla'ot.

Chaim had had to knuckle down, study and work hard to become an accepted rabbi. He had to forego the knitted white skullcap and loose, light-coloured clothes he had favoured in Jerusalem. Here, the congregation did not dance and sing feverishly to welcome in Shabbes and, consequently, proceedings tended to be much more staid.

Everything slowly became more rigid and conservative, including her husband. He threw out all their old pop records, replacing Elvis Costello and The Jam with the sound of famous cantors singing psalms and liturgy.

She took to wearing dark, wintry, neutral shades that made her feel old and frumpy. Her brilliant headscarves in a myriad of hues and textures were exchanged for mop-like sheitels. She put away her bangles, heavy ethnic silver jewellery and her rings encrusted with lumps of turquoise and malachite and wore only her wedding ring. On the outside, she became the model rabbi's wife, a paragon of virtue, modesty and kindness. She visited the sick, she attended Rosh Chodesh meetings, she prayed and baked and cleaned and welcomed and brought up her children in the approved Yiddisher way. She smiled even though her cheeks ached from the effort.

She missed Jerusalem but knew she could never go back. This busy new life left her with little time to think. She did not want to think. It was better to muddle on, to be grateful for the daily routine, for the endless round of holy days and festivals that marked the passage of time. To watch her children grow and become part of a warm, secure, if at times stifling community. The Rebbetzin was lulled into a vague contentment.

Chaim became increasingly pious and formal in his outlook and for the majority of the time, she conceded to follow him, as the supportive spouse. They had little choice. The more they fitted in, the more successful Chaim became. The audiences increased at the lessons he gave. More people attended his services at the local shul. He was no longer just the junior rabbi; he was the next in line. Rabbi Rubowski could not go on forever.

One day, Chaim arrived home to find a shiny green bicycle in the hall. It was a lady's bicycle and had a large wicker basket attached to the handlebars. He tried the bell and it gave off a pert trill.

The Rebbetzin appeared, wiping her hands on her apron. The children were eating an early supper in the kitchen. She watched her husband. He tried the brakes and felt the tyres.

'So, what do you think? I bought it today.'

'Where did you get it?'

'There's a small bike shop in Hampstead.'

'Must have been expensive, no?'

'It's second-hand.'

'Looks new.' He rang the bell again, wheeling the bicycle forward to hear the whirr of the spokes.

'So, where do you intend to ride your new steed?'

She paused warily, alerted by his sarcasm. 'I thought I would ride it around here when I visit anyone sick or elderly. I can bring them a thermos flask of hot soup, or freshly baked chollah in the basket – see it's really useful, plenty of space for my shopping too. It would help me get around quicker. And it would keep me fit.'

Chaim let out a long, tired sigh. Then he faced his wife.

'Rivka, it's a lovely bike and I wish you could ride it, but you know you can't. It's just not appropriate, and by appropriate, I mean modest, for a grown woman, a rabbi's wife no less, to be seen on a bike, pedalling around town.'

The Rebbetzin gritted her teeth, forcing herself to whisper so the children would not hear. 'Chaim, I am going to ride that bike. Whether or not it's appropriate. I am sorry but the community can think what it likes.'

He gazed at her. 'What about what I think? I'm your husband and I don't like the idea of you being seen riding a bike. It's just not right.'

She glared at him. The urge to shout was almost irrepressible, but it would get her nowhere. 'So you are commanding me not to ride it?'

'I am asking you politely and calmly. Please don't.'

'I see . . . so now we live by your rules alone.'

'No, you know that's not true – you rule in the house. HaShem rules over us all.'

'Well I don't think HaShem would take offence at a woman riding a bike.'

'No, but Rabbi Rubowski might . . . and he's due to retire after the Yom Tovim. Listen, ride it on the Heath on a Sunday, no one will see you. We can drive it over in the back of the Volvo. I'll stay with the kids. They can play on the swings.'

Rivka leant against the wall and eyed her husband. His beard was longer and more tangled than ever. There were dark shadows under his eyes. His briefcase was battered and his shoes were scuffed. His tiredness hung over him like a grey cloud.

Still, she was not going to give in. She loved her new bicycle and the freedom it would give her was too tantalizing to forsake without a fight.

'I see. So if I give up this bike, then you should give up watching football on the telly.'

The television was their little secret. Locked away in a heavy pine cupboard in their bedroom, even the children had been warned never to mention it to their friends at school. Chaim and the boys would pile onto their bed to watch football in the evenings if a big match was on.

Chaim's face fell. He loved football. And Rivka loved Eastenders, her guilty pleasure. Yet she was banking on her husband giving in.

'It's not the same. Nobody knows about the telly. It's hidden away in our house, we don't watch over Shabbes, and we don't watch anything inappropriate.'

'Ah, but we all know what Rabbi Rubowksi thinks of television, don't we? It's a vindow of feeelth, it's Sodom and Gomorrah in the home!' She mimicked the rabbi's rant.

Chaim gave her a wry smile. 'Rivka, please, I am begging you now. Don't ride that bike around here. Please, for my sake. For our sake.'

Her husband gazed at her with sad, serious eyes. She could not hurt him by disobeying him. He was changing. They both were. In Nachla'ot he would not have cared if she had ridden a donkey around town.

She stared at the bike; her hand lingered over the narrow leather seat. She pulled away.

'Ok. You win. I'll take the bike back in the morning.'

He clutched her arm. 'Thank you. I'm sorry. But this means a lot to me.'

The next day, she could not bring herself to return the bike. Instead, it remained leaning against the wall, gathering dust. She told herself she would ride it on a Sunday on the Heath. But the Sunday passed by, as did the one after, and the one after that; filled with duties and visits, simchas and prayers.

Eventually, she no longer noticed the bicycle. It had become part of the furniture. Until today. Now she remembered what she had given up and what she had become.

★   ★   ★

The Rebbetzin walked on, brooding. Opposite the station, the shops had changed hands rapidly over the passing years. Several brightly lit sushi restaurants, cafes and a small supermarket had sprung up, serving the needs of the growing Japanese community. She glanced curiously inside the child-like, pastel interior of the café. Everything looked very clean and white – almost like the interior of a spaceship. A television flickered high on the wall.

Several months after the bicycle incident, the Rebbetzin had gone upstairs to watch Eastenders. She groped for the key, her hand disturbing the dust at the top of the cabinet. It was not there. Perhaps it had fallen down the back. The cabinet was too heavy to shift.

She marched out of their bedroom, annoyed that she had already missed the first five minutes.

'Chaim!'

There was no answer. She leaned over the banister.

'Chaim!' she called louder. His beard and spectacles appeared. He was dressed in an apron, his sleeves rolled up. In his left hand, he brandished a cooking spatula.

'Yes?'

'Can you come upstairs for a minute?'

'I'm in the middle of frying latkes with the kids – can't it wait?'

'Where's the key to the TV cabinet?'

'I threw it away.'

'What? Since when?'

243

'Since yesterday.'

They eyeballed each other. Chaim dropped his gaze first, rubbing his aching neck. The Rebbetzin stormed down the stairs and stood opposite him, hands on her hips.

'You threw away the key without consulting me first? Why?' she hissed.

Chaim looked rueful. He scratched his head, tugged on his beard and waved the spatula about. 'I'm the main rabbi now at shul. I can't tell other people not to watch TV if we have one at home, can I? How much of a hypocrite can I carry on being?'

'What about us – your kids? Me? What about our enjoyment? No one would ever have found out! We've always kept shtum, the kids know not to talk.'

Her voice was a furious whisper.

'I know, I know. But next year, Michal will be eleven and we want her to go to Queen Esther, right?'

'Nu? They don't need to know!'

'Come on, we have to sign that agreement when we fill in the application forms saying that we don't have a TV in the house. I'm a rabbi. I can't lie! We have to get rid of it. I'll get Tzaki to come round with his van tomorrow.'

'So, we do what everyone else does – we move the telly into the garden shed whilst we sign the form and move it back into the house when she gets accepted! Technically, that way we are not lying, because it won't be in the house when we sign!'

Chaim pushed his spectacles higher up his nose. He sighed.

'No, I can't do that. I can't lie like that. I am sorry. The TV has to go. It's just not appropriate any more in this house.'

'Fine! You can tell the kids then. Let it be on your head when you tell the boys they can't watch football any more.'

She wheeled round and stomped upstairs.

'I'll miss the footie as much as they will,' Chaim called up after her.

The door to their bedroom slammed with such force that the framed photo of the Lubavitch Rebbe slipped. The Rebbe gave him a lopsided smile, his raised finger now pointing in the direction of their bedroom, rather than at the heavens. Chaim gave him a nod, righted the picture and plodded back to the kitchen.

Over the next couple of weeks, the Rebbetzin retaliated by visiting the station café which had a small television perched on a shelf in one corner. She would drop in during the early afternoons before the children came home from school, nestling in with a steaming cup of tea, as far away from the window as possible.

Whatever was on she watched; it was the act itself that mattered. She imbibed a daily menu of news, second rate soaps, the flogging of suspect antiques in various market towns, or the dullest of them all, darts competitions.

This small rebellion gave her a sense of vindication. The owner of the café began to reserve her seat for her. Soon she was on nodding terms with the other locals, the genteel elderly lady nibbling at her Danish pastry, the school kids bunking afternoon lessons to share a sneaky cigarette over a plate of chips, and the bus drivers who would sit and mutter in a male coven of their own at the back of the café.

Her clothes stank of bacon grease and chip fat but she persisted in her transgression, enjoying every minute. Until Mrs Gottleib, her busybody neighbour from across the street spotted her through the window and marched in to greet her.

The Rebbetzin had been glued to the screen, anxiously awaiting the outcome of a game show when a large, familiar, female shape obscured her view.

'Ahh, my dear Rebbetzin Zilberman, what a surprise to stumble across you here, in this' – Mrs Gottleib took an unsavoury sniff and waved her hand dismissively at the café and its inhabitants – 'unusual, little place.'

The Rebbetzin remained seated, desperately trying to see past Mrs Gottleib's voluminous sheitel. But Mrs Gottleib would not budge. Her stout legs seemed to have taken root amongst the sticky tiles of the café's floor.

'Oh, I just come here to relax a little, find a

moment to myself – I find it so helpful when one needs to recharge, Mrs Gottleib.'

'Really, Rebbetzin Zilberman, I find I can do that at home perfectly well. A ten-minute nap on the couch is all I need – that is if I get the chance. It's a rare thing these days! But I see you are otherwise engaged here, my dear Rebbetzin. I don't wish to disturb you.'

Mrs Gottleib had not turned once to look at the screen. Instead her shoulders braced themselves against the evil transmission bouncing onto her broad back.

The Rebbetzin laughed weakly. 'Not at all, Mrs Gottleib, not at all. How is Mr Gottleib? And your children?'

'Baruch HaShem, thank you, everyone's fine. Well, I must be going, I haven't got time to waste, my Kallah is coming for dinner with her newborn, my sixth grandchild. One must count one's blessings, Rebbetzin!'

'Baruch HaShem, Mrs Gottleib! Do pass on my best wishes!'

Mrs Gottleib gave her a fiendish, self-satisfied smile and ambled out. The café door shuddered as she let it slam behind her. She gave the Rebbetzin a little wave as she passed the window and was gone.

The Rebbetzin sighed. Her tea had gone cold. She had missed the final score. The screen flickered and spoke to her but she could not focus. She was for it now. Mrs Gottleib was the most reliable form of communication the community had. Her secret would reach Chaim before supper-time, she was sure of it.

She had been in the midst of scraping the remains of supper into the pedal bin, when Chaim approached her. Michal stood next to her, loading the dishwasher whilst Avromi chased Moishe around the table with a damp dishcloth.

'Rivka, can I have a word next door please?'

She played for time. 'Can't it wait? I'm clearing up!'

'Now, please.' His voice was insistent and stern. She dropped the dirty cutlery into the sink and let the plates slide in with a clatter. She followed her husband into the lounge. He shut the door and turned to face her, his face a grim expression of biblical doom.

'Please sit down.' He indicated the sofa but remained standing.

'No, I'm not one of your Torah pupils, Chaim. Tell me what's going on.' She stood where she was, a tea towel dangling limply from her right hand.

'I had a phone call today from Mrs Gottleib. She said she happened to be walking past the station when she saw you in the café, watching television.'

He stopped to glare at her.

'So? So what? You took the telly away, I'm a grown up, I make my own decisions what I do with the small amount of spare time that I have. Besides, you never said don't watch television. You just removed ours from the house. That doesn't mean I can't watch it elsewhere.'

She knew that it did. She wanted to provoke him, this holy husband of hers. The Rebbetzin watched as his face went through several distortions as he attempted to master his anger.

'You know *full* well you shouldn't be watching TV anywhere! How could you do this to me? To us? Don't you care about our reputation? Your reputation? This is so irresponsible of you, so selfish.'

'SELFISH? I'll give you selfish! You're the selfish one. I've followed you blindly into Yiddishkeit, doing as you asked, forsaking many things that give me pleasure. I'm *sick* of being controlled like this. This was not what I bargained for.'

She spat out the words, not thinking of what she was saying. They welled up from deep inside her and she was borne away by her resentment.

Chaim's face crumpled. His shoulders slumped. 'I thought we had made a pact to go into this life together. Why are you turning against it now? After all these years.'

'I'm not turning against it! It's just not like it was, at the start – in Jerusalem – where everything felt so alive, so meaningful. Here it's all about the surface – we have to be seen to be doing the right thing. I hate it. I feel like Big Brother's watching me all the time. Why can't I enjoy a bit of telly now and then? I'm a grown woman, for God's sake!'

'Rivka!'

'Sorry, Chaim – no, I'm not sorry! I don't believe HaShem would be offended by a bit of Blockbusters, would He? Come on, this is all so trivial! I do what really matters. I am a good person, a good Jew! I do my mitzvot, I daven. I go to the mikveh, to shul – what more do I need to do?'

They heard a creak outside the door. Chaim crept towards it and flung it open. The children hurled themselves up the stairs, falling over each other and giggling.

'Kids! You should be in your rooms, doing your homework already!' he called up after them. He shut the door and turned back to her.

'Great example you're setting our children. Say one thing, but do another. You need to be more careful. Go to another café, if you have to, go to one further away on the Finchley Road.'

'No. I'm sick and tired of all this hiding and pretending. I'm not saying anything or doing anything. I'm just trying to live a little. Why can't we just be ourselves again? Like we were in Jerusalem before – before, everything else . . .'

Chaim sighed. He turned away, his hands in his pockets. 'I know it's been hard for you, but we've made our choice and we have to stick with it.'

'Well that's easy enough for you to say now that, you're the rabbinical flavour of the month.'

He winced. She felt cheap stooping so low, but the bitterness still seethed.

'Well, I am sorry you feel like that. I've always counted on your support and love. I've tried to do my best by you and our children. I am sorry if the life I have provided is not to your liking.'

He turned towards the door and left the room. The Rebbetzin sank into the sofa and rubbed her eyes hard with the heel of her palms. She felt spiteful and petty, but the truth was hard. They had tiptoed around it for so long.

CHAPTER 18

CHANI. BARUCH.

June 2008 – London

Chani hovered by the reception desk feeling foolish. The hotel clerk had offered his assistance in a neutral voice but his eyes had scanned her plain, shapeless outfit in a way that suggested he had come across her ilk before. Her restless manner and nervous glance had given away her purpose. He had left her in peace after that. And she had continued standing by the desk, clutching her handbag, starting at every hiss of the sliding doors.

The hotel foyer hummed with the force of the motorway just beyond the parking lot. Thick glass windows deadened the roar, but she could still feel a gentle vibration through the soles of her shoes. The floor shone reflecting the glare of the halogen spotlights above. She was on an island of gleaming chrome and white Formica, a combination so cold and clinical that she felt like she was in a hospital.

He was late. Chani checked her watch every few seconds. Out of the corner of her eye she saw movement at the bar. A man was standing at the dark wooden counter speaking to the barman. Her heart lurched. She sidled closer and hid behind a giant cheese plant. To her horror, she realised that she knew this man – he had been the dreary widower from her last shidduch. He was twenty years older than her and had rejected her on the premise that she had been too young and flighty, although he had seemed very keen on her youthful appeal before they had met.

A girl sat on a barstool facing a small circular table. She was short and rotund, her fat little legs dangling in mid-air. Her hair was a mass of auburn ringlets. Dinah Kahn, one of Chani's old class-mates. Dinah turned sensing Chani's stare. Chani fled to the ladies. Where was Baruch? She knew she would have to re-emerge but the safety of solitude was a balm. She scrutinised her reflection and decided she was wearing too much lip-gloss. She wiped off the excess with tissue. Then feeling a little naked, she applied a fresh layer. Her eyes seemed brighter than ever but her face appeared flushed so she ran a tissue under the cold tap, and balling it up, used the soggy fibres to blot her skin. She glanced at her watch and panicked. She had to get back to the foyer.

She forced herself to exit the toilets calmly and blinked as her eyes adjusted to the grey light. He was there. A tall, thin young man dressed in a uniform black suit and white shirt leant against the reception desk. He pulled back his cuff to glance at his watch. Chani could not see his face. It was hidden by the brim of his hat.

She moved towards him. Baruch swivelled, alerted by the clip of her modest heels. He tried to smile but his facial muscles had frozen into a rictus grin. Chani approached and stopped at a respectful distance. She glanced up at him and then looked down at the floor. Baruch became horribly aware of his enormous feet. His brogues covered half the floor space between them.

'Hi, I'm Baruch –'

'Hello, are you Baruch?' Their voices collided, Baruch's emerging as a squeaky falsetto. Chani dug her nails into the palm of her hand to suppress the urge to shriek with laughter.

'I'm sorry I'm late – I was just –' he continued.

'Oh no, not at all, it's fine – I was just,' rattled Chani.

'– stuck in traffic –'

'– in the ladies –' She flushed scarlet. Talking about bodily functions was frowned upon and alluding to them on a shidduch was very bad form indeed. She was mortified.

Baruch beamed. 'Oh never mind,' he said, 'We're both here now.'

'Yes, Baruch HaShem –' said Chani hurriedly.

They stared at one another for a few seconds. With a rush of relief, Baruch recognised her as the girl from the wedding. He had agonised over what he would have done had it been the wrong girl. His fears allayed; he studied her as closely as manners would allow. He wanted to stare at places other than her face but disciplined himself. Her shape was hidden under layers of loose fabric. She was very pretty. Baruch admired Chani's translucent skin and full, pink mouth. But what was that stuck to her left cheek? It looked like a shred of tissue.

Very tall, thought Chani. Perhaps a little too tall. It was like standing under the shade of a thin, shaggy palm tree. She eyed the trio of pimples that clung to his jaw-line like limpets on a mossy rock. Perhaps if he grew his beard it may provide camouflage.

She smiled up at him, her neck cricked at an unnatural angle, revealing the small gap between her front teeth. The defect disconcerted Baruch, for he had dreamt of her as perfect, blemish-free, aware that his own imperfections were alarmingly obvious. She was real after all. He decided that her wonky teeth were charming.

'Shall we go and sit down?' he suggested.

Chani nodded, suddenly mute. Her back prickled with the awareness that their entrance had been noted. Turning, she bestowed a regal nod upon Dinah and her date and with her head held high she pattered after Baruch, delighting in the fact that the other couple had looked glummer than a plateful of cold Shabbes leftovers.

By the end of the date Baruch knew he wanted to see her again. There was a delightful pertness, a brightness about her that hovered behind her quiet smile. There were moments when it broke free and he saw a flash of mischief in her eyes before it vanished, hidden behind a veil of modesty. They covered all the usual topics: family, levels of observance, yeshiva, school and even their closest friendships. The conversation pattered back and forth, hesitant at first but with time the awkwardness eased. He sensed that Chani was holding herself back for there were instances when she had been about to elaborate but had let the subject drop.

He wanted to know everything about her. Riding home in a cab he stared unseeing at the flickering neon lights and the billboards that seemed to promise the world. Lulled by the drone of the North Circular he examined every nuance, every thread in order to glean another morsel. He tried to decipher every look and smile. Did she like him? She had given nothing away at their leave-taking. He agonised over whether he should have asked her out again then and there but that was not the form. But she had agreed to him calling her. That was indeed something.

Before he knew it the cab had deposited him outside his house. Light streamed onto the grav-elled drive as he crunched up to the front door. He had forgotten about the security lights. His parents would be alerted to his return now. He would have to face them. He let himself in.

'Baruch, is that you?' called his mother from the lounge.

'Yes, Mum.'

'Nu, how was it?'

He entered the lounge to find them seated closely on the sofa, gazing at him apprehensively.

'It was great,' he beamed. Better leave it at that.

His parents exchanged a look. His mother had started to twitch. His father placed a steadying hand on her arm, which she swiftly removed. She began to vibrate.

'So does that mean that you will see her again?' she enquired.

'If she wants to see me, yes, I'd like to.' Baruch shifted from foot to foot. He had braced himself for the usual barrage but he wasn't ready to have his memory of the evening intruded upon or spoilt.

His father grunted. 'What's she like then? Is she a nice girl?'

His mother eyed him like a hawk. He let his features fall into a bland, neutral expression.

'Yes, she is a very nice girl. Very nice indeed.' That was all they were getting. He turned towards the door. 'Night then.'

'But are you going to –' spluttered his mother behind him.

'Enough, Berenice, let him go to bed. The boy needs his rest. Tomorrow we'll talk. Yes, Baruch?'

'Yes Dad.' The lie slid out easily. He had no intention of discussing Chani in detail with them. She was his, or at least his choice and he had no desire to contaminate his impression of her.

Shutting the door quietly behind him, hearing

the uneasy mutter of their voices, he sprang up the stairs and finding himself in the welcome privacy of his room, flung himself onto the bed where he laid hands behind his head, grinning up at the ceiling.

Chani was not so sure. Baruch appeared perfectly pleasant, courteous and keen. But was she attracted to him? The pimples and the nerdy glasses still bothered her, as did the alarming difference in height. In his favour, he had pulled out her chair for her, listened intently and smiled warmly at her feeble jokes. It had become easier and easier to talk. She had felt comfortable with him. If only he were better looking.

She entered the kitchen where her parents were seated. The remains of dinner lay strewn across the plastic tablecloth. Her father was craned over a book and did not notice her come in. Her mother had Yona in her lap and was flicking through a recipe book. Yona blinked sleepily at her.

'How was it?' her mother asked.

'Um, it was good. I think. I'm not sure.'

'Not sure? Yankel, Chani went on a shidduch and she's not sure.' Her mother elbowed her father in the ribs. He lifted his head from his book and stared mistily at her.

'Oh yes, any luck? Nice boy? Do we know him?'

'The shadchan knows the family,' replied Mrs Kaufman.

'Good, good, the unstoppable Mrs Gelbmann,

258

eh? What would we do without her?' Having made the right noises he turned back to his book.

'Why aren't you sure, Chani-leh? Does he like you?'

'I think so. He asked if he could ring me.' It *was* a little thrilling to have a boy chasing her.

'So give the poor boy a chance. Is he a mensch?'

'How can I tell, Mum? I've only known him for five minutes.'

'I knew your father was a mensch the minute I laid eyes on him.'

Rabbi Kaufman leant closer towards his book. His nose was almost touching the page. She knew he was pretending not to hear to avoid being dragged into the conversation.

'Yankel!' Mrs Kaufman employed her elbow again.

Her husband looked up dazedly.

'Yankel, she's not sure, your daughter. Tell her something.'

'About what?'

'The boy she has just met! Oy Yankel! Why don't you listen a little? Your daughter has been on a shidduch and the boy wants to call her but she isn't sure.' Yona squirmed in her mother's lap so she let her down. She pattered towards Chani, hauling on her skirt to be picked up.

Her father stroked his beard thoughtfully.

'Mum, leave Dad alone.'

'What is it you're not sure about?' he asked.

'What he looks like. He's very tall; much taller than me. I feel silly next to him and . . .'

She felt embarrassed to go on.

'Nu?' cried Mrs Kaufman.

'He has spots.'

'Spots! What are a few spots in a husband? You silly girl!' Her mother's jowls quivered with indignation.

'Mum! It was my shidduch and it's my decision!' snapped Chani.

'Leah-leh, if she's not sure, she's not sure. She's right. Let her decide for herself.'

'But she's nineteen already,' whined Mrs Kaufman.

'Mum, please don't – not tonight –'

'What is nineteen? A number that's all. Let her live a little,' advised Rabbi Kaufman.

'And so she will be on my head all my life. Unmarried. Has Veh Sholem! Now let me tell you something, Chani-leh. You are going to give this boy a chance.'

Chani rolled her eyes.

'He likes you. And he's an Or Yerushaliyim student. So don't look a gift pony –'

'Horse,' corrected her father.

'– in the mouth,' finished her mother, giving him a grateful nod.

'Ok, ok, I will think about it. Now if you don't mind, I'll go to bed.'

Chani turned to escape when her father murmured, 'Or Yerushaliyim, did you say?'

'Yes, Dad, he's got a place there starting next year.'

'Most impressive,' her father ruminated. 'The place did not exist when I went to Jerusalem to study but I would have loved the chance to study there. He must be very talented, your young man.'

'He's not my young man!'

Rabbi Kaufman grinned. 'Give him a chance, Chani. These young men have not been so kind to you, remember.'

'You should listen to your father!' sang Mrs Kaufman.

Chani sighed. She was too tired to react. 'I know, Dad. Night, everyone.'

Detaching herself from Yona, she dragged herself up the stairs wondering whether Baruch's skin would improve with time. Admonishing herself for being so superficial, she determined to give him another chance if he called her.

In truth, he would have been happier to carry on simply getting to know her. He knew that he could not date her ad infinitum. He had to make a decision or she would feel slighted. Three dates, possibly four, was the limit. Some couples got engaged after merely two – a terrifying concept but perfectly acceptable in the community's eyes.

It did not bother him that she had not attended sem. She had given her reasons and he had accepted them; he had not probed, not wishing to appear impolite. She was very bright and he sensed that she was hiding her light under a bushel. On no occasion had he sensed an intellectual gap between them, but there were moments when he had caught her looking at him strangely. He had even gone so far as to ask her if anything was wrong and she had hurriedly looked down, brushing aside his enquiry. He sensed that she was assessing him and he had squirmed under her scrutiny, feeling horribly self-conscious about his physical flaws. Silently he had pleaded with HaShem to make Chani like him even if he liked her more. He sought comfort in the fact that she had agreed to go on three dates with him.

There was only one way to find out. First he needed to inform his parents of his intentions, a task he was dreading. However there was no law that prohibited him marrying Chani. If she accepted and the rabbis agreed, nothing could deter them from entering wedlock. Not even his parents. However much he loved and revered them, he was prepared to sacrifice their desires to his own. He was confident that they would come round to Chani once they had met her.

After his third date with Chani he decided to bite the bullet. His sisters were at school rehearsing for the school play and his mother was serving up dinner. The latest appliances whirred and the black granite worktop sparkled in the glare of the halogen lights. Sleek white drawers sprang open to her touch and the microwave resembled a spacecraft. His mother's heels echoed on the marble. He waited for the crashing of kitchenware to abate, for his mother to take her seat and for his father to recite the appropriate blessings.

His father whizzed through the sanctifications with his usual aplomb, his mouth barely moving through the fuzz of beard.

'Amen,' sang out his mother.

'Amen,' whispered Baruch. Come on HaShem. I really need Your help now.

'Let's eat,' said Mr Levy, heaping steaming potatoes onto his plate.

Baruch stared at the greasy slab of schnitzel, his stomach recoiling in horror but to please his mother he took a bite. He could not swallow. So he chewed. And chewed a bit more.

'Everything ok, Baruch?' queried Mrs Levy, sawing at her chicken. 'There's plenty more in the pan. Have a pickle.' She thrust her chin at the jar on the table.

'Not just now, thanks. It's delicious, mum. Excuse me a moment.' And he left the table.

His parents exchanged looks. Mr Levy shrugged and shovelled another forkful into his already stuffed mouth. Mrs Levy patted hers with her napkin and abruptly stood up. She crept along the room towards the open door.

'What are you doing now, Berenice? Can't you just sit down and let us enjoy our dinner in peace for once? You're always jumping up disturbing things,' grumbled Mr Levy.

'I'm checking on him,' hissed Mrs Levy as she

continued to sidle out of the room towards the small lavatory under the stairs. She hung onto the kitchen door to prevent it slamming and put her ear up against the toilet door.

Hearing the rumble of the flush, she fled back in.

Baruch emerged seconds later, wiping his mouth guiltily with the back of his hand. The toilet had whisked away his mouthful of schnitzel and he felt better.

He took his seat and gripped his knife and fork. He stared at his parents. His father was too engrossed to notice. His mother's fork was suspended in mid-air. She waited for him to speak.

'I have something to tell you,' he began.

Mrs Levy kicked Mr Levy hard under the table. He looked up from his plate, jaws working furiously. He was a noisy eater.

'Yes, Baruch darling, do go on. We're all ears,' chirped Mrs Levy. Inside, her heart sank. She knew what was coming and like a runaway freight train, it was beyond her power to stop it.

For the past few weeks it had not escaped her attention that her son had drifted about the house like a lovesick cloud and she regretted acquiescing to the shidduch. She only had herself to blame. Her husband had been of little support in the interregnum, refusing to discuss the matter further until Baruch publicised the outcome. So Mrs Levy had tried to ignore her son's moody silences, his sudden bouts of giddiness, telling herself it would pass, that things would fall through.

She had restrained her natural tendency to pry, for fear of unleashing the unpalatable truth and had wrestled with her inner self in a bid to accept her son's preferences for his sake. But soul-searching had never been her forte. She thought of the sniggers that would occur behind her back, the delicious schadenfreude of her enemies. She simply could not accept the girl. Finally she had prayed – in vain as it appeared in hindsight, for now her worst nightmare was coming true.

Baruch cleared his throat. The cutlery was beginning to slide in his grasp.

'I want to marry Chani.'

His father stopped chewing. His mother mewled.

'But darling, don't you think –'

'Not now, Berenice! He hasn't finished!'

Baruch nodded his gratitude. 'I like her. I was planning to ask her on the next shidduch.'

'And you're quite sure she'll have you?' said Mr Levy.

'Yes, darling – how do you know she wants you?' squeaked Mrs Levy as her world began to tilt.

'Quiet, Berenice!'

'Dovid! He's my son too.'

'I think, I think she'll say yes. I get the feeling she was hoping that I'd ask already –'

'Do her parents know? Have you met them?'

'No, of course I haven't.'

'*We* have to meet her first. And them.' interjected his mother, scrabbling for time. 'And only then will we see if she's truly suitable.'

'She is, Mum. I promise you. You'll like her. She's pretty and clever and funny and . . .'

'Frum? Modest? The right sort of girl for a boy like you?' asked Mr Levy.

'Yes Dad. I really feel she is.'

His mother looked as if she was about to cry. His father patted her cheek.

'It could be worse, Berenice . . .'

'I know. I had such hopes. Libby Zuckerman –' she snivelled into her napkin.

'I don't want to marry Libby blooming Zuckerman!' said Baruch through gritted teeth.

'Baruch.' Mr Levy thumped the table with his fist, making the plates bounce. Several peas rolled overboard into Mrs Levy's lap.

'I'm sorry, I'm sorry – I want to marry Chani and that's it. This is my choice. I have to live with my wife-to-be for the rest of my life, not you.'

His mother snorted.

'We have to live with the consequences and all the ties that she comes with,' intoned Mr Levy. 'But Baruch, we respect your decision and as long as her family agrees and we get on reasonably well with them, so be it.'

'On your head be it!' quivered his mother.

'Berenice, let's meet them and the girl first and reserve our judgment until then. If this is what our son really wants, then who are we to stand in his way?'

Baruch offered up a silent prayer for providing him with a father who was capable of being reasonable. His mother remained in an altogether different category.

'Thank you, Dad,' he whispered.

'And if the rabbonim agree –' continued Mr Levy.

'The rabbonim! What about his mother?' shrieked Mrs Levy.

'Please Mum, this is really important to me.' Baruch put an arm around her.

Mrs Levy sniffed. 'Ok then darling, we'll meet her and her parents if that's what you really want. Whoever said being a mother was easy?' But already in her head the cogs had begun to whir.

'Thank you so much, Mum. This means everything.'

'I hope you're right there,' mumbled Mr Levy. 'Pass the vegetables please, Berenice.'

CHAPTER 19

AVROMI

April 2008 – London

Avromi woke disorientated. His mouth was parched and his head reverberated with each heartbeat. He was also stark naked, which was an unusual sensation for someone who always slept in pyjamas. Nor was he alone. The sound of gentle snoring reached his ears. His right leg was crushed by something warm and heavy. Cracking open an eye, he shifted, rolling away from the burden. Shola stirred and turned towards the wall.

The room was bathed in a dim red glow, as the morning shone through Shola's maroon curtains. Avromi sat bolt upright. What had he done? He must leave immediately. But how could he face his parents? He must daven. Repent. Pray for forgiveness. Perhaps a dip in the men's mikveh would absolve him of this abomination? He felt frightened at the suddenness of it all.

The act came back to him in flashes. The shedding of clothes, the grabbing and holding, the overwhelming need to be as close as possible. Then he remembered the slippery heat of her body and how he had shuddered and sighed. And how it had been over, so quickly, too quickly. How she had smiled up at him and he had felt such delight in her, in this strange, violent new unity. He had not wanted it to end. They had fallen asleep in a tangle of limbs.

She was not his wife. She was not even Jewish. Which in a strange way was something for which to be grateful. Had she been Jewish, he would have had to marry her.

He could not locate his underpants, but found his trousers and stumbled into them, forcing both legs through one hole. Shirt on, he shoved bare feet into his shoes and, picking his way through Shola's strewn clothes, made for the door.

'Avromi?'

Shola's sleepy voice halted him in his tracks. She was watching him from under her duvet.

'Where do you think you're slinking off to?'

'I've got to go home.' He could not meet her eye.

'Right. So you weren't even going to say goodbye?'

'I was going to ring you.' He felt full of self-loathing at using such a pathetic excuse. Shola was cocooned in her duvet, her hair standing on end as if she had been electrocuted. She looked small and lost against the sea of white.

He sat down on the edge of her bed. They were silent for a long while.

'It's all right, go home, Avromi. We made a

mistake. Don't blame yourself. Blame the drink. We can just try to forget about it.' Her voice shook a little.

Avromi reached for her hand. She was the last person he wanted to hurt.

'You know I've never done this before? Do you understand how big a deal this is for me?'

She nodded.

'Do you understand that the only girl I am supposed to touch, let alone sleep with, is my wife, once we are married?'

'I know.'

'Shola, I'm really confused. And scared. I know what I've done – what we've done – is a sin in the eyes of my religion. But I like you. A lot. Not just physically, but as a person, a friend.'

She squeezed his hand but did not dare look at him.

'And if I am really being honest, I've wanted to be with you like last night, for a long time.'

Shola's smile broadened. 'That's nice, but I hope you're not proposing?'

He laughed. 'No, I can't marry you. You're not Jewish.'

'Avromi, I was joking.'

'Oh.'

'You're blushing. You've gone so red, you match my curtains!' Shola was giggling.

'Argghhh! I am such an idiot!' He fell sideways, onto the bed, hiding his face with his hands.

'Yup. But it takes two to tango.'

'I guess so. So you seduced me?'

'You kissed me first!'

He thought back to the early hours of the morning. 'I did, didn't I? Wow, no longer a virgin and an experienced drunk. All in one night.' He fell silent. 'Did we, um, use anything?'

'I'm on the Pill. For my periods – it helps them to be less painful.'

'The Pill?'

'Oh God, Avromi! Don't tell me you've never heard of it!'

'I've heard of condoms.'

'Bravo! Well, the Pill stops a woman from ovulating, so she can't get pregnant. It is a tiny tablet I have to take every day, full of hormones that interrupt my normal reproductive process. So I don't produce an egg each month. That means if I have sex, there is nothing there to fertilise.'

'An egg?'

'Yes, an egg.'

He stared at her.

'Avromi!' Shola grabbed a pillow and hit him around the head. 'Don't tell me you weren't taught the facts of life at school?'

He looked sheepish. 'Well, not really. It gets glossed over at the type of schools we go to.'

Shola flopped backwards and stared at the ceiling. He sat up to gaze down at her face.

'But I enjoyed learning about them last night.'

'Oh, did you now? I'm surprised you can remember.'

'That's because you're such an inspiring teacher.' He swooped in and gave her lips a tentative peck.

Shola eyed him warily. 'Is that all I am to you, then?'

'No, you know you're not. I think about you all the time.' He stroked her cheek, tucking a stray curl behind her ear. 'But in my community, guys like me are not supposed to have girlfriends. It's nothing until marriage.'

'So, what are we going to do?' Shola asked.

'I don't know.'

'Neither do I. Anyway, you'd better go. Your parents.'

'Yes.'

They kissed again and he felt himself melting once more. Shola pulled away.

'Avromi, go home. Now. I don't want you to get into any more trouble.'

'Ok. Can I call you later?

'Of course you can. I'd like that very much.'

CHAPTER 20

BARUCH. CHANI.

June 2008 – London

Mrs Levy had a plan. The next day she swallowed her pride and rang Mrs Gelbmann.

'Mrs Gelbmann, it's Mrs Levy here. I was wondering if you could help me . . .'

'Ah Mrs Levy, how nice to hear from you. How are you? And moreover how can I be of assistance?' purred the matchmaker. She had known the bird would return and had been patiently biding her time waiting for the call.

Mrs Levy clutched at the phone wire as if it were an umbilical cord.

'Baruch HaShem. I have a problem. They've had three dates as you may well know and now Baruch wants to marry Chani and I'm not happy about it at all. You know the reasons why.'

Mrs Gelbmann settled herself more comfortably into her armchair. A smile wreathed her waxy features. This would need careful handling but it was well within her capability. She prepared to flex her persuasive muscles.

'I see, Mrs Levy. I understand you. But what would you like me to do?'

Mrs Levy could hear the shadchan smiling down the phone. She paused.

'I want you to dissuade Chani. I want you to put her off my son. Tell her mother he's not interested any more if you have to.'

Ah how the mighty have fallen, mused Mrs Gelbmann.

'But Mrs Levy, you know I can't do that. They like each other, so that means HaShem has given his approval to the match. I can't interfere with fate . . . only HaShem can.'

Mrs Levy bit her lip.

'I'll pay you,' she hissed. Shame spread through her like the heat given off by strong liquor.

Mrs Gelbmann worked hard to disguise her delight. A chuckle of glee morphed into a cough.

'Do excuse me . . . now Mrs Levy, I understand your predicament but you know very well that I do not accept bribes. I have my excellent reputation to think of –'

'A thousand pounds up front. That's what I'm offering. Take it or leave it.' She was filled with a desperate urge to be excused but hung on grimly.

Mrs Gelbmann hesitated. She thought of the expensive hotel in which she would luxuriate the next time she visited her daughter in New York.

Yet if they got married she would earn more, albeit in instalments. Not a lot more but enough. She would sit it out.

'Mrs Levy, I cannot accept. I am terribly sorry.'

Mrs Levy slumped. The fight had gone out of her. 'I see, Mrs Gelbmann,' she sighed.

Now was time for the shadchan to show a little compassion. 'Mrs Levy, you are not the first mother to come to me and ask me to try and interfere with the course of events. Usually it all turns out for the best. Perhaps you should just meet the girl first?'

'Perhaps,' said Mrs Levy. 'Please do not let this conversation go any further,' she added hastily.

'You can have complete confidence,' crooned Mrs Gelbmann.

'Thank you, Mrs Gelbmann. If my husband were to find out –'

'No need to worry. He won't.'

'Ok then.'

'All right, Mrs Levy.'

'Goodbye for now.'

'Goodbye, Mrs Levy.'

Utterly dispirited, Mrs Levy curled up on her cream leather sofa and wept softly into its cracks.

Mrs Gelbmann jumped nimbly out of her arm-chair and reached into her secret drawer. The box of Belgian truffles awaited. After all, she deserved a little reward. Then she relented and opened her prayer book. First she would thank HaShem for showing her His Favour.

Mrs Levy slept a little. When she woke she felt calmer. Vigour restored, she racked her brains for another way to thwart her son's impending engagement. Try as she might she could see no other option but to seek celestial guidance. Rebbetzin Zilberman might have a solution. Perhaps Rabbi Zilberman could speak to her husband and then to Baruch? Obviously if the rabbi agreed with her about Chani's unsuitability, Mr Levy would return to his initial opinion of the match. With God on her side, she felt adamant that they could coax Baruch out of it. The rabbi and his wife were her last resort.

She dialled the Zilbermans' number.

'Ah, Rebbbetzin, it's Mrs Levy here. I wondered if I could come round for a little chat. I need your advice.'

'Of course. With pleasure. Are you free now? It's just the children. My husband will be back later –'

'Yes. I'll come now.'

The Rebbetzin replaced the receiver and wondered what this was all about. She rested her hand on her stomach, rubbed her tightening waistband and smiled softly to herself. Whatever it was, nothing could be as monumental as her own good news. She hugged herself in delight. She would tell Chaim that evening.

The doorbell rang, interrupting her reverie. There stood Mrs Levy resplendent in her copper sheitel. A jacket of the softest chocolate leather hung casually from her shoulders. Around her neck glowed a row of enormous pink pearls.

'Baruch HaShem, Mrs Levy. Do come in,' said the Rebbetzin warmly.

'Thank you so much for seeing me at such short notice,' simpered Mrs Levy.

The Rebbetzin beamed at her. Mrs Levy noted the rosy smoothness of the Rebbetzin's cheeks. Her eyes were clear and bright. She looks remarkably well thought Mrs Levy. But isn't she rather old for that? Quickly she banished any negative thoughts. After all, she needed the Rebbetzin on her side.

'Can I get you a cup of tea?'

'Oh yes please. No milk please but two sugars.'

The Rebbetzin showed her into the living room. Mrs Levy noted the dirty net curtains as she sank into the shabby sofa. She looked around her at the rows of leather-bound books inside the large glass cabinet. There was not a lot else in the room apart from a few sticks of furniture that had clearly seen better days. Yes, this was the place to get proper holy help.

The Rebbetzin reappeared holding two steaming mugs. She clutched a pack of biscuits under her arm.

'Here we are then,' she said placing the tea and biscuits on the little coffee table and taking her place on the sofa next to her guest. 'I always find there's nothing like a good biscuit or two to cheer me up. Or three.' She let out a giggle.

Mrs Levy felt herself relax. She was safe here. Lulled by the sweetness of the Rebbetzin and the informality of her surroundings she warmed to her subject. The Rebbetzin sat and listened keeping her eyes fixed on her guest's face. From time to time her expression wrinkled in sympathy with Mrs Levy's woes.

The Rebbetzin thought back to the time of her own engagement. Chaim's parents had not been overly keen on her either. She had no degree or profession and had no real means of her own. At first they had seen her as another burden to add to the embarrassment of having a son who had suddenly 'turned frum' and wanted to be a rabbi in Jerusalem. They had wanted him to come home. She remembered her first terrifying meeting with them; how much she had wanted them to like and accept her. She looked at Mrs Levy in her expensive clothes and perfect make-up and wondered if the woman had any idea how intimidating she would appear to a young, naïve girl like this Chani Kaufman. Well, she assumed that Chani was naïve. She had not heard of her before, although she was aware of Rabbi Kaufman and the whereabouts of his tiny synagogue.

'And do you see, Baruch just can't marry a girl like that, Rebbetzin,' moaned Mrs Levy. 'So I was wondering if you could speak to your husband and perhaps he could persuade Baruch not to ask her.'

'But Mrs Levy, there's nothing in the Torah to prevent their marriage. It's entirely proper. My husband wouldn't be able to do anything.'

'But he could just speak to my husband, couldn't he? Or even Baruch?' Mrs Levy felt herself clutching at straws.

The Rebbetzin saw the strain beneath the powder and paint. She felt truly sorry for Mrs Levy. She hated to see anyone suffer and she wondered what she would do if Avromi voiced a desire to marry a girl of whom she did not approve. Fortunately nothing of the sort had happened but one never knew.

She would try to offer the only comfort she knew.

'Sometimes HaShem challenges us by making life difficult. We are given a choice to get angry and resentful with Him or we can learn and grow from the problem He has given us. Maybe Mrs Levy, HaShem is trying to tell you something?'

Mrs Levy twitched impatiently. This was not quite the support she had hoped for.

'Yes, but Rebbetzin, I can see that it will all end in tears for the pair of them. Surely HaShem can see that? I'm not thinking about myself here but about Baruch. And Chani of course,' she added hastily.

The Rebbetzin reached for another biscuit in order to hide her amusement.

'Perhaps you could see it as a mitzvah to meet the girl and see the best in her? How do you know she's as unsuitable as you think?'

'Because the whole kehilla knows who we are and for my son to marry a – a –'

'Nobody?' ventured the Rebbetzin.

'Exactly,' squirmed Mrs Levy.

'So who in your eyes would be the perfect girl for Baruch?'

'Libby Zuckerman,' said Mrs Levy without a moment's hesitation.

'Libby's engaged.'

'Since when?' cried Mrs Levy. 'How come nobody told me?'

'It isn't common knowledge but I am telling you because you obviously harbour a hope there. Mrs Zuckerman told me last night. She's going to marry a distant cousin from Manchester.'

How provincial, thought Mrs Levy, her hopes now in tatters. 'So it clearly wasn't meant to be.'

'That's why you should try to embrace Chani if she accepts. Welcome her. Be nice to her. Make a special effort and you might be pleasantly surprised.'

'Oh. Well wouldn't that be rather false on my behalf?'

'Not if you go with an open heart. At least meet the girl and then decide.'

It was clear, thought Mrs Levy, that the Rebbetzin had never suffered from her children's poor taste. She stood up to take her leave.

'Thank you Rebbetzin, you may be right. I will meet her and will try my best to reserve judgment until then. After all, it seems I haven't got much choice, the way things are going.'

'Don't be so pessimistic. You never know . . .'

Mrs Levy knew. Being a resourceful woman, she

had already decided on a new tack. Yes she certainly would meet Chani.

The Rebbetzin lay in bed waiting for her husband to finish saying his prayers. She had already said hers and she lay curled up on her side listening to his familiar muttering. Car beams bounced across the ceiling through the gaps in the curtains.

Finally he pulled her close and kissed the nape of her neck.

'Night, Rivka.'

'I've got something to tell you. I've waited all day.'

'So tell me.'

'Well, it's come as a bit of a shock – a good shock.'

'Tell me – now I'm on spilkes.'

'Ok . . . I'm pregnant.'

She felt him go very still. Then he sat up and stared down at her. She couldn't see his face in the darkness of the room.

'Are you sure? When did you find out?' he whispered.

'Today. I was two weeks late so I did a test.'

'That's amazing . . . after Moishe we were so sure we couldn't and now . . .'

'I know.'

He sank back and wriggled his hand under her nightdress to rest it on her belly. The silence was filled with wonder as he smiled into the darkness, their differences and lingering resentments forgotten in the elation of the moment.

'If it's a boy, let's call him . . .'

'Shh. Let's wait and see if we get that far.'

'B'srat HaShem.'

She squeezed his hand. After a while she felt his heartbeat slow and his breath lengthen. She had forgotten to tell him about Mrs Levy's visit. All that seemed irrelevant now. Moving gently across the bed, she arranged her limbs more comfortably and stared at the ceiling thinking about the life that had begun inside her.

Her mind drifted back to Mrs Levy's conundrum. She thought about the girl and felt sorry for her. She wondered what she was like and whether she would ever get to meet her. It seemed highly unlikely. The Mrs Levys of this world usually got their way. Poor Baruch, he must be feeling very resentful. The Rebbetzin hoped she would never cause Avromi similar pain. Her mind circled sleepily and soon she nodded off.

CHAPTER 21

CHANI

July 2008 – London

Chani plodded along, the fierce afternoon sun beating down. It had been a long, monotonous day in the classroom, cleaning paintbrushes and tables. She lingered in the shadows and thought about Baruch. He had called her to arrange another date and it was just a few days since they had last met. This could only mean one thing. She liked him but did she really want him? The answer continued to elude her. She wished she had more time but the pressure was mounting and she sensed a decision was imminent. Her life seemed to condense. This past month had been the most significant ever and if she made a false move, all would be lost. She had never been on three consecutive dates before.

A large black car was parked at the kerb outside her house. Suddenly the door swung open and an elegant stockinged foot encased in a beige patent stiletto reached for the pavement. A glossy copper sheitel emerged as its owner slid gracefully out of the car and blocked Chani's path. The woman wore huge sunglasses, which she lifted a fraction to peer under.

'Chani?' said the woman.

'Yes?'

'I am Mrs Levy, Baruch's mother.'

Startled, Chani dropped her bag and its contents scattered over the pavement. She fell to her knees and made a grab for her possessions. Mrs Levy looked coolly on.

Perhaps this was just a bad dream. She blinked, but no, Mrs Levy was all too solid.

Mustering the last remnants of her dignity, Chani straightened up and forced her lips into a smile. She looked Mrs Levy in the eye.

'How nice to meet you, Mrs Levy. This is rather a surprise.'

'As I knew it would be, Chani. But I think it's high time we met, don't you?'

Chani was not entirely convinced but managed to conceal her misgivings through some eager nodding.

'Would you like to come in, Mrs Levy? I'm sure my mother would be very pleased to meet you,' she replied.

'No, not this time, Chani, if you don't mind, I was hoping we could have a little chat on our own first. How about going for coffee somewhere?' Mrs Levy added.

All Chani wanted to do was go home and jump in the shower but she dared not refuse Mrs Levy's invitation. Something was obviously up.

Curiosity and good manners compelled her to accept.

Cream and red wicker chairs and matching tables spilled over onto the crowded pavement cafe. A matching awning provided ample shade. Although the café was deserted, Mrs Levy ducked inside and chose a private nook at the back.

'So what would you like to drink?'

Chani glanced at the menu and noted the cheese and ham toastie.

'A Diet Coke please.'

The waiter came and took their order. Alone again they faced each other. Mrs Levy fiddled with her pearls. Chani stared at the condiments. To her chagrin, Mrs Levy found her very attractive, though a little on the skinny side. Her son had good taste, she would grant him that.

'Why are we here?' ventured Chani.

'Well, I was hoping you would ask. Chani, this is not easy for me and I realise it won't be easy for you but I feel what needs to be said must be said.'

Chani's heart began to pound.

'I realise Baruch is rather keen on you,' continued Mrs Levy, feeling her way.

Chani did not react. She stared at Mrs Levy, barely breathing, waiting for the death knell to toll.

'What I am trying to say is that I think Baruch would like to marry you.'

A small smile hovered at the edges of Chani's mouth. She knew it! The waiter arrived with their drinks providing a moment's respite.

'And I imagine you are going to accept.' This was a statement not a question but faced with the reality of the situation, confusion hit Chani once more.

'I think I will accept. I mean I do like him a lot – at least I think I do. I just wish there was more time to decide. To get to know each other.' She could not lie.

Mrs Levy looked visibly relieved. She suddenly realised how thirsty she was. She took a gulp of her soda water. 'Ah, so you're not sure. Well, maybe that's a good thing.' Mrs Levy's smile reminded Chani of a barracuda.

'Why's that?' she asked. Beneath the table her slippery fingers pulled at her tights. She had forgotten all about her Diet Coke.

'How shall I put this? You and Baruch are very different. You come from very different families, both frum and proper – but different. And different is not necessarily a good thing.'

The girl was staring at her again and Mrs Levy sensed the challenge in Chani's light brown eyes.

'What do you mean by different exactly, Mrs Levy? I don't sense that difference. We get on well enough.'

'Yes, but Baruch is not necessarily the best judge of what is right for him. You come from a respect-able, traditional Hasiddisher family, your father is a local rabbi of a small shul. All this is well and good but there are things missing that I would like present in a daughter-in-law –'

'Such as money?' It wasn't hard to guess.

Mrs Levy looked thoroughly uncomfortable. 'Yes. But not only money –'

'What else then?' snapped Chani.

'You haven't been to sem. The right sort of girl for Baruch would be one that has attended. He needs someone on his level to assist him in his rabbinical duties, for as you know we have plans for him to become a rabbi.'

'I am well aware of those plans, Mrs Levy and so is he. Unfortunately.'

Mrs Levy frowned. This was not going the way she had planned.

'For your information, Mrs Levy, I didn't go to sem because I didn't want to. Not because I couldn't get in. I went and had an interview and was accepted on the spot. My grades are excellent –'

'Yes, I know but –'

'Excuse me, Mrs Levy, I was talking.'

Mrs Levy opened her mouth and then closed it.

'As I was saying, I chose not to go because I realised it was not for me. I wanted the real world. I believe you can be frum and still live in it. Well, as close to it as I can get it at any rate. I wanted a small job – maybe in child-care or as a secretary – and some independence whilst I waited to get married. But jobs are hard to come by if you don't have any training, so I'm stuck helping out at Queen Esther. So I have come to a decision. If I don't get married soon, I will take my savings and use them to fund my studies at a local college where I will learn art and eventually become a proper art teacher.'

The speech may have been entirely improvised, but it had tripped as lightly off her tongue as if it had been fermenting in her mind for months. She was rather proud of it and indeed the idea seemed possible should things with Baruch fall through. It was at this moment that she knew she didn't want things to fall through. She would not let Mrs Levy get in the way. This was her chance of escape and suddenly Baruch – even with his spots – had become precious. She would fight.

Mrs Levy was looking at her with a queer mixture of distaste and admiration. 'Isn't that rather a modern path to be treading?' she queried.

Chani shrugged. 'Probably. But I would rather be fulfilled doing something worthwhile than become a burden to my parents if I don't get married.' She looked at Mrs Levy. 'Does Baruch know you are here?'

Mrs Levy had not expected this. She tugged at her pearls. 'No. Not quite.'

'I see,' said Chani. 'And Mr Levy, does he know?'

'That's none of your business!' My, the girl was impudent!

'Really? Well then it's none of your business to be prying about my family or finding out where I live. Snooping on one's future daughter-in-law is not exactly admirable behaviour is it?'

'Look here young lady, I don't wish to fall out with you over this matter but you are not for my son and he is not for you and that is that.'

'Because my family is poor and yours is rich?'

'Yes – no – not only that –' Mrs Levy was floundering. This conversation was most disconcerting. The quicker it ended the better. She prayed for a speedy and agreeable resolution.

'Let me tell you something,' said Chani echoing her mother. 'My father may not earn a lot but he is a good man. He lives his life according to the Torah. There is kindness, respect and honour in my home. There may be a lot of us but we have never gone hungry or cold. My parents always try to do their best even if at times things are not perfect.'

'Chani, I appreciate what you're saying and I respect your family. But Baruch needs a wife who can support him financially too when he is studying or the financial burden will fall on us. Don't you see?'

'I thought you had enough money to spare,' taunted Chani, hackles rising. She didn't care any more. Did the woman think she was the only one permitted to cause offence?

Mrs Levy blushed, cheeks merging with raspberry lipstick. 'We do, Chani. But that is not the point. For a marriage to work the families need to be equal in every sense. And you are not what we are looking for, I'm afraid.'

A dangerous light gleamed in Chani's eye. 'I understand,' she said lightly. 'Maybe it is for the best –'

Mrs Levy looked supremely grateful.

'– that we leave this for Baruch to decide. For after all, it seems that I'm what he's been looking for. Or you wouldn't be here, would you, Mrs Levy? So let's leave it up to him, shall we?'

Mrs Levy's face fell. 'No, that's not what I meant. Rabbi Zilberman is going to speak to him. He agrees that you're not the right sort of girl –' The dishonesty spurred her on. 'And my husband agrees with the rabbi, so we will put a stop to this.'

Chani did not believe her for a moment. A rabbi would not do such a thing. There was no holy impediment to the match. She and Baruch were not close kin. Nor was she waiting for a divorce. She stood up.

'Very well, Mrs Levy. We shall see. I have to go now. It was a pleasure meeting you.' Chani reached for her bag. Mrs Levy was hastily gathering her things.

'Wait, Chani!'

But Chani had marched up to the counter and was paying the bill.

'Don't worry, Mrs Levy, I've paid already,' she called out sweetly and left the café.

Mrs Levy tottered after her, heels skidding on the waxed parquet.

'Wait Chani!' shouted Mrs Levy. Chani did not wait. She left the café and ran to the station where she stopped to fumble for her pass. By the time she had located it, Mrs Levy had caught up.

'Goodbye, Mrs Levy.' Chani stepped through the barrier. Mrs Levy moved to follow her but the barrier closed, forcing her backward.

'Chani, please –'

Chani turned to face her opponent. Mrs Levy was gasping; curls of her sheitel were sticking to her foundation.

'Don't worry, Mrs Levy. Whatever happens, I won't breathe a word about this to anyone. I promise.'

The lift doors opened and she hopped inside. She gave Mrs Levy a little wave and then the doors closed.

Battle-weary and forlorn, Mrs Levy walked back to her car alone.

Mrs Levy was seething with anxiety. She veered between regret and the vain hope that perhaps the girl's boldness was a front and she had succeeded in scaring her off. Eventually regret triumphed. It had all been a terrible mistake. Baruch had asked her to invite Chani and her parents round for dinner; he had made it perfectly obvious that he planned to propose once both parties had met. She was trapped. The girl would be in her house. She would be made a mockery of. She didn't even know whether Chani could really be trusted to secrecy. The whole kehilla probably knew about her bullying tactics. She would be branded a snob.

However, she had an inkling that her reputation for elitism was already widely broadcast.

Life was hard. Mrs Levy stared at her wall-to-wall cream carpet and noticed a large muddy footprint. Baruch. How many times had she told him to wipe his feet before entering the house? Nothing was going as planned today. She had even broken a nail.

And now her dreams of a fitting daughter-in-law for Baruch lay in tatters. All that remained was the dismal prospect of surrender. She lifted the phone and dialled the Kaufmans' number.

CHAPTER 22

AVROMI

August 2008 – London

The summer months saw Avromi become a practised liar. He no longer had the excuse of leaving home for lectures so he turned to cunning and at times, outright deceit. His desire to see Shola overrode the guilt, which he attemped to assuage by praying more fervently, giving more to charity and performing further mitzvot. He also continued to attend community events, ensuring word got back to his father that he was participating as fully as expected. He laid the blame for his regular absences at the door of public transport, casual coffees that became long discourses on the Torah and, simply, the warm weather and his desire to be outside, in parks, playing football or frisbee with his friends, unspecified acquaintances who could not be traced.

His family appeared to swallow these untruths; the summer had cast a torpor over them all. His mother's advancing pregnancy caused her to become forgetful and lethargic, his sister lingered at her friends' houses swapping gossip at sleepovers, and Moishe went to a summer camp. His father continued to pray and work, the rhythm of his days as predictable as a metronome.

Once afternoon prayers had been completed, Avromi would slink off to laze away humid afternoons with Shola, hidden in the long, swaying meadow grass of the Heath or Kensington Gardens, his trousered legs entwined with hers, bare and brown, talking and kissing until the sun became a fiery ball and the shadows had disappeared.

London was their playground and Avromi became an eager tourist at Shola's side. Her enthusiasm for all the splendours the city had to offer was contagious. They explored the South Bank, cultural festivals, museums and pubs. Often they simply walked, discovering historical lanes or bold new architecture as they wandered. Avromi fell in love with his own city that until then had been a stranger to him. The narrowness of life in Golders Green was hard to return to.

He took pains not to fall asleep in her bed – loath though he was to leave her – making sure he was home well before the last bus. But as it swung into Golders Green depot, the familiar angst would return. He would pull out the strings of his prayer shawl, straighten his kippah and don his black jacket, which had been slung over his shoulder for most of the day.

As he turned into his road, his heart would

beat a fearful tattoo, the excitement of the day quickly draining away. His mind would be racing with ready excuses for his late home coming. If all was dark and quiet within, he would whisper a grateful prayer to HaShem and creep upstairs to his room.

The Rebbetzin lay in a tangled heap of bedclothes. The close night air had robbed her of sleep. Chaim slept soundly. All the windows were open but their bedroom remained stuffy. She heard the crunch of feet on the garden path and then the click of the front door opening. Avromi was home. She glanced at the alarm clock and saw that, yet again, it was almost midnight. This was the second time in a week she had heard him creep in.

She wondered where he had been. She sensed she would not like the answer. Her son was an adult and she did not wish to pry, but uneasiness filled her heart. She listened to her son moving quietly about his room, opening and closing his cupboard, and, finally, the squeak of bed springs as he lay down. Then silence.

The Rebbetzin turned onto her side and closed her eyes. Her hand rested on her stomach. Whatever he was up to, it was his business. He had probably been at a friend's house and had walked home. Nevertheless, she was glad that Chaim had slept through it. Her son was changing, becoming his own person, and as long as his nocturnal activities did not disturb the domestic peace, she would let him be. After all, he was a good boy and she had no reason to doubt him. Something still rankled at the edge of her consciousness, but she brushed it aside as her eyelids began to droop and she succumbed to sleep's pull.

CHAPTER 23

CHANI. BARUCH.

July 2008 – London

The Kaufmans approached the Levys' house, Chani sardined between her parents. Mrs Kaufman moved at a ponderous pace forcing daughter and husband to a crawl. Chani itched to propel her mother's bulk up the drive. They had parked a few streets away because Mrs Kaufman was ashamed of the family's dilapidated Volvo Estate.

'Hurry up, Mum. We're going to be late. We were supposed to be there ten minutes ago.'

Mrs Kaufman panted in reply. Her husband spoke for her. 'Just a moment Chani, your mother needs a rest.'

Chani rolled her eyes. Her mother was puffing and blowing like a sperm whale. Her father's shabby jacket and creased shirt made her heart sink. He hadn't even combed his beard and now it resembled tangled vermicelli.

Her mother waddled across the gravel with purpose as the front door came into view. The house loomed ahead making even Mrs Kaufman feel small. Suddenly white light blazed down on them. Rabbi Kaufman looked around him excitedly in the hope of a divine visitation. The door opened and there stood the Levys, immaculate in their Shabbes best although it was only Wednesday. Baruch towered over his parents, an Orthodox giraffe in black and white. He beamed at Chani but she could only see his silhouette.

The Kaufmans blinked stupidly like rabbits in headlights. Mrs Kaufman shuffled closer to Chani for comfort. Her father shook hands with Mr Levy.

'Ah, welcome. Come in,' cried Mr Levy heartily pumping Rabbi Kaufman's hand. Rabbi Kaufman winced.

Mrs Levy's painted lips were stretched into a wide smile.

'Hello Mrs Kaufman. Hello Chani. How wonderful to meet you at last,' she cooed. As her eyes met Chani's, she quickly looked away.

'Baruch HaShem, yes thank you, Mrs Levy,' gasped Mrs Kaufman.

'Ah so this must be Baruch. You're very tall, aren't you?' said Rabbi Kaufman.

'Yes Sir. Sorry about that,' grinned Baruch amiably.

Her parents touched and kissed the chunky gold mezuzah as they crossed the threshold. Chani did likewise, for now more than ever she needed HaShem's protection. Baruch hung back to hover at her side. They exchanged shy little grimaces.

The Levys led them through the glossy hall into

the lounge. Mrs Kaufman paused in the doorway to gaze at the oceans of cream carpet and white leather furniture set before her. Chani gave her mother a nudge. Mrs Kaufman moved on.

Once they were all comfortably seated, drinks were offered.

'A sherry would be lovely, thank you, Mr Levy,' said Mrs Kaufman. Chani eyed her mother warily. Mrs Kaufman was known to get tiddly easily but she was too busy scrutinising Mrs Levy's sheitel and stilettos to remember to take a sip. Mrs Levy was trying to estimate how much Mrs Kaufman weighed. It was a miracle that such a large woman had produced such a shnippsy daughter. But perhaps this meant that Chani would balloon in later life?

Mr Levy was worried that Rabbi Kaufman had noticed that he had taken a swig of whisky before blessing it. But Rabbi Kaufman was in a world of his own, chattering inanely in a nervous attempt to be sociable. Chani groaned inwardly.

'This is most pleasant. What a lovely room. Where did you say this whisky comes from, Mr Levy?'

There seemed to be nothing to talk about. The obvious topic of conversation was being clumsily side stepped. Mrs Levy twitched. Her husband growled jovially. Baruch perched on the wing of his parents' sofa and tried not to stare at Chani. The Kaufmans sat squashed together on the opposite sofa. Then to Mrs Kaufman's enormous relief, the home help announced that dinner was ready.

The vast dining room table was covered in peach cloth. Matching napkins sprouted from wine glasses. A gilded chandelier cast a pearlescent glow on proceedings. Chani felt as if she had been trapped in blancmange. Her mother's maroon jacket resembled an ominous bloodstain.

'Oh how lovely,' breathed Mrs Kaufman, sinking into a chair pulled out for her by the home help. She noted the girl's tight jeans, low cut top and large gold cross that swung between her tanned bosoms and wondered what Mrs Levy must be thinking allowing such impropriety in her house. In front of Baruch too!

Noting her guest's look of disapproval Mrs Levy felt the need to clarify: 'Oh yes, this is Ava – our wonderful Polish help. What would we do without her, I just don't know. The right help is indispensable one finds these days – wouldn't you agree, Mrs Kaufman?'

'That is, if one finds that one needs help. Generally we manage just fine, Mrs Levy,' retorted Mrs Kaufman. She would not be cowed by Mrs Levy's ostentatiousness. The woman had a nerve.

An uneasy silence fell. Baruch and Chani stared at their plates in desperation. Their parents were making a hash of things already. Two aproned minions arrived and began to place steaming dishes on the table. Mrs Kaufman raised an eyebrow as Mrs Levy ordered them about.

'Usually I use Hermolis when I need caterers but they were fully booked, so I had to use Esti Finkelbaum's people today instead – such a shame because Hermolis does exquisite chopped liver.'

Rabbi Kaufman blessed the food and they tucked in. For a while all that could be heard was the squelch and clamp of masticating jaws and clinking cutlery. Baruch pushed his food around his plate and Chani did the same.

'So it seems our son has taken a shine to your lovely daughter,' boomed Mr Levy suddenly. His wife simpered and reached for her wine glass. Baruch bowed his head and wished his parents' triple pile carpet would swallow him up.

'Yes – we are delighted! And he's an Or Yerushaliyim student to boot. Marvellous, just marvellous. He starts next year, if I am correct?' enthused Rabbi Kaufman.

'And Chani appears to be a fine, healthy young lady – a good haimisher girl it seems.'

'Oh indeed, Mr Levy. My Chani-leh is as fit as a fiddle. Hardly ever ill.'

And so the grown-ups proceeded to discuss their children as if they were not there. The dishes came and went and Mrs Kaufman's eyes bulged with every passing delicacy. Carrot and coriander soup was followed by lamb with chopped apricots and prunes served with heaps of hot, fluffy couscous. As Mrs Kaufman reached for her third helping of honey-glazed parsnips her daughter asked to be excused.

'If you head up the stairs on your right, you'll find the guest bathroom,' trilled Mrs Levy. Her husband momentarily wondered why his wife had not directed Chani to the downstairs lavatory but his doubt was quelled by the arrival of dessert, a splendid lokshen pudding – his favourite.

'And if they were to marry, we would prefer the reception to take place at the Watford Hilton – obviously if you have no preference of your own, Rabbi Kaufman,' declared Mr Levy as a mound of glistening noodles was dumped on his plate.

'Dad,' groaned Baruch. 'Please – not now.' His ears glowed crimson. He hadn't even proposed yet and here they were blithely discussing wedding venues. Mrs Levy had half risen, making as if to leave the table but tarried to hear the Rabbi's response. Rabbi Kaufman blotted his perspiring brow and carefully considered his answer. The Hilton. He would be ruined. He glanced at his wife and saw that she had stopped chewing in shock. Oh hurry up your dithering old fool, willed Mrs Levy. Chani would be at the top of the stairs by now.

'We – er – my wife and I that is, have always found the Gateway Inn on the North Circular perfectly adequate for all our daughters' London-based, er, nuptials.'

'Oh no, no, nooo, that just won't do – I mean, we would prefer the meal and the dancing to take place somewhere a little more upmarket –' shrilled Mrs Levy. The Gateway was a shabby little motorway motel. Never in a hundred years would she deem to set foot in such a hovel.

Mrs Kaufman choked gently into her peach napkin. Rabbi Kaufman reached for the sparkling water and poured himself a glass, completely unaware of his wife's discomfort.

'Don't worry, Rabbi Kaufman. I will ease things considerably for you,' gloated Mr Levy, patting his pocket where he kept his wallet. 'Our children deserve the very best, don't they?'

Rabbi Kaufman nodded glumly. He couldn't face his pudding. In need of sugary comfort, Mrs Kaufman launched her spoon into his plate.

Matters resolved, Mrs Levy jumped up and making her excuses, fled upstairs.

The thought of being related to those people! Mrs Kaufman – a Zeppelin in maroon and her feeble-minded husband in his threadbare suit. So unkempt. So undignified. No; it would not do at all. Mrs Levy leapt up the stairs, hell-bent on one final desperate attempt at sabotage.

Now where was the girl?

Upstairs the house was quiet and gloomy. All doors onto the corridor were shut to prevent light fading the gilded wallpaper. Chani wandered through the dimness, gently pushing at doors as she tried to locate the toilet. Mrs Levy stopped on the landing and held her breath watching

Chani's progress. Then she began mincing towards her, the carpet deadening her footfall.

Just as Chani was about to push open the right door, Mrs Levy called her name. The girl flinched and wheeled round to face her. Chani could not see Mrs Levy's expression; she was a velvet silhouette. All she could make out was the wavy bouffant of her sheitel.

'Yes, Mrs Levy? I've just managed to find it –'

'Yes, of course dear, I was just coming to check you were all right.'

There was something in Mrs Levy's tone that lent itself to suspicion. Chani wanted to get away from the woman as quickly as possible but good manners prevented her from disappearing immediately.

'Oh, yes, I'm fine. Your house is lovely, Mrs Levy.'

'Indeed.'

An awkward pause ensued. The woman seemed to be waiting for something but Chani could wait no longer. She pushed open the door and stepped inside.

'Do excuse me, Mrs Levy. I won't be a moment,' she said.

As she was about to shut the door, her hostess's foot shot out, preventing closure. Chani stared down at Mrs Levy's pointed shiny toe. She did not know what to do next.

'Before you go, I'd like a word,' hissed Mrs Levy through the gap. The menace in her voice was unmistakable.

'What about?' chirped Chani. Her hand had gone clammy around the door handle.

'You know very well. Let's drop the pretence, shall we, Chani? I was wondering if you'd had an opportunity to reconsider our little chat the other day?'

'What little chat?' Her mind raced. How long could they spend up here before someone noticed their absence?

'Don't make this any more difficult than it is already,' said Mrs Levy. She could make out the whites of Chani's eyes in the darkness. The lemon pinafore dress the girl wore glowed in the shadows. She looked about twelve years old.

'I'm not the one making it difficult,' said Chani. She sounded resolute but inside she was shaking.

'Let me make this easy for you,' breathed Mrs Levy, leaning closer. Chani could smell her heavy, sweet perfume and the garlic from the couscous on her breath. 'There are plenty of other nice, young men out there. I'll help you find one if you like. As long as you steer well clear of my Baruch.'

So this is what it had come to.

'I haven't changed my mind, Mrs Levy. And I don't need your help.'

'I see,' said Mrs Levy icily.

'I do sincerely hope so, Mrs Levy.' The woman's foot had not budged. 'Now if you'd just excuse me –'

Mrs Levy remained where she was.

'Mrs Levy, I wouldn't want to be put in a

position where I felt I had to disclose any of our little chats.' As she uttered the words, Chani gently but firmly increased her pressure on the door, squeezing Mrs Levy's expensive shoe against the frame.

Mrs Levy inhaled sharply but bore the strain. Chani leant against the door.

'Ow!' yelped Mrs Levy, retrieving her foot just as the door slammed. She pounded on the door but it remained closed.

'Chani!' she hissed through the keyhole. 'Come out right this second! I haven't finished!'

'Mrs Levy, I think I've made things very clear. One more word from you is all it will take. I will see you downstairs in a moment.'

Mrs Levy was trumped. If her husband were to find out about her deviousness, he would never forgive her – not to mention the strain it would place on her relationship with her son. Damn the girl for her insolence.

'And who do you think my husband and my son will believe – you or me?' said Mrs Levy in desperation. She was now kneeling outside the bathroom, fervently hoping no-one would come upstairs and discover her.

'We'll find out soon enough, Mrs Levy,' Chani said. The strangeness of the situation made her head spin. She had never thought she would have to blackmail her way into marriage.

Mrs Levy was silent as she considered her next move. But there was nowhere left to go.

'I understand. We shall have to make every effort to get on, I suppose.' It hurt her to say it.

'Quite right, Mrs Levy. That would be for the best, I feel.'

'Im yirtzeh HaShem.'

'Im yirtzeh HaShem, Mrs Levy.'

Chani waited until the soft tread of Mrs Levy's footsteps had become inaudible. Then she slumped against the cool tiles, waiting for her heart to still.

Mrs Levy plodded downstairs, pausing on the half-landing to collect herself and smooth down her sheitel. She had always been a poor loser. Alas, she thought, needs must. Exposure was unthinkable. No one would want her for a mother-in-law and she still had two daughters to marry off. For their sake she bitterly conceded defeat, an horrific, yet unavoidable prospect. Steeling herself, she re-entered the dining room.

'Hello my dears,' she twinkled. 'Everything ok?'

'Just fine, Mrs Levy,' murmured Rabbi Kaufman, still looking as if someone had hit him over the head.

Her husband looked at her quizzically. She had been gone rather a long time.

'Rabbi and Mrs Kaufman, isn't your daughter wonderful?' said Mrs Levy in a voice that was not quite her own.

The Kaufmans beamed. Mr Levy frowned.

From the end of the table Baruch piped up, 'I knew you'd like her, Mum.'

'And here is the delightful young lady herself,' said Mr Levy as Chani hovered in the doorway.

'Ah, Chani-leh,' cried Mrs Kaufman. 'There you are. I was worried about you.'

'No need for that, Mum. Everything's just fine.' Chani smiled serenely as she resettled herself at the table. Mrs Levy busied herself with rearranging her crystalware to best effect.

'Anyone for more pudding?' said Mr Levy, ogling the last slice.

'If you wouldn't mind, I'll have a little more –' replied Mrs Kaufman, proffering her bowl.

'Tell you what, Mrs Kaufman, let's share it, shall we? As a sign of things to come, perhaps?'

'As you wish,' said Mrs Kaufman. Deference to a higher power was a lifelong habit.

Later that evening as they were preparing for bed, Mr Levy felt it prudent to question his wife about her protracted absence at dinner. His wife was absorbed in brushing out her sheitel.

'You were rather a long time away from the table this evening . . .'

Mrs Levy deliberated mid-stroke and then grasping her wig from within, she resumed her activity with renewed viciousness.

'Oh, Chani and I were just having a little chat –'

'I'm sure you were, Berenice,' he replied, sounding a note of warning. She met his stare.

'She certainly knows her own mind, that girl – I'll give her that.'

'It takes one to know one,' murmured her husband.

The Kaufmans were subdued as they returned home. The house seemed dingier than ever after the extravagance of the Levy residence. The walls were discoloured and their feet stuck to the linoleum in the hall.

Chani watched her mother bumble off upstairs. She turned to her father as he hung up his jacket.

'Dad.'

'Yes, Chani-leh?'

She noticed a hairline crack in one of his lenses. Her father looked tired and frail. His shoulders were poking through his faded jumper and his hands trembled slightly as they hung from his sleeves. She knew he was itching to get back to his books and prayers. Suddenly she wanted to fling herself at him and engulf him in a wild hug, but those spontaneous gestures of affection had ceased a long while ago.

Instead they stood close but without touching, in the dim light of the hall. There was something sad and vulnerable about her father that made her protective of him. Chani thought of loud, brash Mr Levy and found her father infinitely superior, despite his lack of worldly confidence. He was always a good, kind man.

'What did you think of Baruch?'

'He seems a very nice and decent boy. A little quiet but considering the circumstances.'

'And his parents?' The image of Mrs Levy towering over her flared in her mind's eye.

Her father stroked his beard. Chani knew he was choosing his words carefully.

'They are different to us. But well meaning enough, I should think. It is hard to tell at these sorts of events. The main thing is the boy, Chani. He seems a studious and serious young man. You could do a lot worse.'

It was hardly high praise but then her father had barely spoken to Baruch. She wished he could be more precise but vagueness was her father's default setting.

'So you think I should say yes, if he asks me?'

Rabbi Kaufman blinked wearily. His daughter's pale anxious face hovered before him. He reached out and patted her cheek clumsily. 'Yes, perhaps you should. He's been the closest offer you have had yet. Let's see if his intentions are true. I believe they are, judging by tonight.'

Then he turned and slowly made his way to his study. Chani stood alone in the shabby hall. She examined herself in the dusty mirror. A small, thin figure gazed back. Her pinafore looked ridiculous. She hated it and had only agreed to wear it for her mother's sake. She wished she owned something more sophisticated to wear. Like Mrs Levy. She thought of the woman's foot in the door and smiled. Baruch wanted to marry her. Mrs Levy had been forced into submission. The thrill of triumph made her shiver. Her eyes glowed in the dark glass.

The years of being taken for granted by her parents, of being reprimanded by Mrs Sisselbaum, criticised by whining teachers, all fell away. She felt as if she were on the cusp of something adult and significant. A boy had chosen her over everyone else, despite his mother's objections – she was sure Mrs Levy had voiced them loudly and clearly to Baruch. At that moment, the fact that she hardly knew this boy was inconsequential. The future lay before her and she had fought her way towards it and won.

Now all the boy had to do was ask.

Indigestion and night-thoughts prevented Mrs Kaufman from finding solace in sleep. She burped softly into the darkness and listened to her husband's gentle snores.

Rabbi Kaufman was in the midst of a very exciting dream. He was Moses and was leading the Israelites out of Egypt. Just as he was about to part the Red Sea, his wife elbowed him in the ribs and he woke up with a start.

'Yankel, wake up!'

'Can't a man sleep in peace a little?' he moaned.

'Not now, Yankel, I need to talk.'

'Not again. Can't this wait until tomorrow?'

'It's already tomorrow. Yankel, listen, this is important.'

Rabbi Kaufman groaned in surrender. 'Ok, Leah-leh, I'm listening.'

'I'm worried about Chani.'

'You're always worried about Chani. Chani is fine, believe me, that one can look after herself.'

'I've been such a terrible mother –' said Mrs Kaufman. She ended her pronouncement with a loud wet sniff. Her husband fumbled for the light switch. They blinked in the electric brilliance.

'Leah, *please* don't start that nonsense now – I forbid it.' said Rabbi Kaufman.

'Ok, I won't,' said Mrs Kaufman in a small voice.

'Good, now tell me, what's the problem?'

'I don't like those people.'

'I knew you wouldn't like them. They're not our type and we're probably not theirs.'

'That woman, I don't trust her. Those shoes and that dreadful sheitel – she looked like a – a –' quivered Mrs Kaufman.

Her husband reached for her hand. 'Don't say it, Leah-leh, it's beneath you. But I know and I understand.'

'I can't bear the thought of Chani marrying into a family like that – she won't fit in.'

'If it's any comfort to you, from the little I saw of him I believe Baruch to be a very nice boy. And he's clearly very talented. He's not like them, I sensed.'

'B'srat HaShem. Let's hope not.'

'It could be worse.'

'It could. But how, tell me, Yankel?'

Rabbi Kaufman stroked his beard. His wife waited.

'They have money.'

'So? Who needs money? HaShem will provide!' cried Mrs Kaufman.

'Leah-leh, you know that isn't always the case – life is not easy if you struggle financially. Look how it's worn us down. Think of all the things we could have given our daughters.'

'I knew it. We should have given them more,' wailed Mrs Kaufman.

'Now, now, we have given them everything we could . . . and they got what they needed most – love and kindness, and a proper Yiddisher upbringing. And they had us . . . we're not so bad, are we?' Rabbi Kaufman wrapped his skinny arm around his wife's massive shoulders.

'No, and as for that Mr Levy – he is not worth the salt in your little finger, Yankel!'

Rabbi Kaufman chuckled and kissed his wife's cheek. 'Leah-leh, if Chani is half as good a wife as you are to me, Baruch will be blessed.'

Rabbi Kaufman tickled Mrs Kaufman under her chins.

'Stop that, Yankel!' she giggled and then sniffed, remembering her woes.

'That boy is very keen on Chani and I think he'll look after her,' said Rabbi Kaufman as Mrs Kaufman rubbed her face against his pyjama buttons. 'And if he doesn't, she can come home again to us. And we will look for another boy for her.'

'Has veh Shalom!' said Mrs Kaufman. Her eyelids were beginning to droop. Her bulk began to relax. Rabbi Kaufman's right arm had gone numb but he dared not remove it until his wife's head started to loll and her breathing came in long, loud rasps. Then, carefully he inched his shoulder out from beneath her and curled up against her warm bottom as they both fell asleep.

CHAPTER 24

BARUCH. CHANI.

August 2008 – London

T he day had dawned bright and blue and swelled into a balmy afternoon. Riding the sweltering tube into town, they had burst through the bubble of the North Circular and surfaced in the heart of summery London, Hyde Park. They strolled along the wide asphalt paths ogling the sights. A female roller-blader whizzed past almost clipping Baruch. He had been staring so hard at her muscular thighs and gleaming shoulders that he had forgotten to move out the way.

His interest had not escaped Chani and she had felt a pang of envy which was quickly dismissed. After all, this was their fourth date and she was sure today he would ask. They had survived dinner with both sets of parents and so far the scheming Mrs Levy had been successfully outmanoeuvred. She pushed the woman to the back of her mind; she would not let her spoil today. Chani had woken with a jolt that morning and little tremors of excitement continued to flutter in her stomach. To help her cause she had davened extra hard.

She had dressed with care, choosing her favourite white v-neck jumper, a black T-shirt to be worn underneath and a flared black linen skirt that swayed gently as she walked. Baruch wore his usual long-sleeved white shirt and black trousers. He had hooked his jacket over his shoulder and loped by her side. On his head nestled the obligatory black velvet skull-cap. Together they resembled a walking chessboard, the only splash of colour provided by the bunch of flowers he had given her. Chani clutched them tightly against her chest. She could not remove them for fear of revealing the large yellow pollen stain that covered her right breast. She looked as if she had been egged. Still, she did not care for today was the day he would ask.

What else would a frum boy and girl be doing so far from home? The exotic venue had sealed her certainty. Any minute now. She was sure of it.

But Baruch was fumbling for the moment. He wanted to say the words but every time he took a breath, something prevented him. They stuck in his mouth. He had played the moment over and over in his mind but he remained teetering on the edge of marital bliss.

He had to do something. Conversation had come to a standstill. He sensed the expectancy emanating from the small slim figure to his right. He would ask her before they reached the end of the path. He slowed down.

Round the bend spread the shimmering expanse

of the Serpentine. Small waves lapped the bank. Trees rippled in the breeze. Swans dabbled, their orange webbed feet paddling comically beneath them. But Chani was blind to the beauty spread before her. Why was he taking so long? What was wrong with him?

Baruch had an idea. He would take Chani boating in a pedalo on the lake. He would pedal out to the middle where it was calm and pictur-esque and there he would propose. He would pedal and Chani would sit in the hollow next to him. How blissful, how serene the Serpentine appeared! Why hadn't he thought of it before? There was no one to see them and pass judgment. No fear of reproach. They were free! Unless of course Chani did not want to.

He could but ask. He turned to her. She turned to him, gazing expectantly.

Baruch plunged in. 'Have you ever been in a pedalo?'

'A what?' She frowned.

'A pedalo. One of those funny boats over there.'

She followed the direction of his arm to where a man looked as if he was cycling across the lake in a pudding bowl. A woman sat next to him, her knees moving up and down in a mechanical fashion. The bowl proceeded forward sedately.

'No, no. I haven't. Have you?'

'No, but how about giving it a go?'

'Now? You and me?'

Chani looked at him askance. She pursed her

mouth, reminding Baruch of his grandmother. 'Are you sure that's wise? I mean, is it OK for us to get in one of those together?'

She watched the large round plastic boats move slowly across the lake. Laughter drifted over. The people in the pedalos did indeed look happy and excited. A breeze stroked the water; it looked cool and inviting. Here was something new and different.

'I don't see why not. We wouldn't be touching. I'd pedal and you can enjoy yourself. How about it?'

Why not? She could swim should anything happen. Pretence might provide an altogether more thrilling scenario however. It might even force his hand. She had a sudden vision of Baruch churning up the waters in a manly crawl whilst she flailed helplessly, her long skirt twisting around her legs, her mouth opening wide as she screamed for help. She saw herself lying wet and bedraggled on the shore and Baruch kneeling by her side.

Chani turned to him grinning. 'OK. It looks fun. Who would know about it anyway?'

'Exactly.'

They smiled at each other shyly, brimming with excitement. Walking briskly over to the shed they met the manager and Baruch paid.

Life-jackets on, Baruch and Chani followed behind the manager over the small decked jetty to where their carriage was waiting. It was pastel blue and had a small white '22' painted on its stern.

Baruch was the first to clamber into the cockpit. The pedalo rocked violently and he wobbled. He swiftly sat down. There was not a lot of space but he had no problem reaching the pedals. His knees bent at right angles making his legs look like pipe-cleaners.

'In you go,' said the manager offering Chani his hand which she blithely ignored. She placed her right foot into the pedalo with care, found her balance and brought her left foot over whilst clutching at her skirt.

'Most elegantly done,' said Baruch.

'Thanks,' said Chani, blushing furiously. She felt ridiculous in her life jacket but at least it hid the pollen stain. She pulled her skirt down well over her knees and clamped them tightly together to prevent it billowing up. She thanked HaShem that she had chosen to wear her black tights today.

'All right, you two,' said the manager 'You've got forty minutes. I will call you in via the loudspeaker. Any unsafe conduct or jumping into the lake will mean that I will come and fetch you personally with the park police and escort you off the premises. Understood?'

'Of course, Sir,' replied Baruch. 'I give you my word of honour that we will behave ourselves.' Chani nodded.

'I should hope so, son.'

The manager gave him a look and shoved the pedalo hard. It swayed in the wash. He nodded grimly and left.

'It's easy, I've got it under control. You relax and enjoy the scenery. I know how to work this thing.' Nothing to it, Baruch figured.

'Ok, are you sure? I feel a bit silly just sitting here doing nothing whilst you do all the legwork. Pardon the pun.'

Baruch chuckled. She had cracked a joke! He was delighted. He took this as a good omen that they were both beginning to relax and enjoy their little adventure.

'Fear not, it's simple. HaShem didn't give me these long legs for nothing.'

Baruch began pedalling and slowly their boat turned right. He pedalled harder. The water churned underneath. It smelt of mildew. Hoping to speed things up he pumped for all he was worth, his legs shuttling as if steam-powered, but the pedalo had only moved a few feet. They were going nowhere fast. Exhausted, he stopped. They bobbed up and down in silence. The water slapped against the side of the pedalo. Baruch looked out over the lake and sighed.

'I think we need to pedal together to make it go faster,' said Chani.

She was right. Why hadn't he thought of it before? There went his idea of playing the gentleman. Chani tucked her skirt around her legs and reached for the pedals. She had never ridden a bicycle let alone powered a pedalo. Doubtless a pedalo would be considered just as immodest but right now she didn't care.

She pushed down and the wheels turned. Baruch joined in. She pedalled harder to match him and the boat began to power forwards. Behind them the lake foamed. A dirty white streak carved across its olive surface.

'Great work, Chani.'

'You too, Baruch.'

Full steam ahead. Faster and faster they pedalled. Baruch admired Chani's prowess. She was good.

Giggling they approached the centre of the lake. Suddenly Baruch shrieked with pain. It was as if an axe had spliced his groin. It was unbearable. He grabbed his knee forsaking the pedals.

'What's wrong? Whatsthematter?' Chani cried.

Baruch was bent double. He was making strange groaning sounds.

'Baruch! Are you ok? Tell me what's wrong? What is it?'

She wished she could touch him, put a comforting hand on his shoulder.

'It's my knee,' came the muffled reply. He could hardly tell her he had strained his groin. Mentally, he apologised to HaShem.

The pedalo had drifted and now they were miles from the shore. Baruch was lowing like a bullock caught in an electric fence. Helplessly Chani looked on. After a couple of minutes of paralysis, Baruch raised his head. He was ashen.

'I'm so sorry, Chani. I think I've done my knee in – hang on I will try and pedal –' he gasped.

'No – no – don't – you'll make it worse –'

Baruch was silent now. He sat hunched and dejected. His plan had failed; the afternoon was wrecked.

'Come in number 22! Your time's nearly up!' boomed the Tannoy.

Baruch was still, as if in a trance. Chani had to try something. She inhaled deeply and attempted to shout a cry for help, but her voice was lost on the breeze. Now she wished she had learned semaphore and not Yiddish.

'Oh for God's sake number 22! Get a move on!'

There was only one solution. Chani sank back into her hollow and began pedalling. They progressed at a snail's pace. Baruch remained a silent lump. He was humiliated and could not bring himself to make eye contact. Instead he stared at his feet.

'It's all my fault. I should never have suggested this mad idea,' he said.

Chani was inclined to agree. He hadn't even proposed. She had nothing to say. Instead she watched the shore and willed it nearer. The sun beat down on her efforts and her calves started to ache. But she kept going, stopping intermittently to catch her breath. The pedalo nosed forward.

'Number 22! I'll be charging you double. Hurry up!'

Now the pedalo gained momentum and with each thrust her sense of indignation grew.

'You can do it, Chani,' said Baruch in a small, hopeless voice.

Chani did not respond, focussed on her task. She could clearly see the jetty. And there was the manager, a blurry figure holding a white megaphone. Her legs felt like lead. They were slowing down.

'I thought I told you two love birds to stay out of trouble.'

Furious, Chani went beetroot. Baruch looked away. She fought the temptation to lash out at him. It was wiser to save her breath.

The pedalo wallowed in the water. It was going agonisingly slowly, but they were still moving. Finally the jetty was within reach. The manager waited, hands on hips.

'Take your time, why don't you?' he snarled.

'I'm so sorry, Sir, but I've hurt my knee and I can't pedal,' confessed Baruch mournfully.

'There's always one. And as always it had to happen on my shift. Right. No point grumbling. I'm going to throw the young lady a line and hopefully she'll catch it and tie it to the steel handle on the side of your pedalo. I can haul you in. Ready?'

Chani nodded. The line flicked through the air across the water and slapped against the side of the boat. She made a grab for it and caught the soaked end. Her fingers worked at the cold slimy hemp until she had tied a proficient knot. She pulled as hard as she could to secure it. The manager watched her, a dour look on his face.

Satisfied, he started to pull. The pedalo moved

slowly and smoothly. Chani and Baruch were dragged in sideways. As they neared the shore they suffered the curious stares of fellow boaters. The pedalo bumped against the sawn-off rubber-tyres flanking the wooden posts. The murky water sucked and oozed. Delicate water weeds drifted by like sprigs of parsley in chicken soup. They had made it.

Baruch limped after Chani.

'Wait, Chani. Please wait.'

She halted obediently and turned to watch as he hobbled along. His face was a picture of anguish. The anger withered inside her. All she wanted was to go home. Mrs Levy hovered menacingly at the edge of her thoughts. Chani realised that she had survived trial by fire but not by water and now it appeared that Mrs Levy had won.

Baruch caught up with her and slowly they made their way to the nearest Tube in silence.

The ride home was a dismal affair. They sat opposite each other staring glumly into space. Baruch tried to engage her in conversation but her replies were monosyllabic and he gave up.

The stops trundled past. He was barely aware of the doors opening and closing or the rush of passengers scrambling for seats. A businessman blocked his view. He could no longer see Chani and soon he would never see her again. He had missed his chance.

Chalk Farm. Belsize Park. Hampstead. The train roared out of the tunnel into sunlight. In a few seconds they would be stopping at Golders Green, his stop. Too soon. He wasn't ready to leave her.

The doors opened and Chani turned to say goodbye.

'I think I'll stay on and see you to your stop,' Baruch said.

'All right then.'

The train shunted off. Chani appeared indifferent, her pale face glazed with tiredness. The flowers had long since been abandoned and she sat with her arms crossed, her small handbag at her feet. Baruch stared at the tunnel wires as they rose and fell in unending waves outside the carriage. He had to think fast.

Brent Cross came and went. The next stop was Chani's. The train clattered into Hendon Central. Chani got up and moved towards the doors. He followed her onto the platform.

She turned to say goodbye.

Baruch opened his mouth. 'Will you –'

Beep! Beep! The sound of the doors closing obliterated his words.

'What?' said Chani irritably. What was it now?

He took a deep breath. 'Will you marry me?'

Chani's eyes widened in shock. Her face lit up. Exhaustion was replaced by incredulity. He had asked!

'Do you really mean it?' She had to ask. Maybe he was proposing out of guilt?

'Yes,' said Baruch with greater conviction than he felt, 'I mean it.' He brushed aside his doubts and stared down at the excited girlish face in front of him.

'Ok, then,' said Chani. 'I accept.' And she beamed up at him.

'Oh, good,' said Baruch. 'Shall I walk you home?'

'I'd like that if you can manage it.'

So, on platform two of Hendon Central Station, their fate was sealed.

CHAPTER 25

AVROMI

September 2008 – London

On Yom Kippur, the Day of Atonement, Avromi took his place next to Baruch amongst the fasting, swaying men of the community. It was mussaf, the mid-afternoon prayer and Avromi was lagging. A tightening band of pain gripped his forehead. He was beyond hunger but the thirst was terrible, his mouth a parched aperture. The shul's narrow benches and aisles were congested with worshippers, the atmosphere muggy and oppressive. From the benches at the back and from the women's gallery above, came a constant undercurrent, a murmuring of whispered admonitions to bored children, the rustling of long skirts and the patter of feet on stairs.

For each named sin, he struck the left side of his chest with his right fist in rhythm with those around him. The sins were endless. Harsh speech, insincere confession, denial and false promises, scorn, bribery, idle chatter, gossip mongering, baseless hatred, obstinacy, haughtiness and vain oath-making. He felt he had committed them all.

With every pounding of his chest, he was assaulted by another memory of her. The silken texture of her thighs, her tongue, her taut calves and pert buttocks.

'We have rebelled, we have provoked, we have turned away, we have acted wantonly, we have persecuted, we have been obstinate, we have been wicked, we have corrupted, we have been abominable, we have strayed.'

Baruch bobbed and dipped next to him, unaware of his friend's inner turmoil. He envied Baruch's innocence, the peace of mind that came from remaining pure. Baruch, in his pursuit of Chani, was following the well-trodden, approved path towards matrimony and eventual sexual enlightenment. All the twists and turns encountered on his way seemed inconsequential, almost laughable, compared to the emotional mess he had created. Baruch would marry a good, frum girl. For a blissful moment, he allowed himself to daydream about how things might have been had he met Shola under different circumstances. If only he had not been born frum. If only he was not Jewish. If only she was. But fantasising like this only served to heighten his dilemma.

He thumped his breast harder and bowed lower. He screwed his eyes shut and pleaded with HaShem for forgiveness. Every word seemed to have been written for him. He was a fornicator. He had acted wantonly. He was deceitful. Could HaShem see right through to his very heart and soul? His hands shook as he held his machzor. Could the men around him and the women above him read his very thoughts? Beneath his suit, he felt utterly naked. His skin was soaked in a layer of cold, clammy sweat.

But still the images came hurtling through his feverish mind. Her body over his, her hands on his chest, her hair tickling his face, his hands roving over her spine, the echo of their laughter, the delicious taste of intimacy, the long, leisurely conversations that spanned the length of afternoons.

'We have turned away from your commandments and from your god laws but to no avail,' moaned the congregation. His father's voice rumbled out, louder than all those around him. Rabbi Zilberman's tallis hung in neat, triangular folds from his rounded shoulders; the black and white stripes, unerring in their repeated pattern, seemed to reflect the harsh reality of his own situation.

Avromi shuddered. If his father were to discover his relations with Shola, he was sure to be disowned. They could not marry. There was no future in their relationship. He could never leave the kehilla. Nor did he want to. It had to end.

He knew he would miss her terribly. Her kindness, her friendship, her humorous warmth and honest opinion, her sharp mind and her bold, charming spirit. There were no girls like her in the frum world. She was so alive, so vibrant. She had introduced him to so many new experiences. The new music she had played to him, the books and magazines they had perused together, the cafes and bars they had frequented. He had ventured into art galleries with her, foraged amongst flea markets and explored parts of London that he had never known existed. He could never hope to find someone to match her.

Avromi feared the dull loneliness that life without her would bring. He wished he could find a way for things to continue. Conversion to orthodoxy was out of the question; his world was not for her. Shola valued her freedom and independence, and as she had already told him, she was not ready for marriage. She had laughed when he brought up the subject.

Baruch nudged him. He had been standing still, lost in his woes, chest thumping suspended.

'You ok, Vrom?'

Avromi nodded, too tired to whisper. He forced himself back to the present, to the never-ending task of confession and adulation of HaShem.

'For all these, O God of Forgiveness, forgive us, pardon us, atone for us,' he muttered in unison with the congregation. He would have to do what was right, however much it was going to hurt. He would go and see her as soon he had broken his fast.

As twilight gathered in Golders Green and Hendon, the members of the community walked home from shul, the sound of the shofar announcing the end of Yom Kippur still ringing in their ears. Jubilant and purified, they returned home to consume platters of soft, white buttered bread and golden honey cake, washed down with hot, sweet tea.

The talk flowed as families and their guests ate, slowly regaining their strength. A contented weariness settled over the community, coupled with a sense of relief that Yom Kippur was over for another year. HaShem had listened to their prayers and they were starting a new year with a clean slate.

Avromi waited for the right moment to present itself. He had barely eaten. Moishe sat slumped at the table, picking at sweets and sliced fruit. Michal was helping their mother to clear away the piles of dirty crockery as Rabbi Zilberman entertained the last of the guests.

Avromi slipped on his coat in the hall, twisted the latch and padded silently down the garden path, his gut in knots as he contemplated the miserable task ahead of him.

The next morning, Shola woke early. For a few minutes, she remained burrowed beneath the covers and allowed the events of the previous evening to seep back into her heart. She had accepted his reasons without argument or question, having understood from the start that his faith would inevitably jeopardize their romantic involvement.

Perhaps she had simply not believed that his world would still hold sway over her secular world of university, liberated youth and independence. She had shut her eyes and thrown herself in, thinking he had done the same. And so it had seemed until yesterday.

It was not enough. There were questions to which she still needed answers and suddenly she was annoyed that she had acquiesced so easily. Had she mattered to him? She knew full well that she had, but how much? Did he love her? He had never said it but she was sure he had felt something close to love for her. Or perhaps she had been mistaken. Was it a mere dalliance? The sudden rush of hurt and shame at that bitter thought made her kick off the duvet and jump out of bed.

As the train roared through the tunnels towards Golders Green, Shola began to feel uneasy. She had wheedled Avromi's address from an acquaintance in the Admissions Department, but what if he wasn't at home? She should have called him first but he may not have answered or, even worse, declined to meet her. For obvious reasons he had never invited her to his home, so why should he welcome an unplanned visit? He would find her presence an intrusion. What if his parents were there? They knew nothing about her.

But then again she had every right to know how he had really felt about her. Avromi had not been the only one in the relationship and she was not the sort of girl to be slighted, cast aside like a used Kleenex. No, he would bloody well have to stomach her turning up at his front door.

She rattled through Hampstead station and out into the surprise of daylight as the train surfaced above ground. Quickly, she pulled out her compact and dabbed at her nose, wiping away the traces of shine. Shola wore very little make up; a delicate flick of black eye-liner at the corner of each eye, followed by a swipe of cocoa butter to make her lips gleam.

The doors slid open and she stepped out, thinking that the platform – with its green and cream wrought iron pillars and benches – looked very rural. She had never been this far north before, having been born and brought up in Bermondsey.

Outside, she glanced at her iPhone for directions and having orientated herself, made her way swiftly up the high street, barely noticing the shops or passers-by in her adrenaline fuelled haste. The bright September sunshine flickered across her path as she sped past shadowed shop fronts. Soon she became warm, so she slowed her pace in a vain attempt to present an unruffled and collected front.

The crowds thinned until she reached a residential stretch. An elderly Orthodox Jew tottered past, a maroon velvet bag edged in gold tucked under his arm. She stared, fascinated by his black suit, by his grey ear-locks that coiled like heavy phone wires from beneath his old-fashioned hat. His small round glasses took her in with one dismissive glance. Then he looked away, making her feel ashamed at her rudeness. She wondered if he knew Avromi.

Soon Shola was in Avromi's street. She slowed down, observing the ordinary little houses, their front gardens overgrown and unkempt or paved over with concrete. Many houses had several bins parked outside. The road was quiet and unremarkable. No cats or barking dogs, no sign of life apart from a solitary magpie screeching from a shorn elm. A yellow privet hedge obscured her view of Avromi's house.

She paused before opening the garden gate. She had expected something grander than beige pebbledash and a weed-filled path. It all looked so normal. It was hard to believe that he lived here. She raised her hand to ring the bell but was momentarily stymied. There were two bells, or so it seemed – a small, brass diagonal box fixed to the doorframe and a separate, lit buzzer beneath. She pressed the latter hesitantly. The curtains in the front room were drawn but a light came on in the hall, fragmented through the opaque, knobbled glass of the front door. Someone was home.

CHAPTER 26

THE REBBETZIN. AVROMI.

September 2008 – London

The woman stared at her blankly. She was tall and slim save for her pregnant belly. Her hair sat in an odd low, thick line above her brows, hiding her forehead. She was dressed in a long, dark denim skirt that swept the floor and an oversize, navy shirt with pearl buttons.

'Yes? Can I help you?' she said.

Shola floundered for a moment, her courage waning. The woman had Avromi's olive complexion and sharp bone structure. She must be his mother.

'I'm looking for Avromi. I am a friend of his from uni, from his tutor group.'

The woman looked startled for a moment then appeared to collect herself. A spark of recognition glowed in her dark eyes.

'Ah, I understand,' she said quietly, almost to herself. 'So you're the reason behind my son's late nights and his moodiness.'

Shola was speechless. She blushed, giving the Rebbetzin a nervous smile. The Rebbetzin crossed her arms and leant against the doorframe, taking in the girl's sepia skin, almond-shaped eyes, tight, copper curls, and finally, her long legs. Her skirt barely covered her toches. With reluctance, the Rebbetzin ushered her in, before the curtain twitching began next door.

The hall darkened as the Rebbetzin closed the front door. 'I'm afraid Avromi isn't here at the moment. He's gone to a lesson at his father's synagogue.'

'When will he be back?'

'An hour or so at the earliest. It depends how long the discussion goes on for afterwards.'

The girl's face fell. She seemed to sag as she stood awkwardly on the doormat, exposing a fragility that the Rebbetzin had already sensed lay behind the bold facade of biker jacket and mini skirt. She had not imagined that Avromi could be attracted to someone so different to him. Yet in many ways their connection made sense. The girl was the antithesis of the frum prototype he was expected to marry and Avromi was her son after all. Had she not surprised and disappointed her parents by giving up her degree and choosing Chaim and a religious life?

'Why don't you come in and wait for him in the living room? I'll make you a cup of tea. I'm his mother by the way. My name's Rivka.'

The girl's face lit up. 'That's very kind of you, as long as you're sure it's no trouble. I'm Shola.' Shola offered her hand, giving the Rebbetzin a timid smile. For a moment, the Rebbetzin hesitated, unused to shaking hands, even with other women. Then she grasped Shola's palm.

Shola sat on the ancient sofa in the living room. She folded her long legs beneath her, tucking herself up as neatly as possible, and sat very still, taking in her surroundings. She strained at every sound, hoping for Avromi's arrival but all that could be heard was the roar of an electric kettle and the tinkling of teaspoons.

The room was shabby and bare. Shola noted the absence of pictures or ornaments, walls stained by faint handprints and, here and there, the scribbled evidence of a felt-tip pin. The room needed a lick of paint. A glass book cabinet took up an entire wall to her left. The books were heavy, bound in leather, and had gilt Hebrew lettering embossed across their spines. They filled every inch of each of the cabinet's five shelves. There were few in English, mostly religious reference books.

Next to the cabinet stood a small antique dresser. Family photographs were crammed on its dusty surface. She searched for Avromi and found him with his arm around a smaller and more sombre version of himself. Must be Moishe. Both boys were dressed in the customary black and white. Avromi looked happy, buoyant, his smile wide and genuine. He had not been smiling the last time they had met.

The Rebbetzin entered the room carrying a tea tray and Shola, embarrassed to be caught gawping at the photos, rushed to help her. An awkward silence fell. The two women sipped their tea, their heads full of unasked questions.

'So Sho-la,' said the Rebbetzin eventually, trying out the girl's name. 'Why don't you tell me about it?'

Shola tensed. The woman was a complete stranger and although she had the opportunity to unburden herself to the person who probably knew Avromi best, the situation felt very strange. The Rebbetzin stared at her. Shola squirmed beneath her dark, penetrating gaze.

'Shola, my son has been behaving rather strangely recently. He's been returning home very late, sometimes in the early hours of the morning. Sneaking in and out like a thief. He has been irritable and withdrawn and when I ask him what's wrong, he won't tell me. And now you've turned up on my doorstep looking for him. I may be a religious Jew but I'm not naive.'

Avromi's mother had spoken in a soft, gentle voice. The woman was looking kindly at her. Shola suddenly felt exhausted and tilted her head back to fight back the tears. The Rebbetzin laid a warm hand on her forearm. 'Take your time,' she said. 'I don't mean to sound condescending but I think it might help us both if we talked.'

What had she got to lose? Shola took the plunge.

'All right. Avromi and I are more than just friends. But he ended it yesterday, because he said there is no future in it. It ended so suddenly. I didn't see it coming and there are questions I wanted to ask him. I just need to see him one last time. I'm sorry.' The tears threatened to fall again.

'It's ok, Shola. Look, I know it hurts, and perhaps I'm biased, but I genuinely think that Avromi did the right thing. Look at me. Are you prepared to live like me? To swap your mini skirts for floor sweepers and wear a wig once you are married?' The Rebbetzin gestured at her sheitel.

'I don't understand,' Shola said. She had not realized the woman was wearing a wig. 'Why does it have to be so black and white?'

'Because Avromi lives in a world where there are very firm rules and ways of doing things. If you want a future with Avromi, you would have to convert to Orthodox Judaism. Conversion can take anything from three to seven years of hard study. You would have to live with a religious Jewish family, to ensure you keep kosher and learn our customs. You would not be able to have any physical contact with Avromi until you become his wife. The rabbis would turn you away several times, testing whether your wish to become an Orthodox Jew stemmed from something other than a romantic relationship. They hold little faith in those who convert for someone else. The motivation needs to be pure and holy and yours alone.'

Shola had known it all along. Avromi had told her, but she had not taken it seriously. She had laughed, saying she was far too young to marry.

The Rebbetzin waited patiently.

'I guess Avromi did mention conversion and marriage,' she said. 'But it all seemed so unbelievable, so strict and far away from what was happening between us.'

'I can imagine. But are you prepared to go that far for him, Shola?'

Shola paused. She did not have to think for long. 'No, I guess not. I'm only twenty, and I don't want to get married yet. I don't even know if I believe in God. My parents brought me up as a Catholic and I went to mass at school, but that's as far as it went.'

'For Avromi, God is part of everything he does, even down to what he can and can't eat. He needs someone with whom he can share that life.'

'I know. I just wanted to see him one last time.'

'Is there any point in prolonging the agony? I think a clean break is best for both of you. If it's any consolation, I've never seen Avromi so down before. He must really care about you.'

'It does – at least I know I'm not the only one moping about.'

'No, you're not. Shola, I don't want to sound patronising, but when you're ready, you'll find someone else, more suitable and from your own world.'

'Maybe, but he won't be Avromi.' How would she ever find a boy as unique and fascinating as him? Or as considerate and gentle? She wished she could throw her arms around him, pull him close and dissolve against him, just one last time.

'No, he won't be. But I hope he will allow you to stay as you are.'

Shola looked around the drab, austere room. There was not even a television. 'You're right,' she said.

As Shola was leaving, a tall, thin man dressed formally in a black suit and overcoat was coming up the garden path. He regarded her with wary eyes from beneath the shadow of his fedora. There was something rigid and foreboding about the set of his mouth, a tightness in his jaw that his ashen beard did little to disguise. He gave her a peremptory nod and stepped off the path to allow her to pass. She murmured her gratitude but sensed his gesture had less to do with chivalry than disapproval of her presence. He held himself stiffly until she had passed, making her hasten towards the gate, glad to leave.

The Rebbetzin stood at the threshold watching Shola depart. Her husband was coming up the path and she observed their little dance with a heavy heart, having hoped to keep Shola's visit from him in order to protect Avromi. But as he made his way towards her with his mouth frozen in a grim, tight line, she sensed trouble ahead.

Rabbi Zilberman hung up his coat and hat and turned to her without so much as a greeting. 'Nu, who was that girl?'

'A university friend of Avromi's.'

'I wasn't aware he had any female friends let

alone those that favour mini-skirts. What was she doing here, displaying her wares for the whole street to see? So this is what he gets up to at that university of his, instead of studying? Admiring the goyim in their skimpy clothes!' The Rabbi's eyes flashed as he marched into the kitchen. He began opening and closing cupboards as if hoping to find evidence of other young women flaunting themselves immodestly inside.

The Rebbetzin sighed and trailed after him. There was nothing for it; she would have to tell him. She could not lie to him.

That night neither the Rebbetzin nor Rabbi Zilberman could sleep. The after-shocks of her husband's explosion over Avromi's affair still reverberated through the house. The air trembled with the echo of his harsh words. She lay curled up on her side staring at the pale outline of the door, a pillow between her knees to relieve her back of the burgeoning weight of the baby, and listened to her husband toss and turn in his exasperation. When she shut her eyes, she saw her son's wounded expression and remembered the way he had flinched as if to avoid the blow, when her husband had accused him of desecrating HaShem's name.

Rabbi Zilberman had ranted and railed the length and breadth of the kitchen. Then he had stopped, gripped the back of the kitchen chair and blasted her with the full force of his wrath.

'Rivka, this is all your fault! You insisted that he

attended a real university – this would never have happened if he'd enrolled on an Open University course like the rest of the kehilla! Oh no – you had to have your way. And stupidly I gave in. I should have stuck to my guns and sent him to yeshiva.'

She stared down at the sticky plastic table cloth trying to shut out his fury, gathering herself to reply whilst attempting to stem the rising tide of her own anger.

The alarm clock ticked away the minutes and hours of lost sleep. The Rebbetzin was aware of every sound her husband made. Every cough and grunt served to increase her misery and irritation. Despite the ache in her right side, she refused to roll over and face him. She sensed he wanted to talk but the anger he had ignited within her still curdled in her veins.

Suddenly he spoke out in a hoarse whisper. 'What will people say if this gets out? It will affect everything. My standing in the kehilla. People will stop coming to the shul. Everything I have worked for will be jeopardized. Have you thought of that?'

Rabbi Zilberman was lying on his back, arms folded over his chest, his profile in silhouette against the grey half-light. His beard wagged as he spoke. He had known she was awake all along.

'I can't believe your selfishness! What has happened to you since you came over here? All you care about is the kehilla and your job! What about us, what about Avromi?'

Chaim lay as still as an effigy considering her words.

'Whatever he has done, he's our son and he deserves our support. He is heartbroken. You were young once, Chaim, and I know you slept with non-Jewish girls. Don't you remember what it was like falling in love and breaking up with someone?'

Her husband sighed, 'True, but Avromi was born frum. He knew what was forbidden to him and he still flouted all thought of HaShem – that's what really hurts.'

'So what are you going to do? Sit shiva for him? Come on, Chaim, it's over! He had the foresight to end it. You could at least give him credit for that.'

'Not until he shows me he has redeemed himself through davening and going to a proper yeshiva in Jerusalem.'

The Rebbetzin hauled herself upright.

'Well, I'm sure he'll thank you for your under-standing and support later on in life,' she spat. 'Your lack of compassion disgusts me.'

She rolled onto her feet and snatched her dressing gown off the back of the door.

'Where are you going?'

'To sleep on the sofa.'

His father had demanded that he give up his degree and attend a yeshiva in Jerusalem. Avromi conceded and his father had begun making enquiries on his behalf. He had lost the heart to pursue his studies. Jerusalem seemed far enough away from London and university – and his father. His only desire was for his world to return to normal, even if it was a duller existence. He welcomed mundanity; his previous life seemed more appealing than ever in its lost tranquility and blameless sleep. At times, his father could barely look at him and when he did, Avromi sensed glowering disapproval. Sometimes his father was unable to contain himself and stormed out halfway through dinner, leaving the rest of the family to pick at their food in subdued silence.

The house had become a gloomy prison and through its thin walls he could hear and sense the tension he had created. Even Michal gave him the cold shoulder. Outraged, she would march past him on the way to the bathroom, her nose in the air, slamming the door behind her. However, despite her disapproval, she did not speak of his shame outside the family and for her loyalty he was grateful. Only Moishe remained unchanged, demanding gritty detail about Shola and what she looked like naked, which Avromi refused to divulge.

Avromi was expected to attend every family meal and accompany his father to shul three times a day. Whilst he prayed, his father's eyes raked over him. When he looked up, he saw bitterness and disappointment etched into his father's face. His cheeks had become hollowed and a permanent groove had appeared between his brows, giving him a haunted, fearsome look. His congregants began to ask after his health but his father brushed aside their enquiries with a slight nod and placatory response. His mother, her belly rising higher with every day, continued to shuffle up the stairs to his room, to keep him company and commiserate with him. She seemed to be the only person who understood his despair.

One afternoon in the week that followed his exposure, she knocked on his bedroom door with a cup of tea and a plate of buttered toast. Her visits were a welcome respite. It had been a lonely, sombre day. The rain lashed his window and the russet leaves had danced past, whirled by gusts of cold wind.

His mother sat on his narrow bed, leaning back against the wall. She had kicked off her slippers. He noticed that the big toe on her right foot was poking through her tights. His reading lamp cast a comforting, halogen glow over them, the rest of the room melting into twilight shadow. His bed felt like a small boat, warm and safe in the midst of a nighttime sea.

'You know, you're not the first person to fall in love with the wrong person. It can happen to anyone,' she said.

'Well, it doesn't really happen around here, does it?' he said.

'Course it does. We're all human and therefore we all make mistakes. They just get brushed under the carpet in our community. I hear about them from time to time . . .'

'So I'm not the first to fall for a shiksah?' He spat the word out bitterly.

'Don't use that word, Avromi. It's beneath you. Shola was worth more than that.'

'Well, that's what Dad called her. I heard him shouting downstairs last night.'

'He should know better and I told him so. You probably heard that too?'

'Thanks for sticking up for me Mum. I know I've caused a lot of trouble between you and Dad. I'm sorry for all the upset I've caused.'

His mother reached over to smooth his hair and for once he allowed her, feeling like a small child again. 'It's all right, Avromi. I can handle it. Someone needs to put your Dad straight when he goes too far.' The Rebbetzin grimaced momentarily. 'And to answer your question, no, you're not the first. We live in London not Mea She'arim! Although try telling your father that.'

The Rebbetzin sighed. Avromi's face had clouded over again. He sat up in bed and reached for a piece of toast. She was pleased to see him eating.

He munched meditatively. 'I really miss her,' he said.

'I know. It's going to take time. I know she misses you too.'

'Don't tell me that, Mum.' He looked up and she saw the sadness in his eyes.

'I'm sorry, I shouldn't have said it. Give yourself

some time. Daven hard, go to Jerusalem if you feel that's the right thing to do. Getting away will probably do you good. See your friends when you're ready. I'm here for you, whenever you need to talk, or if you just fancy some company.'

Avromi nodded and squeezed his mother's hand. 'Thanks, Mum. But what about Dad?'

'I hope in time he will get over it and forgive you. As he should. But who knows with your father these days.'

A hard, angry look flickered across the Rebbetzin's face. She sighed, tilted her head to one side and gave Avromi a watery smile. Then she heaved herself upright and reached for the empty plate and mug. Avromi got up and held the door open for her. He watched her carefully as she waddled downstairs. His mother looked haggard. It was clear that the current drama, not to mention the increasing demands of her pregnancy, was taking its toll. Once again, he was the one who was to blame. He reached for his siddur and turned to the east.

CHAPTER 27

CHANI. THE REBBETZIN.

October 2008 – London

After the miscarriage, the Rebbetzin retired from her duties. Her presence in synagogue dwindled. Her seat in the women's gallery, the fourth in the third row allowing a clear view of the bimah, remained folded and dust had gathered in its hinges. The air buzzed with rumours. The women nudged each other and averted their eyes when she entered a shop or strode down the street; or rather, she shuffled, her step hesitant as if she was unsure of her direction or had forgotten her purpose altogether.

Chani had heard the whispers and was loath to believe them. She had only met the Rebbetzin a few times before she had rung to cancel her next lesson. She had liked what she had seen of her and was disappointed. She had found their lessons engaging. The Rebbetzin had begun to lift a veil on all that until now had remained hidden. She had spoken with clarity, managing to combine gentle dignity with warmth and even humour. Chani had started to relax in her company, opening up, allowing her natural curiosity to pour forth. She had not expected to enjoy her learning, but these conversations, although spiritual were also intimate and intense. Chani had begun to feel she could ask her anything – well, almost anything. And then they had abruptly stopped. Her mother had nagged her to learn with someone else but she had remained obstinate in her loyalty. She knew the Rebbetzin would not let her down. So she had waited. After what had seemed like an aeon of silence, the Rebbetzin finally called.

Chani rang the doorbell, a knot forming in her stomach. She peered through the oval of frosted glass for signs of life. A blur of a face appeared, broken into hazy facets. The door swung inwards, revealing the Rebbetzin's daughter Michal, dressed in her school uniform.

Chani had assisted students in Michal's class at school and Michal, knowing the reasons for Chani's visits had smirked and giggled at her arrival causing Chani to squirm with embarrassment. This time Michal did not meet her eye. She muttered a greeting and directed Chani to the living room.

Inside the Rebbetzin stood at the window. She had been watching through the dirty net curtains. She gave no sign that she had heard Chani enter, although Chani had knocked. She stood with her arms crossed so tightly it was as if she was embracing herself or holding herself together. Her shoulders were rigid, her back as straight as a plumbline. Her clothes were dark and sombre. The room was silent but a terrible sadness hung in the air.

The Rebbetzin remained where she was. Chani cleared her throat.

She was finding it hard to breathe, let alone speak.

'Hello, Rebbetzin Zilberman – I'm here –'

The Rebbetzin turned slowly, reluctantly. Her eyes were boreholes, their gaze listless and unfathomable. Her skin was sallow and the flesh appeared receded, with dark hollows where once her cheeks had been smooth and plump. She reminded Chani of a goses, one who was close to death. Chani shivered.

'Hello, Chani, do sit down. How've you been?'

The Rebbetzin attempted a smile but only her mouth cracked open. Her eyes remained empty like the windows of a deserted house. She shambled towards the sofa. Chani followed wearing a tight, bright smile.

The lesson stumbled along. Chani tried to follow the Rebbetzin's teaching, but the woman sitting by her side stared down at the book on her lap. Where once the Rebbetzin had smiled, enthused and even charmed Chani with her lively explanations and quick wit, now she hid behind the stiff curtain of her sheitel. Her wig smelt musty and had lost its shine.

Her voice was a low jerky monotone and Chani dared not interrupt with her usual torrent of questions. She held her breath and sat as still as the Rebbetzin. She focused on the Rebbetzin's forefinger as it trembled over sentences.

The Rebbetzin stopped reading. She spoke slowly but her voice regained some of its former precision, the words dropping like pebbles in a pool. 'When you visit the mikveh after your bleeding has stopped you are performing a great mitzvah: the protection of your husband's soul. To have relations when you are niddah would be a terrible sin, Chani – you would both be considered "kareth" – cut off from HaShem and all things spiritual. You would be lost. When you bleed, the blood you shed is a little like a small death. Instead of a baby growing inside you, your body is empty and it is ridding itself of the blood it no longer needs for the baby's survival and so this blood is considered "tamei", ritually impure; not because it's dirty or you are dirty but because this blood signifies a type of lifelessness, where once it had the potential to sustain life. It is like a corpse when the soul has flown.'

The Rebbetzin paused for her words to sink in. Chani silently urged her on. Once again the veil was lifting. Not even her mother had spoken so intimately to her.

The Rebbetzin gathered herself. 'If he were to come into contact with your menstrual blood it would contaminate his soul with its lifelessness. So it is your duty to purify yourself in the mikveh. This is the cornerstone of your marriage and the most important law you must abide by. The mikveh has the power to change you completely, to cleanse you. You come out feeling brand new, pure as a newborn. It is so powerful that when a person converts to Judaism they must immerse themselves in the mikveh.'

Her tone had strengthened with the significance of her words. The Rebbetzin turned to stare at Chani for a moment, her voice a raspy whisper. 'It is your responsibility as a woman and wife to count the seven days and nights after your bleeding has stopped and visit the mikveh. Some less obser- vant couples touch but maintain a purely platonic relationship during this time. But that is not for you, I imagine,' the Rebbetzin hurried on, 'although of course that decision is only for you and Baruch to make. Most frum couples separate their bed or sleep in single beds in the same room. But once you visit the mikveh, then and only then, may you return to your husband's full embrace and because you have had time apart, your relations will be sweeter and more joyful than ever – like on your wedding night.'

On my wedding night. It was as if the Rebbetzin had read her mind. Chani turned gingerly towards the Rebbetzin, bracing herself to ask a question, when a tear fell onto the open book on the Rebbetzin's lap, magnifying the print beneath like a glistening lens.

Both women sat in silence staring at the smeared page. Another large, pendulous drop fell and then another. Chani dug frantically in her cardigan pocket. She handed a crumpled tissue to the Rebbetzin. The Rebbetzin nodded her thanks. This small act of kindness made her heart ache and a deluge threatened. Dabbing her eyes, she sprang to her feet knocking the book to the floor. Then she left the room leaving Chani staring after her. Her suffering had shocked Chani. She had naively thought that someone of her status and poise would not falter in the face of difficulty. A fine husband – a respected and admired rabbi. A comfortable house. Three children. The Rebbetzin enjoyed a revered place in the community. And yet here she was, another woman locked in her misery. Just like her mother. Why were the two most influential women in her life so depressed? What hope did she have of a happy married life if such sadness was inevitable?

The door opened and Chani sat up feeling guilty. The Rebbetzin attempted a watery smile. Her eyes were red-rimmed and her nose was pink and swollen. It was a relief to see some colour return to the Rebbetzin's face. She returned to the sofa, easing herself down next to Chani.

'I'm so sorry, Chani,' she muttered, 'I don't know what came over me. I'm having a bad day. Not feeling my usual self at the moment . . .' She broke off with a strained laugh. The Rebbetzin was on the verge of tears again.

'It's ok, honestly, we all have bad days, Rebbetzin Zilberman.'

'Please call me Rivka.'

'I can't call you that. It feels weird, wrong somehow . . .' stuttered Chani. She had only ever thought of the Rebbetzin as the Rebbetzin, even when they were discussing things as private as the time of niddah.

'No, I'd prefer it. Really. You've been very patient and kind – and well – after you've seen me in this state – it just seems a bit silly.'

Chani met the Rebbetzin's gaze.

'Ok, Rivka,' said Chani feeling out of her depth.

Sensing Chani's discomfort, the Rebbetzin returned back to business. 'Shall we continue from where we left off?' She picked up the book that Chani had lain facedown on the arm of the sofa and tried to focus. But once again she was filled with an overpowering sense of loss; for her husband, for herself, for the intimacy they had once shared. She pressed her hand to her belly and with a sharp intake of breath the pain of its emptiness jolted her back to the present.

The gesture was so familiar to Chani. Instinctively she wrapped an arm around the Rebbetzin's angular shoulders, disturbed by her fragility.

'My mother has lost three babies,' she whispered.

The Rebbetzin tensed. She shifted away from Chani gently removing the girl's arm and looked her full in the face. Her eyes hardened.

'I don't want to talk about it. It's none of your

business, Chani. Whatever they're saying about me out there, I don't care. Let them talk all they like.' She spoke between gritted teeth.

Chani flinched. 'I'm sorry – I didn't mean to intrude.'

The Rebbetzin saw the hurt in Chani's burning face and relented. She squeezed Chani's arm.

'Oh Chani, I didn't mean to snap – I'm being too defensive – I'm ashamed, that I've let myself go like this. Like your mother, many women lose a baby. It's very normal, especially in our kehilla, you hear about it all the time. But for some reason I just don't seem to be able to pull myself together.'

The words came out in a rush. The Rebbetzin seemed to be battling with herself. She was silent for a few long moments.

'This baby, this last one, I knew, I believed it was my last and it had come as a complete surprise to both of us, an amazing blessing. I never thought I would have another but there it was, I found myself pregnant at forty-four and I thanked HaShem over and over for this incredible gift and then, then one night I woke up to find the baby was lost – and there was no time, no time at all to try to save it, not that it could be saved – and after that . . .'

The Rebbetzin was staring into space, her lips slightly parted. It was as if she had completely forgotten that Chani was still with her.

'Many years ago when we lived in Israel, I had

a son, my angel, my first. He died aged three. His name was Yitzchak.'

It was time to remember, to probe at memories that had been buried so deep they had spread silent and toxic, fermenting in the darkest recesses of her mind. After Chani had left she could not stop herself remembering.

CHAPTER 28

THE REBBETZIN

March 1986 – Jerusalem

It was Purim and the narrow streets of Nachla'ot swarmed with people, many of whom were dressed in gaudy costumes. Even some of the younger more daring women had shed their usual sober attire and blossomed into glittering queens or angels. A witch jiggled a pram as a baby bawled inside. At every corner, drunken Hasidim danced in wild circles, some so intoxicated they had begun scribbling on each other's foreheads with marker pens. They reeled and plunged, caught up in a bacchic trance, swigging from hipflasks and wine bottles. Small boys soaked each other with water pistols or sprayed each other with foam. Girls shook noisemakers or beat on pots and pans. Whistles, squeals, laughter and car horns clashed to form an orchestra of merry discord – a soundtrack to the riotous explosion of pent-up energy that signalled the arrival of spring.

Dusk had fallen and a rainbow of festive lights swayed overhead. Chaim and Rivka strolled through the crowds, Rivka gripping Yitzchak's hand. Her husband was dressed as a clown, replete in a scarlet candyfloss wig, white grease paint and a red mouth. He wore stripy pantaloons and matching braces. Pinned to his over-sized lapel was a plastic flower that squirted water. He was tipsy, stumbling over his floppy yellow shoes. He sang and hiccupped, greeting acquaintances whilst trying to steer Yitzchak's buggy. Yitzchak had refused to sit in it. He was agog, eyes bulging with excitement, his little head turning this way and that, squealing and pointing in delight. He had insisted on being a clown too but had already lost his red plastic nose. He had quickly forgotten all about it and now he strained at the leash. Rivka pulled him up short.

'Yitzchak! Stay with Mummy.'

'Mummy, I wanna go see – see –'

'Not now. We have to get to Shifra's for the party, please darling.'

The glitter on her face was making her cheeks itch. Her witch's hat was too large and its brim obscured her view. She could feel her stripy stockings sagging. She was hungry and her temples throbbed.

'Hey, Rivka.'

She turned to see her friend, Dafna, dressed in a kimono. Her sheitel had been teased into a quiff and chopsticks stuck out of the back.

'Hey, Dafna, how are you? Love the costume.'

'Thanks – isn't it crazy out here today?'

'Yup, everyone's gone totally meshuggah. We're

on our way to a party at the Feingold's house. Come with us?'

'I can't, I have to organise supper and Shaul's so drunk, he's bound not to come home till about two in the morning. Last year, he dressed up as the Queen and lost his sceptre. He curled up on the couch and cried himself to sleep –'

'Same with Chaim. He usually comes home sobbing and then he wakes up in the worst mood, with the worst hangover. He doesn't remember a thing – and guess who has to clean him up, all the cuts and grazes –'

'Same with us. I hear you. So where's Yitzchak today?'

He had been there a minute ago. Her hand was empty.

'He was here – a second ago – Yitzchak!' She twisted away from Dafna, frantically pushing against the human tide.

'*Yitzchak!*'

Chaim's painted face re-appeared anxious beneath the garish patterns.

'Where's Yitzchak?' he demanded, his voice suddenly sober.

'I don't know! I don't know! I had him, just here, a minute ago and then I saw Dafna.'

'Yitzchaaaak!' Chaim yelled. They pushed through the crowd.

Suddenly she caught a glimpse of her son. He was tottering on the kerb mesmerised by an enormous yellow bird cavorting on the other side of the street. Its owner's legs were just visible beneath the feathers. Before she could reach him, Yitzchak had darted out from between two parked cars.

'Yitzchak – *Yitzchak!*' Rivka tore through the crowds, tripping over her skirt, Chaim behind her. Brakes screeched and then there was a sickening crunch of metal.

In the middle of the road, a huddle of men, ordinary Israelis in their work-clothes. They spoke in urgent Hebrew, guttural and fierce. One was wailing. She reached them and thrust herself into their centre.

A small crumpled clown lay on the tarmac, inert.

She grabbed her son's body deaf to the protests of the men. She knew already.

A terrible scream rent the air. Arms grabbed her as she fell to the ground.

She was woken the next morning. They dressed her and ripped her garments for her; she had refused to do this herself. She sat slumped on her hospital bed as Chaim knelt at her feet to put on her shoes. Unseeing, unhearing she allowed herself to be led home.

The day was unusually oppressive. A white heat trembled over the dusty cemetery as the mourners stood in their black garb. Cyprus trees grew like charred fingers, motionless in the still air. Somehow Chaim stumbled through the Kaddish, horribly aware of the perverseness of having to read it for his son. Then the wailing began all around him. She swayed next to him, her parents holding her upright.

When the small body wrapped in its shroud slithered into the grave, all she had wanted was to throw herself in. To curl up in the cool, moist earth next to her son. To lie still and quiet as the earth fell on top of them, slowly covering them up forever.

The mourning period passed like a hellish dream. She huddled on a three-legged stool and allowed herself to be consoled by faceless visitors. The mirrors had been turned to face the wall. The house overflowed with mourners and vibrated with the sound of whispered prayers. People came day and night bearing warm pots of freshly cooked food. She did not eat. Her parents, who had flown in from England, sat next to her, ageing almost overnight. Her father looked ill and weak. Darkness engulfed her as she sat close to the ground, stinking and numb.

Over the following weeks the kehilla surrounded them. It carried them. Friends came to sit in silence and to weep. Neighbours cleaned their flat and the fridge was kept stocked. On Shabbes, they forced themselves to rise and attend shul but inwardly she raged. Only Chaim continued to daven.

Yehai shmai rabba m'vorakh l'olam ul'almai

almaya. May His great name be blessed forever and ever. Amen.

The chant echoed through her head. She mouthed the response but her heart was as empty as the cot in Yitzchak's room.

Slowly the visitors dwindled away and they were left to face their grief alone. The flat seemed vast. The old stone walls and high ceilings that had once concealed them from the heat now resounded with oppressive silence. There was nothing to talk about, nothing worth discussing, nothing that would fill the black void between them. Rivka had never felt so alone.

They ate in silence, sitting opposite each other, but avoiding eye contact. Yitzchak's high chair remained between them, drawn up to the table. Rivka still wiped it clean after every meal. She could not stop herself.

Everything reminded her of him. She could not bring herself to throw out or give away his clothes or toys. His little coat hung with theirs on the coat rack. His scribbled pictures still graced the fridge. And when she entered his room, it always seemed for a heartbeat that he was there, asleep in his bed; a small huddled mound, a smooth dark head on the pillow. She imagined she could hear his gentle breathing.

They avoided the road where he had died; taking a long detour was preferable. She did not see Dafna any more. And sometimes when they walked in the streets they saw a child who for a breathless moment looked just like Yitzchak, making them falter and stare. Or they would hear another child prattling, the sound so desperately familiar that her heart would lurch.

Their lives continued in a hollow, meaningless fashion. Chaim continued to study at yeshiva but he had lost his passion for learning. Rivka tried to study but she could not focus. Nothing really mattered to her. Not even HaShem. She had stopped davening and did not go to shul. Only Shabbes retained its power over her; she could not bring herself to break its laws.

At night they clung to each other as if the bed was a liferaft and they were the sole survivors of a shipwreck. They did not make love. In the morning, their pillows were sodden. They woke dry-eyed to another empty day, the same as the one before. There was no need to separate their bed for her periods had stopped. She was rake thin. The clock had stopped inside her, sterility mirroring the vacancy at her core.

A year passed and they erected his headstone. They did not speak about him but he was always there, invisible and silent. His absence was so palpable it had taken his shape so that if she concentrated hard enough she could feel him. A pudgy hand clasped her own. Silky hair slipped through her fingers.

She had to get away.

★   ★   ★

365

One afternoon, Chaim came home to a stack of suitcases standing in the hall.

'Rivka?' he called.

She was in their bedroom dragging clothes off hangers and throwing them onto the bed.

'What are you doing?' he asked.

She did not reply. Instead, she yanked at drawers, freeing them from their runners, tipping their contents into a case.

'Rivka!' he protested. But she would not stop. She marched into their bathroom and swept the toiletries off the shelf. She burnt with purpose.

Chaim grabbed her by the shoulders and swung her to face him. 'What's going on?' he demanded.

'We're leaving. I can't stand this place any more. There's nothing left for us here. We have to go back. I'll go alone, if you don't want to come with me,' she said. She looked him full in the eye and he saw that she meant it.

He paused, thinking it through. He sat down heavily on their bed amongst their things. She continued to sort and chuck; bottles clinked and thumped as they hit the bin.

'You're right,' he said. 'I guess there's nothing left.'

She came back into the bedroom and stood over him. 'We – I – need to get away. We could start over, perhaps? I need England, my parents. Home. Less memories.'

'Yes. I see that.'

'I've booked us onto a flight. It leaves tomorrow evening. We can sell or rent out this flat.'

Chaim looked shell-shocked. As she knew he would. After all, she hadn't even consulted him.

'Ok,' he said slowly. 'And do you think we'll come back?'

'No,' she said tersely. 'I won't,' she added quickly.

'So it's final then?'

'For me, yes. What you do is your decision.'

He gazed up at her. 'Do you want me to come with you?'

She paused. She didn't know any more. Their marriage felt broken in its emptiness. But he was still her husband and Yitzchak had been his son too.

'Yes.'

And that was it. They fled Jerusalem, leaving Yitzchak in his dusty little grave. They buried their pain deep inside and tried to move on.

In London soft grey drizzle replaced the harsh light that had punished the eye and scalded the skin. People were polite, patient and spoke in her mother tongue. Red brick surrounded them instead of ancient bleached stone. Everything was green, lush and damp.

The mild English community supported them with quiet stoicism. They sold their flat in Jerusalem and bought a small house with help from their parents. Chaim qualified as a junior rabbi and started to work under the auspices of an older experienced rabbi. Rivka kept house. Her mother visited her daily. They went for walks and with time the familiar soothed and a rhythm was established.

When she fell pregnant with Avromi she felt as if she had woken and for the first time in two years she began to hope again. She davened with renewed fervour and passion, covering her face with her open siddur as the gratitude spilled forth.

CHAPTER 29

CHANI. THE REBBETZIN.

October 2008 – London

Their strange conversation had taken place three days before, but Chani still felt haunted. She wished there was someone with whom she could share the burden of the Rebbetzin's revelation, but, respecting the Rebbetzin's wishes, she had kept it to herself.

The Rebbetzin welcomed her for the next lesson as if nothing had happened. An eerie serenity wreathed her features, although the glazed look in her large, dark eyes reminded Chani alarmingly of her mother, the difference in size of the two women notwithstanding.

'Do come in Chani,' murmured the Rebbetzin. She stood stiffly in the doorway dressed in the same dark suit as before. A headscarf pulled her forehead taut.

'Thank you. How are you feeling Rebbetzin Zilberman?' Was this the right question to ask?

'Baruch HaShem. And you?'

'Baruch HaShem, I'm ok, thanks.' Chani perched

on the edge of the lumpy sofa and waited for the Rebbetzin to set the agenda.

'So today we are going to talk about hair covering,' said the Rebbetzin, her gaze glued to a spot on the wall above Chani's head.

'Is it true that Jewish women that dress immodestly are responsible for sin in the world?'

The Rebbetzin frowned. A heavy line etched the skin between her brows, but her glassy stare was fixed on Chani. 'Who told you that?' she asked.

'Oh, school. It was in a video. But it sounds like rubbish to me.' She watched the Rebbetzin for a reaction. She wanted a reaction. Where was the fire and intensity of last week? Where was the real Rebbetzin? The connection had been lost. Having spent all week worrying, she found she missed it.

'I wouldn't call it that exactly. But maybe it is going a little far. A Jewish woman must speak, eat and dress modestly as it is said in the Torah,' recited the Rebbetzin. 'So must a man. It is immoral to do otherwise. But it is more important for a woman that she does not expose herself by wearing something improper that is considered fashionable by others. Chani, you know as well as I do that fads are not for us. So once married, we cover our hair because our hair is a symbol of our sensuality and beauty, something another man may find alluring. But in front of your husband, when you are alone, is another matter.'

'So, what happens when a husband and wife are alone together?'

Chani suddenly felt very warm. She dropped her eyes to her lap and waited. The woman was gazing softly at her.

'Chani, I know you need to know. I know how scared you are. It's ok. But I can't answer that question. I wish I could but I am not your mother. You will find out soon enough. It won't be as bad as you think. Just try to relax and enjoy the intimacy you will soon share with your husband.'

It won't be as bad as you think! She was doomed.

'Why can't anyone tell me? I've tried my mother already. No one tells me the truth. It's not fair.' She heard her own whining voice and was ashamed. She hated grovelling.

'A husband enters his wife and places his seed inside her.'

Nothing new there. She was getting nowhere. 'Yes but how?'

'How what?' The Rebbetzin played for time whilst she thought of an appropriate reply. This was more than she was used to. The other girls had never dared to ask such questions, allowing her to gloss over the details. 'When the time comes, you'll find out.'

'But I need to know now.'

'You don't need to know everything. Trust in HaShem. Trust in Baruch. What will happen will happen naturally. And it will be okay.'

Chani gazed down at her siddur and rolled her eyes. It will be okay! Even the Rebbetzin was not telling her the whole truth. And to think the Rebbetzin had been so open about her own life last week. Chani had expected more honesty from her. Sensing, however, that it would be wise not to pursue her quest further, Chani relented.

'And if HaShem blesses you, this seed will create a child within you.'

The Rebbetzin's voice cracked. Chani glanced anxiously up at her.

'And hopefully you will have many children. B'srat HaShem.'

'But I don't want lots of children!' blurted Chani.

The Rebbetzin swallowed noisily and fished a tissue from her sleeve.

Oh no not again, thought Chani.

'You'll be lucky to have them,' whispered the Rebbetzin, pulling the tissue to pieces.

'I'm sorry, Rebbetzin Zilberman – I should have thought –'

'It's not your fault . . .'

'It's just that you don't know what it's like.'

'What do you mean by that?'

'To be one of many. It can be sheer . . . hell.'

The Rebbetzin shifted in her seat.

'Sorry, I shouldn't have said that.'

'You obviously needed to.'

'Yes. I think I did. When you have lots of siblings,

you can get lost in the crowd. My parents simply don't have time for me any more. I don't mean to belittle your loss by saying this, but Rebbetzin Zilberman, it can be really hard on the kids, let alone the parents.'

'I know. I mean I can imagine,' muttered the Rebbetzin. She sighed. 'I wouldn't have let that happen though.' She had seen the grey faces of the women who had large broods, witnessed the chaos of their homes but she had never heard a child's opinion on the matter. Still, she would have given her eye's teeth to have had all her children alive and healthy. Five would have been perfectly manageable. But eight? Nine? Or even twelve like the Krupniks? Sometimes it seemed that these couples were breeding competitively for the sheer kudos of having multiple offspring.

'That's what they all think. But then the babies just take over and it is impossible to give each child an equal share of attention or affection. And the older ones take the strain. I take the strain.'

'Yes, it must be tough,' conceded the Rebbetzin.

'Sometimes my mother doesn't even notice I am there. I don't meant to speak badly of her though –' she added hurriedly.

'Of course not. You're not, Chani,' said the Rebbetzin.

'It's just that when she had the last one, Yona, it was really too much for her. They had hoped it might be a boy after so many girls. So the disappointment nearly broke her. It was really frightening. I felt like I had lost my mother. It was as if she had disappeared into herself for a while.'

The Rebbetzin sighed. She knew how that felt. She thought of Mrs Kaufman, her martyr's smile, her air of resignation, and the envy she had tried to suppress eased a little. Her thoughts returned like a scratched record to her own empty womb.

'I think I want just four kids. Then I could give them all the love and attention that I missed out on. My parents did their best by us all but some days it's just not enough. Sometimes I just want them to notice me more and listen to me and only me. Spend time just with me. I know they love me. It's just impossible to give so many children the same amount of love. Mum hasn't got it easy. Some days she doesn't know what's flying. When two of them need to go and the baby is screaming and Chayale is demanding that you check her homework and supper needs to be ready . . . and then there's the washing to sort . . . and I've got a coursework essay to finish . . . So I've decided.' She felt a little better now. It was good to talk to someone who was prepared to listen even if she did not supply all the answers.

'We can't choose Chani.'

'I thought there were ways.'

The Rebbetzin sensed she was entering dangerous territory. She did not want the wrath of Mrs Kaufman on her head. The woman was large.

'That is something for you to discuss with Baruch and your rabbi. Now let's turn to page two hundred and fourteen in your bride's siddur and let's discuss which psalms and blessings you are going to recite leading up to your wedding,' she said as firmly as she could.

Defeated, Chani bent her head to the task. Inside, the frustration surged but there was nothing she could do to quash it.

She could not remember how long she had been sitting there. Chani had left hours ago. The Rebbetzin stood up, joints clicking. The children were playing next door, their muffled shrieks and thumps coming through the thin plasterboard wall. It was nearly supper time. Chaim would be home soon. For the first time since the miscarriage she needed him. It was time. They had to talk about Yitzchak. She needed to exhume the sacred memory of their first son in order to move on. She could no longer deal with the old pain alone. This second loss had sparked a painful renewal of all that had been buried deep in her heart. It was no way to live.

First she would cook his favourite dish. Slow cooked lamb, golden, crusty potatoes and a cabbage and sesame salad. Gripped by a new urgency, she rummaged inside cupboards and pulled out her pots and pans. She stirred and poured, sliced and fried, her mind whirring, sifting through words, selecting the right ones.

Chaim had just drawn the bedroom curtains. He shrugged off his jacket and was hanging it up. She sat at her dressing table rubbing cream into her hands.

'Chaim, I've been thinking a lot recently about –' she began. Her voice trembled.

'Tell me.' He sat down on the bed behind her relieved she was talking. Their eyes met in the mirror.

'About Yitzchak.'

He dropped his gaze and stared down at the rumpled duvet. She could not read his expression. His silence perturbed her but she pushed on.

'I just think that it would be a good idea to – considering what we have been through recently – well, I just feel that – that it's time to talk about him. Remember him. He may not be here any more but he still exists in our minds and our hearts . . . well, he does in mine,' she finished.

Chaim said nothing. She waited. The seconds stretched into eternity. She began to feel uneasy. She shouldn't have mentioned him. Her hands moved restlessly over each other until they were sticky with friction.

He stood up and walked to the door. 'I don't want to talk about Yitzchak,' he said, each word precisely enunciated.

'But after what's happened, I can't stop thinking about him. It's a sign, don't you see?'

'No, I don't.' His tone was almost nonchalant. It stung her like a slap.

She twisted on her stool to face him. 'But why not? Why can't we talk about our son after all these years?' She was pleading now.

'Because I don't want to.' He moved towards the door.

'Please,' she whispered. 'I need to.'

'I don't.' He wheeled around to face her, his eyes blazing. 'I don't want to bring up the past. It's done and dusted. Haven't we got enough to deal with, what with Avromi and that girlfriend of his? And with you being so depressed after the recent mis – our loss?' He couldn't bring himself to say the ugly word.

'But don't you see? It's the same thing. We've lost two now. We had a child a long time ago – we called him Yitzchak – he was our firstborn.'

'Stop, Rivka! Just stop.' Chaim's hands were over his ears. Suddenly aware that the children had gone to bed, he dropped his voice. 'I don't want to talk about it. I just can't.'

She stared at him in pity. At that moment she found him pathetic, cowardly. His shirt was undone and his braces swung from his waist. His hair stood in tufts around his skullcap. He looked feeble and worn.

'It may help if we could just face the past. I'd feel better.' One last try.

'I'm sorry, Rivka. It's too much for me right now. I'm tired of all our troubles.'

'Ok, then.'

'Ok.'

He left the room and shut the door. Rivka sat and stared at herself in the mirror, a wave of fury churning inside.

He knew as soon as he had left the room that he had been in the wrong. He had let her down again. What was wrong with him? Why couldn't he just be a mensch and talk to her? Chaim stood on the landing, lost once again in the wavering realm of indecision that he seemed to have entered on the night of his wife's miscarriage. He turned towards their bedroom door, his hand outstretched towards the door handle.

But he did not feel like raking up the past. The truth was he could not face it. It was all such an effort. He wanted to move on, to forget the recent miscarriage and the painful hullaballoo of Avromi's transgression. He wanted things to return to the way they had been. He wanted his wife back. He wanted to hold her and caress her, make her laugh, bury his face in her hair, in her skin. Talk like they used to. But when was the last time that happened, even prior to the miscarriage? Chaim could not remember.

He braced himself, fumbling for the right words to form an apology. Then he thought of the abyss in which he had buried all his memories of

Yitzchak, and let his hand drop. Chaim stood still, listening for a sound from within, but the bedroom was silent. Then he went downstairs. Snatching his coat and hat, he stepped out into the night. He needed the sanctity of his office, where he could think clearly without distraction. It was almost midnight. The building would be quiet and empty. Chaim quickened his pace, his shoes tapping smartly against the pavement.

It was a peaceful night, cool and moist. Puddles gleamed against the kerb like miniature oil fields. Inside the modest houses lining both sides of the street, lights glowed and here and there, a human silhouette strode from room to room. The cars stood motionless in their bays, their windows and bodywork covered in a fine mist.

Without warning, a memory swam to the surface and broke through to shatter the calmness of the night. He was carrying Yitzchak on a silver tray. The tray was heavy and awkward and he remembered feeling anxious that he would drop his son before he reached Rabbi Yochanan. Yitzchak was a month old. He mewled and dribbled, his little hands reaching for Chaim whilst his soft, tender feet kicked at the air.

He proceeded with caution, his knuckles white with the effort of gripping the handles and bearing his son aloft. On either side, family and friends stood watching, smiling encouragement. Some of the men were davening. The women stood nearer the back but Rivka stood next to the rabbi. She was grinning at him proudly. Rabbi Yochanan leant against the table patiently. He held a prayer book in his hands and swayed lightly on the balls of his feet, his fleshy, wrinkled face grave and attentive beneath his hat.

A foot away from the rabbi, Yitzchak's face crumpled, turned scarlet and he began to kick and bawl. Chaim hastily set him down on the table. Rivka stepped forward to soothe her son. She stroked and patted him, whilst Chaim watched with delight.

His son settled once more and Chaim cleared his throat and announced, 'This is Yitzchak, the first born son of his mother, Rivka.'

The memory blurred. In his pocket, a jingle of silver coins minted especially for the purpose of redeeming his firstborn, buying him back from HaShem, for all first things belong to Him. The rabbi's blessing as the coins were passed over Yitzchak's head. And Yitzchak was handed back to him, blessed and celebrated as the first fruit of Rivka's womb. The sturdy weight of his son's wriggling body in his hands. The warmth of his son's body radiating through his prayer shawl as his heart had swelled with joy and pride. He lifted the child up and the guests whooped and clapped.

He had never felt that sweetness as fiercely as he had done with Yitzchak. Nothing came close to holding his firstborn, freshly redeemed and sanctified. There had been only hope ahead of them. Perhaps had he lived, Yitzchak would have been the son to eclipse all his children and his goodness and greatness would have blunted the bitter disappointments that followed.

Rabbi Zilberman halted, blindsided by sudden anguish. His throat constricted and his chest ached. The pavement was a blur. He took off his glasses and fumbled for his handkerchief. He would talk to Rivka. He would make amends. Tomorrow, before Shabbes came in.

CHAPTER 30

AVROMI

October 2010 – London

Two weeks after breaking up with Shola, Avromi visited his tutor to tell him that he would be giving up his degree. The professor expressed surprise and regret at Avromi's decision, believing him to be academically gifted.

Avromi wandered out of his tutor's office feeling numb and a little dazed. The corridor bustled with carefree student life. Excitable voices bounced off the tiled walls as young women shrieked with laughter and middle-aged lecturers strutted past, like plump wood pigeons, notes tucked safely under their arms. He felt a million miles away from it all. He did not know where to go next but he was loath to return home. His feet carried him towards the café.

It was after lunch and a few stragglers remained. The serving staff clanged together empty trays. A few lonely chips remained baking under the heat lamps and he caught the dismal whiff of over-cooked broccoli and cauliflower. There were many empty tables and as he gazed across the room searching for a quiet spot, he saw Shola. She was hunched over a notebook writing intently, her frothy hair hiding her profile. A cup of tea steamed at her elbow. She paused to stare into space. Avromi froze, half in horror, half in delight. He had known she might be here. He had wanted to find her.

Something in her expression prevented him from rushing over. She looked forlorn in her solitary state, a little dreamy and pre-occupied. Suddenly, he did not wish to intrude. It would be a pointless exercise anyway. Avromi stepped back. He took one last look and turned on his heel and forced himself to keep walking from the café. When he reached the swing doors that marked the exit of the law faculty, he stumbled through them like a blind man.

He had resisted temptation and for that he was grateful, but the sad, melancholy ache had returned. Avromi buttoned up his coat against the October chill and headed towards the Tube, threading his way through the blue early evening.

CHAPTER 31

THE REBBETZIN

November 2008 – London

The Rebbetzin marched on leaving the bustle of humanity behind. She entered the quiet sanctity of the park, leaving the rush-hour traffic behind. The café buzzed with mothers and children. Pensioners pursed wrinkled mouths to sip steaming tea. Pigeons weaved and bobbed between tables, hoping for crumbs.

Clouds gathered in soft, grey blooms and the drizzle became mist. The moisture clung to her face and cooled it. She was hot now but did not slow her pace. She strode on past the immaculate flower beds, the evergreen shrubs in their barrels and the prized oriental trees until she reached the deer enclosure, her restless mind finding solace in the mechanical rhythm of walking.

The deer watched her pass, her reflection made miniature in their large, dark eyes. They stood still until they were quite sure she was no threat and then began to graze once more. She liked their wildness and pitied their limited freedom. If she had her way, she would set them free to roam

Hampstead Heath as they had done for hundreds of years.

The Heath. That was where she was headed. Her feet found the paths instinctively. The asphalt petered out and became a dirt track, shingled with gravel. She crunched along until fallen leaves and soft earth dulled her footfall. The park receded as ancient oaks closed over her head, creating a pagan cathedral. Damp ground, rustling leaves, corrugated bark and stillness. Not the twitching quiet of a congregation but something even older and deeper. These trees had thrust skywards before any shul in Golders Green had been built or even contemplated.

Here she could think. Away from custom and ritual, from blessings and mitzvot, from her children and her husband. Respite from the world.

Brambles snagged at her skirt and the path dissolved as a clearing appeared. The earth was moist and coated in late autumn debris. She sank to the ground, propping her back against an old beech and crossed her long legs at the ankles, pushing her skirt beneath them. A shaft of watery sunlight pierced the clearing and was gone. A magpie in its sombre butler's uniform swooped nearby. The bird pecked at the ground, regarding her with a beady eye and in a flash of black and white, soared skyward.

A man appeared, a shifting figure, melting into the shadows about a hundred yards ahead of her. He did not see her. Minutes later another man appeared, following swiftly until he too dissolved in the distance. She knew what they were up to and felt no fear. She wished them luck and smiled wryly. A Charedi woman should not know of such things. But she did know, had always known. After all, she had not always been Charedi. Was she Charedi now? She did not know.

Over the previous few weeks her thoughts had circled like buzzards and now she forced herself to pay them full attention. She was living a double life. There was the surface where she appeared to do and say all that was required of her. Then there was the turmoil that churned beneath and could no longer be ignored.

As hard as she tried, she could not be certain of the path she had chosen so many years ago. The kehilla gave her little comfort or sense of belonging when she needed it most. She felt an outsider but no longer one that looked on, longing to be included. How could she fit into a community where the pain of her loss was swept under an endless tide of prayer?

She was expected to return to the fold, to carry on as normal. To keep smiling and praying. To return to the mikveh and her husband's embrace. To do HaShem's bidding. What for? What was the point? One was expected to be happy, to celebrate HaShem's presence in all things at all times. The drug of spiritual bliss had worn off and she had little appetite for the next fix. HaShem had His reasons. She had hers.

Chaim was not the man she had married. That man had faded into a monochrome shadow of his former self. He was a good man, a kind man and model Charedi husband. But when she had needed more from him he had withheld it. He had become intolerant and unbending. She could not forgive him for the harsh way he had treated Avromi. She knew he felt guilty but guilt was not good enough.

If she turned her back on him he would crumble. A rabbi whose wife deserts him would lose respect in the eyes of the community. It would not be good for his career. He would not cope without her. She felt the tightening of the manacles of expectation and duty. He was her husband after all and she had loved him fiercely once. She was sure she still loved him but love alone would not suffice. Not like before. They had both changed.

She pulled out her mobile. It was quarter to four and growing dark. The Rebbetzin had pins and needles from sitting still for so long. Standing up, she made her way back to the path. If she rang Chaim now she would catch him before he went to shul. She did not want to make the call. Dread pooled in her stomach. She punched in the number.

'Rivka? Are you ok?'

The concern in his voice shook her. 'I'm fine, I'm –'

'Where are you? I thought you'd be home by now, you know, the kids are back already and the oven's cold –'

'I know. I'm still out.'

'But Shabbes is coming really soon now –'

'I know, Chaim.' Her tone was terse. He remained silent. 'I'm not coming home tonight.'

There was silence on the other end of the line. She could hear the harsh intake of breath. She waited for the explosion. But it did not come.

In a small voice, he eventually said, 'I knew this was coming. I knew there was something wrong this afternoon. So when will you come home, if not tonight?'

'I don't know. I can't say right now. Maybe never.'

'Do you really mean that? Is this what you want?'

'I don't know what I mean right now. I'm very confused. I don't even know whether I can go back to a Charedi life.'

'Not even for my sake? What about us?' His voice caught and she knew he was crying.

'I feel trapped. I don't feel like it's real any more. I don't believe any more. In anything.'

'Is this because of my refusal to discuss Yitzchak? Because of your miscarriage? Or is it because of how I dealt with Avromi?'

'Yes and no – not exactly. It's more than all of that. I've been feeling this way for a while.'

'Rivka, you know I am sorry. You know that I love you.'

'I know.'

'Doesn't that mean anything to you any more?'

She could not swallow. Something was blocking her throat. 'You know it does.'

'So come home. We can talk.'

'No. I don't want to come home right now. I want to think about things alone, away from you and the children. Away from the kehilla.'

'What if we came to a compromise? You come home and lead any sort of life you feel you need to. And I'll turn a blind eye.'

'You know you can't do that. It means too much to you.'

'Well, I wouldn't mind if we still kept kosher and Shabbes and you dressed modestly . . .'

'That's exactly what I can't do right now. I've been doing it all for too long and it means nothing to me. I'm like a robot. I feel hollow inside.'

'But maybe if you just carry out the basic mitzvot, with time, you'll regain your connection . . .'

'I don't know. I have to go now. And you have to get to shul.'

'Where will you stay tonight?'

'I'll find a hotel.'

'What about the children? What do I tell them?'

'That I need a break. Tell them the truth. It will be tough but I think they're old enough to cope. They know I've been unhappy for a while. Tell them I love them and I will be in touch soon – in a few days. I just need some time.'

'How soon?'

'Chaim, stop it.'

'But we have guests coming tonight – who's going to cook? Who's going to light the candles? Come on, Rivka, it's your home.'

She paused. 'Michal can manage all that.'

'Rivka, I –'

'I'm sorry.'

The Rebbetzin hung up and switched off her phone, leaving the clearing in the direction of the road, a tall, stark silhouette moving towards the headlights.

CHAPTER 32

CHANI

November 2008 – London

The chair lurched and hung lopsided for a terrifying moment. Chani gripped the edges of her seat while her friends scurried to and fro in their struggle to carry her towards the mechitzah. She wore her sheitel for the first time and could feel the rising heat trapped beneath its fibres. Shuli had forced extra grips around her hairnet to ensure the wig remained secure all night. Chani had moaned about the soreness they had caused her scalp but was now grateful for their presence.

The musicians in the men's section played faster and faster. The pounding of feet shook the room like a drunken military tattoo, as the revellers grew heated and their efforts more strenuous.

In the women's section, bodies rebounded like dodgems at a fair. There was no choreography involved. Those who thought they knew the steps crashed into those who clearly did not. The circle grew wider until all the women whirled and clapped together, moving into the centre and back out again in a semblance of unity.

All was sweet chaos. Her friends shrieked. Shulamis barked orders at a small group of girls who were desperately trying to keep Chani afloat.

'Shoshi, come this way and hold the front right leg –'

'I'm helping Rina at the back – I can't leave her or she'll drop her!'

'Esti then, grab this bit and push her up – no! Hold her steady!'

'I'm trying!'

Once again the chair bucked and rolled and Chani came dangerously close to sliding off. She wanted to get down but she knew she had to stand the ordeal a little longer.

'Hurry up!' she hissed. 'I can't hold on much longer – can you try and keep me a bit straighter please?'

'We're doing our best, your Majesty!'

Shulamis' face was moist and pink with her efforts but she was clearly enjoying being in charge. 'When it's my turn, I'll make sure I've put on at least a stone –' she said through gritted teeth.

More women ran to help hoist the chair and soon she was airborne. The chair moved haphazardly, tilting and rolling towards its destination. She began to look around her and enjoy herself. This was her throne, her bride's privilege. She had helped to carry so many other brides and now it was her turn.

The women's backs were braced against the chair's weight. Her dress flounced and her ankles and shoes became visible. She grabbed a handful of material and held it down but once again the chair dipped alarmingly and she let go to grab the edges with both hands.

After another step forward and she suddenly forgot her fears for spread before her was a clear view of the men's section. A forbidden world to all but the bride on her throne.

And there was Baruch hanging on for grim life, his predicament much the same as her own. His discomfort was clear to see, his long legs dangling over the edge of a seat that was clearly too small for him. He resembled a puppet, limp and lifeless. His face had turned a worrying shade of grey.

She wanted to call out or wave but it was not the done thing. Instead she stared at him, willing him to look up.

The men swarmed like rats in a sea of black. Fedoras, shtreimels and black velvet yarmulkes bobbed in its midst. The men sang and stamped, a repetitive melody, simple and rhythmical.

'Ai-yai-ya – ya-ya-ya-yaiiii!'

'Moshiach! Moshiach! Moshiach!' Messiah! Messiah! Messiah!

'Ai-yai-ya – ya-ya-ya-yaiiii!'

Suddenly she sailed through the air as the women thrust the chair high over the barrier for the men to see. She clung to the seat in desperation, anticipating the next wave. Her petticoats flew up despite her efforts and a great roar came from the men's side as Baruch's chair drew alongside her own.

'Moshiach! Moshiach! Moshiach!'

Baruch looked at her mournfully. He was clutching a white handkerchief in his left hand but had not dared to let go of his seat.

'Closer!' bellowed the men. 'Move him closer!'

As his chair brushed the mechitzah, it shuddered and threatened to topple. Suddenly a long, spindly arm shot out towards her, frantically waving the white handkerchief. The women jockeyed to position her. She held out her hand and leaned towards the white fluttering flag thrust at her, more it seemed in a plea of surrender than a desire to connect. The waiting bed – the flash of white sheets – was he thinking of them too? Was he as frightened as she was? The handkerchief still fluttered insistently between them. She hovered mid-air. What would happen if she just ignored it? But the guests demanded their satisfaction. She must not delay.

She snatched at it and grasped a corner. The handkerchief sashayed between them over the barrier. Connected but separate, they rode their chairs as custom demanded.

Her mother and her sisters looked on from a safe distance. A frown creased Shuli's brow as she watched the immodest display of the bride being tossed above the barrier for all the men to see. Rochele jiggled her son on her hip, swaying in time to the music with Devorah. There was something strange about her mother's expression. She was smiling. Another jolt and her mother disappeared from view. Chani wanted to see her again to make sure she had not been mistaken but she was flung forwards to face the grinning, sweating countenances of her bearers and her mother was lost in the frenzy. The Rebbetzin was still nowhere to be seen.

Seated at her table Mrs Levy eyed proceedings. Her privilege as mother-in-law had secured her a ringside seat and she had refused to move from it. Today was not her day for merry-making. It was decidedly more dignified for someone in her maligned position to sit out the dancing. Besides, she did not wish crease her new suit. Her cronies had abandoned her to career around the floor. Fools – imagining they are eighteen again! She snorted as Mrs Wasserman wobbled past her, arm-in-arm with Mrs Schatz whose hat had fallen over her eyes.

Her gaze returned once more to the Kallah. The girl looked unbearably happy which only served to increase Mrs Levy's sense of affliction. Up there on her perch, Chani had every reason to gloat and the thought of the girl's triumph forced Mrs Levy to seek comfort in another glass of champagne. She was not an accustomed drinker and the fizz seemed tainted with a metallic tang. She pulled a face in disgust and reached for a napkin.

'Ah, Mrs Levy, the proud mother-in-law. I am pleased to find you at last!'

Mrs Gelbmann had manifested at her elbow. Uninvited the shadchan pulled up a chair and reached for a chocolate. On top of her sheitel she wore a vile concoction of black feathers and crocheted wool. Clearly she had treated herself with her winnings.

'Baruch HaShem Mrs Gelbmann, how nice to see you. Are you enjoying yourself?'

Odious woman. She had been forced to invite her since it was she who had sealed the match. And she had her remaining daughters to think of. One had to play by the rules.

'Oh very much so, Mrs Levy. The Kallah looks the picture of radiance, don't you think? A pretty girl like I said.'

She would not rise to the bait. 'Yes she does look lovely. But looks are not everything in our world are they, Mrs Gelbmann?' said Mrs Levy smiling benignly at the shadchan's plain, wrinkled face.

'As you would know, Mrs Levy.' Touché, thought Mrs Gelbmann. 'A woman must be virtuous, modest, diligent and dutiful of course – amongst many other things. I am sure your daughter-in-law possesses all these qualities and more. And she will be a blessing to you.'

'Baruch HaShem, Mrs Gelbmann,' replied Mrs Levy drily. How much did the witch know? What had she heard? Her sources ran the length and breadth of the community grapevine. Had Chani squealed? Her foot tingled in memory.

'And her mother, Mrs Kaufman, is a most pious and admirable woman, is she not? I'm sure Chani will be no trouble to you at all having come from such righteous stock.'

'Let us hope so,' murmured Mrs Levy. 'Do excuse me, Mrs Gelbmann. I need to do my rounds and greet my guests.'

'Of course Mrs Levy, don't let me stop you enjoying yourself. After all, it is your big day.'

Mrs Levy inclined her head and gave Mrs Gelbmann a withering smile. She turned to leave but a bony claw restrained her. The shadchan's grip was surprisingly strong.

'A word before you leave Mrs Levy.'

'Yes?'

'The little matter of the money you offered me.'

'I don't know what you are talking about.'

'I think you do.'

She wished the woman would unhand her. Trying to pull away, the claw dug deeper. She turned to face her foe.

'What is it you want, Mrs Gelbmann?'

'A little token of appreciation would secure my utmost confidence. Our little phone conversation a couple of months back . . . would be deleted from my memory, Mrs Levy.' The shadchan's eyes glittered with malice.

'How much do you want?' hissed Mrs Levy.

'Ah, let me see. I need to visit my daughter in

397

New York this weekend and I had in mind a first-class seat on British Airways . . .'

Sometimes one must buy one's freedom, thought Mrs Levy bitterly.

'Very well, you'll find the money in your bank account tomorrow. Now I really must go.'

'Oh don't let me stop you, my dear. And do get in touch when you start looking for Bassy and Malka. I have some very fine boys on my books at the moment.'

'No doubt, Mrs Gelbmann. You will be my first port of call as always.' Never again, she swore to herself. She would find each of her daughters a suitable husband on her own, even if it entailed travelling to New York and traipsing from door-to-door herself.

'Mazel tov, Mrs Levy!' responded the shadchan glibly.

Choosing to ignore this last jibe, Mrs Levy went off in search of the ladies' room in the vain hope that a reapplication of war paint would raise her spirits.

CHAPTER 33

CHANI. BARUCH.

November 2008 – London

Her feet on firm ground once more, Chani lost herself to the delights of dancing. She forced herself to jump and whirl and spin and jig and clap even though the weight of the dress proved cumbersome and exhausting. The stays gouged into her hips with each turn but she ignored the pain.

This way she did not have to think too much. The familiar faces swirled around her as a different friend took her hands. Together they spun round and round leaning backwards, creating a vortex at the centre of the circle.

She was safe here amongst the women. Her mother shuffled forward to dance with her and Chani slowed down to accommodate her. Her mother's paws dripped with sweat making them difficult to grip. They rotated at a gentle pace. Her mother's eyes were warm and bright and when the time came for them to part, Chani did not want to let go.

She would no longer share the same roof as her

mother or her sisters. How quiet and strange it would seem. How lonely. Her mother's face was lost in a blur of tears. She blinked them away. How would she ever get used to living with just one person?

Before she knew it, her sisters had taken her hands and her feet trod the circle rapidly once more. She was tired now but she had to keep going. As she twisted and turned she searched the room for a particular face. But once again the Rebbetzin had eluded her. Where was she? Chani longed to see her. She wanted the woman who had taught her to become a Jewish wife to see the results of her work. She thought about the lesson that had ended with the Rebbetzin's terrible revelation. How good it would be to see the Rebbetzin smiling and enjoying herself. Moreover she wanted to share the joy of her wedding with her, to dance with her as a friend, released from her duty of education. But the Rebbetzin was nowhere to be found. And neither was her mother-in-law. For this small grace Chani was most grateful.

Avromi observed the men's frantic dancing from the sidelines. He was reminded of the last time he had been a wallflower – at Shola's birthday – and loneliness and anxiety welled up once more inside him. His sobriety did nothing to quell it. He had no taste for drink after his initial experience of inebriation.

He worried about his mother. He had not seen

her since Friday morning and although his father had tried to calm his children's panic by telling them she had gone to stay with friends in Manchester for a short break and would be back on Monday, Avromi had not believed him. Neither had Michal. They had never heard of their parents having friends in Manchester but Avromi dared not question his father, terrified that he would invoke his displeasure further. His father seemed subdued and pensive. Something was certainly wrong. Avromi had repeatedly tried calling his mother's mobile but it had been switched off all day. His parents' marriage had not been healthy for a while and Avromi miserably sensed that his affair with Shola had been the toxic catalyst for its deterioration. His mother's miscarriage had simply accelerated the crisis.

He stared mindlessly at the wild scene before him and thought longingly of Shola in her dusty pink dress. There was a dearth of scantily clad young women for him to ogle, since the only dancers were the familiar, bearded, black suited men of his community revolving in concentric circles at breakneck speed. In the past, he would have been among the first to leap and whirl, to thrust himself into the maddened, joyous throng. Instead, he inhabited a self-appointed purgatory.

He was determined to re-establish his place in the frum world into which he had been born. And Jerusalem now beckoned, with a chance to start afresh, and all the possibilities that that entailed.

Two weeks prior, he had received an acceptance letter at a yeshiva favoured by his father, which had led to a slight thawing in his father's icy demeanour. He knew very few people in the city – Baruch was one of course – and was grateful for it.

When Avromi had informed him that he had dropped out of university to study in Jerusalem, Baruch had been pleasantly surprised, but also disappointed that Avromi had not completed his secular education, a liberty Baruch openly envied and admired. Avromi had not divulged the real reason behind the sudden switch. He still could not bring himself to confess the truth to Baruch, especially now that Baruch was a respectable married man. There was also a part of him that feared Baruch's reaction.

His old and loyal friend had acquired a wife. It was bound to happen to one of them sooner or later, but the shy scholarly Baruch had shown a bewildering aptitude for pursuing his chosen bride against all the odds. Good old Baruch. He had shown them his true mettle in the end. Avromi searched the heaving black sea for his friend. He spotted him being dragged along as if caught in a revolving door. Baruch's head was dangling, his arms limp and his whole body that of someone who had spent the day in the village stocks. Avromi steeled himself to mount a rescue. It was the least he could do.

Like whirling Cossacks the men spun round and

round, shoulder to shoulder, their coat tails fanning out behind them. Baruch was lifted off his feet with the force of their momentum. He felt faint and nauseous and wished he could sit down to catch his breath but the human whirligig showed no sign of abating. He was flagging as the sweat streamed down his face. He stumbled causing the man behind him to kick the back of his knees. He had no idea who these men were. Here and there he spotted a recognisable face. He wished he had not eaten so much. The salmon fillet threatened to swim to the surface. He wished he had not drunk so much. The two glasses of champagne that had seemed such a good idea at the time now churned in his belly.

Suddenly arms pulled him to safety. Avromi disengaged his tangled limbs and led him to a seat. He was so thankful he could have kissed him then and there. Avromi produced a bundle of napkins and wiped Baruch's face. Then he disappeared and returned with a jug of water and a couple of glasses.

'Thought you needed a break, old chap. You looked like you were losing it in there.'

Baruch paused while his breathing returned to normal.

'Take your time.' Avromi poured him a glass of water and Baruch drained it in one gulp.

'What would I do without you, Vrom?' he gasped and held out his glass for a refill.

'Whoa, easy does it, B'ruch. You'll be sick if you drink too fast.'

'Already feel sick.'

'Maybe you need some fresh air?'

'Great idea. But how do I get out of here?'

'We'll just tell them the truth.'

'Ok.'

Baruch rose unsteadily and followed Avromi as he crossed the dancefloor, in itself a dangerous exercise. They manoeuvred themselves carefully around the various flying limbs and garments and made for the exit.

A hand fell heavily on his shoulder: 'Where are you going, my son?'

Mr Levy resplendent in crisp white and jet black barred their way.

'Dad, I need some air. I'm feeling a bit ill –'

'Ah, come on, Baruch, it's your wedding day – you can't leave in the middle of the dancing! What would your guests think?'

'Dad, please – I really need –'

Baruch's face had taken on a ghastly pallor. His eyes bulged and his hair stuck to his forehead.

'Mr Levy, I think he's going to –'

Dodging his father, Baruch made a dash for the doors. They swung shut behind him. All was cool and quiet in the thickly carpeted corridor. The carpet was a lurid olive green with a snaking black pattern. The print writhed before his eyes and before he knew it he had grabbed the first receptacle available, a large bronze urn, one of a pair guarding the doors to the ballroom, and vomited copiously into it.

Avromi gingerly patted his back. 'There, there. You'll feel much better now.'

Another heave and a fresh onslaught erupted from his stomach. He waited a moment, breathing heavily into the urn. When it seemed safe, he straightened up and let Avromi lead him into the men's toilets.

The cool, white tiles and drip of water were a balm to his throbbing senses. He ran the cold tap and leaning over the basin he washed his face and hands. He gargled and spat out the stale taste in his mouth. Avromi waited patiently leaning against the next basin.

'You've overdone it, B'ruch.'

'I know,' moaned Baruch. He stared at himself in the mirror. A wretch stared back. He examined his bloodshot eyes and stuck out his furry tongue. 'I look awful. What's Chani going to think? Probably smell awful too.'

'You can wash later and brush your teeth. Here have some gum.'

Baruch leaned against the mirror and closed his eyes. The fear of performance overwhelmed him.

'Vrom, how am I going to –' He paused not knowing how to phrase things.

'Do it?' suggested Avromi.

'Yes,' replied Baruch grateful for his friend's intuitive response. He unwrapped the stick of gum and shoved it in his mouth. Avromi joined him. After a few chews, he spoke again.

'I really don't know, B'ruch. But I'm sure you'll

manage. Later on, you'll feel calmer and better when it's just the pair of you in the room.'

Baruch groaned.

'You can just lie back and think of England as they say.'

Baruch opened one eye and squinted at his friend. 'What's that supposed to mean?'

'Just something I heard said once. I think it refers to the girl actually not the guy. You know she has to lie there and think of something else while you get on with the job.'

'You make it sound so enticing. Why on earth would Chani want to think of England?'

'Not really sure. Come on, B'ruch, cheer up! You're lucky to be getting the chance to actually do it with a real, live girl!'

'Do what exactly? That's just the point. I don't know what it is exactly I have to do, do I? I mean how I am supposed to know what needs to go where? So how can I do it?'

'All right, all right, calm down.'

They remained in silence for a few moments, chewing meditatively, each contemplating the act that was required of Baruch.

'I admit it's a little bit problematic,' said Avromi finally.

'Yup.'

'But if your parents managed it. And my parents managed it – then we should be up to the job.'

Baruch thought of his mother and father managing it. The bile rose in his stomach again.

'Great advice, Vrom. But I'd rather not think of my parents, if you see what I mean.'

'Yes, I see. Could put one off. Sorry, B'ruch. Was just trying to help.'

'I know, Vrom, I know . . . we best be getting back!'

'It will be all right on the night!' Avromi gave Baruch's shoulder a playful punch. Baruch smiled wanly and made for the door.

CHAPTER 34

THE REBBETZIN

November 2008 – London

T he Rebbetzin stared at the grey, concrete façade. From the outside, most of the rooms were dark and appeared vacant. Here and there a subdued light glimmered from the otherwise lifeless exterior. A battered sedan idled in the stony forecourt.

The rain was falling heavily. The hotel would have to do. She went in. The foyer was dusty and forlorn. Blinds fell in uneven slats across the large, dirty windows. The carpet had atrophied under years of accumulated dirt. She looked up and saw that the ceiling light had become a mortuary for hundreds of insects, their small black corpses piling up along the inner edges of its glass bowl.

'Hello, anyone here?' she called out.

Something stirred from behind the desk. A small, ash-grey Asian man shuffled into view. He had been slumped in a corner behind the desk so that at first the Rebbetzin had been completely unaware of his presence. A small television flickered silently on the counter. He had been watching her all the time.

'Yes, ma'am, can I help you?' He eyed her wet wig that had begun to mat in clumps. His gaze took in her over-sized coat, wrinkled, soggy tights and scuffed loafers. The Rebbetzin fiddled with her wedding ring. She was a married woman and perfectly respectable but still she saw the question in the man's eyes.

She cleared her throat and spoke as boldly as she could. 'I'd like a room please. A single room.'

'Of course, ma'am. Can I take your name, ma'am?'

The man's fingers began to tap at an ancient computer on the shelf below the counter.

'Yes. The Reb – I mean, Mrs Zilberman. That's Z-I-L-B-E-R-M-A-N.'

'How many nights, ma'am?' He made the question sound as if she might reside in this dusty forgotten hole forever.

'I'd like to stay the whole weekend if that's possible, including Sunday night. How much is it per night?'

'Certainly, ma'am. It's sixty pounds per night and that includes breakfast.'

She paused, thinking of the obscene waste of money to which she was about to commit, just so that she could lay her head on a dirty pillow. She thought of her old mahogany bed at home and sighed. Then she handed over her credit card.

Moments later she was holding a plastic key fob embossed with the number thirty-one.

'Just go down the corridor, you'll find the lift at the end and press number three for the third floor. Your room is on the right. I'll bring your luggage up for you in a moment, ma'am.'

'Oh that won't be necessary, thank you. I have no luggage.'

The receptionist leant over the counter and peered at her feet just to make sure. He tried to resume his previous blank expression but his eyebrows had remained stranded in surprise. The Rebbetzin blushed furiously. She drew herself up to her full height, nodded her thanks, and strode towards the lift leaving the receptionist staring in her wake.

'Breakfast is served in the dining-room on the first floor between seven and ten,' he called after her. She did not reply but stepped into the lift and pressed the button for her floor.

She had become an outcast, a nobody, an eccentric middle-aged woman who wore a wedding ring but arrived alone. She *was* alone. Casting her eyes around the newly bought cell, there was no doubting her solitude. This was the freedom she had longed for. The room was as silent as a morgue. She ran a finger along the sill just to confirm her suspicions. The room was as she had expected. Tired and soulless.

The Rebbetzin allowed herself a bitter smile. As she sat down, the bed springs creaked a warning, which prompted her to stand and investigate the bathroom. The shower curtain was stained brown and had stuck to the bath. Two dead bluebottles lay belly up, their tiny legs brittle and stiff. She ran the tap. It gurgled and vomited a rusty gush that eventually ran clear and whisked away the flies.

Discarding her wet things, she stepped into the tepid running water as the bath began to fill. A half used mini bottle of green shampoo and a slither of soap rested in the soap dish. The Rebbetzin pulled off her sheitel and the hair net it concealed, releasing the tight coils of hair. The water reached her shoulders and was finally pleasingly hot. She slipped below its surface hearing the clank of rusty pipes, her hair spooling around her like seaweed.

Afterwards, wrapped in a towel, she blow-dried her hair with what looked like a ribbed hose pipe, a relic from the seventies. Her mother had had one. She had not told her that she had left Chaim and the children. She considered calling her but it would be enough of a shock for her mother to receive a phone call during Shabbes; she would think there was some sort of emergency. She would contact her after Shabbes went out and hoped that her mother would not ring Chaim before she could tell her what had happened.

The Rebbetzin suddenly felt exhausted. She did not want to think any more. Easing herself into bed, she spread her damp hair across the pillow, curled up on her side and closed her eyes. She heard a distant door slam and the rumble of suitcase wheels.

She fell into a fitful sleep in which she dreamt of her husband and children. They were walking down Brent Street, coming towards her, but they made no sign that they recognised her. She called out to them but they remained deaf to her cries. They walked straight past her as if she was a ghost. When she stared after them, she realised that there were five figures not four. Another woman clung to her husband's arm. She turned round and the Rebbetzin saw the swell of her belly. The woman laughed scornfully at her and turned her back.

On Saturday morning she woke late. She had not eaten since Friday lunchtime. She scrambled into her clothes and out of habit donned her sheitel.

Outside, the Rebbetzin wandered along the grim and noisy Finchley Road until she found a café that appeared reasonably clean and peaceful.

The waitress handed her a menu and reeled off the daily specials: 'We've got spaghetti bolognaise, jacket potatoes with a topping of your choice, either cheese, tuna and sweetcorn, sour cream or bacon, mushroom soup with a fresh roll and butter. Or spinach and onion quiche. So what would you like?'

The Rebbetzin could not bring herself to eat treif but everything was non-kosher here, even the plates. She ordered the soup and bread roll as it seemed like the most neutral option. When it was set before her, she hesitated and muttered a quick prayer before she dipped her spoon. By now her family would be home from shul and would be sitting down to lunch. It felt strange to be eating alone. She used the bread to mop up the remains of her soup and fished out her mini prayer book from her pocket and whispered grace.

The rest of the day stretched emptily before her. She needed clothes, a toothbrush and paste, some shower gel. There was nothing for it but to go shopping. She had not shopped on Saturday for years and a guilty shiver of excitement ran through her as she headed for the Tube and into town.

On her return, she laid out all her purchases on the hotel bed. The Rebbetzin pulled on her new jeans, enjoying the strangely familiar roughness of denim against skin. The jumper was soft and its collar covered her collarbones, which she was still reticent to expose. She regarded her reflection and on impulse, yanked at her wig and, ignoring the pain, sent the grips flying. She shook out her hair. It fell in soft waves over her shoulders and down her back. She looked ten years younger. Her reflection smiled back at her.

Eight o'clock. Too early for bed but nor was she ready to take off her new clothes. She wanted to go out and show them off but what does a single middle-aged woman do on her own on a Saturday night?

* * *

An hour later, clutching an enormous box of popcorn, the Rebbetzin settled into her velvet seat and watched the curtains open. The screen flashed and music blared. All around her were courting couples but she felt far from lonely. She shovelled another handful of popcorn into her mouth, let her head loll back against the seat and waited for the film to begin.

When she stepped out of the cinema it was still early. Although it had grown dark, there was an air of expectancy and spontaneity in the air. Couples dawdled in front of shop windows and groups of teenage girls and boys loitered outside Nando's. The weekday rush had been forgotten and the night stretched before them. It seemed to the Rebbetzin that all of London was out on the town.

It was too early to return to her miserable cell. She had not eaten supper and could not bring herself to eat treif again. The Rebbetzin thought longingly of the houmous and falafel joints on Golders Green Road. Better still would be juicy lamb shwarma dripping in tachina, wrapped in a fluffy, warm pitta.

Her stomach growled but she could not risk it. What if someone recognized her? But then again, so what if they did? What was the worst that could happen? Her appearance would simply generate more grist for the rumour mill but she could survive that. But could Chaim and her children? What if she bumped into them? It was unlikely.

Avromi would be hiding in his bedroom and she felt treacherous for not being there to cheer him up. Michal and Moishe would be at friends' houses. Her husband would probably be at home. Her heart tightened at the thought of him, sitting at the kitchen table alone, worrying about her whereabouts. She wondered what he had told them and hoped it was plausible enough not to cause them concern, for she doubted he had told them the truth. She squared her shoulders and strode towards the bus stop. Within minutes, a number 13 pulled up and she was chugging towards her old world.

She leapt off at the station. The wind whipped her hair and it fluttered, banner-like in her wake. The Rebbetzin buckled her husband's trench coat tighter to ward off the icy fingers of an early autumn breeze. Shabbes had gone out and Golders Green would be busy. She braced herself, holding her head high as her heart pumped faster with the thrill of trespass. Starbucks, Costa Coffee and Caffé Nero; the strange, old-fashioned clothes shop, full of furs and kitsch; the Middle Eastern grocer's; and the all night chemist with its glamorous adverts promising the illusion of flawless skin. She was still in neutral territory. But soon enough she passed a kosher bakery and the cafes loomed, their windows bright and cheery as the great and the good met after Shabbes to gossip over cheesecake and cappuccino.

The pavements were filling up. From a

double-parked people carrier, several young frum girls emerged wearing identical navy quilted jackets. They slammed the doors and ambled towards the kerb, heedless of the enraged hooting coming from the cars held up behind them. The Rebbetzin approached them warily. Sure enough, she spotted Michal's classmate Sissy Ross. The girl was a gawky bundle of nervous energy, and whilst not a close acquaintance of her daughter's, a face she knew well. The Rebbetzin edged past the group, staring into the middle distance. Sissy was far too busy chattering to notice.

Her route wormed its way under the railway bridge that spanned the road. Young African men exchanged news outside the shabby internet café and call centre that was squeezed into an alcove in the bridge's shadow. A Polish couple gazed longingly at the display in the window of the discount shoe store next door.

The faded front of the Dizengoff café appeared on her right. Small pockets of customers huddled within its gloomy interior, beneath the large, perennially dusty, glass photos of 1980s Tel Aviv. To the Rebbetzin's horror, trundling towards her were Mr and Mrs Schwartz, regular shul goers and keen participants in her husband's lessons. She had even taught their daughter how to use the mikveh. It was too late to cross the road. The Rebbetzin held her breath. She could not help but stare at Mrs Schwartz, who was leaning heavily on her husband, due to her arthritic hip. Her face was twisted with painful effort. She was a kindly, benevolent soul and it unsettled the Rebbetzin to see her struggling. The couple passed within a foot of the Rebbetzin. They gazed at her, blinked, but showed no sign of acknowledgement. Instead, the pair continued to shuffle forward, Mr Schwartz gently encouraging his wife. Within seconds, they had passed her by. The Rebbetzin sighed and walked on.

The woman had stared straight through her. There had been no dawning of recognition, no greeting uttered. The Rebbetzin felt invisible, a ghost of her former self. She drifted on, perturbed yet relieved. Perhaps since she was no longer dressed in frum attire, she no longer existed for her community; they only saw what they wanted to see. In her jeans and loose hair, she was not of their ilk and therefore unimportant, merely another obstacle to negotiate as they progressed along the street. She may as well have been a lamppost. What a strange, blinkered world they inhabited.

Solly's beckoned and she pushed open the heavy glass door to join the queue. The bored Israeli youth took her order with insouciance, barely glancing at her. She handed over her money and in return received a warm bundle of meaty spices and dough. Once outside, she tore open the paper and bit into tender, greasy lamb, allowing the sauce to coat her chin.

On Sunday morning the Rebbetzin lay in bed. She stretched languorously, enjoying the space, her mind replaying choice scenes from the film. Reluctantly, her thoughts turned to home and her husband and children. The guilt and the worry returned and her mind swung like a pendulum between them. She began to feel sick with anxiety. How could she walk out on them? She thought of Moishe, his skinny body, his messy hair that he refused to comb flat, his teenage fits of pique – he needed her. And who would listen to and comfort Avromi? He needed time and her careful encouragement in order to heal. Lastly, she thought of Michal – her sensible, pragmatic daughter on the brink of adulthood: despite her maturity, Michal still needed a mother's guidance.

What was she thinking of by abandoning them?

She sat up and reached for her mobile but could not press the buttons. She stared at the lump of plastic in her hand, knowing that as soon as she heard their voices, she would be rattling back home in a cab within minutes.

If she moved out, she could find a small flat nearby, in Swiss Cottage or West Hampstead. She could still see her children every day. Michal would finish school this year and begin sem at Gateshead or in Jerusalem next September. She was on the cusp of adulthood. Avromi would survive. He was a balanced young man and although he was suffering, he would start afresh in Jerusalem in January. Hopefully he would learn and grow from his mistakes, and at least he would still be at home for a while to keep an eye on Moishe until they had all adjusted to the situation. They could visit her whenever they wanted, stay the night or just have dinner with her. For that, she would need to keep a kosher kitchen. Her mind raced with possibilities, faltering at complications. Fine, she could keep kosher at home – it was no real hardship.

What about Chaim? What would he be doing today? She did not have the strength to talk to him again just yet. With a jolt, the Rebbetzin realised that he would be officiating at Chani's wedding and she had promised Chani that she would be there. The Rebbetzin groaned. Shul was the last place she wanted to be. But a promise was a promise.

Then she had an idea. The ceremony was at two. She had plenty of time.

CHAPTER 35

CHANI. BARUCH.

November 2008 – London

The doors of the lift closed with a discreet rumble. Chani and Baruch stood in silence as the machine soared to the sixth floor. Baruch allowed Chani to exit first. The corridor was empty and hushed. Chani's dress rustled over the plush carpet, which was emblazoned with the same pattern that had writhed before Baruch's eyes hours earlier. Wall lights cast a dim glow emphasising the black swirls, creating the illusion of the pattern rising to meet them.

Chani followed half a step behind her husband. Baruch clutched the key card and led the way. They passed room after room, each door a full-length mirror reflecting them in its dark glass depths, giving Chani the sensation of being accompanied by the ghosts of the previous brides and grooms to have walked the corridor before them. How had they fared? Chani was wide-awake, her previous exhaustion forgotten. Her stomach gurgled loudly but Baruch did not seem to notice. She imagined he was equally nervous; he had barely spoken or looked at her since they had taken leave of their parents.

The room was magnificent. Palatial in size, its décor was heavy and traditional. Floor length brocaded curtains were held back by twisted gold ropes ending in fringed tassels. A chandelier dangled from an ornate ceiling rose. A mahogany dressing table stood in the window bay. Her every-day wig stood on its stand in front of a framed looking glass, a faceless woman watching them closely. A large basket of kosher treats sat on the writing bureau to the right. Their suitcases had been stored beneath.

In the centre of the room stood a huge four-poster bed. Their nightwear had been laid out on it. She approached the bed and gingerly sat down, the thick mattress barely denting under her weight. Baruch copied her causing the bed to sag and Chani to lean towards him. They giggled and glanced shyly at each other and looked away.

'Big, isn't it?' said Baruch.

'Very,' agreed Chani.

'Might get lost in it. Should have brought a map.'

Chani was silent. Baruch reddened as his joke flopped. 'Are you tired?'

She looked up briefly at him. 'No, not all. I don't believe I'll sleep at all tonight.'

'Me neither.' He reached for her hand and so they sat for a few moments until the silence became unbearable and Chani broke away to pretend to examine the gift basket.

'Are you hungry?' she asked.

'No, couldn't eat another thing. Are you?'

She shook her head. 'Definitely not.'

The sweat had congealed into cold patches under his arms and his mouth felt full of sand. He needed a wash but what was the correct protocol in front of one's newly acquired wife?

'I guess we should get ready for bed.'

Chani did not move. She stared at the gaudy pink bow stuck to the cellophane of the basket.

'Would you prefer to use the bathroom first?'

She nodded. 'Can you help unbutton my dress at the back?'

'I'll do my best.'

She turned her back as he towered over her. The buttons were small and fiddly but he bent to his task. They gave way and slowly Chani's slim pale back was revealed to him. He wanted to stroke the length of her spine but as soon as he was done, she grabbed her nightdress and fled to the bathroom. The door locked and he was left waiting.

From within came the whir and hiss of the shower. He stood up and wandered around the room, opening drawers and examining their contents. Writing paper, envelopes and menus – nothing very interesting. He flicked the switch on the electric kettle just to see it glow red. Then he peered at himself in the mirror, breathed on it and grimaced as he caught a whiff of the stale odour. He had to brush his teeth. Baruch HaShem he had not tried to kiss her yet. But how was he supposed to kiss her? Does one move one's lips against the other person's? Or do they remain stationary, merely pressed up close? And what does one do with one's tongue? He had seen kissing on television. The men and women had devoured one another. He had thought it had looked thoroughly unpleasant. But perhaps that was what was meant to be done? Maybe Chani would like it?

The lock slid in the bathroom door and it slowly swung open. Chani emerged through the steam, a large fluffy hotel dressing gown dwarfing her frame. Her hair was wet, her feet were bare and she clutched her wig in both hands. She looked very young and vulnerable.

'Um – I just need my toothbrush and toothpaste. I'll be done in a couple of minutes.'

'Sure. Take your time.'

She fumbled with the zips on her suitcase, stuffed in her wedding wig and pulled out her wash-bag. Then she flitted back inside, locking the door once more. Baruch paced the bedroom, hands behind his back.

In the humid privacy of the bathroom, Chani scrambled into her bright pink bra and knickers. She had hidden them in her wash-bag, wrapped up in her old shower-cap. The material shone brighter than ever and seemed utterly incongruous against the plain white cotton of her nightdress. Perhaps it had been a bad idea to have bought the set after all. Still, she was enjoying the slither of satin against skin. She fastened the small buttons of the nightgown up to her collarbone and pulled the sleeves over her wrists. Her secret concealed, she brushed her teeth, whispered a quick prayer and opened the door to find Baruch styling his hair in the mirror. He spun round.

'Your turn,' she said.

'Thanks,' he muttered, grabbed his pyjamas and wash-kit and retired to the sanctuary of the bathroom.

What does a bride do now?

She had hung her dress on the wardrobe door and was curled up in the armchair, feet tucked beneath her. She was cold. The room was large and draughty. Baruch was taking his time. Her siddur had been placed on the dressing table for her by her mother but praying was the last thing she felt like doing. On the coffee table lay the remote for the television. She would just switch it on for a second. She pressed the large red button and pointed it at the screen. The screen flashed and cleared to reveal a couple writhing in a passionate embrace on a beach. His hand crept up her thigh and she arched her back against him, moaning softly. He covered her neck with kisses and her hands gripped his muscular back.

Chani was glued to the screen when Baruch stepped out of the bathroom. He cleared his throat and in a panic she reached for the remote, knocking it flying. The couple continued to moan and groan as she scrabbled for the device under the sofa. She stood up to find Baruch entranced by the display of passion enacted before him. Immediately he turned away, blushing furiously. Hurriedly she switched off the machine and silenced the couple.

'I only meant to see what's on,' she rattled. 'I hadn't thought it would be that sort of thing –'

'Yes, most inconvenient,' said Baruch.

'So,' said Chani. 'What shall we do now?'

Her dress trembled a little on its hanger. In the thick darkness it appeared almost luminous. The only other point of light came from the television opposite, an unblinking red eye in the gloom. They lay in the enormous bed separated by a vast expanse of Egyptian cotton, each cleaving to their side of the bed. Neither stirred and they remained frozen, staring at the canopy above them.

Chani's feet were numb with cold but she dared not move them. She waited for Baruch to make the first overture. But her husband continued to lie inert and silent. She sensed his breathing in the gentle rise and fall of the covers.

Baruch contemplated his situation. He must penetrate the girl lying next to him but his member had curled up in fright, rendering the act impossible. All the manuals he had consulted in the library had not prepared him for this. He longed to sleep off the nightmare but he knew he must perform his duty. The longer he lay there motionless, the harder it was to begin proceedings. His limbs felt pinioned to the mattress. The girl was waiting.

Chani grew restless. She wanted it over and done with. She had waited and worried for an eternity only for Baruch to suffer stage fright. She knew he wanted her. She had seen the way he had stared at her when he had thought her unaware. It was fear that had paralysed him, the same fear that gnawed at her. Something had to be done. She reached out a hand towards the large, silent mound to her left. He was still too far away. She wiggled over until she was within reach.

An icy little hand stroked his shoulder. This was not how it was meant to be. But in his cowardice he was grateful that she had made the first move. The small hand continued to caress. He could feel light feathery movements through his pyjamas. She was touching him! It was really happening. Emboldened, he turned towards her and reached over. He was met with more material but there was something undeniably soft and pliant beneath. Her breast? His penis twitched. No. It was merely her upper arm. Gingerly he started to explore. Her hand had begun to rove the whole length of his arm and friction had made it warm. He shifted nearer to her and to his joy she did the same. Their arms continued to writhe like tentacles but their bodies remained stubbornly apart.

Chani shuffled closer. He could just make out her eyes in contrast to the whiteness of her pillow. He gazed at her face, enjoying the warmth emanating from her body still inches away. Suddenly a cold, clammy foot began to prod his upper shin, rubbing along his pyjama leg. Taking this as an invitation, he pressed up against her and pulled her in close. Her heartbeat raced through the thinness of her nightie. She leant over him. Damp locks of hair brushed his face. Then she kissed him, soft lips nudging his own. His arms locked around her and his hands began to explore the length of her body.

They pressed and squirmed against each other. The air grew hot and moist beneath the duvet but they remained fully clothed. Baruch ached to rummage beneath her gown but Chani was almost on top of him and he could not reach to pull it up. A moment later, her hands crept beneath his pyjama top and furtively stroked his chest. He thought his heart would burst with joy.

She was pleased with her findings. Baruch was not hairy in the slightest. His skin was seal-smooth save for the odd wisp just above his sternum. Beneath, ribs and muscles flexed and she enjoyed the energy in them. His body was a thrilling new land to her.

A large pair of hands grasped her bottom. She froze. This was happening more quickly than she would have liked. She was not ready to remove her gown. She wriggled free but Baruch took the opportunity to manoeuvre himself alongside her and now his long fingers were rubbing urgently along the front of her gown. Soon they plucked at the placquard of buttons and each one surrendered with a little pop. He kissed her face clumsily like an exuberant dog. She wanted to wipe her chin and cheeks but did not want to offend him. She placed a placatory hand against him pushing him away.

Startled he pulled back. 'Are you ok? Have I done something wrong?' he whispered.

'No, not all. A little less kissing that's all. Please.'

'I'm sorry – I have no idea how to kiss –'

'Neither have I. But let's try a little more slowly and gently.'

'Ok,' he said. He was useless, as he had known he would be.

They lay separately, breathing hard. He felt himself deflate. She squirmed towards him once more.

'Come on, let's try again,' she said.

He became lost in a sea of Chani. Enmeshed by her soft, slender limbs and silken flesh, he kissed, licked, stroked, fondled, nuzzled and probed. He became only fingers, mouth and tongue. His universe began and ended, marked by the parameters of the small, delicate frame beneath him. She responded in a similar fashion – perhaps a little more restrained, yet her enthusiasm seemed clear enough. Now and then she emitted small moans and fluttery sighs. Encouraged he struggled to remove her bra. He pulled at the straps and tugged at the underwiring but it stubbornly remained in place.

Her gown had long been cast aside as had his

pyjama top. His fumblings were leading nowhere. She lay patiently before him.

'Can you help me out here?'

She grappled behind her and in seconds the bra lay discarded on the floor. Chani was disappointed that he had not even seen her in the new bra. She had yearned to be admired and appreciated but it had not made the slightest bit of difference to Baruch. All he had wanted was to play with what it had concealed. A flicker of pleasure raced through her. Whatever he was doing it was quite delightful. She arched up to meet him and soon something hard and hot was pressing urgently against her knickers. Perhaps the Rebbetzin had been right after all.

He had to be inside her. He had no idea of how to accomplish the feat. His penis pressed and throbbed and ached against the flimsy scrap of material preventing him from achieving the union he craved. His pyjama bottoms lay cooling on the floor.

The girl lay under him, a writhing mass of skin and bones. Her hipbones were sharp and thin against his abdomen. A hand moved between his thighs as she reached down to remove her knickers. He shifted his weight off her momentarily. Then with a gasp he returned, his member poking wildly at the warm, hairy mound beneath him. He pressed and pushed but was met with a hot wall of muscle. He looked down at her. In the darkness, her eyes gleamed. Her teeth were gritted, bared in pain. She was a wild animal caught in a trap; but still he could not stop.

Chani lay braced beneath Baruch's weight. Her knees jutted out and she felt like a beetle that had been dropped on its back and could not right itself. She could barely breathe. She tried wriggling a little up the bed but before she knew it something throbbing and insistent was thrusting against her. His snout.

At first she felt nothing. But as the pressure increased so did the pain. She bore it, eyes shut, teeth clenched, opening herself for him. But still he pushed and pressed. He panted and groaned on top of her. She opened one eye and saw his huge shadowy form hanging over her, his hair a mass of wild curls. He did not look like the boy she had married. She could not see his face. He could be anyone.

A sudden burning stab of pain caused her to cry out. She shoved at him with all the force she could muster and pushed up the bed, so that her back was pressed against the headboard. He reared backwards in shock. A terrible moaning, sighing sound escaped him. Her feet were sprayed with warm liquid. And then Baruch sank into a torpid, lifeless mass amongst the disarray of bed linen.

She lay there, the liquid congealing between her toes. She could not move. Her hands were clamped between her legs, pressing down at the unbearable soreness he had caused. It had been worse than

430

she had imagined. The Rebbetzin had lied to her. There was no pleasure in such pain. She hated the Rebbetzin and her mother at that moment. But most of all she hated Baruch. She had to blame someone, however unfair she knew it was. He was the cause of her physical misery. And if this was what marriage was, she wanted nothing of it.

Shame engulfed him as he lay there exhausted by his pathetic efforts. He was a failure. A sticky mass coated his belly. He had not sown his seed within her nor even entered her. Worst of all he had hurt her. She had yelped in pain and pushed him away. Horrified at what he had done, he dared not raise his head to look at her. Minutes passed and neither of them moved. The darkness was filled with a low whining sound. It was not coming from him. He jerked upright and fumbled for the light. It blazed, blinding him momentarily but when the fuzz cleared he saw Chani. She lay in a tight curled up ball, hugging her knees into her chest. An arm was flung over her face.

'Chani?'

She did not answer but the keening sound grew louder. He was terrified. What had he done? Had he damaged her irrevocably? His wife of only a few hours was not moving or speaking. He crept closer, leaning over her and gently plucked at her arm. She shifted away from him and he caught the glitter of tears on her cheek.

'Chani! Are you ok?'

Still no reply. The sobbing grew louder. Her mouth gaped beneath her hands. He moved to embrace her but she pushed him away. She did not want him to even touch her. Should he ring for an ambulance?

'Chani, I'm so sorry – what can I do to help?'

She stood up and grabbed the quilt off the bed. Wrapping it around her, she stumbled towards the bathroom as it trailed behind her, an echo of her wedding dress. The bathroom light bathed her retreating figure in harsh neon. The door slammed, was locked and she was gone.

Baruch waited. Minutes passed but still he sat immobile on the edge of the bed, naked and cold. He looked down at his withered member with disgust. Finally he pulled on his pyjamas to cover his shame. There was no sound from the bathroom. He tiptoed towards the door and listened. Nothing. Should he knock? Something told him to leave her be. But it was his duty to look after his wife and she was in distress.

'Chani?' His voice sounded idiotic.

No reply.

'Chani? Are you ok? Please tell me you're ok. Is there anything I can get you? Is there anything I can do?' His words were drowned out by the sound of the flush and then the splutter and gush of the taps. He tried the handle although he knew it was locked. 'Chani, please talk to me.'

'Just leave me alone.' Her voice was wretched.

'I can't leave you alone. We're married now. You're my wife.'

Silence.

The shower whirred and he was blocked out once more.

She washed away every trace of him. She soaped it all away – his saliva, his sweat, his seed, his touch. She wanted to be clean and new again. He could wait.

Baruch sat slumped on the floor, his back against the bathroom door. He would wait until she came out. She had to come out sometime. He had not thought it would turn out as badly as this. What a mess. The door clicked behind him and before he could scramble to his feet it opened, unbalancing him. She stepped backwards allowing him to clumsily unfold. Then she walked straight past him.

'Chani?' He followed her. She pulled out her suitcase, opened it and drew out several garments. She began to dress.

'What are you doing?'

'I'm leaving.' She did not even look up at him.

'But – but – you can't – we're married –'

'I know and I want to go home to my parents.' Her voice was clipped and hard, a tone he had never heard her use before.

'Chani – please – it's six in the morning! They'll be asleep – you can't go back now! Please – stay – we can talk –'

'I have nothing to say.'

She continued to pack with her back turned to him. Baruch moved towards her and reached out a hand. He could barely see her for tears. She had become a watery pixelated blur.

'Please,' he croaked. 'Please stay and talk. I'm sorry. It's my fault.'

'It's no-one's fault. We don't know each other but we are expected to go from nought to sixty in a night. It's pathetic!' She gave a hollow little laugh.

'I know. I tried, Chani, I really tried. I went to the library to work things out for tonight –'

'Well, you were obviously looking at the wrong books!' she snapped. 'What good are books in this situation? Always blooming books! It's all the same – we're told one thing but the reality is so very different –'

'I agree. But maybe we can work on things . . . take our time. Try again.'

'Try again? After tonight?' She stared at him.

It was all so unfair. Why should all the blame fall on him?

'Look, Chani – it's not all my fault – I know as little about these things as you do – I had no idea what I was doing –'

'Clearly!'

The rebuke stung. He did not deserve it. Suddenly he was furious.

'*Fine then!* Walk away – run off home – blame it all on me, if it's easier for you!' He stomped off towards the bathroom to hide his hurt.

Chani watched him go. 'No, Baruch. It's my fault. I should never have married you. I should have listened to your mother when she tried to stop me –'

He stopped dead in his tracks. 'She did what?'

She had not meant to say it. 'Nothing, forget it.' She plucked her everyday sheitel from its stand. She could not bear to put it on. It seemed a lifeless, repellent thing. Hair that had once belonged to someone else flopped and slithered over her fingers.

His head pulsed. He could not believe what he had just heard.

'No, Chani. You have to tell me. What did my mother do?'

Baruch stood, hands on hips, his face a mask of fury and determination. Chani suddenly felt frightened. He could do anything to her here in this vast prison of a room.

'It really doesn't matter now. Forget I said it –'

'I can't. You did say it. So tell me. You at least owe me that.'

'Ok. Your mum ambushed me on my way home from school –'

'Ambushed you? What do you mean?' His mother in a balaclava and army fatigues, carrying an Uzi, flashed across his mind.

'She was waiting in her car in front of my house and when she saw me approach, she got out and introduced herself.'

'When was this?'

'Just before you proposed.'

'I see. And what did you do?'

'I got in her car. She asked me to.'

'And then?'

'We drove to Hampstead and sat in a café and she told me I was not the right sort of girl for you. That our families were too different. And that I should move on.'

Baruch made a horrible strangled sound. His fists were balled. He turned to face the wall to contain himself. 'And what did you say to all this?'

'I refused to give you up. I told her my family were just as good as yours.'

He turned to face her. His eyes were moist and red. 'Thank you' he said. 'For not giving up on me in front of my bloody mother.' His voice shook with anger.

But now she had started she could not stop. He may as well know the whole truth and then he would understand what she had been through and why she wanted to abandon their marriage.

'That's not all.'

'Well, don't spare me, Chani – you've got this far!' His sarcasm spurred her on.

'Ok then. You remember the dinner with my parents and your parents?'

'How could I forget it? Best night of my life!'

'Your mother followed me upstairs when I needed to be excused and cornered me in the bathroom.'

'She did what? I don't *believe* it. When she had your parents waiting downstairs – and my father –' He began to pace the room, his pyjamas flapping with the force of his stride. He stopped dead and whirled to face her. 'And? What else happened?'

'She offered to help find me another more suitable boy if I would leave you alone.'

'My God! She's incorrigible! I knew my mum was the meddlesome type but this really takes the biscuit! If my father had known – if he were to find out –'

The pacing began again.

'No, Baruch – please don't say anything – I shouldn't have told you.'

'Oh, you can bet I am going to say something! But first of all tell me the rest. How did you get rid of her?'

'I crushed her foot in the door.'

He stopped and stared at her in disbelief. And then his face crumpled and he collapsed into spasms of laughter.

For Chani the confession had been no laughing matter. Baruch's outrage at his mother's audacity indicated he would not let it slide. Lord knows what the woman would be capable of if stirred to revenge. It occurred to her then that if she were to return home now, Mrs Levy would have won. She was caught between the devil and the deep blue sea. She was exhausted. She did not care any more. All she wanted was her own bed.

Baruch clung to an armchair, still convulsed with

laughter. He seemed to have forgotten her. She crammed her wig into her pocket, slammed her suitcase shut and dragged it towards the door.

'Chani! Don't go! Please wait, let's keep talking –'

In a single bound he was by her side, his face wrinkled in concern.

'Well, you seem to find my predicament funny,' she retorted.

'No, I don't. It's just the thought of you –' The giggles threatened again. He looked away and wiped his mouth.

'Seriously, I want us to work things out. Not give up so quickly.'

'Why? Your mother has plenty of more suitable girls lined up for you to meet.'

'Don't be cruel. I'm not interested in other girls. I want to be with you. And she knows that.'

So he had fought for her too. His glasses winked down at her. She could not see his eyes behind them, but a large, warm hand reached for her own and this time she did not shun his touch. They stood by the door holding hands, her suitcase at her feet.

'I don't want to try again tonight,' she said.

'Neither do I. I told you already.'

'But we don't have a choice. We have to do it tonight.'

'Who says?'

She shrugged. 'Everyone.'

'They won't know if we do or we don't. It's between us now.'

'What about HaShem?'

He had not thought about HaShem. He decided to give Him the benefit of the doubt on this occasion.

'I'm sure HaShem will understand if we took our time.'

'But what about the Shevah Brachot? By keeping apart we'll be lying to all those people who are hosting us.'

'Like I said, if we don't tell them, they won't know. It's none of their business. Let them think what they like. They'll think what they always think.'

'Ok. But if we stay together, we will have to sleep together at some point . . . and I don't want to go through what I went through tonight.'

'Chani, I wish we had never tried. Honestly – we can try again but at your speed. Much more slowly. Take our time. Talk. Get to know each other more. Till we feel really comfortable.'

'But then we'll need to repeat the Sheva Brachot. How can we keep apart otherwise?'

'We'll manage. We're not animals.' He thought of Rabbi Zilberman and his beasts of the field. 'It will be practice for when you are really niddah. We can go out every night to a different kosher restaurant and celebrate privately.'

'People will talk.'

'People will always talk. We have to be ourselves and do what is right for us.' He could not believe how mature and responsible he sounded. Baruch the married man. He grinned. She turned towards him. He edged a step closer. He opened his arms and she moved into them.

'And there's one more thing I need to talk to you about.'

'Oh? Tell me then.'

It was about half past six on Monday morning. The curtains were still drawn and Chani sat cross-legged on the bed, bundled into her hotel dressing gown. Baruch lay stretched out on his side, still in his pyjamas. His large feet hung off the edge of the bed. The covers were strewn with plastic wrappers and scrunched up foil, ransacked treasures from the kosher basket. Chani's right cheek was daubed with chocolate. She was halfway through an apple. Baruch helped himself to another strawberry flavoured wafer.

'I don't want a baby just yet.'

There was a pause in Baruch's munching. He swallowed noisily. 'Well, I don't want one either. Just yet.'

'Really? Do you really mean that or are you just saying it for my sake?'

He rolled his eyes in imitation of her. 'No, Chani, I was just saying it to please your Royal Highness. I'm not ready for children. I can't think of anything scarier! I am only twenty.'

'But the community expects, our parents expect –'

'So? Let them expect. It's our decision now.'

How strong and sure he sounded. He wished Avromi could hear him. But Chani was frowning and picking at her apple.

'Ok. But what are we going to do to avoid me getting pregnant so soon?'

He had not thought this one through. 'I think there are ways . . . I think we need to go to a doctor and ask. But firstly, I guess we will have to ask the rabbis for permission. I heard they'll give you up to a year off.'

A year seemed a long, long time to both of them. They grinned shyly at each other. Chani sighed. 'I knew it. We're never really going to be free to decide for ourselves, are we?'

'No,' said Baruch sadly. 'But we'll do our best. Besides, we'll be new in Jerusalem and for a while that might give us a bit more space and privacy.'

'And I only want a maximum of four.'

'Four is plenty. Too many even!'

'Really?'

'Really.'

Marriage was improving by the minute. In all, he was not a bad catch. Mrs Levy had a point. She wiped her sticky hand on her gown and reached for his fingers. She stared down at how tiny her hand looked against his and giggled.

Later that morning, Baruch woke up in need of the lavatory. For a moment he did not know where he was. He stared up into the shadowy folds of the canopy and listened to the gentle snoring coming from the small huddle to his left. Chani. He moved carefully not wishing to wake her, but could not resist examining what she looked like when asleep. She was curled up on her left side, the covers pulled up to her chin. Her eyelids flickered in response to her dreams. What was she dreaming about? He hoped it was something pleasant. Her puckered mouth quivered with each inhalation. Her cheek was flushed and her mussed hair hid her forehead. She looked about twelve. He gently stroked away the hair glued to her skin. His wife. So she had stood up for him. She had given his mother what for.

His thoughts returned to the miserable events that had led to their first disagreement. He shivered. Baruch HaShem she had stayed. He would make it up to her. Even if it took a year to consummate their marriage. Well perhaps not a whole year. He had hoped to lose his virginity a little sooner. But Chani was the most important thing in his life now. He hoped in turn to be hers. He eased himself off the bed and made his way towards the bathroom when his left foot skidded on something soft and slippery. He found his balance and groped at the carpet, locating a sliver of satin material. He opened the bathroom door and examined the fabric in the light.

A shocking pink bra. It could only be Chani's.

He thought of her wearing it under her prim nightgown and began to feel aroused. He wished he had seen her in it. Perhaps he could ask her to wear it again for him sometime.

Perhaps.

CHAPTER 36

THE REBBETZIN

November 2008 – London

The Rebbetzin crept up the back stairs leading to the women's gallery. The men's voices could be heard through the thick walls. A violin whined the first notes announcing the Kallah's entrance. She sprang nimbly up the last steps and found a discreet seat against the back wall. No one had observed her entrance. She fervently hoped that would remain the case. The first two rows of the gallery were crowded. Women craned forward, straining to catch a glimpse of the bride. Some had risen from their wooden seats and dared to lean over the balcony. Chani had entered the shul but the Rebbetzin's view of her progress to the wedding canopy was obscured.

Chaim would be somewhere beneath the chuppah. She wondered how he was, how he was feeling. How he looked. He usually enjoyed officiating at weddings and she hoped her behaviour had not spoilt his joy. A sense of shame and guilt spread through her. Of course it must have done. She

444

shook her head, as if to eject the negative thoughts, trying to focus solely on Chani.

The women grew very still, prayer books forgotten, as they gazed at the bride gliding below. The chazan's voice rose mellifluously.

The Rebbetzin wished she could see her. Closing her eyes, she sent up a passionate prayer for Chani's future happiness, hoping that Chani's marriage would fare better than her own. And then, having done her duty, she slunk quickly from the gallery before she could be noticed.

The Sunday crowds surged like a sea in front of her. Taking a deep breath, the Rebbetzin plunged into the swaying tide. Her feet quickened and soon she kept pace. An onlooker could have just made out the familiar rigidity of her back and shoulders under her husband's old raincoat, her hair fluttering as she walked. And then her figure grew gradually smaller until finally she became an indistinct blur, one of the masses, alone in her ordinariness, pursuing her freedom.

YIDDISH–ENGLISH GLOSSARY

Ashkenazi – a Jew of East European descent

Baruch HaShem – (exp) Blessed be God, thanks to God

Bedeken Room – the room where a bride waits for her husband-to-be to verify she is the right girl

bimah (Hebrew) – an elevated platform, a little like a pulpit, from which the Torah is read and sermons are given in synagogue

blintzes (pl.) – fried, crispy pancakes stuffed with cream cheese or fruit or potatoes

Bobover – member of Hasidic group within Charedi Judaism, hailing from Bobowa, Galicia (Southern Poland). Most of them now live in Brooklyn, New York.

brachot or broches (pl.) – blessings

brocha – a blessing

broiges (adj) – sulky, moody – in a bad mood

B'srat HaShem – please God (let this happen) . . .

Chanukiah – the nine branched candelabra used during the winter festival of Chanukah

Charedi – ultra-Orthodox

cholent – a stew cooked overnight on a slow cooker from Friday afternoon and eaten on Saturday (Shabbes) for lunch

chollah – sweet, white bread eaten on Shabbes

chuppah (Hebrew) – the wedding canopy a wedding party gathers under for the ceremony

daven – pray

Fahr-Shpiel – an afternoon of humorous sketches, songs and games put on by the female friends of the bride to entertain her, shortly before her wedding day

frum – religious, observant (adj)

frummer/frummah – a religious person – can be used for a man or woman

ganif – thief

gaon – genius, great scholar

goses – someone who is at death's door

goy (male) / goya (female) – a non-Jew (can be derogatory – but can also just mean 'other', as in someone who is simply not Jewish)

goyim – non-Jews

goyishe (adj) – non-Jewish, not Jewish

haimisher (adj) – homely, traditional

hasanah – a wedding

HaShem (Hebrew) – God (literally 'the Name')

Hasid – a follower of the pious Hasidic sect. Hasidism is generally thought of as a happy, exuberant and positive teaching, where followers display their love for God and the Torah through joyful song, dance and passionate prayer. The other side of the coin is fanaticism

448

and rigidity – where stones and bottles are hurled at those who transgress (eg by driving a car on Shabbes). The men are dressed in long black coats, white shirts with no ties and wide-brimmed black hats. They have full beards and many have ear-locks.

Has veh Sholem! (exp) – God forbid!

Hossen – bride-groom

Im yirtzeh HaShem – if God wills it

Kaddish – mourner's prayer for the dead

Kallah – the Bride

kehilla – the frum community

keine hora – expression used to ward off the evil eye / envy

Kiddush wine – special kosher wine used for blessings

kippah or kippot (pl) – the Hebrew word for a skull-cap that a boy/man wears to cover his head in the presence of God

kneidele – dumplings served in soup

kosher – 1. fit to eat according to religious, dietary laws or 2. legitimate or 3. genuine

kvell – to glow with pride

kvetch – to complain or fuss

lokshen pudding – a pudding made out of noodles and sultanas

mache – a big shot, an important, powerful person in the community

mechitzah – movable barrier made from screens used to separate men from women at religious and social events

meshuggah / meshugganeh – both are variations on 'crazy/crazy person'

mezuzah – small, oblong box containing the Shemah (holiest prayer written on a tiny prayer scroll) fixed to a door frame, used to bless the house and its inhabitants upon entry

mikveh – the ritual bath for women

mincha – afternoon prayers

mishpocheh – family

miskenah – a person who deserves our pity – literally 'poor thing'

mitzvah – a good deed in the eyes of God

mitzvot (pl) – good deeds in the eyes of God

mazel tov! – congratulations!

mensch – man of fine qualities, a good human being

naches – the sense of pride and affection you get from your children and their accomplishments

nebbuch – fool, also an exp of sympathy, as in 'poor thing'

niddah (adj) – when a woman is menstruating/bleeding due to miscarriage or birth and is forbidden to a man

nu? – well? so?

oy vey! – Oh dear! Oh dear!

peyos – side-curls worn by orthodox Jewish men and boys

Rabbi/rebbi – spiritual leader and teacher

rachamim – pity

Rebbetzin – the rabbi's wife

rogellach – sweet pastries

sem – short for seminary, a religious college for girls – the equivalent of a yeshiva for men

Sephardi – Jew of Spanish/Portuguese/Moroccan origins

Shabbes – the holiest day and time of the Jewish week, from sundown on Friday to sundown on Saturday.

Shabbat – modern Hebrew for Shabbes

shadchan – match-maker

sheitel – the wig a married woman wears to cover her real hair and preserve her modesty. A married woman's real hair is only for her husband's eyes

Shemah – holiest prayer in Judaism, one all Jews know

Shevah Brachot – the 7 dinners spread over a week that a newly wed couple must attend in their honour to keep them separate after their wedding night because the Bride has bled following the loss of her virginity and is therefore considered 'forbidden' to her husband until the bleeding has stopped

shidduch – an arranged blind date, usually orchestrated by a match-maker

shiksah – non-Jewish woman (derogatory)

shiur (Hebrew) – a lesson on the Torah or other spiritual matters

shivah (Hebrew) – the traditional mourning period of a week, where mourners come to visit the house of the deceased to pay their respects

shloomp – frump or slovenly person

shnippsy – small and skinny

shomer nageah – the law observed by religious Jews of not touching the opposite sex unless they are your spouse

shoyket – butcher

shtiebel – a small, neighbourhood synagogue – often the building is an ordinary house, where men gather to pray – unlike the large, purpose-built, official synagogues.

shul – synagogue

siddur – prayer book

simcha (Hebrew) – a happy occasion, like a wedding or a barmitzvah

Simchat Torah – a joyous, giddy religious celebration that marks the completion of reading of the Torah for that year and the beginning of reading it again for the new Year.

spilkes – on tenterhooks with suspense/restlessness/fidgetiness

tallis – a large striped prayer shawl with tied fringes worn by men only. Even very young Orthodox boys, will wear a thin undershirt with tied fringes (tzizzit) against their skin, from the moment they wake until they undress for bed. The tied fringes are left dangling on the outside, visible to the world. The knots are specifically tied and are always the same number, giving a mystical significance to the garment.

Talmud – basic body of Jewish law and tradition studied at yeshiva

tefillin – leather phylacteries that an observant,

male Jew binds to his forehead and left forearm during morning prayers

toches – bum

treif/trayf – non-kosher

tzaddik – righteous man

tzaddikim – righteous men

tzedakah – charity

tzimmes – a stew-like accompaniment of fruit or vegetables

tzurris – worries, troubles

yarmulke – the skull-cap a boy wears to cover his head in the presence of God (Yiddish)

yeshiva – religious college for men (after school)

yeshiva bocher – a talented yeshiva scholar

Yiddishe – Jewish

Yiddishkeit – Jewishness

Swansea Libraries

#		#		#		#	
1		25		49		73	
2		26		50		74	
3		27		51		75	
4		28		52		76	
5		29		53	6/18	77	
6		30		54		78	
7		31		55		79	
8		32		56		80	
9		33		57		81	
10		34		58	4/19	82	
11		35		59		83	
12		36		60		84	
13		37	8/19	61		85	
14		38		62		86	
15		39		63		87	
16		40		64		88	
17		41		65		89	
18		42		66		90	
19		43		67		91	
20		44	3/17	68		92	
21		45		69		Community	
22		46		70		Services	
23	10/17	47		71			
24		48		72			